A DANGEROUS ROAD

A DANGEROUS ROAD

Kris Nelscott

St. Martin's Minotaur ♊ New York

MYS

www.minotaurbooks.com

Library of Congress Cataloging-in-Publication Data

Nelscott, Kris.
    A dangerous road / Kris Nelscott.—1st ed.
      p. cm.
    ISBN 0-312-26264-7
    1. King, Martin Luther, Jr., 1929–1968—Friends and associates—Fiction. 2. Parents—Death—Psychological aspects—Fiction. 3. Inheritance and succession—Fiction. 4. Private investigators—Fiction. 5. Afro-American men—Fiction. 6. Memphis (Tenn.)—Fiction. 7. Race relations—Fiction. I. Title.

PS3564.E39 D36 2000
813'.6—dc21

                         00-025137

First Edition: July 2000

10 9 8 7 6 5 4 3 2 1

For my brother, Fred Rusch, with love

It's a winding, meandering road. It's really conducive for ambushing. . . . That's a dangerous road.

—Martin Luther King, Jr.
April 3, 1968

ONE

The rioting is finally over, and the fires have burned out. Washington, D.C., is a blackened ruin, and so are the west and south sides of Chicago. Pittsburgh, Newark, Hartford, and Trenton have all suffered serious damage. So have many other major cities.

Jimmy and I drive the green Oldsmobile that belonged to Henry's church and listen to the news. We hardly speak to each other any more. There isn't much to say. Martin Luther King, Jr., is dead, assassinated in our hometown, in our neighborhood, and both Jimmy and I played small roles in his death. Inadvertent roles, of course, but roles nonetheless.

We drive through fallow cornfields, the ground muddy with spring thaw. Some of the areas smell of manure as the farmers prepare for spring planting. I keep the windows of the Oldsmobile down despite the chill. I need to do something to stay awake. I have been driving for two weeks straight, and I am getting tired. Soon we'll have to find a place to stay—Jimmy needs stability, as all ten-year-olds do—but I haven't found any place that I feel safe in. The nearby cities are ruined—the black neighborhoods destroyed—and the two of us wouldn't fit into small-town

America, at least not here, where we are driving, in the center of the Midwest.

Jimmy doesn't know it, but I have backtracked several times, afraid to cross the Mississippi. I know little of the western United States and what I do know, I don't like. So every night, after we find a roadside motel (I've been following the old gospel route, stopping in places that I know will accept us), I stay awake and pore over maps, hoping to find a home.

I despair of ever finding one.

I know I'll have to choose some place soon. The money is running out. I need to make some decisions for both of us, decisions that will determine our future.

But my mind doesn't focus on the future. Instead, it latches onto the past. The last two months are so fresh that I dream of them. With the clarity of hindsight, I can see the warning signs, the ones we missed—the ones all of us missed, from Martin's lieutenants to the Committee on the Move for Equality, which we called COME, to the Memphis Ministers Association.

I'm the one who failed the most. I'm the one trained to see patterns, the one who made his living putting pieces together, and I knew that something was going to happen. I simply hadn't expected that something to be Martin's death.

I tell myself, as I clutch the big heavy steering wheel and sit upright in the Oldsmobile's soft plastic seats, that I couldn't have seen it. The case I was working on was personal and absorbing; it took all of my attention. But that lie is breaking down under two weeks of strain.

Is that my fault? I don't know. I wasn't in Martin's inner circle. I wasn't in anyone's inner circle, although I probably could have been. But joining wasn't—isn't—my nature. It hasn't been since I was Jimmy's age, back in the days when Martin and I were friends, when I called him M. L. just like everyone else did, when he was nothing more than a little boy with powerful eyes and an even more powerful father.

Those days ended in a single night for me, the longest night of my entire life: December 16, 1939.

But all the seeds for everything that followed were sown two days earlier. That night, I used to believe, inspired Martin to his life's work—and perhaps it also influenced mine. That night, the Old South and the New met face-to-face in a way that they wouldn't do again for nearly twenty-nine years. They would meet again on April 4, 1968—a little over two weeks ago. Then the New South faced the Old and lost, as an assassin's bullet tore into Martin's throat—the home of his golden voice.

The night of December 14, 1939, wasn't as dramatic, at least for most of America. But in Atlanta, it was the biggest single event of the twentieth century. That night, Atlanta began two days of parties to celebrate the premiere of the movie *Gone with the Wind.*

And Martin and I were there.

The festivities actually began the evening before, as Hollywood's biggest stars rode through the cobblestoned streets of Atlanta. I had snuck out of the house—my father didn't cotton to all the hoopla surrounding *Gone with the Wind,* which he (rightly, as it turns out) saw as perpetuating the white myths of the Old South. In the middle of the afternoon, I secured a spot on the corner of Peachtree and Ellis.

It was December and cold, but people began lining up as early as noon for a parade that wouldn't start until four. I wasn't the only black on that corner. Right beside me were the daughters of the Grand—John Wesley Dobbs, the unofficial black mayor of Atlanta. He too would have been angry if he had known his daughters were there. I had heard him say only the day before that the book *Gone with the Wind* was not a great literary piece and it wouldn't last long. The Grand was right about many things in his life, but not that.

In those days, Atlanta was a small provincial city, with a

population of perhaps 300,000. There had to be that many people in the streets that afternoon, many of whom had driven in from rural areas of Georgia. Strangely, the crowd didn't shove or push. We stood, talking softly among ourselves as we waited, hoping to catch a glimpse of the stars we had watched on the big screen.

I didn't care so much about the movie, but I wanted to see Carole Lombard, who I thought was the prettiest woman I'd ever seen—a sentiment I'd once expressed to my aunt when she was visiting. She slapped me. Hard. Little black boys like me didn't ogle rich white women like Carole Lombard, not even on the big screen. I learned that lesson early, and I learned it well.

But that didn't stop me from standing on Peachtree Street, right in the center of the route from Candler Field, where the stars had landed that afternoon, to the Georgian Terrace Hotel, where they would stay for the next three nights. The street was all lit up, and ahead were klieg lights, brought in special for the premiere. Banners and balloons hung from every balcony, and most buildings displayed the Confederate flag.

It was not my celebration, and yet I cheered with the rest as the first of thirty convertibles appeared, flanked by police motorcycles. Confetti fell like snow and somewhere a band was playing "Dixie." I held up my hand and waved, until I realized that seated in that car were people I didn't know. Behind them was a car filled with Daughters of the Confederacy, in period costume. My hand went down, and so did the hands around me. We waited until the stars started showing up: Laurence Olivier (Vivien Leigh's husband) and Olivia de Haviland in a convertible with feathered banners on the windshield, Evelyn Keyes in another, and Vivien Leigh herself riding with David O. Selznick and Governor Eurith D. Rivers.

Around me the cheers and whistles and hollers grew. I screamed with everyone else, standing on my frozen toes so that I could see the Gables as they passed. And they finally did, in a car with Mayor William Hartsfield. Clark Gable was closest to me, wearing a cloth coat, his hair slicked down, his head bare despite the cold. He waved his hat and grinned as if he were really enjoying himself. The men flanked Carole Lombard, and all I saw of her was a fleeting, rather nervous grin, a leather-clad hand making a small, almost hesitant wave, and the flash of her famous platinum blond hair.

And then they were gone. Beside me, Geekie Dobbs complained that the cars were going too fast; she hadn't been able to see. Her sister June shushed her as a male voice beside me asked them what had they expected—the stars to get out and walk? We watched the rest of the parade—young men wearing their grandfathers' Confederate uniforms, more cars carrying more luminaries, most of whom I didn't recognize—and then we waited as the crowd dispersed.

I don't remember what I told my father when I came in the house, confetti on my coat and in my hair. He must have known where I had been and what I had done, but he said nothing. Later he did deliver a lecture at dinner about black history—one of his favorite topics—and the lecture centered on the portrait of Abraham Lincoln my parents kept in the dining room.

At the time, I wondered if M. L. got the same lecture. Looking back on it, I doubt that he did.

I saw M. L. the next night as we gathered in the basement of the Ebenezer Baptist Church. The sixty-voice choir, under the leadership of M. L.'s father, Martin Luther King, Sr., known even then as Daddy King, had agreed to perform at the most prestigious event of the premiere: the ball held by Atlanta's Junior League.

The Junior League was the center of white Atlanta society. Run by southern matrons so staunchly conservative that they often didn't admit wealthy members of their own community, the Junior League sponsored many of the "important" social events, including the debutante ball. A girl who did not debut properly in white society was never admitted into the Junior League and, ironically, one of those girls whose debuts failed to impress the league nearly twenty years before was Margaret Mitchell, the author of *Gone with the Wind*. Because she had been so badly and consistently snubbed by the league, Mitchell didn't attend the Junior League ball on Friday night—snubbing them in return—but the rest of Atlanta did, including several hundred blacks.

Only we didn't go as invited guests. Some of us were hired as chauffeurs to take whites in period carriages to the Atlanta Municipal Auditorium, where the ball was being held. Others served as ushers, and the rest of us performed.

The Ebenezer Baptist Church Choir had been assigned its costumes, and we put them on in the chilly basement of the church. The women wore patched dresses with aprons and Aunt Jemima kerchiefs over their hair. The men wore torn pants too short for their legs and shirts with the sleeves rolled up to reveal powerful arms. M. L. and I wore miniature versions of the men's clothes, with one addition: straw hats that were coming apart on top. The adults were dressed as slaves; we were dressed as pickaninnies.

When we arrived at the Atlanta Municipal Auditorium, Daddy King made us take off our shoes and leave them by the back door. We spent the rest of the night barefoot, because he wanted to make sure our costumes were authentic.

Five thousand rich white people attended that event—the cream of Atlanta society. When we went out on stage, there were tables on the floor. The heads of Atlanta businesses sat at those tables—and would later move to the balcony, among them the famous golfer Bobby Jones, former mayor Robert F. Maddox, and former judge Shepard Bryant, along with their families. Slightly behind them were well-known northerners: William Paley of CBS, Harold Vanderbilt, and Laurance Rockefeller. I learned who all of these people were much later.

I was more concerned with the stage. It looked like a reproduction of a Greek Revival plantation home, with four eighteen-foot ionic columns. My stomach fluttered at that; I knew that standing in front of it, the Ebenezer Church Baptist Choir would look even more like the slaves we were dressed as.

Surprisingly none of the adults balked at performing. M. L. made a soft sound of protest in his throat when he saw it, and I thought of my father and knew I could never tell him of the humiliation I had volunteered for.

What made things worse were all the people in Confederate and Old South attire. Women wore their grandmothers' hoop skirts; men their grandfathers' gray uniforms. The surviving members of Atlanta's Confederate battalions—doddering old men who couldn't walk without help—were honored with front row seats.

The auditorium smelled of sweat, pine needles, and mothballs. It was cold in there—or perhaps it just seemed that way because I was barefoot on a tile-covered concrete floor. We stood backstage as the master of ceremonies, Clark Howell, publisher of the *Constitution*, introduced the luminaries. The crowd laughed when he called Clark Gable "Mr. Carole Lombard," and that phrase sent a surprising spurt of jealousy through me.

I grew restless during the introductions—dozens of them—and shoved M. L. He shoved me back, then put a finger to his lips. "Don't want Daddy seeing us," he whispered, and he was right. The last thing we wanted to do was anger Daddy King.

So we watched and we waited. And, when the signal came, we filed onto the stage like we filed into the choir loft in church. Bright lights nearly blinded me: all I could see were the faces of the white men in the front row, smiling at us as if we were babies doing a good deed. I scanned the seats for Carole Lombard and saw only darkness.

Even though Daddy King was our leader, Mrs. King was our director. She clapped her hands together for attention. We focused on her, and she led us through our repertoire— spirituals all, starting with "I Want Jesus to Walk with Me," and ending with "Plenty Good Room." I had a solo that night, a small one, something that was supposed to sound like an impromptu descant on "Get on Board Little Children," and as it approached, I felt my hands grow clammier and clammier. I had to sing in front of people I usually watched in the darkness. I had to sing while they watched from darkness, unable to see their faces, just as they were unable to see mine from that screen in the movie house.

When my solo came, I stepped forward into the light and sang with a passion and fervor I would never have again. For the first and last time in my life, the whole white world— the world that I knew—focused on me, and I put my entire soul into impressing them.

Then I stepped back, and there was a smattering of polite applause. The choir left the stage, our performance done, and was allowed to huddle around the edges of the auditorium as other blacks, dressed in the clothes of house slaves, cleared the tables and set up for the ball.

Kay Kyser's Orchestra put our little accomplishment to shame. To this day, I can't hear big band music without seeing a parade of Atlantans walking slowly in front of the crowd, the women in their crinolines clutching dried flowers and the men standing tall in Confederate gray. Some of the women were so nervous that when the spotlight hit them they would trip, and their men would have to hold them upright. Flashbulbs glinted off swords and brass buttons, and I pushed against the wall, decorated with banners and evergreen bows, wondering why I had bothered to come to this place that mourned a past I was glad was gone.

8

After a long time, the dancing started. Clark Gable, looking dapper in his tux, graciously led off with Mayor Hartsfield's daughter, and Vivien Leigh, wearing a long black gown with black and white feathers for sleeves, danced with the mayor himself. As Atlanta society slowly made its way to the dance floor, Daddy King gathered us up, took us to our shoes, and told us to go home.

Strangely, I never talked to M. L. about that night. It was as if we hid it in a secret pocket of ourselves, to be forever remembered and never discussed. It wasn't a part of his official biography, and I never mentioned my Atlanta days to anyone. His father was censured by the Atlanta Baptist Ministers Union not only for performing at a segregated event, but also for performing at one that included the sins of dancing and drinking.

Daddy King never apologized for his involvement, and my daddy never found out about mine. Not that he would have had time to punish me even if he had.

The next morning, my father found himself in the middle of a mess larger than anything he could have imagined—and two days later, he and my mother would be dead.

For me, that was the end of everything, and the beginning of something I have only recently come to understand.

If that night had gone differently, I wouldn't be sitting here now, in this car, Jimmy at my side, a cold wind in my face, and terrible news on the radio. If that night had gone differently, I wouldn't be here—and maybe, just maybe, Martin wouldn't be dead. I might have seen what was in front of me, and I might have changed it.

Instead, I solved the central mystery of my life, and in doing so, forfeited everything I held dear. Everything, including someone I hadn't realized I still cared about.

Martin.

TWO

Some people will tell you the end began on January 1, 1968, when Mayor Henry Loeb took office. Mayor Loeb did all he could to antagonize Memphis's black community, and was hated for it. Still others will tell you the end began on February first, when two black garbagemen were accidentally crushed to death in the compressor unit of their ancient—and malfunctioning—truck. That incident was the unofficial beginning of the sanitation workers' strike, the one that brought Martin to Memphis, where he died less than two months later.

For me, though, the end began on Monday, February twenty-sixth. That was the day I saw Laura Hathaway for the first time.

She showed up at 9 that morning. My office was on the second floor of the Gallina Building on Beale Street, the center of black commerce in Memphis, and home of the blues. Sometimes, late at night, I could hear blues coming from the clubs below, ever so faintly, accompanied by laughter and the sounds of revelry. Those sounds had grown softer over the years—most of the music clubs had moved to West Memphis—but I still heard them, and still treasured them.

The Gallina Building was seventy-seven years old and had

housed several businesses, from a saloon and twenty-room hotel to a gambling den to a dentist's office that had just closed when I rented my room near the top of the stairs. I had been a practicing private detective for over ten years, and until that day, I had never seen a white woman come through my door.

Laura Hathaway was tall and slender and in her late twenties. She carried a coat over one arm and a white clutch purse under the other. She wore an ever-so-proper pullover angora sweater and trim skirt that went modestly—and unfashionably—to her knees. Her little white boots didn't do much to protect her feet against the garbage that had been pushed against the curbs below. Around her neck, she wore a strand of pearls. Her blond hair was cut shoulder length, ends flipped outward in a style that looked as if it took a lot of care. She had on just enough makeup to enhance her conventionally pretty face, but not enough to suggest she was willing to do anything immoral, illegal, or both.

I stiffened my shoulders, but didn't stand. I was six feet tall, muscular, and broad-shouldered. Sometimes my physical presence frightened white people, especially white women. There was no percentage in scaring her, at least not right away.

I figured she was either another observer from the Civil Rights Commission—one of their observers had been injured Friday morning, and they weren't taking too kindly to it—or the fifteenth reporter who was trying to find out what I had seen from my window.

On Friday morning, we had had what the mayor's office was calling a "riot" and what the sanitation workers were calling "a march that had gotten out of hand." The mayor had set Thursday as the last day the strikers had to come back to work, or they would be fired and replacement workers would be hired. The city council opposed the mayor and had promised to vote on Friday morning to support the strikers. But Friday came, and the council didn't vote as planned.

So the union members marched in protest back down-town, and somehow the march grew violent. Men, women, and children—bystanders and participants—were maced, clubbed, and bloodied.

I was in my office that day, and I had a great view of the mess. Only I didn't watch. I went to the window, saw the mêlée, and decided I would only get hurt if I went below. I waited until things calmed down, then I finally went to the street, helping up people who couldn't see because their eyes were swollen shut and tearing, cleaning the blood off a young girl who had met with the wrong end of a truncheon, and generally cleaning up anything that looked like it needed cleaning.

That was how I saw myself: as a man who didn't get involved with a crisis, but who did clean up other people's messes—usually for a price.

I had offered no opinion on the strike to the reporters who had talked to me over the weekend, and I wasn't about to now.

"What do you want?" I asked the woman.

She raised her eyebrows, which had been plucked and then marked over with a darkening pencil. "Mr. Dalton?"

"Yes," I said. "I'm Smokey Dalton. And you are?"

"Laura Hathaway." She said the name as if I should know it. I didn't.

I threaded my fingers together. I could wait for the infor-mation. Patience usually threw off white reporters. It often irritated white members of the Civil Rights Commission. I'd see which one she was.

"Your real name is Billy Dalton," she said. "Not William. Billy. Right?"

Only good friends knew my first name, and very few of them used it. She was not a good friend. I kicked my chair back so that it rested on two legs. "Look, miss. I only deal with people through referrals. So unless someone told you about me—"

"The only person who told me about you was that man who works valet parking at the Peabody," she said.

Roscoe Miller. I kept my expression carefully neutral. Roscoe Miller owed me. He wouldn't send just anyone my way. And he was conscious of the debt. While I had never been able to locate his daughter's rapist, I had been able to raise enough money to fly her to Switzerland and pay for the legal abortion. Roscoe didn't do favors for white people, not after what happened to his daughter. And he never turned on me.

"What did he tell you?"

"I asked him where your office was," she said. "He told me."

"Really?"

She nodded, and I thought I might be seeing nerves beneath that made-up exterior. "He didn't really tell me about your office, not until I asked exactly where it was. Then he wanted to know what I wanted with you."

That was the Roscoe I knew. She obviously had some important business then. "And what is that?" I asked.

She raised her chin slightly. "I'm Dora Jean Hathaway's daughter."

Again, she spoke as if the name meant something to me. It didn't.

"So?" I asked.

Something flashed through her eyes, so quick that I almost didn't recognize it. Surprise. She expected me to know the names.

"Earl Hathaway was my father."

I kept my face impassive, let two fingers tap on the desktop as if I were tired of the conversation. I wasn't. I finally felt as if we were getting somewhere. I just didn't want Miss Laura Hathaway to know it.

"I need to know," she snapped, "why my mother believed you were entitled to a payment from her estate at the time of her death."

"Your mother's dead?" I asked.

"Yes."

"I'm sorry."

Laura Hathaway swallowed hard, so hard I could see the movement in her long and lovely throat. When she did speak again, her voice had an edge of disbelief. "You didn't know her, did you?"

"I never knew anyone named Dora Jean Hathaway," I said carefully. "When did she die?"

"Just before Christmas," Laura said.

"Where are you from, Miss Hathaway?"

"Chicago," she said.

"I've never been to Chicago." I put my chair back on all four legs. "Are you sure you got the right Dalton?"

She swallowed again. It was a subtle nervous gesture that probably no one saw when she wore high-collared sweaters against a midwestern winter. But here, in the warmth of my office, her rising nerves were as palpable as humidity in June.

" 'A Negro named Billy, not William, Dalton, known as Smokey, of Memphis, Tennessee.' Is there anyone else in this town that answers to that description, Mr. Dalton?"

Negro. At least she didn't say nigra. Or nigger.

"Not to my knowledge," I said. "How old is the will?"

"Updated last June, but the lawyer assured me that clause has been there since my father died."

"And he died when?" I asked.

"Nineteen sixty," she said. "January."

My tapping fingers froze, and I had to concentrate in order to relax them. I didn't want her to see my reaction.

"How much money did your mother want to give me?" I asked.

"I would really rather not say, Mr. Dalton."

"Enough to bring you down here, though," I said. "Enough to make you investigate me. Why didn't you hire a private detective, Miss Hathaway? It would have been easier."

"I wanted to see you myself," she said.

"So your private detective found no connection between me and your family."

She flushed. I had caught her. "I didn't say that."

"It's always interesting to listen to what folks don't say."

At that moment, my door opened. Jimmy Bailey peeked around it. He was ten but his scrawny body made him look younger. His eyes looked older.

"Smokey?" He sounded plaintive.

I stood. "Jimmy? Why aren't you in school?"

"I was goin', but I—"

At that moment, Laura Hathaway turned her head. Her movement made the old chair squeak.

Jimmy caught his lower lip with his teeth. "Never mind," he said, and pulled the door closed. His footsteps echoed as he ran down the hall.

"Excuse me," I said. I hurried to the door, yanked it open, and ran toward the stairs. I made it in time to see Jimmy disappear out the front door.

I ran down, but by the time I got to the street, Jimmy was gone. I put my hands on my hips and sighed. Jimmy was a good kid, smart. I'd been keeping an eye on him, unofficially, since I caught him crying near my doorstep three years ago. His mother was a hooker who started the work to make ends meet, and who lost herself somewhere along the way. The day I first met Jimmy, she'd been arrested and the cops had been violent. They'd ignored her son and shoved her in their wagon, leaving him and his older brother to fend for themselves.

It had been the first time Jimmy had witnessed such a scene, but it wasn't the last.

The February air was cold and I shivered once. I'd see if I could track down Jimmy later. But first, I had to deal with the white woman in my office.

As I went back up the filthy marble stairs, I tried to suppress the feeling of unease that was growing inside me. The money, the dates, had to be more than a coincidence. But I didn't want to jump to any conclusions.

I pulled open the door to my office. She still sat in the chair, clutching her purse. "Is the boy all right?"

As if she cared about a kid like Jimmy. "Show me a picture," I said.

She frowned, not making the mental leap.

"Of your mother," I said. "Maybe I'll recognize her then."

"Oh." She flushed slightly. She knew I wasn't going to talk to her about Jimmy or anyone else. She flicked the clasp on her white clutch purse, opened it, and pulled out a photograph. It had the tiny wavy edges and white border so common to snapshots taken in the 1950s. She handed the photograph to me.

I took it to my desk and sat down. Then I leaned back in my chair and studied the picture.

It was black and white, a candid shot of a woman seated at a glass table, a cup of coffee before her. She wore long white gloves and a Mamie Eisenhower hat that covered her short curly hair. Her face had the same planes and lines as her daughter's, but the features were different. Dora Jean Hathaway had small eyes, a pug nose, and a wide mouth. It almost looked like someone had grafted parts of various heads together to form hers. Yet hers was a formidable face, a memorable face, the face of a woman who seized life and held it. I tried to imagine it without its character lines and wrinkles, and found that I couldn't.

"Do you have another photo?" I asked. "Something taken when she was younger?"

Laura Hathaway was watching me. "You don't recognize her?"

"Not from this shot. Give me something older."

"I don't have anything older with me."

I shrugged. "Then I can't help you, Miss Hathaway."

She sighed, and glanced around the room, and I saw it through her eyes: the pull windows, their outsides covered with the grime of decades of city dirt; the high ceilings; the papers scattered everywhere. There were piles of paper on the floor, the filing cabinets tilted against the scarred wood paneling, and a shabby coat rack on which I had hung two shabby coats. My desk had its own stack of papers and there were two chairs—the wooden one in front, and the metal one on wheels that I used to annoy my downstairs neighbors.

"What exactly," she asked with just the right note of curiosity, yet somehow maintaining a touch of distaste in her voice, "is it that you do here?"

She wouldn't have been able to tell from the door. It had the frosted glass, but no name stenciled in. No number. I liked the anonymity. It allowed me to control who became a client and who didn't. "Your detective didn't tell you?"

She turned toward me. Her eyes were flat, her gaze cold. "I expected him to find some connection between our families. I had assumed we were distant relatives, going back to the days of slavery, and that you were blackmailing my mother to get some of the family money."

My palms had grown wet. I took up a napkin from my desk and wiped my hands slowly, deliberately, wondering what good it would do to never invite another white person in my office again. I really wasn't a supporter of Black Power. When I thought politically, I thought like Martin did, that integration would be a good thing. But I never really acted on it. I had no white friends.

Now I knew why.

"I'll take that to be another no, that your detective failed again," I said. "I hope you didn't pay this idiot very much money. He sure as hell didn't find out anything useful for you."

"He found you," she said.

"Anyone with a Memphis phone book could have found me."

"So what do you do?" she asked.

I almost continued the games. I almost taunted her about

her sources, about her decision to come here instead of sending someone else. But it was that decision that stopped me. For all her good-girl manners and her condescending ways, she had taken that long two-block walk from Union to Beale. She had sought me out.

"I do odd jobs for people," I said, the official answer, the answer I gave white people, coming out of my mouth so fast that I didn't have to think about it.

"Odd jobs." She frowned. "From an office?"

"Why not?" I asked.

"Seems strange, that's all." She tucked her clutch purse under her arm and started for the door.

"I'd hold that if I were you," I said.

"What?" she asked.

"That purse," I said. "I'd hold onto it, at least till you cross Gayoso, and maybe even after that."

It was as if she were reassessing me each time she looked at me. "All right."

"And I'd move from the Peabody," I said. "A woman like you shouldn't stay in this part of town."

"A travel agent recommended it. She said the ducks—"

"Are great for tourists. But you're not one, are you, Miss Hathaway? And as you can tell this neighborhood isn't the best."

"I thought the Peabody wasn't in your neighborhood." She flung that at me just as I was warming to her.

I shrugged. It wasn't my concern whether the lady got followed from Beale, mugged, and put in her place. The Peabody was a grand, expensive hotel in Memphis, but I expected trouble there and soon. It had just desegregated as part of a union concession, although that fact wasn't well known, and I was afraid that when the first blacks registered, there'd be hell to pay.

It is amazing how wrong I was.

"I'll bring an older photo for you," Laura Hathaway said. "See if it jogs your memory."

"Why bother?" I asked. "This means nothing to me."

"I'm obligated to make sure you get your cash." Her eyes clouded for a moment. It was beginning to look like disposing of Momma's assets had become a tricky and uncomfortable proposition.

"You know," I said, "sometimes people should be allowed their secrets."

"Do you think so, Mr. Dalton?" she asked, and this time there was no condescension in her voice. "Do you really think so? A man like you who takes odd jobs? Do you allow people their secrets? Or do you just want to hang onto yours?"

Then she let herself out, closing the wooden door gently behind her. Her shadow moved across the frosted glass, and then she was gone.

I stared at the door for a long moment, and then I stood up. I finally had a lead in a personal quest that had bothered me for eight years.

I was going to go to work—for myself.

THREE

After she left, I picked up the phone and called Jimmy's school. He had been marked absent which, the secretary said, wasn't that unusual anymore. Her tone had a touch of blame to it as if I were the one responsible for the boy. He had a mother, such as she was, and a brother who was older. They were supposed to be looking out for him.

I wondered why I was always the one who did.

Before I faced the feelings that Laura Hathaway's visit had stirred, I wanted to find Jimmy. His abrupt departure bothered me. Jimmy rarely came inside my office, and when he did, he slipped in like a wraith. This morning, he had barged in, and my response, along with my client, had frightened him off.

With luck, he'd be waiting for me across the street, beneath the statue of W. C. Handy and his famous trumpet.

I left the office. The late-morning sun shed a pale cold light on Beale Street, revealing the garbage piled on the curbs. Several shoppers hurried by, their faces tense and harried.

The daily march to the courthouse was over, and near Handy Park, I saw several men carrying placards. They were going somewhere else with them, holding the signs horizontally so that I couldn't read them. But I wasn't really trying to. I was looking beyond the men to the center of the park, just behind the statue.

Jimmy's brother, Joe, sat on one of the concrete benches. He was as thin as his brother, and five years older. Joe should have been in school too, but of course he wasn't. No wonder Jimmy was skipping. His brother had already shown him that it was all right.

I crossed with the light and walked toward the park. As I got closer, I saw that Joe wasn't alone. An older man in a black beret was talking with him. Their heads were bent together and the discussion looked serious.

They stood as I walked into the park. The man with the beret turned and headed toward Union. Joe came toward me.

"Don't say nothing, man," he said as he passed me. "You don't understand."

His hostility surprised me. I hadn't seen Joe since January, and although he often got defensive with me, he had never before been hostile.

I turned around and caught up with him. "Jimmy isn't in school today."

"Yeah? So?"

"He's too young to be on his own all day."

"Someone should tell our momma." Joe glanced at me. He was as tall as I was these days. That was disconcerting. "I ain't got time for this, Smokey."

"Joe—"

But he was already weaving his way through the crowd, walking so fast that I would have had to run to keep up with him. I stopped instead and put my hands on my hips. Going to their mother would do no good at all. If she was home. If she wasn't entertaining. Calling the cops wouldn't help either. They'd put Jimmy in some foster home, probably white-run, and he'd be even more miserable than he was now. He'd become one of the lost, as my friend Henry called them. Although I was wondering if he wasn't becoming one of them already.

I crossed back to my side of Beale. I couldn't spend my entire day searching for Jimmy, but I could do my other work and look for him at the same time.

Besides, my meeting with Laura Hathaway had left me with some unfinished business.

I went back across the street. My office was on the south side of Beale, closer to Third than it was to anything else. The Gallina Building held a lot of history and some of that history still showed in the three-story façade. It had exquisite brick work, including massive arches that framed the third-story windows, and an orange terra cotta cornice at the top of both sides of the structure. But the building was falling apart. The brick work was dirty and the arches were crumbling. One of the downstairs tenants, the owner of the Memphis Meat Company, once told me he had trouble putting in his Double Cola sign: he was afraid the attachment would cause serious damage to the building's front. It didn't. That happened a month later, when one of the newer businesses put a Schlitz sign next to the rusting fire escape staircase.

Still, for all its decay, it was more home to me than my own house was. I had spent years there developing my business in the time after I returned from Korea. Just going inside relaxed me, and entering my office, messy as it was, made me feel like I could accomplish something. Not much, maybe, but enough.

I didn't close the door all the way, in case Jimmy was lurking in the hallway. Then I stopped on the far side of my desk, turned the telephone around, and dialed Shelby Bowler, one of the most eccentric lawyers Memphis State University ever produced. Not surprisingly, he answered his own phone.

"Been thinking I'd hear from you," he said. "I settled a case this morning and got the afternoon free. You wanna come down to my place? I ain't too fond of yours."

He said that every time I spoke to him, which wasn't often. I first met Bowler in June 1960 when he came to my office and handed me a check for $10,000. Attorney-client privilege, he told me, prevented him from revealing my benefactor. And no matter how hard I tried, I hadn't been able to pry the information from him.

I waited almost a year before I cashed the check; I thought there was some trick attached. I investigated everything, including Shelby Bowler, and learned nothing, except that, for all his eccentricities, Shelby Bowler could be trusted despite the lightness of his skin.

I drove to Bowler's office, taking the long way, searching for Jimmy. Black kids clustered throughout the downtown, some of them carrying signs, others looking for trouble. It seemed like there were more kids out of school than usual—or maybe I was just paying attention for the first time. Either way, it bothered me.

I cruised all the hangouts I knew, and didn't see Jimmy. I wondered what had brought him to my office that morning. I knew what made him leave. My tone when I asked him about school, and Laura Hathaway's presence.

I was worried about him, but I also knew that he'd been on his own before. If he ran true to form, he'd find me again, and we'd talk about whatever it was.

I left the neighborhood and headed south.

Bowler's office was on Highway 51, right near the border of Tennessee and Mississippi. Bowler liked having his office that far out of town. It was his way of controlling his clients, just like word of mouth was my way of controlling mine. He once told me he could tell who would be worth representing just by the way they reacted to the drive and the neighborhood. The location benefited me, especially when I first drove there, in July of 1960. There weren't a lot of neighbors around to worry about what a black man was doing in that part of town. I didn't like going to a lot of white people's offices, but I didn't mind going to Bowler's.

I drove a white Ford Falcon that I paid cash for in 1961. The car was battered and its underbelly had a coating of rust, but the car and I, we took a liking to each other. It wasn't too fancy, so it didn't broadcast my windfall in the days when people like me didn't get windfalls, and it got me around Memphis easily. I liked the shift on the steering column, and I even liked the old push button radio with the button for WDIA so loose that it always threatened to come off.

Bowler's office was a square building made of sand-colored brick. The original layout was long gone and almost impossible to guess at. Bowler had ripped out and remade the interior into four rooms: the reception area, where his legal secretary usually sat and barked at people; his associate's office, often empty because the junior lawyers came and went as soon as they learned just how strange Bowler was; a conference room that doubled as a law library; and Bowler's private office, which was filled with antique mahogany furniture he once told me had been carved by slaves.

I parked on the gravel lot that stretched behind the chain-link fence that protected the office from the road and let myself inside. The office smelled of Bowler's cherry pipe tobacco and dusty legal tomes. His secretary, a woman who'd been with him since he first hung out a shingle, looked up from her typewriter and grunted. I took that for the greeting it was and slipped through the door to Bowler's private office.

He was sitting behind the mahogany desk, nearly hidden by thick green books, all of which were open and stacked on top of each other. A pencil was stuck in his silver hair, and earlier that day, he'd spilled tobacco on his gray suit and failed to wipe it off. His pipe was resting in a tin ashtray and looked as if he'd filled it, then forgotten to light it. When he saw me, he waved me in.

"Been expecting you," he said.

"That's what you told me on the phone." I headed toward one of the mahogany chairs. It had been reupholstered in dyed red leather and looked damned uncomfortable, although I knew from personal experience that it wasn't.

"Lucinda!" he yelled. "Shut the door."

His secretary got up and walked toward the door, grabbing it and pulling it closed, not before she shot me a filthy look. I couldn't tell if it was because I should have closed the door myself or because she just didn't approve of me. I suspected the latter, but knew if I said anything, Bowler would claim it was the former.

"Some private detective from Chicago called me three days ago to ask if you were still alive."

I sank into the chair. Laura Hathaway really should have asked for her money back. The detective had done nothing that she couldn't have done herself.

"Did he say why he thought I was dead?"

Bowler picked up his pipe and tamped the tobacco down. Then he placed it in his mouth but didn't light it. "That's what I asked," he said, "and he made some comment about us killing lots of you folks down here the last few years."

"Stupid," I murmured.

He took the pipe out of his mouth and stared at me for a moment. "He's from the North."

"That's no excuse for one-sided thinking."

"Television—"

"Doesn't create all our evils."

He rolled his eyes. "We've had this discussion before."

"And never finished it."

He stared at me, then put his pipe back in his mouth and lit it with a gold monogrammed lighter. He puffed, and blue smoke smelling of rancid cough medicine filled the room.

"This private detective," I said, "he wouldn't have anything to do with the money I got in 1960, would he?"

"Smokey, I got lawyer-client privilege—"

"Laura Hathaway visited my office this afternoon," I said.

He leaned back in his leather chair. It squeaked. He took another puff off the pipe, then removed it ever so slowly, cradling it in his left hand. That was one of his courtroom tricks, making him look relaxed and calm, while in reality it gave him time to think.

"Laura Hathaway," he said, using the repetition as another stall.

"She was the one who hired the detective, or didn't he tell you that?"

"Oh, he did." Bowler put his pipe back in the tin ashtray. "I was getting to that."

Actually, he had been startled that I knew her name, only he didn't want me to know that.

"She says her mother left me some money in her will," I said. "You know what this is about?"

"Why would I know?"

"Why would the detective call you?"

"I was your lawyer."

"No, you're not. I have never needed a lawyer. You're someone else's lawyer who just happened to pay me money."

"People've got my name before," Shelby said. "Maybe he called lawyers till he found one who'd heard of you."

I shook my head. "Sounds like a lot of legwork. This investigator doesn't believe in legwork."

Shelby's eyes narrowed. "How do you know?"

"I've been on the receiving end of his work all day, and it's clear." The smell of cherry pipe tobacco was getting thick. I rubbed my nose and resisted the urge to sneeze.

"What're you here for, Smokey?" Shelby asked.

"You said you were going to call me," I said.

"To warn you about the detective. I didn't know what it was about."

"And you thought it could be bad."

"Hell, Smokey, most things are bad these days." He set his pipe in the tray. The tobacco still glowed red, but the embers would die in a moment, and Shelby would have to relight it. "What are you really here for?"

"I've only received money that I didn't earn once in my life," I said slowly, "and you're the guy who gave it to me."

"It was from a client."

"I know," I said. "And now I'm about to receive more money I didn't earn, this time as part of a will." I leaned back in my chair. "I have a hunch, Shelby, that this money comes from the same source."

His left hand fidgeted with the pipe stem. The expression on his face didn't change. He said nothing.

I crossed my arms. "Shelby, your client is dead. Confidentiality doesn't apply any more."

"That's never been adequately determined." He spoke, and then he flushed. It was the flush that gave him away.

"Why is this Hathaway family interested in me?"

"You're the detective."

I smiled slowly. "I do odd jobs."

"That too." Shelby picked up his pipe, tamped the tobacco down, and picked up his lighter. Then he must have realized he was fidgeting, for he set the entire mess down.

"Look, Smokey." He folded his hands and rested them on the desk, giving me that fatherly lawyer approach he was famous for. "I had a hell of a time forcing you to take that money eight years ago. I think one of the reasons you did was because I wouldn't tell you who your benefactor was. Now it looks like you might get some cash again. Let me give you some advice. Take it. Take it, and pay off your house—"

"I did that last time."

"—or put it away for your retirement, or buy a new car for chrissakes. But don't question it. Don't worry about it. Just take it."

He seemed so sincere, his blue eyes watering and his face still slightly flushed. But we'd had this go-around eight years ago, and I hadn't changed since then. I finally took the money then because Shelby threatened to use it to pay off my bills—which were considerable in those days—without my permission. I told him to give the money to charity, and he refused, saying it belonged with me, and he would dog me about it for the rest of my days.

I took the money. I paid off my debts and my house and bought my car.

I tried not to think about what kind of trouble I was buying.

I let that windfall put me on the right road. But I'd been cautious with money ever since, and I didn't need money this time. I could afford to be ethical.

"We're different, you and me," I said.

Shelby closed his eyes. Such an eloquent way of expressing disgust. The movement was slight—his eyes opened a half second later—but not before I saw it and understood it.

It didn't stop me. "You come to this world with a sense of entitlement."

"Smokey—"

"Let me finish." I'd never told him this. Not in the eight years we'd known each other. In 1960, speaking of such things black to white was unthinkable. We'd come a long way since then. A long, long way. "You get money like this, you think it's a windfall and you don't question it—except maybe to find out who to thank. I get money like this, I want to know what the strings are. I want to know who's gonna pull the rug out from underneath me before somebody does."

"I thought you said this Hathaway woman is dead."

"But her daughter isn't. And I don't know how many other relatives are alive. These are *white* people, Shelby. Rich white people. They may not like it that their mother or their grandmother is giving money away to blacks they don't know. In fact, the girl already don't like it. She shows up at my office wearing angora and pearls and acts like the whole place smells bad."

"It does smell bad, Smokey," Shelby said. "It smells like Mississippi River rot and mold. That building should be condemned—"

"You know what I mean."

Shelby closed his eyes again. He pushed his leather chair back and placed his folded fingers across his soft stomach. He appeared to be in deep contemplation. Finally he opened his eyes, and when he looked at me, they were clear and blue and filled with light.

"You're right," he said. "I don't know what you mean. I look at you and the way you live and the choices you have and I think a bit of money will help. If you can't use it, I'm sure you know folks who could. A little bit of cash in the right hands can do a lot of good, Smokey."

"You used that argument on me in 1960."

"And you took the money."

"There wasn't some prim white woman looking down her nose at me, wondering what my connection was to her mother."

"What was your connection to her mother?"

"Damned if I know." I squirmed in that soft leather chair. "The girl even showed me pictures. I didn't recognize the mother, but that doesn't mean a thing. I've lived an interesting life, Shelby."

He smiled. "Been around a lot of older white women, have you?"

I shrugged. "It could have been a job, or it could have been when I was in the army or it could have been at Boston University or it could have been some connection I don't even know."

"Is that what's got you worried? That you don't know who this woman was and what her connection to you is?"

"Haven't you been listening?"

"I've been listening. You've been complaining about a lot of things, some of which make sense and some of which don't. It seems to me that you should just take what's offered."

I stared at him a moment. He was a good man, an ethical man for all his liking to play devil's advocate, and things weren't always straightforward with him.

"Would you take the money?"

"Yes," he said, with a touch of impatience.

"Wouldn't you want to know where it came from?"

"Of course, but that wouldn't stop me from taking such a lucrative gift."

"Sure it would, Shel," I said. "If the circumstances were right. If you were running for public office, you wouldn't take a gift like this."

"That's different."

"Is it?" I stood and walked toward the large windows in the back of the office. They were covered with heavy velvet curtains. You couldn't tell that it was daylight outside. "Those are the kinds of strings I'm talking about. In everyday life, you never think of them. I do."

"So," Shelby said. "You've got the girl. Ask her."

"She doesn't know. I doubt she'll be back."

"Then do some investigating on your own."

I turned. "That's what I'm doing. And I'm starting with you. Did that first check come from someone named Earl Hathaway? Or his wife, Dora Jean?"

Shelby's eyes had gone flat, the light gone from them. It was that look that made him such a good attorney. He could pin anyone with that look, from the governor to the lowliest criminal.

But he wasn't pinning me. I waited.

"What if it did?" he asked.

I got the game. He wasn't going to say yes, and he wasn't going to say no. He was going to tell me all that he could, while retaining the ability to deny everything.

"Then I'd have to ask to see any correspondence that came with the bequest."

"That wouldn't be possible." Shelby flattened his hands against his stomach. "Confidentiality again."

"Of course, that assumes there was correspondence."

"It would be odd to receive such a bequest without it," Shelby said. "But normally, such correspondence only contains instructions for the attorney."

"Do you think any correspondence in a case involving the Hathaways would be normal?"

He smiled. The movement was small, but it was there. "I don't see how it could be anything but."

"Would it be normal in such correspondence to explain *why* someone would get such a bequest?"

"Most people know why they would get such a bequest."

"What about anonymous bequests?"

"Most anonymous bequests prefer to remain anonymous. Doling out any information about the bequest might destroy that anonymity."

I'd had enough of the games. "So all these years, you've only had a letter instructing you to find me and give me the money? No explanation, no nothing?"

"I've told you that much before, Smokey." Shelby's chair was tilted so far back the edges of his gray hair brushed his bookcase.

I sighed and returned to my chair. "Didn't you investigate who this money came from?"

"I knew," Shelby said. "I just couldn't tell you. And I still can't, although I think you have some suspicions."

That was as close as he would ever get to confirming what I knew.

"You have no explanations?"

"None, and even if I did, I wouldn't tell you."

Although he would have tried, now that the daughter was here, now that she was looking for me.

"Why didn't you send someone out to investigate this?"

"There's no point, Smokey. Attorneys handle anonymous payments all the time. It's not ours to question why. It's ours to do the job." He ran his fingers through his hair and dislodged the pencil. It tumbled down the side of his head before he caught it against his suit. "Smokey, is there going to be trouble between you and this Laura Hathaway?"

I froze. No matter how much you trusted a man, he could still ask a question that made you doubt everything about your relationship. "Trouble?"

"If she doesn't give you the money—"

"I think she has to. She wouldn't be here otherwise. I'll wager giving me that cash is tied to her getting the rest of the estate."

He smiled and set the pencil on his desk. "You'd've made a good attorney."

"Because I see things?"

"Because you understand human nature and how it pertains to the law." He stood, clasped his hands behind his back, and made his way around the desk. "What if she does have to give you the money?"

"I won't take it without knowing why. Forgive me, Shelby, but I won't be beholden to a white woman for anything."

"If she has to give you the money, that might be trouble in and of itself." He stopped near me. The scent of cherry tobacco wafted off him. It wasn't so offensive when he wasn't smoking.

We were the same height, something that always startled me. He was heavier than I was, and the net effect was to make him look shorter and rounder.

"I really don't expect to see her again," I said. "I think she just wanted to check me out, and now that she knows I have no idea what this is about, she'll disappear."

"But she told you about the money."

"She saw my office."

"Meaning?"

"She knows I can't hire an attorney to come after her."

Shelby's smile grew. "I'd take the case, on a contingency basis. It's intriguing enough."

I patted him on the arm, then headed toward the door. "No need, Shel. Taking someone else's money once in my life was plenty. I'm not sure I want to do it again."

His smile remained. It made him look eerily like the Cheshire Cat. "Then why did you come here?"

"Because this thing has bothered me for eight years, and I thought I might finally get an answer from you."

"And?"

"I hate a mystery," I said, putting my hand on the doorknob.

"Yes." His smile faded, followed by a look of such deep compassion that I had to turn away from it. "But there are some things in our lives that will remain a mystery forever."

"I know that," I said. "But I don't like it."

"Someday you will have to accept it."

I turned back to him a bit more fiercely than he deserved. "I've been told all my life to accept things, and usually they are ugly, unfathomable things. I decided a long time ago to accept nothing."

"Then you'll be tormented, my friend, by things that most people would never give a second thought to."

I wasn't his friend. I took a deep breath so that I didn't snap at him. "I'll make a deal with you. If Laura Hathaway reappears and offers me the money, I'll find out why her mother felt I deserved it."

"And if you don't find out?"

"I'll take it anyway. I've done my best."

"You'll live with the mystery."

"I'll have to either way. At that point, taking the money is the sensible thing."

His smile returned. "I'm glad you see it my way."

"Actually," I said, "I think you're beginning to see it mine."

FOUR

I drove back to my office slowly, watching for Jimmy and thinking about my conversation with Shelby. I always felt frustrated after leaving his office, even though this time he had given me more information than he ever had before.

I parked in front of the office, on Beale. The street was a mess: garbage piled against the curbs, people stepping over it. The city had hired scabs to pick up the garbage, but the crews were small and unable to hit all the neighborhoods. Of course, the black sections of town got the least attention, partly, I believed, to hasten the end of the strike, but others thought it was yet another example of discrimination.

I got out and went inside, half expecting Jimmy to be sitting in front of the locked door. He wasn't. I stared at the frosted glass for a moment. I had a lot of work to do, but I didn't feel like doing any of it. Most was report writing, which I hated, even though it meant I would get a much-needed check, and the rest was legwork on half a dozen small cases that I had pending for the black lawyers and insurance agents who hired me regularly.

I turned away from my door, went outside, and walked east to Wilson Drug.

I had a handful of regular places that I stopped by for a

meal or a beer. I'd been on Beale a long time and had a large network of acquaintances, even though I once vowed I would have no roots. The way I met people, it seemed, was in restaurants and bars. Somehow it seemed to work.

Three blues musicians braved the cold in Handy Park. They were jamming, playing something rhythmic and dark, completely lost in their music. I tossed some coins into the guitar case—I always tossed in money, because I wanted the musicians to come back—and then I moved on.

The music followed me past the New Daisy Theater and all the way to Wilson's. Wilson's had been around since the 1940s, and still had that sweet plastic odor that newer drug stores lacked. The pharmaceuticals and personal items were just inside the front door, but to the left was my favorite part of Wilson's. The soda fountain.

The soda fountain was in its own section, complete with counter and a ledge on which six swivel stools rested. Just beyond that, hiding behind the combs, barrettes, and plastic rain bonnets, were five tables and two wooden booths built against the wall.

Martha, the day waitress, came up beside me, her rubber shoes squeaking against the tile. She smelled faintly of sweat and perfume. I smiled at her. She was an old friend. She was married, although not happily, and struggling to make ends meet.

"You have company," she said, nodding at one of the booths.

I looked at the booth. Reverend Henry Davis had squeezed himself into it. Henry was probably my best friend in Memphis, although neither of us acknowledged that. We were too different. He had his parish to run, and I had my own quiet life.

Lately I'd been avoiding him. He'd been getting more and more involved with the strike, and he wanted me to get involved too. He'd asked me to go with him to several union meetings, and each time I had been conveniently busy.

I suppressed a sigh and then glanced at Martha. "You still got soup left?" I asked.

She nodded.

"Bring me some and half a turkey sandwich."

"I could have guessed," she said.

I raised my eyebrows.

"It's Monday."

"I'm not that predictable."

She grinned and turned away. Apparently I was that predictable. I went to the booth and sat down.

Henry was finishing the last of a cheeseburger. "I was beginning to wonder if you broke routine and went to the Palace."

He meant the King's Palace Cafe which was right next to my office. I shook my head. "I was tracking down some information."

He took a final bite and wiped his mouth with a paper napkin. "I thought I'd keep you up to date."

"Henry, I don't want to be up to date."

"No one would have been injured Friday if you'd been in on the planning," he said.

I smiled. "You're trying to flatter me."

"I'm telling the truth."

"I thought the march was an impromptu thing that happened after the council meeting."

"You'd have counseled against it."

"You wouldn't have listened."

It was his turn to smile. He had a broad, friendly face and warm eyes. His congregation loved him, even though he wasn't a good orator, in a town filled with excellent orators. He had compassion, which I always thought was in short supply, and he had heart.

"What do you think I need to know?"

He leaned back as best he could in the small space. "James Lawson has put together a biracial committee of ministers to work on this strike. We're going to bring both sides together and get the community even more involved."

"The community is involved."

"Not in any constructive way."

"And what do you think you'll accomplish?"

Martha stopped with my soup and sandwich. The soup was depression soup, one of my favorites. I took a large spoonful of tomato-based broth, hamburger, and okra.

"We're going to get this settled," he said.

I swallowed. "Does the mayor know that?"

"The mayor doesn't approve of anything. The more people who get involved, the better off we'll be," Henry said.

I set down my spoon. "And you've come to me because . . . ?"

"Like it or not, Smokey, you're a well-known member of the black community. Your support would mean a great deal."

I shook my head. "You know I don't get involved in political issues."

"Yes," Henry said, "and I don't understand why."

Our gazes locked for a moment, and then I looked away. "I don't like to be noticed."

"Like it or not, Smokey," he said, "you always get noticed. And right now, everyone's noticing that you're not helping."

"This one's explosive, Henry. I don't like where it's going."

"I know," Henry said. "That's why we need cool heads."

I smiled at him. "You've got one."

"It'd be nice to have another."

I had no response to that. I wouldn't be pressured into working on this strike. I cleaned up messes. I didn't help create them.

He sighed and picked up his check. "Promise me you'll think about it at least."

"I can guarantee the answer won't change," I said.

He shook his head. "I hope it will someday, Smokey." He slid out of the booth and walked to the counter, handing Martha a dollar for his meal and tip.

I finished my soup and sandwich. I did have a level head, but part of it came from my detachment. That detachment let me look at the world clearly, and it kept other people from looking at me.

I had avoided attention as long as I could remember, and my foster parents believed it was their fault. They kept my presence quiet for the first year I was with them, following the Grand's suggestion. They were trying to protect me, and I believe they did.

But as I got older, they regretted the way they'd kept me close. My foster mother even told me once that she believed their influence was the reason I never used my prodigious education.

I felt as if I *were* using that education. I had a bachelor's from Howard and a master's from Boston University, and I got better training in the army after I completed both degrees. I discovered that I liked solving puzzles and being active, and a man couldn't do either as a professor at one of the nation's few black colleges. I didn't make the living they expected, and I didn't have three point four children like the culture said I should, but I was content with my life. It was small, it was contained, and it was mine.

Still, my foster parents' disappointment in me, subtle as it was, distanced us. I rarely spoke with them and I hadn't visited them since they moved to Atlanta a few years before. They were good people, but I felt as if all we had in common was our history.

I finished lunch and headed back to the Gallina Building, feeling better than I had earlier. The musicians had left Handy Park and in their place was Jimmy. He sat on the cold concrete beneath the statue of W.C., and he looked as cold as the stone. His coat didn't quite fit anymore. He clutched a schoolbook in one hand, but he wasn't looking at it.

"Jimmy?" I asked.

He raised his head, then ducked when he saw me. I came over and crouched beside him.

"I've been looking for you. What did you want this morning?"

He shrugged as if it were no longer significant.

"You can tell me," I said.

He pressed his lips together. In the hours since he'd come to me, something—or someone—had changed his mind about talking.

"It seemed important this morning."

His hands clutched the schoolbook tightly. It was an ancient American history text, its cover scratched and ink-stained. The binding was ripped and some of the pages were coming loose.

"Jimmy?" I asked again.

"Who was that lady?" He looked up at me, his brown eyes wide.

"A client," I said.

"She wasn't no cop?"

I smiled. "Did she look like a cop?"

He shook his head.

"Were you worried because you weren't in school?"

He looked down again. Wrong question.

"Was it something else, then, Jimmy?"

"I didn't 'spect to see no one, s'all."

I rocked back on my heels and studied him. Thinner, blue shadows under his eyes, skin gray with fatigue. He wasn't ill, but he would be if he kept this up.

"Have you had lunch?" I asked.

"Naw."

And probably no breakfast either. I put a hand on his shoulder. I could feel the bones. "Come on," I said. "Let's see what they've got at King's Palace."

His eyes lit up, then he lowered his lids and shook his head. "I gotta wait here."

"For what?"

"Joe."

"Why?"

Jimmy shrugged. What did Joe have him involved in? I remembered the man in the beret, and didn't like how this was going.

"I'm sure he won't mind if you have lunch," I said.

"He said I gotta wait."

I squeezed Jimmy's shoulder. "You're cold and hungry. I think you've waited long enough."

He sighed as if he'd been hoping someone would say that. Then he got up slowly, the cold making him move like an old man.

We crossed the street and entered the arched doors. The restaurant was mostly empty. We took a table near the bar, and when the waitress came, I ordered a meal along with Jimmy so that he didn't feel the weight of my charity.

He didn't talk much, and he kept glancing over my shoulder as if his brother were going to come in and drag him out. When the food finally came, he ate like he hadn't seen food in a week.

"It's getting late," I said. "Too late to take you back to school. You want to come home with me?"

Jimmy wiped his mouth with the back of his hand. I could see the longing in his face. Then he shook his head. "Gotta see Joe."

"Can I come with you?"

"No."

I stared at him for a moment. He still had one hand on the history book as if it were a lifeline. He and I had talked about the importance of school several times. He was one of the smartest kids I knew, and I was afraid that the circumstances of his life would prevent him from using his mind.

"All right." I couldn't quite keep the disapproval from my voice. "How about I pick you up in the morning, get you some breakfast and take you to school?"

"Don't need you feedin' me all the time, Smokey." The protest sounded half-hearted.

"It's an excuse for me to have a big breakfast. What do you say?"

Finally, he grinned at me. A little boy grin, full of mischief and delight. "Okay."

Then, as quickly as it appeared, his grin faded. He was looking past me again, and I knew that he had seen Joe through the restaurant's large windows.

"Gotta go," Jimmy said, slipping out of the chair. "See you tomorrow, Smokey."

"All right." I put some cash on the bill and then walked to the door, making sure it didn't look as if I was following Jimmy. He was already in the park. Joe was shaking a finger in his face. I debated crossing the street but was afraid I'd make things worse for Jimmy. Then Jimmy handed Joe a small brown package.

My heart sank.

Joe grinned and clapped his brother on the back. Then he led Jimmy through the park, and they disappeared into the alley behind Paul's Tailoring.

If I followed, I wondered if I'd see a man in a beret. I wondered if he would get the small brown package and then hand Jimmy another package to deliver to someone when he should really be in school.

But I wasn't going to follow. I didn't dare let anyone see me. I was Jimmy's last hope and he had to trust me. He wouldn't do that if I got his brother in trouble.

Still, it was hard to cross the street and pretend I hadn't seen anything. By the time I got inside the Gallina Building, my stomach was in knots.

Most of the day was gone and I still hadn't done my reports. I unlocked the office and let myself inside, catching the familiar scent of dust and Mississippi River mold. As I shut the door behind me, the phone started ringing.

I picked it up.

"Mr. Dalton?"

I recognized that voice already. "Miss Hathaway."

"I have found some more pictures. I would like to show them to you. I'll be in your office tomorrow at ten A.M. sharp. Will that suit you?"

It wasn't really a request. It was an order. But that was all right. I was curious enough to continue this. "I'll be here," I said and hung up.

FIVE

The next morning, I pulled up in front of Jimmy's apartment building. It was an old four-story brick from the turn of the century, and hadn't received much care since. I arrived early, hoping to have a few words with Jimmy's mother, but Jimmy was waiting outside in the cold morning air. He clutched his books to his chest as if he were using them to keep warm.

I had no choice. I reached across the front seat and opened the door, and Jimmy got in.

We went to Pantaze Drug. I asked him about his classes and he told me which ones he liked. He was getting behind in math, he said, although he didn't tell me why. I waited for him to explain why he'd wanted to see me the day before, but he didn't. I thought of mentioning Joe and the man in the beret, but I decided it wasn't time yet.

When we finished, I took Jimmy to school and waited at the curb for ten minutes after he went inside. He didn't come back out, which I saw as a good sign. If he could get to school, he would stay there.

It wasn't even eight o'clock yet. I stopped at the Salvation Army and looked for coats. The winter coats, one of the volunteers told me, had sold long ago. What they had left disappeared once the strike started. They had a few in back that had arrived the day before. I looked at them, found a small man's pea coat that would be too big for Jimmy, and took it anyway. Better to get lost in a coat than to have one that he couldn't fit into at all.

By ten proper, I was in my office, just as Miss Hathaway ordered. The pea coat hung on my shabby coat rack next to the other coats, and it looked like something a client had forgotten. Next to my hand was a Styrofoam cup filled with coffee that was slowly going cold. I had a file open and I was trying to peck out a report, but my mind wasn't on it. I kept thinking about that small brown package in Jimmy's hand and the way that, no matter how hard I tried, the boy seemed destined for the streets.

Then I thought about Laura Hathaway and her inheritance, her self-assurance, and the way she spoke to me, as if I were someone she had charge of. She probably thought all little black boys ended up like Jimmy. If she gave it any thought at all. She didn't see how the community fought for each and every one of them, and cried when they were lost.

I thought Jimmy had had a chance. His mother, irresponsible as she was, loved him and his brother used to look out for him. I had a sense Joe wasn't looking out for him any more.

Then I saw Laura Hathaway's shadow outside my door. She turned the knob as if she were trying it, then pushed the door inward. She wore her raincoat open and clutched her gloves in her left hand. Beneath her coat, she had on a long-sleeved dress with a high collar. A black purse hung over her right forearm and matched her black ankle-high boots. Pearls were clipped to her ears. I wondered how much luggage she had brought with her to Memphis, and then decided that I didn't want to know.

"Well," she said. "You're here."

"You ordered me to be here." I wasn't in the mood for her attitude.

She closed the door gently as if there were someone outside whom she wanted to protect from my rudeness. "I brought the pictures."

She remained by the door. I wondered if she wanted me to come and get them.

"All right." I stayed in my seat. She pulled her purse even tighter, and came closer.

"It's warm in here," she said.

"Take off your coat."

"How long do you think this will take?"

I shrugged. She pulled off her coat and put it over the only other chair, instead of hanging it on the rack beside the pea coat. She wrinkled her nose as she did so. The pea coat had a faint odor of mothballs that the heat was bringing out. I hoped the smell would be gone later in the day.

Then she opened the clasp on her purse and removed a small manila envelope. She set it on my desk.

I lifted the flap. Inside were a fistful of photographs of all shapes and sizes. Most dated from the forties, and several were of the same woman Laura Hathaway had shown me the day before. Only this woman was younger. She still had the same homely features, and I realized what I hadn't the day before. What I had seen as age was resignation.

Why would a woman like this, a rich white woman, look so defeated?

"My parents moved to Chicago when I was a little girl." Laura Hathaway had come around the back of the desk and was looking over my shoulder. "They didn't have a lot of money in those days. My father was one of the few men his age to stay home from the war—some old eye injury—and he got a lot of work. They put all the money away that they could. They made some good investments early, and by the time I was a teenager, we'd moved into a house in one of the nicer neighborhoods."

I was staring at a photo of Dora Jean Hathaway, her arms protectively around Laura, who had to be only three. The look in Dora Jean's eyes hadn't been put there by poverty. It had been put there by fear.

"How did your father learn about investments?" Poor people didn't save their money and invest it. Poor people spent as much as they could to live as well as they could. I knew that from personal experience.

"His father taught him, he said once."

"So your paternal grandparents were rich?"

"I don't know," she said. "I never got to meet them."

"Never?"

She shook her head. "They were dead by the time I was born."

I nodded and went through the photographs. The fear never left Dora Jean's eyes. In the fifties' family portrait, clearly done by a reputable studio, the look had etched itself into her skin. I had never seen this woman before, not when she was young and not when she was old. I was certain of it.

I was less certain of Earl Hathaway. The older version of him—a tall stately man with a receding hairline and fleshy gray skin—had a familiar brightness around the eyes. There was only one picture of him as a younger man, and that was blurred. He was holding Laura, who had to be about four, and he was turning his face from the camera. I saw the same receding hairline—he had apparently started to lose his hair relatively young—a narrow face with a strong jawline, and a powerful neck, the kind weight lifters, boxers, and football players have. He looked like the generic 1940s white man, the kind who would be used as an extra in movies or an office employee in a magazine ad.

"What?" she said, noting my interest. "What is it?"

"Where did your folks come from?"

"Chicago," she said, as if I hadn't been listening.

I decided to let the tone slide. "Before that."

She didn't answer.

"You said they moved to Chicago when you were a girl. Where did they move from?"

"The South." She spoke hesitantly, almost as if she didn't want to. Finally, we were getting somewhere.

It was my turn to give her a meaningful look, my turn to put sarcasm in my voice. "I understand that most northerners think the South is a small and provincial place, but we're actually quite a large region of the country."

"I don't know exactly," she said, color rising in her cheeks. "They never said."

I set the photo of her father on my desk. "They never said?"

She shrugged. "I got the sense there was some bad blood with my grandparents. I'm not just here for you, Mr. Dalton. I'm also here to see if I can find any remaining family. I'm not sure my grandparents are dead."

I waited. She stared at me. The color in her cheeks had gone from a soft rose to a deep red. If she had been black, she would have asked me outright to help her. But she wasn't, and she expected me to offer, and because of that expectation, I wouldn't.

"You think they're in Memphis?"

"You're in Memphis."

"I lived in Atlanta until I was ten. Then I moved to Washington, D.C., and lived there for eleven years. I was in Boston for a couple of years, and then I went to Korea. Your parents could have known me from anywhere."

"My parents had nothing to do with the war. They remained in Chicago. I told you that."

"You did." I picked up the family portrait. "I don't remember seeing them in Memphis. If our meeting was significant, and it must have been for your mother to want to leave me money, I would have remembered her face."

Laura's eyes narrowed. She apparently thought I'd insulted her mother.

"It's a striking face," I added.

Laura's expression softened. "Yes," she said. "It was."

She reached for the portrait. I moved it just out of her grasp. "Your father, on the other hand, seems somewhat familiar." I gazed at her. Her eyes were wider than his—although some of that could have been the effect of the eye-liner and the false eyelashes. Her nose was softer, up-turned in the way every white American parent wants a daughter's nose to be. She had lips so bow-shaped that she didn't have to use lipstick to mask their form.

"I suppose there could be a family resemblance," I said, "something I'm not quite seeing."

"I look more like my father than my mother," Laura said primly. That much was obvious. Laura was conventionally pretty. Her mother, in later life, was one of those women who would have been called handsome if someone had to find a kind word to say at all. "But I really don't look like either of them. I sometimes wondered if I favored another relative. . . ."

She let her voice trail off. Again, I could have offered—and was probably expected to—to help her. But I wasn't about to.

"The South," I said, reflectively. Laura's initial impression was probably right. I was probably a shirt-tail relative, and her mother, keeping step with the times, felt guilty and wanted to share part of the family windfall with the darker, less fortunate relations. But that didn't feel right. There would be no reason to hide that information from Laura, would there? Except, perhaps, the stigma of being distantly related to someone like me. "What was your mother's maiden name?"

"Jones." She looked away from me as she said that.

"Dora Jean Jones? Someone gave a child a name like that?"

"It was—"

"The South, I know," I said.

She shook her head. "I was going to say it was a slip of the tongue. Or it could have been. She only told me once, and that was when I went for my driver's license. They asked me, and I didn't know, and I asked her and she shrugged and said, 'Jones.' "

"And you didn't believe her, even then."

"I told you. There was bad blood with my grandparents."

"I thought it was with your father's parents."

"If I knew which set of grandparents it was, I would understand what was going on," she snapped.

"And your detective?" I asked. "What did he find?"

"I'm not going to hire you, if that's what you want, Mr. Dalton. This is not an odd job." So she had found out what I really did and wasn't willing to tell me. Apparently she had noted my two snubs and was going to snub me in return. Perhaps this woman and I were related. We certainly acted childishly around each other.

"You're the one who came to me, Miss Hathaway, wanting information. I don't know the information, but I could find it out for you. Or you could return to that big city detective who probably charged you way too much money for his call to the operator."

She raised her chin slightly. I was beginning to recognize that look. She wasn't going to answer me.

"So your detective didn't find anything," I said. "Just like he didn't find anything about me."

"This is my personal quest, Mr. Dalton. I don't need you."

"You don't," I said. "But if you want to know how I'm involved in your family, it might make sense to hire me."

"You'll be getting money from my mother's estate."

"So you say."

She snatched the portrait out of my hand. "I'm not paying you anything more than your inheritance."

"You haven't given me any money so far. And you have ordered me about and taken my time." I picked up the remaining photos and placed them inside their envelope. "I guess it's my turn to order you. I'd like you to leave my office, Miss Hathaway."

"We're not finished yet."

"We are," I said. "I don't need you or your family's make-believe money. I've got a lot of other things that need doing, things that are a lot more pressing."

"You're not a detective," she said clutching the envelope against her purse.

"Not like your talented Chicago man, no. I actually get the job done." I almost added that I would have motivation on this project, since I wanted to know the connection between her family and me as well, but I wasn't going to try to sway her. If she decided to walk out the door, that was fine with me.

She rounded the desk and grabbed her coat. I thought she was going to leave. But she stopped halfway to the door. Perhaps she expected me to break down, call her, beg her to stay. But I did none of those things, and that left the choice up to her.

Her shoulders rose and fell in a silent sigh. Then she turned around. The flush was back in her cheeks. "Then it's true, isn't it? You do detective work?"

"Yes," I said.

She still wasn't looking at me. "How much do you charge, Mr. Dalton?"

I told her. I also mentioned a retainer, since I knew she could afford one.

"You'll keep your findings confidential?"

"Absolutely."

She took a deep breath. "My attorneys said I was crazy to come down here. They said their detective could find what I was looking for."

"It was their detective who found me, wasn't it?" I asked. She nodded.

"And you don't like him either, do you?"

"He's old and fat and lazy," she said, and then put a hand to her mouth.

I smiled. "Don't worry. I like it when my clients are honest."

She sank into the chair, letting her coat fall across her knees. "I'm afraid I've been behaving like an ass, Mr. Dalton. It's just that the attorneys said you'd try to cheat me out of the money."

I felt my back go rigid.

"Only you haven't even asked me how much you were entitled to. And you would have kicked me out of your office without a penny."

"Maybe I'm manipulating you," I said without a trace of humor.

"Then you're doing a piss-poor job of it." She raised her head slightly. "I'm sorry, Mr. Dalton."

My breath caught in my throat. I couldn't remember the last time a white person apologized to me. Perhaps one never had.

"It's all right," I said, even though she had done several things that weren't all right, and which she probably wasn't even aware of. It wasn't my job to raise the consciousness of every white person I came into contact with. And now that she had dropped her defensive attitude, I had a feeling we could get along. "You're under strain."

"Yes, I am," she said. "I don't know anyone here, and I'm trying to find out something without having a clue how to go about it. There are no Hathaways in Memphis, at least none with our spelling. And there are a million Joneses."

"There are easier ways," I said. And then, just because I was feeling fair, "I could recommend a white detective if you would feel more comfortable."

"I suppose I deserve that." She pulled her coat closer to her stomach. "I would rather have you. You might remember some things, know some things—I mean, obviously my mother knew who you were."

"Are you sure the connection is with your mother?"

A slight frown creased her forehead. "Positive. The bequest is in her will."

"But your father is dead. Are you sure she wasn't just carrying out his wishes?"

Laura's frown deepened. "I hadn't thought of that. No. I'm not sure. And I don't know where to begin. I really thought you would remember them. I thought you would know." The color still stained her cheeks. "It was the lawyers who suggested that you were probably a distant relation. That's what makes you think I'm a bigot, isn't it? The way I treated you from the start?"

I wasn't going to get into that at all. We were finally communicating, and I didn't want to ruin it. I wanted to find the answer to this conundrum almost as much as she did.

"Did you bring family papers with you?" I asked. "Or do you have access to them?"

"I can get them." She took a deep breath. "What do you need?"

"A Bible with the family genealogy would be nice."

She opened her mouth, but before she could speak, I said, "But I know that's not possible. So let's start with birth and death certificates, the will, medical and financial records, and go from there."

"Financial records?" Even though she had decided to be nice, this obviously wouldn't be easy. She was predisposed to mistrust me, a predisposition that couldn't be blamed entirely on the lawyers.

"Maybe other payments went out." Now was the time for truth. But I couldn't bring myself to tell her I had received a previous payment in 1960; I had trouble enough admitting that to myself. "Perhaps when your father died . . . ?"

That was as close as I would get, and she didn't pick up on it. Instead she closed her purse and hung it on her arm. "I know nothing about the family's financial affairs prior to my mother's illness."

"What about the will?" I asked.

Her shoulders straightened. "What about it?"

"Any other beneficiaries besides us? Any other surprises?"

The tension in her shoulders relaxed slightly. She was trying to control her responses. She was trying to shift her attitude, and that was clearly taking an effort. Her initial reaction to me each time was to bristle.

When she didn't answer, I sighed. "Look, Miss Hathaway. This probably won't work. If you believe that my interest in this thing—as nebulous as it is—would be a conflict, then—"

"The other beneficiaries," she said slowly, "are an organization that helps abandoned children, several church charities, and a large sum that goes to the University of Chicago Foundation. That's twenty-five percent of the estate. Then there's the money that comes to you. The rest goes to me."

"I'm the only other individual mentioned in the will?"

She nodded. "There is no other family that I know of."

"Except your grandparents."

"If they're alive," she said.

"And if they are, will you give them part of the estate?"

She leaned back as if she hadn't thought of that.

"They could be living in poverty. Most people in the rural South are. Perhaps your parents escaped that life and never wanted to go back. Or maybe—" I stopped myself, the thought making me cold.

"Maybe?"

How to explain to this naive white woman the other thought that I had? Maybe her parents weren't white at all, not by racial categorization. Maybe they went north so that they could pass. No one would know who they were, and they would be judged by the color of their skin, not the color of their parents' skin.

"Maybe?" she asked again.

"Maybe they eloped," I said. The comment sounded lame

to me, but I wasn't going to express this new idea. Not yet. Maybe not ever, unless I had proof.

"But you don't think so."

"I don't think anything until I know it for a fact." I took a deep breath. I had to ask the next question, even though I knew it would upset her again. "You need to tell me the amount your mother left for me in the will."

As I thought, she raised her chin, and her entire body became rigid. "Why?"

"So that the cards are on the table, Miss Hathaway. We need to work from equality of knowledge. If you hire me, you hide nothing from me." It wouldn't work that way, I knew, but I had to make a stab at it.

She bit her lower lip.

"Besides, you don't want me thinking I'm going to get half a million dollars when I'm only getting five hundred dollars."

She closed her eyes. Fine lines appeared around her mouth. "Ten thousand dollars," she said, then opened her eyes to see my response. "My mother left you ten thousand dollars."

I clenched my fingers. It was the same amount as before. The dates matched up. These people, now dead, whom I didn't know, had twice given me more money than I would have earned in a year, for no reason that I could understand.

"It's a lot of money." Her voice rose. It probably wasn't a lot of money in the scheme of the estate. If it were, she wouldn't have been quite so defensive about it.

"Yes, it is. Especially for something neither of us understands." I rose. She watched me, without moving. "But it's not enough for you to come all the way here from Chicago, spending money on a private investigator, and searching for me. I'll bet those attorneys told you to put the money in trust until they could find me, and if they couldn't, they would place a provision in your will to give that money to charity after your death."

The look of surprise on her face made her look younger. "How did you know?"

I shrugged. "That's what I would do. No sense finding a man who had no idea he was going to get the money. If you put the money in a trust, you wouldn't have been violating the terms of the will. You would have been using your best efforts, am I correct?"

"That's what they argued."

"And you were being ethical, trying to carry out your mother's last wish?"

"Mother didn't make finding you contingent on anything," Laura said. "She just wanted it done."

"So you're doing it."

Laura swallowed. I saw the high collar move. "I told you," she said, her voice as low as it could get. "I'm looking for family."

"Even if that family is a coal black detective working out of a decrepit building in Memphis?"

"Yes."

"You thought about me," I said. "But what about the rest of the family? What would you do if they were black?"

She held out her hands and laughed. "How could they be? Look at me."

I did look at her. I knew things she didn't. Like the fact that my grandmother was as white as Laura was, only she had dark hair and big brown eyes. Like the fact that wasn't unusual in black southern families. Like the fact that I had friends who came out of the army and didn't go home, disappearing into northern cities, passing for white because life was better that way.

"Do you really think that's possible?" she asked.

"Anything's possible right now," I said. "Get me the information I need, and then we'll see what's actually going on."

She stood, ran a hand over her hair, and then came toward the desk. "You need a retainer, you said."

"No, I don't." I glanced at her. She was shaking. "I changed my mind."

She pulled a checkbook out of her purse, and then cleared a small spot on the back corner of the desk so that she could write. "I expect to be treated like the rest of your clients, Mr. Dalton. I will pay your retainer and you will give me an accounting—how often?"

"At the end of each week. An expense sheet will be attached."

"Very good." She wrote the check, her handwriting flowing and smooth. Then she ripped it off and handed it to me.

I didn't take it. "Miss Hathaway," I said, staring at the check that dangled between us, "there is a possibility that I'll find nothing, the same as your Chicago detective."

"Give it your best shot, Mr. Dalton, and we'll review after a month."

She was such an innocent. I wondered if she had ever managed money on her own before.

"No, Miss Hathaway," I said gently. "You need to put a financial limit on this. Otherwise I could—"

"Bill me a thousand dollars for a call to an operator in Memphis?"

I sighed and stared at that check. A license in my profession didn't mean a thing, especially not when attorneys helped with the billing. "Yes. Or I could find excuses to fly all over the country, looking for your long lost relatives."

"Staying at exclusive hotels?" she asked, raising an eyebrow.

Maybe what I had taken for an attitude was actually a subtle sense of humor. "Exactly."

She set the check on my desk. "You're the first ethical man I've met since my mother died, Mr. Dalton. I think your conscience will limit you enough."

She didn't know how right she was. I took the check, set it in my ledger, and placed it in the top drawer of my desk.

I'd use that check to find out a few things about my client, things she didn't even know I needed to know.

"Where do we start?" she asked after I had finished.

"Let me ask you a few questions, unless you're in a hurry." I looked pointedly at the coat. She scrunched it up slightly,and returned to her chair.

"No," she said. "I'm not in a hurry."

"Good." I sat down too. It felt odd, this subtle shift in our relationship. Suddenly I was in control, and she seemed content to have that happen. Was it two frustrating days in Memphis that did that? Or something else? "You said you moved to Chicago when you were very little. Where did you move from?"

"Rockford, Illinois."

"That's farther north," I said.

She shrugged.

"Were you born there?"

"No."

"Where were you born?"

"Birmingham, Alabama."

I looked at her. "I suppose you've already searched for family there."

"My mother told me they were just passing through."

"A pregnant woman traveling that close to her due date?"

The flush grew on Laura's cheeks. "I never thought of it that way."

"That's why you're going to pay me." I leaned back in the chair, feeling my heart pound. "What hospital were you born in?"

"St. Mary of Mercy," she said.

"And what was the date?"

"November fifteenth, 1939."

I scrawled all of this down. "It would be nice to see a copy of your birth certificate."

"You can't keep it," she said with that damned primness.

This time I expected it. "I know. I just want to see it. Sometimes birth certificates reveal a lot more than you'd think."

"Why mine?"

"Because you have immediate access to it. If you have access to your parents' as well, then I'd like to see them."

"I haven't found them," she said.

That stopped me. No one lacked a birth certificate. A person couldn't get a driver's license without it, or a passport, or other identification.

"You haven't found them anywhere? For both parents?"

She shook her head.

"How old were your parents?"

"Mother was sixty-four when she died. My father was sixty."

That narrowed it a bit. If they were born in rural communities, especially southern ones, they might not have received a birth certificate. But most people their age had something. If they didn't have an official birth certificate, they had a special certificate, often issued years later. She should have found an official piece of paper, some kind of proof of identity.

"And you're sure they were born in this country?"

She chuckled at that, as if I had asked something so preposterous as to be laughable. "Absolutely."

Odd, but not unexpected. People who had something to hide often hid it from their own children even after death.

"Let's start with the papers, and then I'll work from there. What can you get me?"

"I have my own papers," she said, "and I can have the lawyers wire me the rest."

"Let's do that."

She took a deep breath. "I've been going through everything, Mr. Dalton. I haven't found any family references. What do you think you'll find?"

It was a fair question, couched in that imperious tone. I

folded my hands. I would have to get used to the tone. She would have to learn to trust me.

"Patterns, Miss Hathaway. The information you're looking for may not have been on the surface. It may have been underneath. Just like you thought when you saw the bequest to me. There might be other things, things that lurk in your parents' important papers. I've done this sort of search a lot for black folks, many of whom couldn't read or write so the important information was often oral, and I've found things. Papers should make things easier."

"You think?" There was hope in her voice, a hope I wasn't sure I wanted to hear.

"You may not like what I find, Miss Hathaway."

She took a deep breath. "I'm beginning to realize that, Mr. Dalton."

"At any point, you can end this investigation. If I'm digging up things—"

She held up a hand, made a small wave, like beauty contestants did when they rode on the back of cars. Only she meant it dismissively. "Mr. Dalton, I'm sure that I can accept the truth of my family no matter how difficult it is."

I stared at her. Sometimes I wondered if we were ever prepared to face our families' truths. "All right, Miss Hathaway. It's your call. I'll get started with what you've given me today. Can you bring your papers tomorrow?"

She nodded. "And I'll drop off the others as soon as they arrive."

"Good."

She stood, her coat hanging awkwardly over one arm. She glanced at the door, as if uncertain how to make her exit, then smiled at me and came forward. "I'm sorry I was so rude, Mr. Dalton." She extended her right hand. "I'm glad we'll be working together."

I stood too, staring with surprise at her long manicured fingers. Even though she wore other jewelry, she didn't wear any rings.

She must have taken my response as rejection because she started to move her hand back. At that moment, I took it, shook, and smiled.

"I'll do my best to make this work," I said.

"Me, too." She slipped her hand from mine, and then walked out of the office. She closed the door before she stopped to put on her coat.

I watched her, still feeling the warmth of her palm in mine. Beneath that abrasive, arrogant exterior was a very lonely woman. The risks she had taken coming to Memphis, coming to Beale, were signs of how badly she needed this information. I had read her wrong from the beginning. I had thought she resented me and the fact that I was taking money from her. But she now seemed more complex than that.

Her shadow moved away from the door. I sat back down. I knew better than to trust a client without facts. I had learned that lesson the first week I had joined up with Loyce Kirby, the man who taught me the tricks of this trade. He'd given me one of his choicest clients, a man worth a lot of money, who had a poker face as smooth as any I'd ever seen. That man led me on a wild goose chase, then refused to pay me until Loyce got involved. Loyce had done it to teach me a lesson.

The lesson stuck. I picked up Laura's check and studied it for a moment. Then I dialed her bank in Chicago, put on my best white banker's voice, and asked for help verifying funds.

It was such a simple procedure, and no one ever checked to see if you were truly the business you said you were. I verified the check I held, then called back, got a different clerk, and using the same check number, asked for a funds verification of $100,000, and was told a check of that amount would clear.

My sense of Laura Hathaway was right. She had money. That much was true. The rest would remain to be seen. I would spend the rest of the day investigating her before I ever turned my attention to her missing relatives. And then I'd focus on the connection between us. Because, despite what I said to her, I had no intention of dropping this investigation until I knew once and for all why her family felt it owed me money.

SIX

Hours later, I had learned that Laura Hathaway was a twenty-eight-year-old white woman from Chicago who had never held a job. She was divorced from the younger son of one of Chicago's big department store families, and because her attorneys had been as powerful as and more interested than his attorneys, she received a monthly alimony payment of $5,000. She lived in an apartment in a building that she owned on Lake Shore Drive, with a gorgeous view of the lake (the apartment had been decorated by 1965's hot designer and had been written up in the Home and Family section of the Sunday *Chicago Tribune*). She was well known for her support of the arts, and for her successful fund-raising efforts on behalf of the Chicago Symphony. Her divorce last year had placed her down a notch on society's list, but by then, it seemed that she didn't care. Her mother was dying, and Laura devoted her own time to making sure the passage was a peaceful one.

When her mother died, Laura inherited one of Chicago's larger and more secret fortunes. Her parents had been virtual recluses, and they hadn't received attention from Chicago society until Laura's coming-out party in 1957. Even then, her father, Earl Hathaway, had refused to give the usual "I'm so proud of my daughter" interview to the press. Little was known about him, and what was known often came through his attorneys. It was widely speculated, and never disputed, that Earl Hathaway had ties to the Chicago underworld.

I got most of that from the society columnist for the *Tribune*, with a little more from the city editor for the *Sun-Times*. They both promised to have their morgue forward me copies of the relevant stories. I didn't care if I saw the stories or not.

The rest I learned through the bits of information Laura had given me—her checking account number, her address, and her date and place of birth. A few times I had to pose as her husband, once I had to pretend to be his attorney, and another time I was a sympathetic reporter from the Memphis *Commercial-Appeal*. Never once did I use my real name in gathering this information, and never once did anyone challenge my right to ask for it.

Such is privacy in America.

I also learned a few other things. Laura had "gone crazy" since her mother died, snubbing her "friends" and refusing to donate what had to be a considerable fortune to "worthy causes like the symphony." Instead, Laura had become obsessed with her past. Her best friend, a woman named Prissy Gargen Golden, said that Laura was determined to find out her parents' secrets, even though everyone tried to talk her out of it. The attorneys were particularly upset, and Laura had nearly fired them. In fact, Laura took control of her mother's financial affairs in the final year and insisted on maintaining her own expenses, something that "just wasn't done" in their circles. Gargen Golden had apparently confided all of this to the society column at the *Tribune*, leading me to wonder what kind of best friend she really was.

That bit of information—that Laura handled her own money—made me smile. She had patronized me, perhaps unwittingly, and I had done the same to her. Yet it was my concern for her financial affairs that had led her to state that I was the most ethical person she had met since her mother died, a statement I was only just beginning to understand. Somewhere in there, her world had shifted, and that shift had come with an understanding that when you had money, other people wanted to take it from you.

All of that information, while making me feel that I was probably the strangest employee Laura Hathaway would ever have, also made me calmer about working with her. She had layers like anyone else, but her layers had less to do with me than they had to do with things she was dealing with out of her own life. I was supposed to have been a stepping stone to more information. That she decided to pay me for my services meant that I must have, in some way, given her a reason to believe in me. And that, oddly enough, gave me a bit of comfort in our strange partnership.

I hadn't had lunch and my stomach was rumbling. I decided to make one more routine phone call, and then pick up something warm and spicy for lunch. I called an operator in Birmingham and asked her to look up three phone numbers for me: public records, city hall, and St. Mary of Mercy Hospital.

"I have no listing for a St. Mary of Mercy Hospital," she said.

"Are you a native of Birmingham?" I asked. Operators were sometimes my best sources of information.

"Yes, sir," she said.

"Can you give me the phone number of the hospital that used to be St. Mary of Mercy?"

"No hospital has changed names that I know of," she said.

"Was there a St. Mary of Mercy there in 1939?"

"No, sir. We have a Catholic hospital, but it isn't St. Mary of Mercy."

"Would you give me their number then?"

She did, and I thanked her for her time. Then I sat at my desk and stared at my black phone. Never, in all my years digging up information, had I ever had someone give me the wrong name for a birth hospital. People lied about towns, they lied about dates, but not about hospitals. If they didn't know, they simply said so, and then I tracked the information down.

But people didn't remember where they were born; this was information told to them, and Laura had hired me to find out about her parents. The mob connection, mentioned by the city editor, seemed a likely lead, although it wouldn't tell me why Laura's parents had lied about their origins.

Unless there was something else in their past, something they were running from that wasn't innocent, something that would be unforgivable if found out. Something, perhaps, connected to the underworld, which had branches from Florida to Los Angeles, with ports in between.

I still hadn't touched my cup of coffee. The Styrofoam had melted, leaving a film on top of the liquid. I grimaced in distaste, put on my coat, and picked up the cup. I carried it with two fingers as I left my office, set it on the ground as I locked up, and then headed to the street, where I poured the offending liquid under the wheel of my car. Then I crumpled the cup and tossed it in the full metal curbside garbage can, not that it would do any good. It was getting to the point where I would have to start hauling my own trash to the dump.

There was music in Handy Park. Four young men wearing bright colors huddled on the north end of the park. Two were playing passable acoustic guitar, another was playing bass, and a third was playing fiddle. They weren't good, but they weren't bad either, and it was always nice to hear some blues, whether it was well done or not.

I glanced at my watch. School was out, but Jimmy wasn't

sitting below the statue. I saw that as a good sign. I'd stop by the apartment on the way home and give him the coat.

It was too late to get a good lunch at Pantaze Drugs—their sandwiches were just passable; only their specials were fine—and I'd been to Wilson the day before. Long about four o'clock the Little Hot House started their evening specials, and if I arrived at the right time, I would get a free taste. It paid to be a regular who appreciated good food.

I hurried past Schwab's, with its cluttered window displays showing nothing of interest to me, then gazed longingly into the windows at Pape's Men Shop. The clothes in there were high quality. I'd once bought myself a suit coat there, back in the days when I was feeling flush, and I was never able to buy anything there again. I promised myself the next time I got a windfall, I'd splurge in the clothing stores I saw every day—particularly Pape's—but the promise felt more like a daydream.

There was a gap between buildings that showed the parking lots and alleys, and then I passed two more doors before getting to the restaurant. It had a greasy menu pasted in the window and its Pabst Blue Ribbon sign was new. Someone had already taken in the sandwich board—which was promising for me—and the interior was light against the late February afternoon.

I slipped inside, inhaled the smell of old beer, chili, and grease so baked in that the place would probably smell like that forever. The floor was wood and uneven due to varied materials used in the Depression when the place was built. The tables were scarred and round, the chairs mismatched, but I loved it inside. You could get some of the best catfish in Memphis here if you were willing to pay a little extra, and the chili was hotter than a four-alarm fire.

There were a handful of booths down the stairs and to the right, and I took my favorite one near the narrow bar.

Suzy, the waitress, was usually on this time of day, and she knew enough to give me my Coke and a filmy glass of water without asking. She also knew enough not to ask me what I wanted if the catfish was fresh, the chili was good, or chicken and dumplings were the special. She didn't want an order, so I knew I'd get one of the three.

I leaned my head back against the booth's high wooden side. An exhaustion headache was building in my temples, probably exacerbated by my lack of food. I think I was dozing when Doc Shann punched my arm lightly.

"Hey," he said, slipping into my booth. "You buyin'?"

I smiled and rubbed my eyes. "Food only."

"Yeah, sure." He put his feet up and waved at Suzy. "Bring me what yer bringing him."

I didn't complain. I'd known Doc since I arrived in Memphis. In those days, he played a mean tenor saxophone and I used to hit the clubs just to hear him. He had a wife and two children, a boy and a girl, and was proud of them. Now he played for change in Handy Park when he was sober. I never found out what happened to his wife; I assumed she left him. His son died in Vietnam two years before. I'd seen his daughter a few times, grown up and professional, fishing her father out of clubs long after midnight.

Suzy brought him a Coke, and he didn't complain. He would when he noticed it, but he had ordered exactly what I had, and she was following that order.

"You been watching the TV?" Doc asked.

I took a sip of Coke, hoping I didn't know where this conversation was going, but fearing that I did. "Not too much, Doc. I've been busy."

"You seen them pictures they been sending back from 'Nam?"

I had. They were getting worse by the day. The offensive that had started on January thirtieth was escalating into something ugly, and reporters were capturing it all on film.

If you didn't catch the news on television the night before, it was rehashed in the morning papers, the still images just as horrifying as the moving ones.

"Yes," I said.

"I don't know what to think no more."

"Me, either, Doc."

"Cronkite's doing a special tonight."

"I didn't know that."

"About 'Nam."

"I figured."

He picked up his straw and shook it at me. "You know Dr. King."

"We went to the same school," I said cautiously. "That's all."

"He called it our sin. He said we sinned in Vietnam."

We'd been having the same conversation since Martin made his most important speech against the war nearly a year before. I suppressed a sigh.

"He said we must all protest. *All.* That ain't right. My boy, he died because he thought we was doing something right."

"I know, Doc," I said softly.

"And if it wasn't right, then what'd he die for? You tell me, Smokey. You know Dr. King. You ask him for me, would you? Please?"

"I'm not close to him anymore, Doc. I've told you."

"I know. I know." He was shaking his head. "But I marched with Dr. King. I been beside him, been talking with him. And I don't know no more. Because if he's right, my boy, he died . . ."

He shook his head again.

Suzy met my gaze from across the room. She had to have heard that last. Everyone had. Doc was raising his voice with each sentence.

"Now there's them pictures," he said. "You seen them pictures?"

"Yes, Doc."

"It don't seem right, but I tell myself it's war. My boy, he thought—"

Suzy came up to him and put her hand on his shoulder. "Your order's done, Doc. I'm going to serve it to you at the bar. Smokey's got some business he's got to do."

Doc didn't protest. This had happened too many times before, and he knew that protesting might get him kicked out of the restaurant. He slide out of the booth and made his way to the bar, leaving his Coke behind.

"Thanks," I said.

She smiled at me, and slipped into the booth for a moment. Suzy and I had a fling several years ago. It had been short, and it ended when I learned that she was married. Her husband left her later, but she wasn't interested in me anymore. I think the demands of raising two children on a waitress's salary had her mind on other things.

"Haven't seen you for a while," she said.

I shrugged. "Been busy."

"Me, too." She glanced at the door. A large party was coming in. "Friday was hell."

She was referring to the riot.

"The place doesn't seem worse for wear."

"I stayed inside." She shook her head. "I just want this thing to be over. I had to drive the restaurant truck to the dump this morning, and I got stopped. They told me I was crossing a picket line. Do you know what a mess it is out back? I have to get rid of this stuff somewhere."

"I know."

"Suzy!" the bartender yelled.

"I'll be back," she said, and slipped out. She went to the large table and took their order, then went into the kitchen and picked up mine. She started to bring it to me, but I pointed at Doc. She set food down in front of him, then went back in the kitchen.

The new party was loud and obnoxious, arguing about

which was better, Motown or Stax. That was my first clue that some of them were outsiders. No one from Memphis would argue in public against our own studio. Motown may have been older, but Stax was the wave of the future.

Suzy brought me chicken and dumplings and the morning papers, which I hadn't seen. I ate and read about the upcoming New Hampshire primary, the latest developments in Vietnam, and the continuing stalemate in the sanitation workers' strike. Someone started the jukebox, playing the Supremes at full volume, and I suspected I was in for a battle of the bands. I didn't mind. It gave me something to listen to while I ate.

Doc passed out on the bar, and the bartender struggled to wake him up. Suzy had her hands full with the new table, the men on one side grabbing at her and the boys on the other laughing just a bit too loud. I'd helped her through a couple of those situations, and usually she got mad at me. She always said gropers gave the highest tips.

It took me nearly an hour to go through the *Commercial Appeal* and another half hour to peruse the *Press-Scimitar*. Then I left my money on the table, along with a generous tip, and stood. It was time to go home, get some rest, and let the brain focus on something other than Laura Hathaway.

I was halfway to the door when I realized one of the faces at the big table was familiar. Joe Bailey was sitting on the end, wearing a beret, a new leather coat slung on the back of his chair. He looked cleaner than usual, though, and happy. When he saw me, he grinned.

I did not smile back. I walked over to the table.

"I took Jimmy to school this morning," I said to him. "Apparently he's been missing a lot of it."

The table grew silent. Several others, older men, were watching me now. One looked very familiar. He pulled his beret over his face and turned away so that I couldn't recognize him. I didn't look at him directly, although I did try to study him out of the corner of my eye. I wondered if he was the guy I saw in the park.

"Jimmy?" Joe asked.

"Your brother." I let the sarcasm show my displeasure.

"I'm not in charge of what he do."

"Really?" I asked. "I saw him meet you at lunch yesterday. He wouldn't have been able to do that if he were in school."

Joe's eyes narrowed. "That all you see?"

I wasn't about to tell him about the parcel, not in front of his friends. "Was there more to see?"

"Jus' me makin' sure he ate."

"I bought him lunch." My tone was flat. Joe had the decency to look away. He knew I'd caught him in a lie.

I leaned forward so that I was as close to him as I could get. I could see the acne on his skin, the shadows under his eyes. Why was it that the Baileys weren't sleeping? "You're old enough to make your own choices. But Jimmy isn't. He's got a future, if you just let him try for it."

"A future doin' what? Whatever some honky tells him?"

That wasn't a sentiment that Joe had ever expressed before. I glanced at the rest of the table. Black Panthers, or wanna-be Panthers. What passed for the Black Power movement in Memphis. I didn't like Joe hooked up with them.

"You want to introduce me to your friends?"

Joe's expression went flat. "They're just friends."

"Mmm," I said. "So this is what the Invaders look like." The Invaders were a group of high school students who were beginning to make themselves known as militants. They had interrupted a few strike meetings already, trying to turn the strike into a Stokely Carmichael type of event.

"We ain't all Invaders," one of the older men said, and the man next to him, the one who had been hiding his face from me, elbowed him.

"Really?" I asked. "So I'm to believe you're Black Panthers who've come all the way from California to little ole Memphis."

"Believe what you want," Joe said.

"I do," I said. "I believe you're poisoning this boy, and you're letting him poison his brother."

" 'Cause he don't like bowin' to the white man?"

"Because he needs to grow up before he makes the choices you're offering him."

"I'm grown," Joe said, sitting up even straighter.

"Not enough," I said. "You don't know what their philosophy will do."

"It'll make our people strong," the older man said.

"That's a bunch of horseshit and you know it." I kept my hands on the table and looked directly at him. The other man in the beret still slouched near the wall. "This 'burn, baby, burn' crap will only get people killed. Good people, like Joe. And maybe like his ten-year-old brother. Our people."

"Careful," one of the men said. "If he ain't with us, he work for the Man."

"I don't work for the Man," I said. "I work for myself, and I pay attention to the black community. But there is a difference between you and me. And the difference is simple: I believe the system can be improved for black *and* white. You think it can only be improved for blacks."

"Was there somethin' about bein' a chil' in Atlanta that makes niggers idealists?" The man who'd been hiding his face pulled his hat down even lower.

I felt a shiver run through me. Very few people knew I had grown up in Atlanta. Most people thought I was from Washington, D.C. They thought my connection with Martin occurred at Boston University, not on Sweet Auburn Street.

I wasn't going to let him see that he had rocked me.

"How can a man who believes in black power use that word?" I asked.

The man beside him grinned as if I had walked into a trap. "We take it over, make it ours, use it so much it ain't got no sting. We take their weapon from them and turn it on them. We do it with words, and we'll do it with weapons. You wait."

"You run the risk," I said slowly, "of becoming just like the white folks you hate."

He shook his head. "You been kowtowing to them so long you don't even know when you're doing it."

"I believe we all have to live together."

"And I believe we can break the system and remake it in our own image."

"You better have an idea which image you're shooting for then," I said. "Because if you're not careful, you'll tear down their system, and rebuild one just like it. Only you'll be the oppressors. You'll become the very thing you hate."

"It'll be different with the black man in charge."

"Will it?" I asked. "Will it really?"

"Yeah, it'll be different," the man said.

"I used to agree," I said, and that got Joe to look up. I wanted to get him away from this group as quickly as I could. But I didn't exactly know how. "Back in the days when people listened to Martin's words on nonviolence. Our people were doing something different. We were doing something better. But now I hear rumblings about Martin in the black community that sound just like those from the white. He don't represent blacks no more, people say. He abandoned us to talk about the war. He don't think of us no more, not when he's trying to take on poverty. But he's right. The whole society is sick, and if you tear it down and replace it with the same sick structure, the wars will continue. Or worse, if you replace it with nothing, this whole country will burn."

Joe glanced at the others, then pounded his fist on the table. "I say let it!"

I stared at him for a long time, so long that his enthusiasm dimmed and his fist unclenched. He continued to look at me, but the light faded from his eyes.

I finally let my gaze leave his. The other men were watching me, their expressions wary.

"The thing about fire," I said, "is that it's very hard to control."

"The thing about fire," said the man who knew me from beneath his beret, "is that it burns clean."

"Not when you want it to," I said. "Sometimes it destroys everything you love, alongside everything you hate."

"You know how to do this better?"

I shook my head. "I'm just one of those guys who knows what doesn't work, not what does. It's my job."

I didn't let them answer that. I turned back to Joe. "You want to come with me?" I asked. "I've got something for Jimmy, so I'll be going your way."

"I'm stayin'," Joe said, and we both knew he wasn't just referring to the Little Hot House.

"Well," I said. "You know you're always welcome to come to me, for anything."

"I know." Joe mumbled that last, as if he were ashamed of it, ashamed of me.

I stood up and nodded at the others. They were no longer looking at me. Apparently, if they couldn't defeat me with words, they'd pretend that I didn't exist.

I wanted to haul Joe out of there, but I had no right to do that. He was a fifteen-year-old boy, but he wasn't mine, and they weren't doing anything illegal, at least not in the restaurant.

So I left the table and let myself out into the growing dark. Beale was nearly empty, in its transition between a daylight workaday street and its nighttime party street. I stood beside Pape's window and took a deep breath of cold evening air. I was shaking, and it wasn't from the conversations. Or maybe it was. I had a feeling of foreboding so deep that I half expected someone to come out of the shadows and grab me.

But no one did. And after a moment, I stepped away from the window and walked down the street, hands in my pockets, listening to my footsteps on the concrete, and I knew I was alone.

SEVEN

On the way home, I stopped at Jimmy's apartment building. Two of the street lights were out and one was fading, making the entire area dark. The cold air smelled of garbage. The piles weren't neat here like they were downtown. They looked as if people had simply thrown their waste on the curb instead of bagging it. Dogs rooted in a heap near the alley. The strays looked healthy this year; the garbage was giving them enough to eat.

I put the pea coat over my arm, crossed the threshold, and went inside. The hallway was dark. Someone had smashed the light above me and no one had bothered to fix it. The stairs were still lit, the fixture so high above them that it would take sheer cussedness to break it.

I climbed them, ignoring the toys and discarded cans that littered the hallway. It smelled of urine and beer. The railing was crusty, so I let it go.

Jimmy's apartment was on the third floor. The building had deteriorated since the last time I had been here. I wondered if his mother would take my help finding a new home. Probably not; a new home would mean giving up her profession and she seemed loath to do that. She said there was nothing else that paid her as well—at least nothing she could get.

The hell of it was that she was probably right.

The third floor hallway was relatively clean. All the fixtures worked here. I could hear children crying in the nearest apartment and B. B. King blaring from the next apartment over. I stopped in front of Jimmy's door. No light filtered under the threshold, but I knocked anyway.

The sound reverberated inside. You could always tell when no one was home. A slip of paper was stuck in the space between the door and the frame just above the cheap lock. I pulled it out. It was a hand-written notice from the super about the overdue rent.

I knocked again.

"It's Smokey," I called, just in case they were hiding from the manager.

Still no answer, and I doubted I'd get one. I knocked a few more times for good measure, hard enough to get the blues fan to open his door.

Finally, I gave up. I wondered where Jimmy was. Joe was at the Little Hot House, and his mother was who knew where, but Jimmy needed somewhere to go. I hoped he had it.

I debated leaving the coat hanging from the doorknob, but knew that wouldn't be wise. Someone else would get it, and Jimmy would go through Memphis's winter chill wearing a coat several sizes too small.

I'd give it to him in the morning. As I went down the stairs, I cursed myself for failing to arrange to take him to school the following day.

By the time I got home, I felt both tired and a bit dirty. My house was small, essentially three rooms on one level, but it had a large porch, a basement that I used for storage, and an even larger yard. The living room was square and arranged badly for company, just one easy chair and a couch big enough for me to stretch out on. A bookshelf ran along one wall, with paperbacks and some bookclub hardcovers, some science fiction, but mostly black authors, from Ralph Ellison to Langston Hughes to James Baldwin. I was half done with William Melvin Kelly's *Dem*, but it didn't appeal to me that night, not after the conversation with Joe's friends. I picked up the second volume in Samuel R. Delany's *Fall of the Towers* trilogy, but that didn't hold me either, so I turned on the television.

I tuned in CBS and watched until ten. I was sprawled on the couch, almost dozing, when *Who, What, When, Where, and Why* flashed on the screen, followed by a subtitle: *Report from Vietnam by Walter Cronkite.* It started with images of Saigon, a ruined city, and reviewed the past month. Cronkite had promised a personal review of the Tet Offensive, and this was it.

This was the program Doc had warned me about.

Cronkite called his conclusions "speculative, personal, and subjective." But they were blunt and captured what I was feeling—probably what the country was feeling. He called the war a stalemate, and said, essentially, that winning would require an impossible price—"cosmic disaster." He called for a negotiated peace, "not as victors," he said, but as "honorable people who lived up to their pledge to defend democracy and did the best they could."

In other words, people who had failed.

Walter Cronkite, the most trusted man in America, was telling us to throw in the towel on Vietnam, just like Martin had done a year before. I wondered what Martin thought. Was he declaring a personal victory tonight or did he even know? I knew Doc Shann would be disappointed—or maybe he wouldn't be. Cronkite might have given him a way to speak about the war without tarnishing the memory of his son.

And me, I tried to ignore Vietnam, but it was hard, when I knew that boys like Joe were the ones on the front lines. I had tried to warn him once, but it wasn't real to him yet. Playing revolutionary with his little friends was. He wasn't draft age. When he was, maybe he would learn the meaning of the rhetoric he was using. I only hoped he survived it.

It took me a long time to get to sleep after that program, and when I finally did sleep, I had the dream.

I am ten years old, lanky and too thin, nearly asleep under a quilt my momma made, my head cushioned against a feather pillow that had just been repacked. It smelled of chicken—a smell that Momma promised would go away in a few weeks, but which I knew would stay for longer than that, invading my sleep and making me sneeze.

The front door bangs open, starting me awake. My momma's voice rises, sharp with fear. My daddy goes into the hall. I can see him in the thin electric light, nightshirt unbuttoned, tying the string on his pajama bottoms. He leans overthe railing, cries, "Who down there?" and when he gets no answer, tells my momma to call the police.

I get up and walk to my door, and he whispers, "Hide, son." I stand there for a moment, and he makes an impatient movement with his hand. I know that movement. If I don't do as he says, I'll get that whupping I've been deserving, the one he don't know about.

I grab my stuffed dog off my bedstand, where I'd been keeping it since I turned ten—a big boy now—and I ease myself into the closet. There's a crawl space in the back that no one knows about but me, a space that I used to fit in a lot better than I do now. I squinch myself inside, wrap my arms around the dog, and listen.

My daddy's made me hide at night before, and it has turned out fine. When I was eight, men came, shouting and yelling and demanding my daddy. The police came too, and everything died down. My daddy had a shotgun he kept near the door, and he took it out whenever he expected trouble.

I just guess he didn't expect trouble tonight.

The door opens, and I hear voices. No yelling. Just voices. Then my momma's voice joins them, and she shouts, "It ain't so! It ain't so!" She screams once, and my daddy hushes her. Then the door closes, and the house is quiet.

It's hot in the crawl space, and my legs fall asleep. I clutch the dog to my stomach and close my eyes, hoping my daddy'll come for me soon. But the house is really quiet. Too quiet. All I can hear is my own heart, pounding, pounding, pounding, and my breathing, harsh and raggedy.

I started awake, sitting up in bed, sweat pouring down my back. My heart *was* pounding, my breath coming hard, just as it always did when I had that dream.

I threw the covers back and put my feet on the thin carpet, noting the differences between this place—my home—and that house in Atlanta. That was the last time I saw my parents. The Grand came for me and told me nothing. No one said anything to me about what happened to my parents. Conversations would cease when I entered the room.

Later, I learned that they had been lynched that night, and I realized that my father's whispered "Hide!" had probably saved my life.

I made my way into the kitchen, fumbled for the light switch, and clicked it on. The bulb was yellow, and the light looked thin. I had white curtains on the window, made for me by a girlfriend who was now married to someone else, and they provided poor cover against the darkness outside. I glanced at the clock on the stove. It read 4:25 A.M. I sighed. I would never get back to sleep, not after the dream, and it was too early to get much done.

Maybe if I calmed myself. Only one thing worked, and it was something that my mother used to do for me when I was very young. I heated up some milk on the stove, added butter and honey, and poured it into a ceramic mug. Then I sipped, slowly, closing my eyes, letting myself return to a time before that awful night, a time when I believed that things like a mother's touch and a sweet night-time glass of milk could make anything better.

I took the mug back to my bedroom and finished drinking. The trick worked: I slept a deep dreamless sleep of the innocent, or perhaps of the man who wanted nothing more than escape.

I was tired the next morning. I got a call from Henry asking me to meet him at Wilson Drug for breakfast. On my way, I drove by the apartment to see if I could see Jimmy, but he wasn't there. The slip of paper was gone from the door, though, so someone had come home.

Wilson's was full that morning, but Henry had gotten there first and found a table. He was already eating his eggs, covered in Tabasco, and sopping up the whole mess with a slice of toast. I ordered my eggs scrambled, and then I sat down.

I didn't really want to talk about the strike, which I knew was foremost on Henry's mind. But I did want to talk about Jimmy. I was beginning to think it was time to see what my options were.

"You aren't going to like this, Smokey," Henry said after we'd gotten past the pleasantries.

I leaned back in the metal chair. It groaned. "I knew that when you called."

"Mayor Loeb and the city aren't budging."

I nodded.

"We been thinking we need national support."

Martha brought me my eggs and a newspaper. I hadn't even seen her when I had come in. That showed how distracted I was. I thanked her, poured catsup on my hash browns, and started to eat.

"You got the local AFL-CIO," I said. "The national will probably get involved."

Henry shook his head. "They're seeing it as a black issue, Smokey, and they aren't that far from wrong."

I knew the arguments. Most of the sanitation workers were black. They barely earned more than minimum wage and they had no workers' compensation. To make things worse, the city operated on the "plantation system" where the mayor and the city council oversaw the work of thousands of municipal employees. Since Loeb, a longtime segregationist, had declared the strike illegal and ordered workers back to their jobs or be fired, things had escalated into an issue that was more about race than fair pay.

"A black issue means they won't get involved?" I asked.

"Not without sanction and even then maybe not," Henry said. "We need some national attention, Smokey, and we won't get it from the unions."

I shoved my eggs aside. Suddenly they didn't look that good any more. Martha came by with the coffee pot and I had her pour some more. I had a hunch it was going to be a long day.

"You've got Reverend Lawson and a lot of other people who have national connections," I said. Reverend James Lawson was one of the founders of the Southern Christian Leadership Conference. He had worked side by side with Martin in the most important decade of his life. If he couldn't get Martin here, no one could.

"That's not the issue," Henry said. "Between COME and the NAACP, we have enough connections to bring in the right people. The key is security, Smokey. We don't want another incident like we had a week ago."

Incident. What a great word for that disaster. "Who're you bringing in?" I asked.

"We're talking about Roy Wilkins and Bayard Rustin. And of course, Dr. King."

"Of course," I said.

Henry put his plate aside. Martha picked it up immediately. I wondered if she was listening. "I'm asking you to provide security."

"Those men have their own teams."

"We could use other eyes."

The eggs weren't sitting well in my stomach. "I can't guarantee anything."

"Just stand in the back," he said. "Watch for trouble during the speeches. Maybe make sure the buildings are clear."

"You need a professional security team for that."

He raised his eyebrows. "Where are we going to find that here, Smokey?"

He had a point. I sighed. "Let me know where and when the speeches happen. I'll take them on a case-by-case. If I'm busy, you'll have to find someone else."

He grinned. "I knew I could count on you."

"I haven't done anything yet," I said.

He grabbed the check. I tried to pull it from his hand, but he wouldn't let me. He was out the door before I remembered that I wanted to talk with him about Jimmy.

I wasn't too happy as I went to my office. I didn't want to be involved in any way. If something bad happened at those meetings, people would see it as my fault. And one man, even an observant one, couldn't stop a group like the Panthers if they wanted to create trouble.

I'd see if I could put together a group and put someone like Roscoe Miller in charge. That would have to be good enough for Henry.

With that decision, I turned my attention to the rest of the morning. Laura Hathaway was coming to my office. Hers was the only case—such as it was—that was completely active right now. Before it went any further, I had to tell her about the money. I had demanded that she be honest with me. I had to be honest with her.

I just wasn't sure how to do it.

She arrived promptly at ten. She knocked, not because I had asked her to, but because she was carrying a small box. I opened the door, and she smiled up at me. Her makeup was perfect except for a microscopic dot of eyeliner beside her left eye. Her hair flipped out as if she had spent the entire evening in curlers, and she was again wearing the pearls on her ears.

I took the box from her and set it on a pile of papers, then helped her off with her coat—she glanced over her shoulder at me with some surprise—and hung it on the coat rack.

She was wearing a white cashmere sweater over a pink turtleneck, a matching pink skirt, and a different pair of ankle boots. She had changed her nail polish to match the outfit. The entire effect was perfect for the Peabody and so out of place here that I wondered why I hadn't said anything until now.

"Miss Hathaway," I started and then stopped, unsure how to finish. We had just reached a comfortable truce. Did I break it by commenting on her clothing?

"I brought some of the records you wanted," she said. "I called the attorneys and they weren't happy, but I insisted. I reminded them that I was the employer and they were the employees and if they had a problem with that, well." She grinned. "You know."

I did know. I had seen that side of Laura Hathaway myself. I grinned in return. Then I let my smile fade.

"Miss Hathaway," I said.

"Laura."

"Laura." I took a deep breath. "That first day, when you came here, I warned you about the walk from the Peabody to Beale—"

"Yes?"

I sighed. "There's a group of professional thieves that work this street. The cops call them the Beale Street Professionals, and you—"

"Look like a target, I'll bet." She laughed. "You're telling me to dress down."

"If that's possible."

Her grin widened. She was beautiful when she smiled. "I have been known to go into a Woolworth's from time to time."

I smiled back, relieved, then went to the box. "Now, what did you bring?"

She joined me. She was wearing a light perfume, so faint that I wouldn't have noticed it if her movement hadn't made the scent drift between us. "What I had. Pictures. Financial records from the last year. My stuff."

"Is your birth certificate here?"

"In my purse. Why?"

I didn't answer her. I wasn't going to tell her anything, yet. "May I see it?"

She opened the clasp on the purse, pulling out another small envelope. The inside of her purse was incredibly neat: a thin wallet, a checkbook with gold pen attached to the leather cover, lipstick, eyeliner, rouge, and a comb. Every woman's purse I had ever seen had been filled with receipts, tattered paper, ancient gum, pens that no longer worked, and makeup that had caked shut. That seemed normal to me. Laura's seemed obsessively tidy.

I took the envelope, opened it, and saw all her important identification. I was about to say something, when she said, "I know. I was trying to be cautious," so I left it at that.

I took the certificate and handed the envelope back to her. Then I walked to my crusted windows. Thin morning light filtered in through the grime and dirt. I held the certificate up to it.

"Is this the original?"

She frowned. She was still standing near the box, clutching the envelope, watching me. "I don't know. It's the one I've used my whole life."

It didn't look like an original. A retyped copy would have all the pertinent information, but would be missing the baby prints that hospitals often took, foot and hand prints. But my certificate didn't have the prints, and it was an original. I didn't know what the customs were in Alabama.

Time and date of birth were duly noted. Laura Anne Hathaway was the name on the birth certificate, daughter of Dora Jean and Earl Ray Hathaway. The attending physician was named Beaumont Calhoun. The certificate was issued from Birmingham in Jefferson County, Alabama.

I stared at that for a moment. A retyped copy, which so many birth certificates were, told me nothing.

"When did you lose your original birth certificate?" I asked her.

Laura turned her head slightly. "I never did."

"Then who requested this copy?"

"How do you know it's a copy?"

"I don't for sure. But originals usually have infant footprints on them or near them. Parents usually kept that sort of thing."

She walked up to the window beside me. "It's the only certificate I've ever seen."

"And you're certain your parents were passing through?"

"That's what my mother said."

"That's interesting," I said.

She peered over my shoulder. "What are you seeing?"

"Note the line next to the attending physician's name."

"Yes?"

"It's blank."

"So?"

"What hospital were you born in?"

"St. Mary of Mercy."

"There is no St. Mary of Mercy Hospital in Birmingham. There has never been one."

I could feel her stiffen beside me. "You're sure?"

"Positive."

"How do you know that?"

"I found out yesterday, just like you asked me to do." I

tapped the certificate with my left forefinger. "That blank line, it's for the hospital's name. Now, not having the line filled out is pretty common for 1939. Most folks, especially in the South, still preferred home births, often with the family doctor attending. But your mother said she was traveling through, and I doubt any doctor would come to a hotel room. I'm pretty sure he'd insist on having a traveling woman come to his hospital."

"You get all of that from a blank line?"

"And the wrong hospital name. And the fact that your folks were pretty secretive about their family."

"You think I was born at home in Birmingham, and then my parents left?"

"It's a start," I said. "It gives me a direction."

I handed the certificate to her and sat down in my chair. She remained standing, staring at the document she had seen all her life as if it had suddenly grown legs.

"Why wouldn't she have told me?"

"There could be a thousand reasons, Laura." I had been looking through the envelope she had given me. I stopped. "You'll have to be ready for anything, you know."

"I am ready," she said, but her voice shook.

This was my opportunity. I hadn't expected it so soon. "All right, let's test your resolve."

She raised her chin. Her lower lip trembled. She bit it to hold it in place.

"In early 1960, I received an anonymous cash payment of ten thousand dollars."

She let out a small breath.

"I was never able to find out who sent it or why. The attorney who dispersed the money wouldn't tell me where it came from, of course, but he did receive a phone call from your detective last week."

Her skin had gone so pale that she seemed to have no blood in it at all. "You think my mother sent it?"

I nodded.

"Why?"

"Hadn't your father just died?"

"Oh." She sat on the chair across from me so hard that it nearly scooted out from underneath her.

"In all these photographs," I said, "your mother looks haunted, somehow, as if she were afraid of something or resigned to it. Do you know what that is?"

She shook her head. "You think they did something criminal, don't you?"

"I think it's likely, but I'm not sure." And then I said softly, "We can stop here, if you want."

She licked her lower lip. "How is all of this related to my messed-up birth certificate?"

"I don't know yet," I said. "You know that the word in Chicago was that your father worked with the mob."

"It's a lie," she said.

"Is it?" I let the words hang between us for a moment, and then I said, "These are the sorts of things you're going to have to look at, Laura. What you may learn may be innocuous—a family feud that led your parents to build a new life in Chicago—or it might be ugly. What if your father had been in prison?"

"He never—"

"What if, Laura?"

She looked down at her manicured hands. She didn't answer me for a long time.

"Laura?"

She raised her head. The color was back in her cheeks. "You warned me," she said. "You can stop now."

"I want to make sure you understand—"

"Oh, I understand," she said. "And I'm ready to know."

I hoped she was. Because the person she would blame if she didn't like what she learned wouldn't be herself or her dead parents. It would be me.

"All right," I said, dismissing her. "Bring me the other

boxes when you get them. And I'll let you know when I have anything."

But I had a funny feeling that wouldn't be any time soon.

After she left, I picked up the phone and dialed the operator in Birmingham, Alabama. These were the times I thanked every god I could think of for my education. I could sound whiter than Bobby Kennedy if I really wanted to.

When the operator came on the line, I asked for Beaumont Calhoun out of Birmingham, then I clarified: Dr. Beaumont Calhoun.

"There's no professional listin'," the operator said. "But I have a Dr. and Mrs. Beaumont Calhoun."

"That'll do," I said, and waited while she read me the number. Frankly I wasn't surprised that there wasn't a professional listing for Beaumont Calhoun. The man would have had to have been a very young doctor in 1939 to still be practicing—although some doctors continued to work until they died. But I wasn't surprised at the personal listing. Doctors were stable creatures; they remained in their communities from the day they settled there.

I dialed the Calhoun number, not really expecting an answer in the middle of the day. I figured I would have to call back later in the evening, after the errands were run, but before the important social events—if there were any in Birmingham—began.

The answer, on the third ring, startled me. A woman's voice with an accent I recognized—the one that identified her as black, the one I was trying to avoid—answered the phone with "Calhoun Residence."

"Doctor Calhoun, please," I said, knowing on the one hand that no self-respecting white man would have a conversation with the maid, and feeling embarrassed at my own brusqueness on the other.

"Ah—jes a minute." Without giving me a chance to say

anything else, the woman set the phone down. I heard her footsteps as she walked away, so crisp that I knew she had to be walking on a wooden floor—probably one she polished daily—and then the murmur of voices—female voices—in the background.

Footsteps came back to the phone, slower footsteps, with a bit of uncertainty in the sound.

"This is Mrs. Calhoun," a deep, rich voice with patrician southern accents said to me.

"I'm sorry, Mrs. Calhoun," I said, "I was calling for the doctor."

"The doctor's been dead nigh these past fifteen years." She spoke with a dryness that suggested she fielded these requests often.

I hadn't prepared for this contingency. I simply decided to move ahead. "My name is—Billy—Dalton. I am investigating a case for a client from Chicago, and I was hoping to get some information from your husband."

"Well now, Mr. Dalton," she said. "You don't sound like you're from Chicago."

"I'm from Memphis, ma'am."

"Memphis, Lordy. That's some distance too."

"Yes, ma'am."

"And you're working for a Chicago man?"

I decided not to correct her. "Yes, ma'am."

"Whatever could my husband have done with someone from Chicago?"

"I have a birth certificate, which your husband signed. It seems a bit odd to me as there is no hospital listed."

"My husband believed in helping women in their home, Mr. Dalton," Mrs. Calhoun said archly. "Although most doctors don't do that anymore."

"Perhaps you can help me then," I said. "I'm dealing with some contradictory information in this case. I was wondering if I might have access to your husband's records in this birth to help me sort things out."

"Such records are confidential, Mr. Dalton, even now."

"I understand, Mrs. Calhoun, but it is the now-grown child on the birth certificate who is requesting the information."

"That sounds a might strange, Mr. Dalton. If he wants the information, why doesn't he contact me himself?"

I suppressed a sigh. "Because this is just one detail in an on-going case, ma'am."

"Well, I couldn't answer any questions over the phone, no matter who was callin' and why. It's not right. I wouldn't know if you are who you say you are."

I gripped the receiver tightly. The last thing I wanted to do was go to Birmingham, Alabama, and try to get some information out of a white doctor's wife. I'd do it, and I'd find a way to make it work, but I certainly didn't want to.

"I understand," I said. "But my client really doesn't want to come to Birmingham. I'd have to be the one—"

"Mercy, there's no need for that," Mrs. Calhoun said. "Just have him send me a letter making a request for his files. That'll keep everything confidential, just as the doctor would have wanted it. It'll still take me some time to get to the information, of course. We don't keep it here. It's in storage, and I'll need to send a man to get it . . ."

Finally I understood what she was about. Old Dr. Calhoun apparently hadn't provided well enough for retirement. "I forgot to ask," I said, working to make sure I sounded polite. "Is there a fee for this type of thing?"

"It's a token," she said. "Fifty dollars covers my man and the expense of sending the file."

It was an outrageous sum and we both knew it. "Forgive me, ma'am," I said, "but I thought the standard fee for something like this was twenty-five dollars."

"Oh it is," she said, her voice fluting slightly, as if discussing money made her happy. "But that's for a working office. Since my husband is gone these past fifteen years, there's extra effort in gaining the information."

In other words, she wouldn't budge. I supposed it could

have been worse; she could have said the files were destroyed. In fact, she probably still could, after cashing our fifty-dollar check.

"The records are intact?" I asked.

"Oh, yes," she said. "The doctor never threw anything out."

I had that much at least. "Well, then. I'll have my client write to you and we'll send a check for the information. May I have your address?"

She gave it to me. As I knew almost nothing about Birmingham—having learned long ago to avoid that place—I had no idea if she lived in a good neighborhood or not. I promised to send the letter and the money and thanked her for her prompt response.

I hung up and put my head in my hands. I had expected a quick and easy phone call on this, not an elaborate game that an elderly woman seemed to like playing with her husband's former clients. But, as I had noted before, our communities were different. No black doctor in Memphis would charge for that sort of information—at least not one of his former patients.

I made notes about the conversation, typed up a letter for Laura to sign, and then set it on my desk along with a check, ready to go.

I put Laura's personal papers in the small cast-iron safe that I used for important things. The safe was hidden by a haphazardly built wooden frame—something I put together to make it look as if there was nothing of value in my office. The safe itself was bolted to the floor and was too heavy for one man to lift alone, but I didn't believe in taking chances. Over the years, my office had been tossed five times, and no one had ever found the safe. I figured her belongings would be fine there.

Then I went outside. As I crossed the sidewalk to my car, I saw Joe in Handy Park. He wore his leather jacket and was smoking a cigarette. Two men I didn't recognize were talking earnestly with him. Jimmy was sitting cross-legged beneath the statue of W. C. Handy, his back to Joe. Jimmy had a pile of schoolbooks on his lap—too many to be his. One was open, but he wasn't looking at it. He was staring at the street as if he wanted someone, something, to save him.

I started to cross the street, but he saw me and shook his head slightly. He didn't want me to come there. I held up a finger, silently asking him to stay, then I went back to my office and got the pea coat.

By the time I came back down the stairs, Jimmy and Joe were gone. I stared at the park for a moment, as if I could make them magically appear, but they didn't.

After a moment, I put the coat in my car and wished, not for the first time, that good intentions made life easier.

EIGHT

A phone call when I arrived at my office the next morning took me away from Laura's case for the day. I freelanced for several attorneys, and one of them needed me to act as a process server for him on a critical case. I spent all of the morning and most of the afternoon tracking down a day laborer so that I could receive the most vituperative dressing down I'd received in weeks. I went back to the office, typed up my bill, and served that to the attorney before I went home for the evening.

I also called Roscoe Miller and asked him to meet me at Club Handy the following night. I still hadn't figured out a way around Henry's request to do security, but I figured Roscoe could help me.

I didn't see Jimmy that day, but I did call the school. He was there. I dropped off the coat and asked the office secretary to make certain he got it. She promised that she would.

The next day, Friday, the first of March, Laura came to my office with the boxes. She wore a short rabbit fur jacket and blue jeans and had her hair long with no styling at all. She carried a crocheted purse. If anything, her style was a bit too hip for a white person on Beale, but someone probably would think her one of the many musicians who came to town and not give her a second glance.

At least, that was what I hoped.

After she set the boxes down, she closed the door, took off the rabbit fur, and hung it on the coat rack. Underneath, she wore a tight ribbed turtleneck and no bra. I made my gaze move toward the boxes.

"I'm helping you," she said.

"I see that." I didn't get up from my desk. Instead, I shoved the letter forward. "Sign this."

She came forward, her kid boots leaving damp prints on the marble floor. She bent over the letter, read it, then frowned and looked at me.

"What's this?"

I explained my phone conversation with the doctor's wife.

"What do you hope to find?" she asked.

"Something in the records that might tell us more about your parents."

"But fifty dollars, isn't that unreasonable?"

I made myself smile. "Very. I tried to talk her down."

"Maybe I should call her."

I shrugged. "I get the sense that the harder we try, the more she'll up her price."

"Why would she do that? She's a doctor's wife. She doesn't need the money."

"We don't know that." I took a ballpoint out of my top desk drawer. The pen was slender and blue. I'd already tossed out a number like it. They tended to leak. I set it on top of the letter. "A lot of doctors, particularly white southern doctors, worked in parts of town that they would never admit to if they were dealing with whites."

"But you're black."

"I didn't tell her that. She lives in Birmingham."

"Oh," Laura said, a slight flush rising in her cheeks.

Everyone had seen the rioting in Birmingham five years ago. The televised images of police dogs going after teenagers and black folks getting knocked over by high pressure hoses stayed with everyone who saw them. I knew people who lived in Birmingham, and they said it had its good points. I just didn't want to find out.

"Will she send you the right information?" Laura asked.

"Or any information for that matter," I said. "That's the $64,000 question."

She frowned. "This doesn't seem very efficient to me. I mean, if she doesn't, we're out fifty dollars."

I smiled. "If she doesn't, we send you down there in your prom girl get-up and have her look it up while you're there."

She wiped her hands nervously over the front of her jeans. "You think that'll work?"

I nodded. "And I have other ideas if it doesn't."

Although I didn't want to pursue them. I figured I would probably have to make a trip to Birmingham, which I wasn't too thrilled about. But I wanted to postpone that trip as long as I could.

"Well, then," she said, and bent over to sign the letter. Her breasts moved independently of each other as she did so, and I felt a sudden surprising desire to touch her.

I stood and turned toward the grimy window. She's a client, I reminded myself, and clasped my hands tightly behind my back.

"You know, Smokey," she said, "I think it might be better if I send a check directly. Having one from your agency looks a bit suspicious, don't you agree?"

I turned. Her hair was swinging slightly against her face, her cheeks were still flushed, and her body was too sharply defined in that outfit. She was beautiful in a way I hadn't noticed before, a way that actually appealed to me.

I could almost feel my aunt's hand on my cheek, telling me that black boys didn't ogle rich white girls. In my mind's eye, I saw Carole Lombard's famous platinum hair against the gray Atlanta sky.

"Smokey?"

"Yes," I said, then cleared my throat. "Um, yes. You're right. It would be better if the check came from you."

Laura rummaged in her crocheted bag, removed her checkbook, and then took my pen. As she leaned over the desk again, I turned my attention back to the window. I didn't want to watch her. I didn't want to be thinking the things I was thinking, and not just because of my aunt, whom I hadn't seen in nearly thirty years.

There was no place for a woman like Laura in my life. Not now. Not ever.

"There," she said. "Did you type up an envelope?"

"Under the letter."

Papers rustled behind me.

"Where's the nearest mailbox?" she asked.

"I'll take care of it." I turned, took my check off the desk and tore it up. Then I set the letter near my coat and made myself take a deep breath. "Are those all the boxes?"

She nodded, biting her lower lip. Her small white teeth tugged a bit at the flesh. Her lips were chapped, something I hadn't noticed before. Usually those lips were hidden under a thick layer of lipstick.

"I got the last ones from Chicago yesterday." With the thumb and forefinger of her left hand, she swept her hair off her face. "I'd like to go through them with you, Smokey."

She was asking permission. I had thought, when she hung up that hideous rabbit coat, that she would simply stay and I would have to work with her around.

I almost said no. I preferred to work alone. But rather than go through boxes that remained from two lives I knew nothing about, it would be better to have her there to answer questions as they came up, to explain documents, and to provide a second eye.

"As long as you don't bury anything," I said. "I see everything."

She nodded.

"That sounds easy, but it might not be. Prepare to be embarrassed, Laura."

She blinked, sighed, and shook her head slightly. "I've already been embarrassed a lot on this trip. What's another few times?"

I studied her for a moment. She seemed subdued this morning. I wondered if she was afraid of what we would find.

"All right," I said. "Have you looked through these?"

"Enough to know everything is out of order."

I had expected that. I also expected the records to be incomplete. Some of the best ways to keep secrets was to make it hard to find them. Hiding them in plain sight, but in such a jumble as to make it time consuming to put them together was one method that I expected her parents to have used. Another was to destroy more incriminating records. I suspected they had used that one too.

I rounded the desk, grabbed a box, and pulled it toward me. Then I sank down on the floor and started digging.

Papers were littered haphazardly throughout the box, mixing with photographs, receipts, newspaper articles, and folders. Dust rose as I pulled everything out, and I resisted the urge to sneeze.

Laura watched me for a moment, then she sat down next to me and grabbed another box. "How do you want to do this?"

"Let's see what we have first," I said. "Then let's sort by year, by month, and by date. Photographs, everything, go in the same piles. This stuff might be related."

"All right," she said. She pushed up her sleeves and dug her hands into her box, pulling papers out one at a time. She paused to look at each.

"Don't read them yet," I said. "Just look for dates."

She nodded and kept digging.

We made piles that ran from 1945 to 1967. There didn't

seem to be much material that was dated before the war. What there was, we put in its own pile, which, I said, could be sorted out later.

It took us nearly two hours to go through the boxes before us. Finally, Laura wiped her face with the back of her hand, smearing dirt and newspaper ink on her light skin. "I'm hungry."

"All right." I stood, brushed the dust and dirt off, and extended my hand. She ignored it as she got off the floor herself, brushing the dust off her jeans.

We bundled up and went outside. I hesitated just for a moment in front of the door. I debated taking her into West Memphis where blacks and whites mingled at the blues clubs, but most of those places weren't open yet. I could have taken her to a few other businesses as well, but none of them were close.

Finally I turned left and headed to the Little Hot House. Part of me was hoping that Suzy was working, and part of me hoped I didn't see anyone I knew. I could have taken Laura to any of my other haunts, but this one occasionally got white patrons because of its proximity to Schwab's. To be fair, all of the black-owned businesses on Beale had white customers. It was simply that the restaurants here were as segregated as the ones in the ritzy white sections of town. The only difference was that here, the segregation was voluntary.

I opened the door for her and let the familiar smells of old beer and grease wash over me. Laura went in and headed toward a small table in the center of the restaurant. I took her elbow and led her to my booth near the narrow bar.

The movement felt proprietary, even though I hadn't initially meant it that way. Laura didn't even seem to notice, nor did she seem aware of how out of place she was. I was the one who was aware of it, just as I would be aware of how out of place I would be as her dinner guest in the Peabody.

Apparently I was more conscious of the eyes following us than she was.

Suzy was working. She watched us walk in, her face shadowed in the restaurant's dim light. I usually didn't like coming here for lunch—the place was as dark as it was at night, and I didn't like the feeling that it was 3:00 A.M. instead of noon. Suzy crossed her arms when she saw me take Laura's elbow. Suzy waited until we were seated before coming to the booth.

She set two torn, grease-stained menus in front of us, chosen, I suspected, because they were the worst in the place. "Today's special," she said, looking at me as if she didn't know me, "is homemade chili with fried cornbread." She snapped her gum, pulled out her notepad, and said, "You ready?"

"I'm afraid I need a minute," Laura said. The Miss Prim voice. She did it unconsciously, but I had only just learned that. I knew how that voice grated.

"Could you bring us something to drink?" I asked and made sure I smiled. Suzy didn't smile back.

"Sho'nuf," Suzy said, exaggerating her accent, and waited.

"Coke-a-Cola," Laura said without looking up.

Suzy looked at me. The flatness of her gaze made me shiver. "Well?"

"The usual," I said, showing her that I recognized her disapproval. I tried to mitigate it. "Suzy, this is Laura."

Laura looked up in surprise. She apparently hadn't expected me to know the waitress. Maybe being on a first-name basis with waitresses wasn't done in her world. Of course, sitting in a restaurant with newspaper ink smeared on her chin probably wasn't done in her world either.

Then she smiled her widest smile, transforming her face from something attractive into something beautiful. No man, black, white, or blue, could have resisted that smile. But it was the wrong wattage for Suzy.

"Hello," Laura said.

Suzy nodded, glared at me, and disappeared behind the bar.

Laura raised her eyebrows. I shrugged.

Suzy brought us our drinks and we both ordered the chili. We were the only patrons in the place. Normally when that happened to me, Suzy, the bartender, or the chef came over and talked. But no one did. The chili arrived and Laura and I ate in relative silence. She finished her Coke before I did—obviously she wasn't used to the chili's heat—and I had to go to the bar to get her another, since Suzy hadn't come back to the table after serving our meal.

Laura seemed to eat with relish, but her movements were dainty, filled with society polish that seemed out of place in this rundown room. She glowed—her white jacket, her hair, her skin. It felt as if she were wearing a neon sign, advertising that she was slumming.

Not that she did anything to make me feel that way. She tried to start a conversation once or twice, but I grunted my responses. I could feel Suzy's gaze on me, the judgment in it, judgment that I usually had when I saw a black man with a white woman.

So I studied my food. The chili was thick, the cornbread fried perfectly. I concentrated on filling the spoon, eating slowly, not making a mess. I didn't enjoy it, though, and I doubted that Laura enjoyed hers either.

When we were done, I paid at the bar and led Laura outside, placing one hand at the small of her back as I ushered her through the door. I was touching her too much. She didn't seem to notice or mind, but I did. Although that didn't make me stop.

The thin gray light on Beale street seemed bright as summer sunshine after the darkness of the Little Hot House. We walked down the sidewalk to the Gallina Building. Laura opened the door, went inside, and it wasn't until she was on the stairs that she spoke.

"I've never been so uncomfortable in my life," she said.

"It wouldn't have been that bad if you'd been on your own." I smiled. "The freeze-out was for me."

"Because of me."

"Yes."

I unlocked my office door and was vaguely relieved to see the boxes and piles as we had left them. We went in, removed our coats, and returned to our places without saying much.

I started a new box. So did she. We sorted in silence, searching for dates on the tiniest scraps of paper. She hadn't asked any questions, although I expected her to. Maybe she understood more than I gave her credit for.

Or maybe she had vowed never to go through anything like that again.

After a few moments, she handed me a folder.

"I don't want to look at anything until we're done separating," I said, handing the folder back to her.

"You need to look at this one," she said.

I took the folder from her. It was officially bound in fake leather, with metal clips holding the pages together. Inside the window flap someone had taped a title and an address:

INVESTIGATION INTO THE WHEREABOUTS OF
BILLY (SMOKEY) DALTON

Report prepared by: Edward Levy
April 18, 1960
The William Kowolski Detective Agency

My hands were shaking. I smoothed the cover of the report with my left hand. Laura had stopped looking through her files.

"I guess there's no doubt the money came from my folks, is there?" she said. "That initial payment, anyway."

"Actually, there is." My voice broke ever so slightly. She

probably didn't hear it, but I did. I cleared my throat, then continued. "Your mother looked for me after your father died. It seems to tie, but it might have been preliminary to doing her new will. I mean, why leave me money if I was already dead?"

"True." Laura set the newspaper clippings down. "Aren't you going to read it?"

I wasn't sure I wanted to. I had filed a number of reports like that myself. I had just never expected to see one about me. But I was on this case now, and this, whether I liked it or not, was part of it. I turned the cover to the front page, saw the same information typed on a fine bond, and turned to the next page which held a table of contents.

1. Overview
2. Education
3. Military Service
4. Employment
5. Financial History
6. Prospects
7. Local Contacts
8. Recommendations

I turned to the Overview section first. There this Edward Levy paraphrased his instructions. He was to find me and determine how I was living. He was to include an address and contacts so that Mrs. Hathaway could donate some money to me anonymously.

Apparently this idea so offended Mr. Levy that he included more than Mrs. Hathaway had asked for. He did so, he wrote fatuously, at no extra charge. My educational history, military service record, life after the military, and my financial history were all included courtesy of Mr. Levy. He felt it incumbent upon him to determine whether or not I would spend that money wisely. Of course, looking at my financial history, my haphazard employment, and my race, Edward Levy decided that I was a bad risk and Mrs. Hathaway should give her money elsewhere.

I was holding the folder too tightly. All my life, I had been judged by white people and found wanting.

All my life.

"What is it?" Laura asked.

"A private detective's report."

"I gathered that much," she said.

"How much did you read?"

"Enough to wonder how my mother had known you."

My heart was pounding harder than it should have been. I hadn't wanted Laura to have read any of this.

"There's no clue from the overview," I said. "I'll look through the rest. Maybe this is the break we've been looking for."

"Do you think so?"

No, I didn't, but I didn't say that to her. Levy was using my background to show Laura's mother how unworthy I was. He wouldn't detail how she had met me, if he even knew.

I flipped through the report, pulling out the bits of paper that had gotten stuck inside of it so that I could look at each page. I didn't like what I saw.

When Levy relayed the facts, the report was accurate, although the information was sketchy. The report's bias showed in his commentary, so I skipped as much of that as I could.

It was strange to see my meager finances from eight years before outlined on a page for someone else to see. I had often done the same thing, calling banks, verifying credit with lenders, investigating a man's life through the details, but it felt very different to see my financial history delineated so coldly. Coldly, and given to a woman I hadn't met or didn't remember meeting, and then analyzed by a man who had no idea of what my life was really like.

I wasn't sure I liked the fact that Mrs. Hathaway hadn't taken his advice. If she had hidden this report, it would have been a curiosity when Laura went through her parents' records. A curiosity and nothing more.

I closed the folder and set the report on top of the 1960 pile.

Laura hadn't moved. "Are you all right?"

I made myself smile. "I've written a lot of those reports. I know what they're like."

"Is it accurate?"

I shrugged. "As accurate as something like that can be."

She tucked a strand of hair behind her ear. "Would you like to stop?"

"Why?" I asked. "Your mother had to find me somehow."

Laura nodded.

"It's only a small piece of the puzzle," I said. "There might be more in here." And more for show than anything else, I reached into my box and removed more papers. I separated them, glancing only at the dates. After a moment, Laura did the same.

It took an effort to make sure that my hands weren't shaking. But I didn't want Laura to know that the report had unsettled me.

I should have known someone was investigating me. I should have caught it. It was my business, after all, to notice such things—especially when they pertained to me.

After a few moments, Laura seemed focused on the task before her. I must have seemed the same way. But all the while I shuffled papers, I was reviewing my life, trying to remember the Hathaways—and failing.

NINE

At four-thirty, Laura put a hand on her back and moaned. "Who would have thought that sorting papers would make me sore?"

I smiled. "Tedious but difficult, that's my business for you."

She had arranged most of the papers into neat piles. At some point in the afternoon, she had written dates on pages from my legal pad, and placed the yellow sheets on top of each pile. She surveyed them now, her expression dissatisfied.

"Why don't you get some rest?" I said. "We can finish this later."

"If I stay—"

"Then I'd have to, and I have a few things I need to do for other clients before close of business today."

"Oh." She bit her lower lip as she often did when she was confronted with a fact she hadn't thought of. She apparently hadn't realized that I was doing other work besides hers. "I can work tomorrow."

"I can't," I said, even though that wasn't true. I could. I just wanted to sort out the feelings I had uncovered this day. The unwelcome feelings for Laura, and the feelings that got uncovered when I held that report. "I need the weekend. How's Monday?"

"Fine," she said, but she sounded a bit lost. She stood. Her knees cracked as she did so. She went to the coat rack and got the rabbit fur, slipping it on, and then grabbing her purse. "Call me if you change your mind."

"I will," I said.

I waited until her footsteps had receded and the door closed on the street level before I stood. Laura was right, sitting that long was hard work.

I picked the report out of the 1960 pile, rolled the folder, and carried it to my desk. I turned on the metal desk lamp— it was getting dark and the fluorescent overhead, put in over a decade before, did not cast good reading light.

Then I spread the report open on my desk and leaned over it. The Education section simply listed my bachelor's and master's degrees, along with my G.P.A. and a few comments from professors who remembered me. The Military Service section read like it had been taken from the War Department's records. Although it mentioned my rank and my service in Korea, it really said nothing else about my time there.

The Employment section covered my work with Loyce and my own business here, although Levy didn't really look beyond the "odd jobs" description I gave white people. That made me wonder if I had ever spoken to him and if I had dismissed him as unimportant, just as he had dismissed me.

The Financial History was depressingly thorough. The debt load I had carried eight years ago had been high and Levy, for all his snide comments, had been right; I never would have repaid those debts working for myself. The windfall had been a godsend, even if I hadn't wanted to admit it to myself.

The Prospects section was insulting, and if I hadn't known that Laura had already looked through the report, I would have ripped that section out.

If the information in his service record is accurate, Dalton received an excellent education before he went to Korea. As noted in the Education section, he graduated from college at the top of his class. Upon graduation from his Master's Program, again at the top of his class, he received job offers, including a teaching offer from a prestigious Negro college in Atlanta. He turned all of the offers down.

Like so many of his race, he lacks the ambition to use that education in any constructive way. Instead, he has become an odd jobs man. He is too lazy to apply for a detective license, although most of his work is in that area. He does not advertise his service and often goes weeks without paying customers. As a result, he cannot make ends meet.

My sources throughout the Negro community like Dalton, but none seem to understand him. Why a man with such a background would return to the South, do odd jobs work, and not try to use his advantages to improve his lot in life is inexplicable.

Dalton's behavior has been like this for several years. I cannot see it changing. An influx of money at this time would only encourage him to work less and to contribute even less to society. He has not been offered a real job in years, and the longer he continues as an odd jobs man the less employable he becomes.

Once Dalton left the service, his days as a valued member of society ended. He is a smart Negro whose unremarkable life and lack of desire will make him a drain upon society as he ages.

Dalton, while a curious subject, has no prospects at all . . .

Of course, Mrs. Hathaway had hired a white detective who hadn't seen past the surface. Yes, I had gotten half a dozen job offers when I left school, all of which required me to move and none of which would have paid my bills. The man who graduated second in our class, a white man, received three dozen job offers, from think tanks to major corporations, and all of them paid a good salary with moving expenses. He had started to discuss them with me when he had seen from my eyes that I hadn't received any of those offers.

He had had the grace to blush and turn away.

Being self-employed in Memphis meant I controlled my own hours and regulated my own pay. Sure, I could have gone on to law school and become the next Thurgood Marshall. And perhaps I did lack the ambition for that. But I did well for who and what I was.

At least, I thought I had.

I almost closed the report at that point, but I made myself continue. The next section, Local Contacts, listed eight Memphis lawyers who were willing to take on black clients. Apparently the detective didn't consider coming to the lawyers in the black community. It was typical of his attitude and, after just reading his assessment of me, pissed me off more than it should have.

Shelby's name was fourth on the list. Apparently three others had been called and, hearing the nature of the work, had said no. I made a note of the names. Most were familiar to me, and all but two were still practicing. One had retired, and the other was on the mayor's staff, actively involved in the strike negotiations. That made a certain sort of sense, I supposed.

I sighed, and with a trembling hand, turned the page to the Recommendations section. I had vowed I wouldn't read it again, but of course I did, my gaze stopping on the same phrase as it had before:

If you are intent upon giving money to him, you might be better served placing the money in trust in case he has heirs. Otherwise, I would recommend that you give the money to a charity of your choice. Dalton will simply spend it and be no better off. If the money must go to a Negro veteran, I'm sure that with time and consideration, we can find a better prospect....

But Mrs. Hathaway didn't search for a better prospect. She searched for—and found—me. And then she sent money to me, and did so again when she died.

And there wasn't a single reason in the report. Not even a clue there, although I had the feeling I was overlooking one.

I went back to the piles on the floor, sat near the 1960 pile, and found the financial notebook. The early entries were in Earl Hathaway's cramped handwriting, shaky in the way of the ill or the elderly. By the middle of January, though, there was nothing. And it wasn't until the middle of February, according to a note in the margin, that Mrs. Hathaway had straightened out the financial records enough to continue the books.

I stared at that note for a long time. It looked like a personal note, or one made to remind oneself of the lapse at tax time. It didn't look like something meant for someone else's eyes.

But it was a strange note nonetheless. To my inexperienced gaze, the Hathaway financial records appeared to be in order. Earl Hathaway had been using a double-entry bookkeeping system, and he kept track of every expense from his property tax payments to the pennies he put daily into parking meters. If the man were that organized, what financial records did Mrs. Hathaway have to put in order?

That was a question to be answered later in the investigation. I thumbed through the ledger until I found the notation I was looking for: check number 3110 made out to Billy (Smokey) Dalton in care of Shelby Bowler, Attorney at Law, Memphis, Tennessee, in the amount of $10,000. Check number 3111 was made out to Shelby himself and covered his expenses, plus a bonus for continued confidentiality. A later notation showed that Shelby had returned the bonus. I smiled. It had probably offended his sensibilities. A lawyer, Shelby would have said, didn't have to be paid extra to do something that was already part of the job.

So one of my questions was answered definitively, the one I already had deduced for myself. The Hathaways had given me money after Earl Hathaway died. But nothing in the report told me why.

The report. I picked it up and dialed the phone number off the label in the front. It was late on a Friday afternoon, but someone might still be in the office.

If the agency was still in business.

The phone rang twice before a woman answered. "William Kowolski Detective Agency."

"Edward Levy please," I said in my best white voice.

"Just a moment." And then silence greeted me as I was put on hold.

My heart was pounding even harder than it had earlier. So the opinionated Mr. Levy still had his job at the agency. I wondered how many other black men he had hurt over the years. How had he conducted himself in cases with black suspects? I had a hunch I knew.

Then the silence ended and a gruff voice said, "Levy."

I almost introduced myself and asked him about his prospects. But while that would make me feel better, it wouldn't get me any answers.

"Mr. Levy," I said. "I'm Robert Hayworth. I'm a private detective in Memphis. How're you today, sir?"

"Fine." He sounded impatient. Ready to go home to the wife and kids. Or out on a Friday night, have a few too many drinks, and tumble into bed before dawn.

"I have here in my hand a report you wrote eight years ago for Mrs. Dora Jean Hathaway." I knew just how to talk to this man. Sometimes my ability to sound like a good ole boy alarmed me. "It was about a Negro fella named Smokey Dalton. Do you recall this report?"

"I'm sorry," Levy said. "Who did you say you were working for?"

"I'm doing some side work for Mrs. Hathaway's daughter, Laura. I can't say much more than that our case also deals with Mr. Dalton. Your report, while thorough, does not mention how Mrs. Hathaway chose Mr. Dalton for her benevolence. Did she know him?"

"It's an eight-year-old case," Levy said. "I have no memory of what I wrote in that report."

Funny, I thought. I knew I'd remember what he wrote for a very long time.

"I expected as much," I said. "I would have the same difficulty. But you do remember Mrs. Hathaway?"

"She's hard to forget." He sounded bitter. "She's the first client who ever laid into me for being thorough."

"Come again?"

"I wrote her the report and she almost didn't pay us. My boss had to get involved. She said she didn't want anything on paper and that I had disobeyed her instructions. My boss assured her that we always wrote reports and I had done nothing wrong. She took the report and all the copies and still stiffed us half the fee."

Very bitter. So the case had caused him grief as well. Good.

"What did she want if she didn't want a report?"

"Simply that boy's name and address and a contact so that she could give him money anonymously. I had to do a month's worth of digging to find the fellow and then I put a lot of work into that report. She didn't like any of it."

Interesting. "So you don't have the report?"

"No," he said. "But I have my notes. I'll have to review them. What did you say you wanted again?"

"I wanted to know how Mrs. Hathaway came to chose Mr. Dalton for her benevolence."

"You should ask her," he said.

"I would if I could." I made my voice very smooth. "But she passed on a few months ago. It's her daughter who would like to know this time."

"So she left him money in her will, did she?"

I didn't answer that. Levy wasn't as dumb as the report had made him sound.

"Tell you what," Levy said after my silence gave him the answer he wanted. "Give me your number and I'll check my notes. I may not have the information you want, but I might. I just can't remember after all this time."

I gave him my phone number—which hadn't changed in eight years—and hoped he didn't compare across when he found his notes.

"I don't have the time to check tonight," he said, "but I'll call next week."

"I'd be much obliged," I said.

"It's no problem," he said. "I'm just glad to hear that the old bat is dead."

His words took my breath away. I hadn't heard about Laura's mother from anyone but Laura. Somehow I had thought her mother had been a sweet downtrodden thing. Instead, she had been a dynamo who made a man hate her when she was crossed.

I thanked him for his time and hung up. The anger I'd been suppressing during the conversation came to the surface. I clutched the receiver against its cradle, using all of my strength to prevent myself from flinging the phone across the room.

Pompous ass. He hadn't even done what his client had asked him to do. He probably thought that Dora Jean Hathaway's judgment was suspect when she chose a black man for her bequest. He hadn't listened to her instructions and he hadn't followed them.

All she wanted was an address and a contact. And nothing on paper. Only one copy of the report remained in the boxes. I wondered where the others had gone.

Nothing on paper. What an unusual request. She had gone to a lot of trouble to find me, and I was still no closer to finding out why. But it was becoming clearer that the connection was not aboveboard.

That didn't narrow things down for me. In fact, it made them even more complex.

TEN

Club Handy was on the second floor of Pantaze Drug Store. The entrance was on the Hernando side of the building. A small neon sign advertised the club, which started almost accidentally in the 1940s.

In those days, black entertainers got stranded in Memphis for lack of work. Andrew "Sunbeam" Mitchell opened the third floor of the Pantaze Building as a hotel for those down-on-their-luck entertainers and let them pay for room and board by performing in the second-floor lounge. Eventually these jam sessions with local and out-of-town entertainers started drawing crowds.

Over the years I'd heard everyone from Little Richard to Lionel Hampton in that lounge. It was one of the few local blues watering holes that still remained on Beale.

I got there early and ordered a beer while I waited for Roscoe. The entire day had unsettled me.

A man couldn't read an analysis like that about himself without wondering if there were some truth to it. After all, I had grown up near Martin. We'd been boyhood friends, until I left Atlanta the day after my parents' death. I didn't see Martin again until graduate school. We went to Boston University at the same time as well, but we didn't see each other much, not after the first conversation in which Martin recognized me, but not my name.

He stayed friendly. I was the one who pulled away. In those days, before he became the famous Dr. King, he simply served as a reminder to me of my parents' death.

That night, B. B. King had come home to Memphis and was jamming with the local band. He sat at the edge of the stage, blending in with the musicians as if he were part of them and not a star in his own right. I met B. B. when he was still hosting the Sepia Swing Club on WDIA. It was at the station that the fans gave him his nickname, "The Beale Street Blues Boy," which later got shortened to "Blues Boy" and then became B. B.

He was a skinny kid then, small and wide-eyed. But success had changed that. He wasn't small any longer, and the look of innocence had long since left his face. Still, he loved the music and he loved Beale Street. He tried to play here whenever he could, and I considered myself lucky each time I heard him.

He raised my mood. Just listening to the wail of his guitar made me remember that there were good things in the world, things that couldn't be touched by a man's prejudice or a woman's anger.

I ordered my second bowl of chili for the day—chili was Club Handy's specialty—and had nearly finished it when Roscoe arrived.

Roscoe was a big man who'd made a lot of money in his youth as a boxer. He'd gotten badly injured in a rigged fight and decided to get out of the business. By then he had a family to support: four sons and his beautiful daughter. I'd known Roscoe for years. I'd been the one to hold him back when his daughter had been found at fifteen, beaten, bloody, and near death, when all she could remember of her attacker was the paleness of his skin and the onions and beer on his breath.

That was three years ago. The whole thing had added

slowness to Roscoe's movements and a visible weight on his mighty shoulders. I knew what it cost him to carry white people's bags all day, to get their cars, and take their token tips. I knew he wouldn't do it if it weren't for the fact that he still had two children at home.

He sat heavily on the wooden chair, told the waiter he wanted a beer and some chili and then peered at me. His familiar round face looked tired, and the scar above his right eyebrow—the one from his long-ago fight—seemed paler than usual.

"You got some trouble, Smokey?" he asked.

"Not yet," I said. "But Henry is getting to me."

He folded his big hand around the plastic water glass and glanced at the stage. The musicians were talking among themselves while the drummer got another beer.

"The strike's trouble," Roscoe said. "There's already been three meetings at work. Management wants us to know we don't keep our jobs if we get caught marching."

I swallowed hard. I didn't want Roscoe to lose his security because he helped me. "I didn't have marching in mind."

Roscoe raised his eyebrows.

"Looks like COME is bringing in some national speakers. Henry wants me to provide security."

"That ain't your job," Roscoe said.

"I know. He wants me to keep an eye out."

"And you won't, so you want me to do it."

He was quick, my friend Roscoe. "I can't go to every meeting. I want to spend the weekend training some strong men to look for troublemakers and stop things before they start. You don't have to be part of it."

"Except to help you find the suckers and train them."

I nodded.

"Shit, Smokey, you know this ain't gonna be good enough. If them ministers want security, they should get professionals."

"From where?" I asked. "And with what budget?"

117

Roscoe sighed. "I can't get many men for free."

"And I don't want someone who is only there for a paycheck."

He nodded. The waiter brought his order, and Roscoe dug in. The musicians were sitting down. B. B. was running his fingers along his guitar strings, but not making a sound.

"I'll have people," Roscoe said. "First thing tomorrow outside Clayborn Temple."

Clayborn Temple was where most of the marches started. It was seen as a home for the strikers.

"No," I said. "My office. We'll find a place to go from there."

The training went well. Roscoe brought eight people, including his twenty-year-old son, and I found five of my own. We instructed them in the art of calming a crowd, getting marchers to walk arm in arm so that no looters could break through, and how to guard doors once a speech was started. We told them techniques for seeing troublemakers in a crowd and ways of keeping those troublemakers at bay.

A weekend of instruction wasn't worth a lifetime of training, but it would do. It would have to.

I spoke to Henry and he said it looked like Roy Wilkins would be speaking in Memphis on March fourteen. That gave me one more weekend to work with the team before the national news people arrived.

On Monday, I entered my office early. I wanted to be there for Edward Levy's call, and sure enough, he called me collect at nine o'clock.

"Mr. Hayworth," he said, "I'm afraid I can't be of much help to you. I have no idea how Mrs. Hathaway chose that boy. She provided me with his name and location. She knew he was in D.C. during the war."

I let out a small breath. "That's helpful."

"But she didn't say why she wanted to send him money. In fact, that became a point of contention between us. I believed she should have found someone else to give the money to. That boy couldn't have handled those funds. He could barely pay his bills. He probably squandered the money. There were other needy ni—"

"I'm sure," I said too harshly. I was gripping the receiver so hard that my hand hurt.

He stopped. "I didn't mean to offend."

I was supposed to say no offense taken, but I couldn't bring myself to do so. "You asked her why she wanted Smokey Dalton to have the money?"

"She never did answer. I remember that as clearly as I remember the words she used when she screamed at me. No matter how much money she had, she wasn't a lady, Mr. Hayworth."

Interesting.

"I got the sense it was personal. She wanted this Dalton to have the money, and she was going to give it to him, no matter what I said."

"I got that." I couldn't make myself sound polite. It was all I could do not to tell him I was "this Dalton."

"I'm sorry I can't tell you any more."

"You narrowed my search," I said. "I appreciate that. If you think of anything else, let me know."

And then I hung up, unable to stomach the obsequiousness that I had just displayed. I wanted to call him back, berate him for his attitudes, let him know that it was *me* he had been talking to. But I didn't. I couldn't. I might still need information from him.

I paced the office, trying to let the anger dissipate before Laura arrived. When she did, still wearing her rabbit fur, I didn't even greet her.

"Were your parents in Washington, D.C., at any time during the war?"

She smiled at me. "Good morning to you too, Smokey. I

had a nice weekend. Thank you for asking. I spent most of it on the phone, but I did find some time to visit the river and the Pink Palace Museum. I even got a cab driver to take me past Graceland, but Elvis didn't appear to be home."

That stopped me. "Sorry," I said. "I just got off the phone with that idiot Chicago detective who wrote the report. He isn't the guy you hired to find me, is he?"

Her eyes widened and the smile left her face. "No."

"Good."

"You didn't tell him who you were, did you?"

"Of course I did," I snapped. "And he said, 'Boy, didn't know your people understood how telephones operated.' "

She flushed. "I didn't mean—"

"I know." My outburst upset me. I was so furious at Levy that I could barely control myself. "You didn't deserve that."

She tucked a strand of hair behind her ear and pulled her coat close.

"I told him I was a detective here in Memphis and he told me that your mother provided him with my name and location during World War II. That's why I accosted you when you came in. There might be a D.C. tie."

My voice had softened. I was leaning too close to her, but she didn't seem to mind. She looked up at me. "I don't remember them traveling."

"Not even your father? On business?"

She shook her head. Her grip on the coat relaxed. "But that doesn't mean it didn't happen."

I looked at the piles behind us. "Well," I said. "If it's anywhere, then, it'll be in the receipts."

"I guess."

"Take off your coat," I said. "This is going to take us a long time."

It did. We spent the next two days going through her parents' files. We started with the financial records.

The ledger system dated back to 1944. Mostly it was

maintained in Mr. Hathaway's cramped handwriting, although Mrs. Hathaway's flowing script covered an occasional entry. In the forties, their income was relatively small, and the things they spent money on logical: clothing, rent, food. An occasional entry would mark the purchase of a toy for Laura and at those she would stop and smile. Apparently she remembered most of them.

I cross-referenced the ledger with the check stubs and found that everything matched. Most purchases were made in Chicago, although they did spend a week in the summer of 1947 in Lake Geneva, Wisconsin. That got me thinking of mob connections again, since Lake Geneva was well known of as a resort community for Chicago mobsters. But that didn't exclude regular folk from using the resorts either. Still, I made a mental note and kept up my work.

I saw no reference to Washington, D.C. The only family trip we could find was the one to Lake Geneva. But there were no calendars in these files. If someone else paid for the trip, we would have no way of knowing about it.

Laura soon grew tired of this tight examination of her parents' finances. Once we confirmed that there were no records of a D.C. trip, she didn't know what I was looking for, but she felt that I was wasting time. I wasn't. Something didn't add up, and I couldn't tell what it was, not from the information in front of me.

It wasn't until I had gone through five years of ledgers that I realized what was missing. Earl Hathaway had never recorded the source of his income.

I reached this discovery in the middle of Wednesday afternoon. I was sitting at my desk, the check stubs in front of me, the ledger open. Laura was compiling the receipts from the earlier years—if you had come in on us, you would have thought we were a married couple going over our taxes—and looking exasperated.

"How exactly did your father make his money?"

"Investments," she said without looking up.

"I know that." I leaned across the pages. "I discovered that much on my own. But the initial money, the money that made that first investment, the money that was the down payment on this large fortune you're sitting on, where did that come from?"

She raised her head, a frown creasing her middle brow. She had a streak of dirt on the side of her face that was threatening to become permanent. Apparently she touched that spot quite often, and newsprint and dirt from the old papers rubbed off there.

"What do you mean?"

"Did he inherit it from his father? Did he work a series of menial jobs, let you all live in poverty, while he put money in the right schemes? Did he run booze for the mob in the thirties? How did he get money to invest?"

She had clearly never asked that question before. She was looking at me as if I were speaking Greek.

"Did he say anything?" I asked. "Most people have stories of their origins. Most people are proud that they've turned ten dollars into eight million."

"He never said anything." Her voice was flat.

"I noticed no mention of anything in his obituary either. Your mother didn't write it up."

"No," she said. "He never said anything."

"And did your mother?"

"No."

"Did he inherit the money from your grandparents?"

"I don't know." Her voice cracked midway through the sentence. The emotion hidden in that small sound made me shudder. Despite her protests, she probably wasn't ready to learn what she was going to learn about her parents. Whatever it was.

"Well, it had to come from somewhere," I said, more to myself than to her. "You might want to pay real close attention to those papers from that period. Maybe there's a clue in there."

She nodded and bent her head quickly, as if going to work would ease the distress she was feeling. I returned to the ledger work, knowing I would have to go deeper than this if I wanted to solve the mysteries left by Earl Hathaway.

ELEVEN

Friday morning, I arrived at my office to find a piece of paper with my name on it taped to the door. I took the paper off carefully and unfolded it.

The words were cut out of the newspaper and taped haphazardly onto the page and formed a single sentence.

Keep to yourself if you don't want to end up like Mom and Dad.

My mouth went dry. My hands shook and I nearly dropped the paper. But I made myself hold it until I took it inside.

I had learned in the army how to stay calm even when I didn't want to be. I shoved the feelings back and carried the note to my desk. I didn't have a lot of time before Laura arrived and I didn't want her to see this.

I turned on the metal desk lamp and looked at the paper. No prints on the tape that held the words in place. No bits of dust or hair either. The words were taken from the *Press-Scimitar* and the *Commercial-Appeal*. I recognized the typefaces.

Slowly I sat down. Then I opened my desk drawer and removed my fingerprint kit. Carefully, I dusted the page for prints and wasn't surprised when I failed to find any.

Only then did I look at the words again. Mom and Dad. No one in Memphis knew about my parents, that I'd grown up without them. I had learned, as a boy, not to talk about Atlanta, and so I never did. Someone had found out and someone was using them to threaten me. The note wasn't very instructive, the threat vague. I had no idea which of my activities I was being warned away from.

I took the note and slipped it into a manila envelope. I put the envelope in my top desk drawer and locked it. I didn't want Laura to come on it by mistake.

Laura. I had tried to keep as far away from her as I could, even though we had been working side by side all week. Sometimes she brought food in, and sometimes I went out and bought us some, but we never went to a restaurant again. It seemed to be an unspoken agreement. The incident at the Little Hot House had made us both uncomfortable.

Just like she was making me uncomfortable. I liked the way she sat cross-legged on my floor, the way newspaper ink smudged her face. I liked her meticulous handwriting and her dainty movements. I even liked watching her manicured fingers sift through the detritus of her parents' lives.

The work had been detailed and was gaining us little. I learned, as we dug through them, that the Hathaways' money grew exponentially over time. I did find stock sheets and balance reports, real estate holdings—many in the lucrative Lake Shore Drive area—and other indications of growing wealth. That made sense to me. It would have bothered me more if I hadn't found anything like that.

I glanced at the door. Laura wasn't due for a while, and rather than accost her as I had done on Monday morning, I had to calm myself. I didn't want to tell her about the note. I wanted everything to seem fine.

I sat down in my usual spot and double-checked Laura's work on the early years. She hadn't found anything, and I didn't either. No indications of payments made. No salary stubs. No dividend papers.

Nothing.

There should have been something.

It was clear from the ledgers that Mrs. Hathaway was in charge of the household, and she handled it alone until 1949, when they hired their first housekeeper. The housekeeper's salary appeared in the ledgers as well, and then so did other household employees—gardeners, handymen, a maid or two—as time went on. The Hathaways moved from a downtown address to a house in the suburbs. Judging from the upkeep and maintenance records, the place was big.

But I didn't learn much more than that, and even that was unusual. I should have learned a lot from those financial records. People's lives are diagrammed by their finances. In bad years, there are overdue notices and in some cases foreclosures, lawsuits, and bankruptcies. In good years, there are increased purchases: larger homes, better furniture, luxury items. And in great years there should be more money than a person knows what to do with—surplus cash, strange investments, luxury purchases never used and often forgotten.

By the time Laura arrived, my mind was completely on the records and the search. The little wave of adrenaline brought on by the note had faded. She didn't seem to notice anything out of the ordinary.

She sat across from me and picked up the pile she had left the night before. She had taken to wearing blue jeans and dark sweaters, which didn't show the dirt as much. Her hair fell across her face as she worked, and I longed to push it back for her.

I made myself focus on the work. It wasn't until I reached 1958's ledger that I realized something else was missing:

The tax returns.

When I mentioned them to Laura, she said, "The accountant handled all that."

"I thought the financial records were to come from him."

"They did," she said, "but not the corporate records."

I almost hit myself in the forehead with the heel of my hand. I had always dealt with black clients, and never had I dealt with anyone of this level of wealth. Well-off clients, yes. Doctors, lawyers, educators, people who had made small fortunes investing in oil or business machines or real estate. But never people with large fortunes, people who had so many assets to hide that they had to create corporations as a tax dodge.

"Can we get those records?"

She shook her head. "I already asked. The corporation is now being run by a board of directors. Daddy never thought a woman should have to do such things."

"And your money?"

"Comes from my parents' personal holdings and a salary from the corporation."

I didn't like the sound of that. Always suspicious, Henry would have said. And he was right.

"What happens if your board of directors runs the company to the ground?" I asked.

A small flush built in her cheeks. I liked that trait of hers. It made her emotions quite difficult to hide. "I'm going to be all right."

"You've thought of that then."

She nodded tiredly.

"And what are you going to do about it?"

"There's nothing I can do," she said. "My parents' will is tight."

"Couldn't you talk to your mother?"

She shook her head. "My mother wasn't the problem. She was bound by my father's will. The board took over after he died."

I set down the papers I was holding. "What kind of corporation is this? What kind of business does it run?"

"Real estate holdings, some construction, a lot of it in the suburbs—the outside edges of the city that are really getting built up now. There's a lot of money to be made, and we're making it." She sounded bitter.

"But you control none of it."

She nodded. "And I even have a degree in business."

"Your father wouldn't have known that."

"But he knew I was interested. He didn't want me anywhere near it. He said, 'We wanted you to have the best life, baby girl. You don't have to work for a thing.' "

I put my hand on a stack of ledgers. "When did your father incorporate?"

She blinked, frowned, turned her head aside. "I was twelve, thirteen? Somewhere in there. Nineteen fifty-one or fifty-two."

The ledgers reflected none of it. That was strange.

"Your father was the CEO?"

"Yes."

"How did he get paid?"

"A check, I guess."

A missing check. The Hathaways' financial affairs were very interesting. I nodded toward the empty boxes now stacked neatly inside each other on the left side of my office. "And you're sure these are all the financial records?"

"These are the only records I know of," she said.

"Call the accountant, then," I said. "We're still missing a lot."

"Like what?"

"Payroll records. Copies of tax returns. And perhaps a thousand other things. See if you can convince the corporation to release some of its documents to aid in our investigation."

"They won't," she said. "I already asked."

"Ask again."

"What do you think you'll find?"

"There should have been clues to your family in here. There are none. I find that very strange." I picked up the ledger I was working on and glanced at it. "You know, we also lack correspondence. Didn't your parents write letters?"

"That's what secretaries are for," Laura said with a smile.

"Not even your mother? No cards, no gifts, no long letters to friends?"

She shook her head. "Mother's friends all lived in Chicago. There was no reason to send letters."

"Give me the name of your father's personal secretary. There are bound to be carbons."

"I'll call her," she said. "I just didn't think of it."

"All right," I said. "Have them sent down."

"If I can."

"You will," I said.

"You sound so certain."

I smiled. "If you can't, then I'll have to get involved."

"You can get them when I can't?"

"Yes," I said. The means wouldn't be legal. They'd require lies I didn't want to tell, impersonations I didn't want to make. I'd do it, though, to get the records.

She took a deep breath and wiped her hands on her knees. The idea of me trying to get the records bothered her.

"I'll get them," she said.

"Good," I said, and returned to my work. Or I tried to. But I found myself staring at numbers, wondering what else I was missing. Maybe my investigation was too traditional. Maybe it wasn't traditional enough. Maybe the Hathaways weren't hiding anything more than most rich people did, and I was too inexperienced to see it.

By afternoon, I was getting frustrated. I was about to say something when someone ran through the hallway. I stiffened, remembering the note. My gun was at home. I was casual about it. I hadn't had much need for it since the service.

Laura looked up at me and my unease spread to her. She started to say something. I put my finger to my lips. There was a shadow in front of my door. Then someone knocked.

Laura jumped. I stood, and as I did, the door opened. Jimmy peered in and saw Laura.

I said, "Jimmy!" not wanting a repeat of the week before, but he ignored me and pulled the door closed. I could hear him run through the hallway again. I pulled open the door and ran after him.

He was halfway down the stairs before I was able to reach him. "Jimmy! Stop!"

He turned, paused for a moment, and grabbed the handrail.

"You wanted to see me," I said, hurrying down the steps.

He shook his head. "Ain't nothing."

"It's something. Now come where we can talk."

"You got one of them city people in your office." He meant one of the city government workers. I didn't know how he pegged Laura for one of them, except that she was white.

"That's the same woman from last week. She's my client. She's from Chicago."

"I ain't going in there," he said.

"You don't have to." I put my hand on the small of his back. He was wearing the pea coat. It was too big on him, but at least he felt warm. I pointed up the stairs. "Let's just go up there."

He shook his head. "Gotta talk alone."

"We will be alone."

He looked as if he didn't believe me.

I sighed. "The offices upstairs are mostly empty this time of day."

"The stairway echoes."

It did too. "Well, we'll have to take our chances," I said.

He shook his head and started down the stairs.

I grabbed his arm. "Jimmy, you're already here. If you're worried about something, you may as well tell me."

He froze, staring straight ahead, as if he were considering

my words. It was a very adult posture on such a young boy. Finally, he sighed, turned, and walked up the stairs, his head down, his movements slow and elderly.

When he reached me, he moved far enough away so that I couldn't help him climb. Perhaps he did that to show me he had grown up; perhaps he did it because he wanted to prove to himself that he was coming to me of his own volition.

He waited for me at the top of the stairs. I pointed in the other direction from my office, toward King's Palace. That part of the Gallina Building hadn't been occupied in some time. The offices were dark and dingy, and cobwebs filled the halls. It was rumored that just before the turn of the last century, several people were murdered in this part of the building. It had been a secret gambling and racehorse den, and it was in fights over money that more than one patron had lost his life.

Jimmy glanced over his shoulder at me as he went deeper into the gloom. I nodded and followed. He stopped near a rotting wooden carton and some sprawled packing straw. This entire portion of the corridor smelled of decay. The lights had long ago burned out, and the only light came from the window that overlooked the roof of the building next door.

I stopped beside Jimmy. He was hugging himself even though the hallway was warm. He too had probably heard the stories about this part of the Gallina Building.

"All right," I said softly. "What is it you wanted to tell me?"

He rubbed his hands along the sleeves of his coat. "It's Joe. He ain't going to school no more."

I suppressed a sigh. I guess I had known that, but I hadn't wanted to face it. "What's he doing?"

"He's with them Invaders. And the new guys."

"The ones I saw in the Little Hot House?"

Jimmy nodded. "They got plans for the strike."

I felt a chill even though the hall was stifling. "What kind of plans?"

"I don't know. Joe says they're going to do important stuff if they get a chance."

This wasn't anything I didn't know. "Why'd you come to me?"

Jimmy looked away. "Joe likes you. He's thinkin' you know what's what."

"He didn't act that way the other night."

"He was with them new guys."

I swallowed hard. "What are they planning?"

"They don't know," Jimmy said. "They been arguing about it. That's why I come to you. Because of Joe."

"He's with them."

"He don't go to school no more. He sits with them and smokes weed and talks all day." Jimmy looked up at me and I finally saw the worried little boy in his eyes. "You said nobody gets to do nothing without school. You said it's the only way to be somewhere. But Joe says you're full of shit. He says you didn't go nowhere."

I winced.

Jimmy didn't seem to notice. "And besides, he says that the world's different now."

"What do you say?"

Jimmy closed his eyes and leaned his head back against the filthy wall. "I think them men're gonna get Joe in trouble."

"I think you're right. But what do you want me to do about it?"

Jimmy opened his eyes. "Talk to him?"

"I don't think he'll listen to me right now."

"Sure he will. He likes you."

I almost smiled. The words sounded so naive. But Jimmy was not even a teenager yet, and he didn't realize that teenagers often rebelled against the people they had once admired.

I couldn't promise to help Joe. The conversations I'd had with him the week before made it clear that he had found someone else to listen to.

But Jimmy hadn't. He'd come to me twice in two weeks. He wore the coat I sent to him.

I said, as gently as I could, "They haven't gotten you involved, have they, Jimmy?"

He shook his head, but a tear ran down the side of his face.

"What are they making you do?"

"Deliver stuff," he whispered.

Drugs, I thought. I had been afraid that was what the brown packages were. "Where?"

"Places around here. The park." He raised his head. "Scary places."

I sighed. "Where's your mom?"

"Tampa."

Wonderful. She had never been much of a role model, but at least she had been there. Now it seemed she wasn't even doing that. "How long has she been gone?"

"Christmas."

I started. The boys had been on their own since then, and I hadn't even noticed. I wondered if anyone else had. "How are you living?"

"Joe's taking care of it."

Yeah. Joe was taking care of it by using his brother as a courier. I wondered if the drug money went to Joe or to the Invaders. Then I remembered the slip I had found on the apartment door and knew I had my answer. Soon Jimmy wouldn't have a place to live. He certainly wasn't eating. And getting to school was becoming a struggle.

It was time to do more than buy an occasional meal.

"Look," I said. "Come back to my office with me. That

lady in there won't hurt you. I'll call Reverend Davis, and he'll find you a nice place to stay, where they won't have you deliver things to strange people and they'll make sure you eat, okay?"

Jimmy was tempted. I could see it in his eyes. They were wider, more hopeful than they had been a moment before. Then they clouded over. "What about Joe?"

"I'll take care of Joe."

"Will you?" There was such a plaintive note in his voice, as if he knew, as I did, that Joe was a lost cause.

I nodded, then put my hand on his shoulder. "Come on."

He bent his head, and I was surprised at how easy it was. Had Jimmy come to me, not just for Joe, but for himself? Did he want me to take charge? Had this been what he wanted all along?

We walked through the corridor to my office, and as I pulled open the door, Jimmy froze again. Something about Laura, seated on the floor, the newspaper clippings scattered about her, worried him.

"It's all right," I said, keeping my hand on his back for reassurance.

He slipped inside and nodded at her, and she smiled at him, that full-wide beautiful grin that made her seem even younger than she was.

"You sure she's not from here?" Jimmy asked.

"Positive," I said.

Laura caught that question, and her gaze met mine. I nodded once and looked away, not wanting her to say something that might destroy the moment.

I led Jimmy to my desk and let him sit in my chair. He frowned at the numbers on the ledger before him as if they were math homework, then swiveled so that his back was to us. He was so small that he got lost in the chair. It was as if he wasn't in the room at all.

I picked up the phone and called Henry. In a few brief well-chosen sentences, I explained Jimmy's situation.

"I know just the right folks to watch him," Henry said. There wasn't much more he could say, not then. He knew it and I did. Henry's voice boomed through the phone line, and Jimmy heard each word. I had let Henry know that Jimmy was there, and Henry knew better than to destroy such a fragile situation with some ill-spoken words. Too many kids were lost with that final straw.

I hung up. Laura was looking at me, a question on her face. I smiled at her, trying to reassure her. Then I crouched beside Jimmy.

"You sure Joe's gonna be all right?" he asked.

I took a deep breath. I could lie to him, give him those platitudes adults always gave kids. But that wasn't fair, not to him, nor to Joe.

"No," I said. "I'll do what I can, though."

"Maybe I should stay with him."

"Have you seen him much lately?" I asked.

Jimmy looked at me sideways, then looked away quickly.

"He's been leaving you on your own, hasn't he?"

Jimmy shrugged. "He's got stuff."

"We all do." I rested my forearm on the chair. "Have you heard at all from your mother?"

Jimmy shook his head.

"She go alone?"

"She said it was a vacation. She said she'd be back." His voice was flat, his tone harsh. He had apparently long ago given up on his mother's return.

"What does Joe say?"

Jimmy looked at me again, that measuring look. "That we have to take care of ourselves."

"He's been doing that? Taking care of himself?"

Jimmy nodded.

"And so have you."

Jimmy shrugged.

I saw Laura through the corner of my eye. Her face had paled.

"Do you think he'll be mad?" Jimmy asked.

I had a hunch Joe wouldn't even notice that Jimmy was gone, not for a few days. "No," I said. "He'll want you to be okay."

"It's been me and him since we were little," Jimmy said.

"I know."

"Them people—" He stopped himself. I caught my breath, hoping he'd go on. But he didn't.

"What about them?"

He turned the chair just enough so that I caught his reference to Laura. He didn't want to say anything around her.

"I told you."

"Yeah," I said.

Then there was a knock on my door. Henry had arrived. Laura got up before me and pulled the door open.

Henry filled the doorway. He wore a heavy coat against the chill of the day and galoshes that squeaked as he walked. He smelled so strongly of cigars—his only vice, he said— that he brought the stench with him into the office.

He looked at Laura like he'd never seen a white woman before. She stepped out of his way.

"Smokey?" he said.

Then I realized he couldn't see me. I stood. He grinned. Jimmy swiveled the chair and gripped its arms as if Henry were the police come to take him away.

"You remember Jimmy," I said.

"Indeed I do." Henry crossed the room and held out his hand. It was a trick I had seen before, one that usually worked with sullen boys. It worked with Jimmy. He stood and took Henry's hand, a look of wonder on his face. Most people didn't treat Jimmy with respect.

"Hear you need a place to stay for a while," Henry said.

"Till my mom comes home," Jimmy said.

Henry nodded. "Well, we have that. You want to come with me?"

Jimmy glanced over his shoulder at me, and I could feel his fear. Laura could too. She reached for him, then clasped her hands in front of her. I found a new respect for her. She knew she was not part of this situation, and she was doing her best to stay out of it.

"You're not going far away, Jimmy," Henry said. "You can see Smokey whenever you want, and you'll still be in your same school. This is just temporary, until you decide how you want to live permanently."

I noticed the way that Henry phrased that last, but I knew Jimmy didn't. Until *he* decided. He would probably decide quicker than he knew. The decision was already made; that was why he had come with me so easily.

"Is there anything you need from home?" Henry asked.

Jimmy shook his head. He had his school books. From the looks of his clothes, I doubted he had any others that fit.

"You hungry?" Henry patted his own round stomach. "I could use some catfish. Want to join me?"

Jimmy shrugged. Then he licked his lips, giving himself away. "Can Smokey come?"

"I don't know," Henry said. "Smokey?"

Henry, bless him, had an ease that made things work. Some of the other ministers in town were too formal or too condescending for a boy like Jimmy.

I glanced at Laura. She picked up her coat. "I was just leaving," she said.

I smiled. I liked this side of her. "I'd be honored to come," I said to Jimmy.

He visibly relaxed. Henry nodded to me over the boy's head.

Laura grabbed her purse and pulled open the door. "I'll see you Monday, Smokey."

"Great," I said. "Thanks."

"It's not a problem." She left and closed the door gently behind her.

Henry looked at the floor. "Do you need to clean up?"

"It can wait." I put a hand on Jimmy's shoulder. It was bony and ridged. "Some things are more important."

"Catfish!" he said.

"Yeah," Henry said, his gaze meeting mine. "Catfish."

And making sure Jimmy went to his new home.

TWELVE

That weekend, Henry moved Jimmy into a new home. He asked that I wait until Monday to visit so that Jimmy could get settled. He asked this at our catfish lunch and Jimmy had looked at me with liquid eyes.

"Is it all right?" I asked him.

He nodded as if he weren't sure. I waited, giving him a chance to change his mind, but he didn't.

Somehow, not being able to see him made the weekend harder for me. I trained my small cadre of security, this time without Roscoe, and I despaired that they'd ever be more than glorified bouncers.

The strike had gotten uglier. During a boycott of local merchants, the Invaders and their parallel organization, the Black Organizing Project, harassed blacks who made purchases at downtown stores. Several Invaders were arrested for disorderly conduct, but I called the precincts. None of the arrested was Joe.

Sunday, March ten, was the hardest. It felt like Reassess Vietnam Day. The *Commercial Appeal* ran a syndicated *New York Times* article that claimed Westmoreland wanted to send two hundred thousand more troops over there to die in what NBC called later that night a futile war. The country was talking about 'Nam now, and they were doing so in a way that mirrored Martin's speeches about the country the year before, speeches Martin had been excoriated for.

People were again bringing up the King/Spock ticket that had first been proposed last April: that Martin should run for office with Dr. Benjamin Spock as his vice-presidential candidate on a peace ticket. Word from the Southern Christian Leadership Conference, the organization that Martin headed, was that he was not interested in running for president. His interests lay in something he was calling the Poor People's Campaign. He believed that poverty was the root of all our social ills, and that unless you stamped out poverty, you had no hope of solving the social problems.

I later discovered that I wasn't the only one who had seen the articles on Martin. The Memphis Ministers Association used them as a final straw: they had been talking about appealing to Martin to help resolve the strike. The articles convinced them to do so.

They contacted Martin on Monday. He promised to rearrange his schedule to see if he could come the following week.

I didn't want him in Memphis. Martin was a greater security risk than any of the other potential speakers. There had already been several attempts on his life, from the dynamiting of his hotel room in Birmingham to being stabbed near the heart in New York City in 1958. He was receiving constant death threats. He joked about them with me once, and I had refused to laugh.

He had not been laughing either. His eyes never smiled.

But I had to deal with other things before Martin arrived. Thursday was the day that Roy Wilkins of the NAACP and activist Bayard Rustin who, among other things, organized the March on Washington in sixty-three, were scheduled to speak.

My security team and I would have our hands full.

———

On Tuesday, Eugene McCarthy came in a stunning second to the President in the New Hampshire primary. The votes were so close that, if you subtracted the Republican write-ins, Johnson won by only 230 votes. The student movement, the peace movement, and the civil rights activists suddenly believed they had a platform.

The New Hampshire primary result left the door open for a hundred possibilities, and I heard, in my haunts on Beale, a bit of hope.

Everything felt better that week. I walked Jimmy home from school several times, but he wouldn't let me inside to meet his new family. I had a hunch he didn't believe he'd stay with them long, and I also knew that he was afraid I'd make the comparison with his real family and find them wanting.

For the most part, though, I holed up in my office with Laura. She was getting more and more frustrated. She had finally reached her father's secretary, and the woman had said that her father's papers had been destroyed—on her father's orders. I made Laura ask basic questions, such as had the secretary actually destroyed everything, including carbons? And the secretary's answer was yes.

Laura asked why her father had given the order, a question that burst from her on her own, with no prompting from me, and the secretary had no answer for that. The secretary did admit that such wholesale destruction was unusual, but then, she had said that working for Earl Hathaway hadn't been like working for anyone else.

Laura didn't follow up on that statement.

I took down the name of the secretary. I would follow up, if need be.

We were still going through the financial records, finding a lot of missing ingredients. I became more and more convinced there was another set of books, and Laura became more and more discouraged.

On Wednesday, I left the office in the early afternoon. I

wanted to check with my so-called security team to see if they were ready for the following night.

I had to walk down to Second—all the parking on Beale had been taken that morning, and I hated parking in the alley in the back. My car was parked on the other side of Capitol Loans, and as I got closer to the building, I saw Joe standing there.

Joe jittered between the two parking meters in front of the large striped awning, looking once at the display of watches and jewelry in the window. Then he tripped on the grate, grabbed one of the meters for balance, and stood for a moment as if he were dizzy.

I shoved my keys into my pocket and walked toward him. He looked up, saw me, and shook his head, as if he didn't want me to come any closer.

I kept walking, though, and got close enough to call his name. He waved uncertainly, and in that jerky awkward movement, I realized what was wrong.

He was high.

I took a deep breath, shoved my hands in my pockets and headed toward him. As I did, an older man came out of the Capitol's double doors at a run, grabbed Joe's arm, and tugged him down the street. Joe looked over his shoulder, then turned south on Second.

By the time I got there, he was gone. And I couldn't resist. I wandered into Capitol, afraid of what I might learn.

Capitol smelled of dust and dirt, tobacco and desperation. The floor was made of uneven wood slates and supported dozens of glass counters filled with stuff people had pawned for a fraction of its worth.

Steve, the man who worked the counter in the afternoon, was a backup musician at Stax and made extra money playing clubs in the evenings. He had the largest afro I'd ever seen, and it looked right with the multicolored dashiki he wore.

"Whatcha need?" he asked, not very welcomingly. Usually

I was tracking some stolen item, and if I found it in this place and could prove the item was stolen before it had been brought in, Capitol lost money. Steve wasn't the owner, but he'd lost enough items to me over the years to get yelled at a few times, and he needed the job bad enough that he didn't want to be yelled at much more.

"Saw that guy run out of here," I said. "You okay?"

Steve raised an eyebrow at me, a surprised and calculated look. "You think I was robbed?"

"I thought it was a possibility."

He nodded. "I thought so too. I think they was casing me. I let 'em see the shotgun under the counter, made it clear I wasn't 'fraida usin' it, and they was gone." He tilted his head. "Ain't never seen that bro before. You?"

"I'm not sure," I said. He could have been one of the older men with the Invaders that night in the Little Hot House.

"But looked like Joe Bailey's with him. That yer interest?"

"Initially," I said.

"He was on something. Too jittery for weed. Thinkin' maybe he was shootin' up."

I was thinking the same thing, and I didn't like it. "Keep an eye out."

"I will. I don't like how thing's goin' right now." He patted the cases. "These babies gonna fill up and nobody's gonna have money to empty 'em."

"Let's hope the strike ends soon."

"May as well hope for a black president of the United States," he said.

I shook my head at his pessimism and left. Outside, I scanned the street for Joe, but didn't see him—not that I expected to. I got into my car and drove to Joe's apartment, the one he had once shared with his mother and Jimmy. An eviction notice, days old, was thumbtacked to the scarred door. Joe hadn't been here in a long time.

I wondered if he even knew that Jimmy was gone.

THIRTEEN

Thursday morning, I found another anonymous note taped to my door. This time, before touching it, I went downstairs and asked my neighbors if they'd seen anyone suspicious in the building. Of course they hadn't. They hadn't noticed anything unusual at all.

I unlocked my office door and got the fingerprint kit. Then I dusted the glass and the area around the note. I saw lots of prints, most of them undoubtedly mine, and nothing near the note.

Someone had wiped the area clean.

I slipped my winter gloves over my hands and pulled down the note. It was the same as the last one: words cut from newspapers, clean tape, no marks.

The message was different, though.

Stay home tonight.

I guess I finally knew what the notes were connected to. The strike. Somehow it made sense.

I took the note inside and put it with the other. I wondered how many I would collect before the strike was over.

I worked with Laura for most of the day, continuing to sort and study. The new records hadn't arrived yet, but we still had material to go through. We found all sorts of messes in those boxes, from old dress ads torn from newspapers to society portraits of people Laura didn't know. She guessed that her mother used those pictures as inspiration; her mother had been horribly insecure when she finally started mingling with Chicago society.

I sent Laura home early. She knew I was going to hear the speeches and she wanted to come along. But there had been disruptions all week—most of them by the Invaders, who blocked traffic and tried to persuade students to leave school. I was worried that there would be more at the meeting that night.

The leaders of COME had assured me that Wilkins and Rustin would have their own personal security. They wanted me to focus on the site of the speeches itself.

Clayborn Temple was an old stone church, pitted and soot-covered, its stained-glass windows covered in grime. It had been the starting point of the daily marches to city hall and the site of several volatile meetings. I was more worried about the location than I was any crazies in the audience. Too many people went in and out of that building all day.

Too many people had access, and too much access meant trouble.

The speeches were supposed to start at eight. My crew, such as it was, was coming fifteen minutes before the doors opened at seven. I arrived at four and went through the church from top to bottom.

I found things in that building that people hadn't seen for years, from old sneakers to moth-eaten choir robes. I investigated the plumbing and the boiler. I shone a flashlight in all the vents and was happy to see cobwebs blowing with the heat. I liked finding dust so thick that it coated my hands and dirt so old that it crumbled at my touch.

No one had planted a bomb, at least not that day. That day, we were safe.

I didn't hear much of the speeches. I spent most of my time circling the outside of the building, making certain that no one tried anything suspicious. A group of teenage boys in leather jackets and berets arrived at eight-thirty. I followed them in just in time to see them line up in the back, under the balcony.

I signaled to Roscoe's son, Andrew, to keep an eye on them. He nodded and signaled his partner, who then signaled another. Some of the training stuck.

The Temple was full that night—a sea of black faces, punctuated by an occasional white face, usually that of a reporter. Television cameras had appeared outside, but were already gone. The only people inside were print journalists, and even they seemed weary, as if they had heard it all before.

The audience wasn't weary. They cheered and whistled, pleased to have speakers of Wilkins's and Rustin's stature involved in this strike.

But the meeting did not go easy. The teenagers were loud and disrespectful. One of them asked loudly how anyone could listen to those "Uncle Toms."

Andrew started toward them to throw them out, but I stopped him. I didn't want a scene if we could at all avoid it.

I was about to leave when one of the boys stepped forward. He put his hands to his mouth and shouted, "When you talk about fighting a city with as many cops as this city's got, you better have some guns! You're gonna need 'em before it's over."

"That's it," I muttered. I signaled my men, and we grabbed the boys, dragging them outside. They didn't resist. They seemed to enjoy the attention, which angered me all the more.

When we reached the door, we shoved them out. They

staggered forward, tripped on the stone steps, and almost fell into the street.

"Stay out," I said.

"Don't like truth, do you, man?" a boy yelled in the dark.

"He don't know it's time to move from resistance to aggression. He'll learn," another said.

"Resistance to aggression," I said, putting my hands on my hips. I couldn't see the boys' faces in the dark. "Why don't you finish the quote? You want to move from revolt to revolution, don't you?"

"Hey, man!" a different voice shouted. "You do know."

"I've heard of H. Rap Brown, same as you," I said. "I just don't believe he knows what makes the world work."

Then I led my team back inside and pulled the Temple doors closed.

We had no more disruptions that night, but I stayed late to make sure we'd have none the next day. Wilkins and Rustin left with their bodyguards and assistants, feeling as if they had inspired and led.

Like it or not, half of me agreed with the teenagers. Speechifying wasn't settling this strike. Involvement from national figures would only entrench Loeb and his henchmen all the more. I was beginning to worry that the garbage was going to pile up until summer, when the heat and the humidity would make people older than Joe ready to listen to the words of H. Rap Brown and Bobby Seale.

I was the last one to leave the Temple. It was nearly midnight. The sky was clear after a cloudy day and the air was cold. I was tired, and the hope I had felt earlier in the week had evaporated when I heard black-clad teenagers talking about guns.

Maybe if I hadn't been so self-involved, I would have seen him. But I didn't. I didn't notice at all until he grabbed my arm and pulled me toward him.

I swung and he caught my fist in his large hand. He was alone. His dark skin looked almost purple in the streetlight. He was holding me like a lover would, a lover who wanted the first dance. Only the tightness of his grip and the look in his bloodshot eyes convinced me that we were involved in a different kind of dance—one that he controlled.

"You've gotten lazy," he said.

I recognized the voice. It was the man who had been trying to hide from me in the Little Hot House the week before. Only this night, he had his beret tilted back, his broad scarred face visible in the pale light.

"Thomas Withers," I said. "The last time I saw you, you were wearing a uniform and praising the work of your comrades in that oxymoronic place, Army Intelligence."

His grip on my fist tightened. "Things change."

"Not that much." That was why he had made me feel uneasy. "What're you doing preaching revolution?"

"I saw the light, Smokey. Maybe it's time you did too."

"What light?" I asked.

"You been saying some things that don't support brotherhood. We got a situation coming up, and we need people behind us, not opposing us."

"Really?" I said. "I'm a little old to be convinced by rhetoric like that. I told you. I don't believe in burning cities."

"It's the only way," he said. "Then we rebuild in our own image."

"Is that why you're here?" I asked. "Does the strike give you grounds to infiltrate Memphis? Do you think that bringing down Mayor Loeb will be the start of a black utopia?"

"You always did have a smart mouth," he said. "I came to get you on our side."

"I don't take sides," I said. "But I tell you, I'd rather work with the Committee on the Move for Equality than you guys."

"All those ministers," he said. "I didn't take you for the religious type."

"I'm not," I said. "That's my point." Then I tilted my head. "And why do you want me? Did I make you nervous, Tom? Think I recognized you and might tell those kids how you lived when you were their age? Should I tell them that you worked for the Man?"

"They know."

"They know you worked for him, not that you enjoyed it." I yanked my fist from his grasp, then shoved him away from me. He stumbled backwards a few steps before catching himself. Even though he was bigger, he wasn't an experienced street fighter. I was. He was easy to move.

"I'm not that lazy," I said.

"You watch out," he said, tugging on his jacket to straighten it. "You don't know who you're touching."

"Threats now. Who am I touching, Tom? Is there some other reason you're in Memphis? Are you still working for the Man?"

"If I was, I wouldn't be teaching Invaders about Black Power." He shook his arms as if I had hurt him.

"Is that what you're teaching them?" I asked. "Or are you infiltrating them? Are you teaching those kids how to disrupt things so that there'll be an excuse for some harsh police action? Maybe just enough to bring in some of your friends from the government and shut this entire section of the city down."

"I never seen a man so cynical as you," he said.

I shrugged. "I remember you, Tom. I remember what you were like."

"I changed." The words didn't sound sincere. He stood, his hands at his sides, ready if I made a move.

"Someday you'll have to tell me what caused the change," I said. "But tonight's not the time. And if you think I'll come over and help you tear this place apart, you're wrong."

"Your loss, Smokey," he said. "It'd be better for you if you were on our side."

"That's the second threat in a matter of minutes," I said. "How come I make you nervous, Tom?"

"You don't," he said. "But some of the kids respect you. They asked too many questions after you left. They don't need you confusing them."

Joe. Maybe I had gotten through, a little. "Seems to me I'm not the one doing the confusing. You'll mess with this place and then you'll leave, and where will they be?"

"They'll be the ones in charge."

I shook my head. "Funny you should come to me, Tom. Don't you remember how much I hated fools?"

"You're the one who's the fool, Smokey," he said softly. "You should listen to Dylan. Times, they are a-changing."

"Bob Dylan's a white man's guru." I grabbed my keys out of my coat pocket. "You give yourself away in the details, Tom."

His eyes narrowed as he watched me. "Leave the kids to me, Smokey," he said.

I shrugged. "You can have them," I said. "If they want to play revolution, it's not my game."

"I have your word on that?"

"On what?" I asked. "That I won't play with the children? Sure."

"And you'll leave us alone?"

"It depends on what you're planning, Tom. Care to share that with me?"

His grin was wide and easy. "Already have, Smokey."

"Somehow I don't think so." I turned the keys outward with my fingers, creating a weapon that I hid against my side in the dark. "You're the one who's been leaving those notes on my door."

He grinned. His teeth flared white against the darkness. They were perfect. The last time I had seen him, in Korea sixteen years before, they'd been chipped and broken. He'd come into some money somewhere.

"You don't scare easy, Smokey. I respect that. I really do."

I crossed my arms. Knowing that Withers was behind the notes calmed me a little. I'd let it slip in Korea that I'd spent time in Atlanta.

"But what do you think your daddy would have thought of that white bitch you're trailing after?"

I almost lunged for him, and then I realized that was what he wanted. "Why do you keep bringing my parents into this?"

Withers shrugged. "Interesting people, your parents."

"How do you know about them?"

His grin faded. "I know more about you than you do," he said. "That's one thing I did learn in the army. Knowledge is power, Smokey. And sometimes the right fact can be mighty useful."

He brought his beret back down over his face. Then he tapped my hand.

"You can put your keys back the normal way now," he said. "I'm not going to fight you. I know when I'm outclassed."

Then he walked away. I watched him go. I had no idea why he was letting me see him now, or what he wanted to prove by it. Except that he had escalated his threats.

They didn't just include me any more.

He had also mentioned Laura.

FOURTEEN

The next morning, I got up early and went to see Henry in his office. My run-in with Withers so disturbed me that I tossed and turned all night.

Thomas Withers and I had had several run-ins in Korea, most of which I didn't like to think about. He worked for military intelligence then and had left to continue his nasty ways with the FBI. I couldn't believe that all these years later he had seen the light and gone to the other side.

He wasn't that kind of man.

His presence made me realize just how complicated this sanitation workers strike had become. I wanted to tell Henry about it as soon as possible, and I couldn't do it at breakfast in public. Nor could I talk to him in my office, not with Laura due at her usual ten o'clock.

I knew that he spent his Friday mornings writing the Sunday sermon. That gave him Saturdays to revise and practice the material. Henry always felt insecure about his speaking skills—probably because the competition in Memphis was so high—and he worked harder on his sermons than almost anyone else. The writing was always excellent, the expressed thoughts brilliant, and the execution a little dry. Henry had been trying to stop reading his sermons aloud, to memorize them instead, but it didn't work. He simply didn't allow himself enough time.

That morning was frosty. Winter hadn't let us go yet. The chill cut down the odor from the garbage, though, and for that I was grateful. The church's parishioners kept the sidewalks clean and made sure that the church's garbage was moved. I didn't know if some brave soul took it to the dump—which many of the strikers would have seen as crossing the picket line—or if the garbage was simply put in another location, waiting until that day, whenever it would be, when the strike was over.

The church was over fifty years old, built of wood and painted white every few years or so. It was due for a new coat. The steeple was small and the only thing that made the church stand out from some of the larger homes in the neighborhood. That, the parking lot in front, and the small sign that had been erected in the lawn with the church's name in white, and the title of the upcoming sermon in small block letters.

This week it read:

Look carefully then how you walk, not as unwise men but as wise, making the most of the time, because the days are evil.

—Ephesians 5:15–16

The words chilled me. I walked past and averted my eyes from them, wishing that they would go away. They didn't. *The days are evil* felt like a warning, a premonition of the time ahead. Or perhaps I was just feeling what everyone else was, the strange unraveling that had started months before and was continuing with alarming swiftness, not just in my life, but in the country as well.

The front doors were open and I went inside, taking the side stairs that led to Henry's office. It was a large, old-fashioned room with a high ceiling and a view of the garden. In the summer, the church held functions there and I sometimes attended them at Henry's invitation, even though I didn't consider myself a religious man.

I found Henry at his desk, poring over a Bible, three concordances stacked beside him. His coat and hat were on a nearby chair as if he meant to put them on and had forgotten.

I stood in the doorway and knocked. Henry looked up. "Smokey." He smiled. "It went well last night, don't you think?"

"That's what I'm here about."

Henry's smile faded. He took his coat and hat off the chair and indicated that I sit.

I did. The spot had a good view of the windows and the winter garden. It was overgrown now, dried leaves providing a bed that was usually grass. The trees were bare; dark lines against a darker sky. It almost looked ominous. Hard to believe that in the summer it was one of the most welcoming places in Memphis.

"Something did happen," Henry said.

I nodded and then I told him about my encounter with Thomas Withers and who Withers had been. I tried to explain the kind of man Withers had been in Korea—a career soldier, the kind who believed all the crap they fed him.

"I'm afraid I'm not making the connection you are," Henry said. "We know that there are outside agitators here. We're a community ripe for it right now. That's why we formed COME."

I hated the acronym for Community on the Move for Equality almost as much as I hated the committee's name. It was unwieldy and didn't represent what Henry had said it would.

"I don't think Thomas is your ordinary agitator."

"Obviously," Henry said.

"No," I said. "You're not listening. I think he's FBI. He

joined up after the service. I can't believe he's left to become a Panther."

"What would the FBI be doing teaching high school students how to revolt against the government?"

"Black high school students," I said. "Didn't Frank Holloman used to be a special agent for the FBI?"

Holloman was the head of Memphis's police and fire departments.

"Yes," Henry said, sounding confused, "but I'm still not following your reasoning, Smokey."

"Mayor Loeb wants to win this strike. What better way to do it than to use it to discredit the entire black community? And what better way to do that than to turn the whole thing violent?"

"But the FBI, Smokey."

I suppressed a sigh. We had disagreed over this before. Despite our upbringing, despite the separate water fountains and the segregated schools, Henry had a naive belief in the power of government as a force for good. Not southern government. Northern government. He said it was the same sort of belief that inspired men like Adam Clayton Powell to run for Congress.

"The FBI has been messing in local politics for the last twenty years," I said. "Ever since someone first breathed the phrase 'civil rights' down here. Well, you guys have started connecting the phrase 'civil rights' to the sanitation strike, and suddenly an old army buddy of mine shows up."

"But he wouldn't go after you if he were government."

"Of course he would, Henry," I said. "He was afraid I would do exactly what I'm doing now. He was trying to convince me as to how much he'd changed. But you know, he never told me what caused the change. If he had, I might have believed him."

"But he's one of us, isn't he?" Henry asked, meaning Withers was black.

"Only on the outside." Anyone could be coopted and

often was. The FBI had a history of using certain blacks to infiltrate civil rights organizations. I was sure Withers was one.

Henry was silent for a long moment. "If what you say is true," he said, "then what?"

"Warn the labor leaders this is going on. That's another reason the FBI could be involved. They don't trust organized labor, and they'll do what they can to bust this up."

"And then what?"

"Be cautious, Henry. Don't put yourselves in any situation that can get out of control. You're still doing daily protest marches to city hall, right?"

"Yes," he said.

"Make sure you know everyone who is marching, and make sure you've got some trained security people of your own guarding the troops."

"All right." He folded his hands on his Bible. "What else?"

"Don't bring in any more national speakers. And hire some professional security. My small team isn't going to be good enough."

"We can't call Dr. King now," Henry said. "He's making Memphis a stop in the Poor People's Campaign. He's going to take this strike and use it to focus on the plight of poor people all over the country."

"It's not a good idea, Henry," I said. "At least have Reverend Lawson call the SCLC. Tell them that the FBI is involved, that we have some internal dissent—"

"They know that," Henry said. "They know about that riot."

"Henry . . ."

He frowned. "You can't tell me that you believe the FBI would hurt Dr. King. They wouldn't allow that to happen."

I sighed. I didn't believe it. "I'm worried about the disruptions."

"We all are. You can stop them. You know what to do."

"Henry, he threatened me and one of my clients."

Henry stared at me for a moment. "And then he recognized that you're not easily intimidated. You're not, are you, Smokey?"

I was silent for a moment. I wasn't easily intimidated, but I also knew that things here were larger than I was. Once Martin was involved, if something spiraled out of control here in Memphis, things would spiral out of control nationally. It had happened before in places that rang with the short, modern history of the civil rights movement: in Montgomery, Birmingham, and Selma. Most of these were great victories, but I had a hunch that Martin was due for a defeat.

I didn't want it to be here.

"Warn the SCLC," I said. "Let them decide."

"What do I tell them?" Henry asked. "That you suspect a man from your past is an FBI officer? That there could be trouble? Smokey, these people know about trouble. They live with it every day."

"Warn them," I said as I stood. "Promise me."

Henry's fingers smoothed the surface of his Bible. "I'll tell Jim Lawson," he said finally. "It would be better coming from him."

I sighed and made my way to the door. I wanted more of a promise, but I understood what Henry was thinking. He was worried that Martin wouldn't come. Everyone saw Martin as a savior. They didn't realize that he was as human as the rest of us.

"Smokey?" Henry said as I started out the door. "One more thing."

I turned.

"I'm worried about Jimmy."

That got my attention. "He's not doing well?"

"Oh, he is. He goes to school. He gets good grades, and he studies hard." Henry took his chair and scooted it forward. He marked his place in the Bible with a piece of yellow legal paper and closed the book. "But more than once, he's gone off campus for lunch and missed the first hour afterwards."

"How's the family?"

Henry shrugged. "They try. But Jimmy is not talking to them. To be fair, he doesn't really know them."

"And Joe?"

"I don't know if there's been contact. I think so. I can't think of any other reason Jimmy would be off campus."

I nodded. "I'll see him. It's time I meet the family anyway."

"They're good people, Smokey."

"I know that." I didn't tell him that my concern was more with Joe, with the jittery boy I had seen outside the pawn shop two days before. "I'll get the address from you tomorrow."

"Good," Henry said. "Jimmy needs you. He needs to have some continuity from his previous life to this one. I'd rather it be you than his brother."

"Me, too," I said and hoped Jimmy felt the same way.

I managed to get to the office shortly before Laura. She was struggling with two boxes small enough that she could cradle them in her arms. I opened the door for her and she came inside, dropping the boxes on my floor.

"What are those?"

"Courtesy of my father's secretary," she said.

I raised my eyebrows. "Those are all the records from his entire career?"

"All that she had."

"Why don't I believe that?"

Laura's gaze met mine. "Because I don't?"

"Well," I said, "at least it's a start."

I gave Laura one box and I took the other. We sat in our customary positions on the floor and began working. The materials inside my box were difficult to handle. Blurred carbons of old letters and tiny receipts with no labels on them. We would be at this for hours, if not days.

After half the morning went by and I found no letter more informative than one that began, "Enclosed please find the memo from last Wednesday," I gave up.

"Laura," I said, "maybe you should go back to Chicago and get what records you can. I'll go through these and see what I can find."

She set down a sheet of onionskin paper and wiped her fingers on her jeans. "I've asked her to send more."

"And she'll find more junk. It would be better if you go."

I didn't want her out of there as much for the records as I did because of the threat Thomas Withers had made. Withers probably wouldn't make good on any threat, but I didn't want to take chances.

Not with Laura.

Laura shook her head. "Not yet, Smokey. I hear Dr. King is coming to town. I'd like to hear him speak. Do you think that's possible?"

Out of the frying pan, I thought.

"Things are volatile here, Laura. I don't think going to Martin's speech would—"

"You know him?" Her eyes widened.

A slip. I had been concentrating on her so much that I hadn't paid much attention to what I was saying.

"We went to school together," I said as I always did. People understood that to mean Boston University, where we did go to school at the same time. But I meant elementary school. I simply never corrected anyone.

"Then you can definitely get me in, Smokey. Please. He's such a great speaker."

I stared at her for a moment. "I didn't think this would be your thing, Laura."

Her eyes narrowed. "Because I'm white?"

I didn't answer her. That was what I meant and we both knew it.

"He has a lot of white supporters, you know. I've been following his career for years. I think he's a great man,

Smokey." She said this last as if she were challenging me to show that she had never had these beliefs.

"Laura," I said softly. "There's been a lot of violence here. The week before you came—"

"I know about the riot," she said.

"And since, there's been trouble as well. It's not going to be safe."

"Surely no one would do anything while Dr. King is here."

Henry had said the same thing. Had most people assumed Martin's profile had gotten so high he would be safe? I didn't think any black man achieved that level of safety, no matter who he was.

"It's possible something could happen," I said.

She shrugged one shoulder. "I'm a big girl, Smokey. I've lived in the roughest city in North America for years. What did Carl Sandburg call it? The city with big shoulders? I can handle trouble. I know how to stay out of the way."

I doubted that. "I don't want to worry about you," I said.

Her eyes sparkled. "Would you?"

I nodded. Just once. It was an admission I didn't want to make.

"You can sit beside me. Then you'll know I'm safe," she said.

"I can't sit beside you," I said. "I'm working with a security detail that night."

"Oh." She smiled. "Then things will be fine."

I wished I had as innocent a view of the world as she did. But I didn't. And I knew that if someone wanted to do something bad, one person—even a prepared person like me—wouldn't be enough to prevent it.

No matter how hard he tried.

FIFTEEN

No matter how much work my small security team and I did that weekend, nothing prepared us for the reality of Martin's speech. And we did work. Hard. Except for a brief stop to listen to Robert F. Kennedy's announcement that he was running for president—something that did not thrill me since I remembered the Robert F. Kennedy who argued against sending troops to Arkansas to protect the students—and a few trips to Jimmy's foster home only to discover the family had gone on some kind of outing, I worked my small team as if they were a military unit and their lives depended on their ability to perform.

Monday morning, I did not meet with Laura. I had a brief meeting with Reverend James Lawson. He assured me that Martin would have his own people, and that there would be a professional security team as well. All my group had to do was watch for local troublemakers.

Which was harder than it sounded. By the time eight o'clock rolled around, the Mason Temple, one of the larger venues in Memphis, overflowed. Crowds sat on the floor, on the stairs, in the aisles, and in the doorways. Hundreds who couldn't get in waited in the streets outside. I managed to find Laura a seat in the middle only because she came with me when I began sweeping the building for bombs. She sat there, a small white figure against a sea of black, looking proud of herself just for being there.

I tried not to look at her. I didn't want her to take my mind off my impossible job.

I looked at this like it was a military mission. The bomb sweep produced nothing, but there was little I or anyone could do if this crowd got out of hand. Reporters and crowd watchers at the scene estimated that there were seventeen thousand people in and around the Temple.

I saw none with black berets. I could only hope that the Panthers and the Invaders had decided to stay away from this meeting.

We had set up a side door for Martin to enter through, and I had planned to wait there, to say hello and maybe have a word or two with him. But as the crowd grew, I knew that wasn't possible. I spent most of my time pacing the perimeter of the building, threading among the people.

I wouldn't have known that Martin had made it to the podium if it weren't for the sudden deafening roar of applause, the stomping feet, and the whistles that greeted his arrival. I stopped in the back of the Temple and watched him, a small man with dark sincere eyes, letting the wave of adoration flow over him.

Hard to believe this was the same person who had played with me as a boy, who had shoved me back at the *Gone with the Wind* premiere, who had worried about his own father's disapproval. He had had something even then, but I never would have guessed that he would have come to this.

The applause continued, a live thing. Martin was loved here. He held out his hands for silence, but it still took five minutes for the crowd to settle down.

As he began his speech, I went back to surveying the building, sure that I could see anything awry before someone else did.

So I only caught snatches of the speech. But through the

whistles and applause, the pounding feet and the shouts of "Yessir" and "All right!," he caught the spirit of Memphis. "We are tired," he said over and over again. "We are tired of working our hands off and laboring every day and not even making a wage adequate with the basic necessities of life. We are tired . . ."

After a long hour, he ended by advocating a massive downtown march on Friday, and he urged all black employees to stay home from their jobs and all black students to stay out of school. The hall erupted into pandemonium. People screamed their approval, waved their arms, shouted how wonderful he was. Martin stepped down to the front row, and the applause went on forever.

By that point, I was watching from a side door. Laura was applauding too, her face flushed with the moment, her eyes shining. She seemed as caught up in this as the rest of them did. Only I wondered what Mayor Loeb would think, and only I worried what a march of that size might do to the city—not the white city, but the black city that had already received so much punishment.

After a moment, Martin went back to the podium. The applause died down. "I've just received a note from two of my lieutenants," he said, "suggesting that I return on Friday to lead the march. The Poor People's Campaign will begin in Memphis! I will see you here in four days!"

The screaming and shouting rocked the building, and I wondered if we would be able to get Martin out. I hurried toward him and his lieutenants. Martin saw me over the crowd and grinned. He mouthed, "Billy!"—he'd never called me Smokey—and I nodded back. His group moved him forward, and I guarded the back, and somehow they got him outside and to a car.

That was the kind of security team I wanted COME to hire for all the marches. People who knew how to work a crowd, how to get in and out of a building. People who knew how to make sure nothing bad happened.

As the car drove away, I stood near the doorway, getting shoved and pushed as the crowd left the building. I was covered in sweat and exhausted, but relieved. No berets in the audience, no bold threats from young voices, no leaflets proclaiming revolution, no flyers on a race war. It seemed like Thomas Withers and his little group had been scared away from this event, as if Martin's presence had indeed been the charm that Laura and Henry thought it would be.

I went back inside to find Laura. She had remained on her chair as I had told her to. Only a couple hundred people were still inside and the hall looked very empty.

She smiled when she saw me. "He's wonderful," she said.

I nodded. He was an amazing speaker and the best leader the black community had seen in my lifetime. But I had a feeling that he didn't understand Memphis. I wasn't sure more confrontation was what we needed. I had hoped, I suddenly realized, for a bit more diplomacy.

I had hoped that with this speech, all the turmoil would come to an end.

SIXTEEN

But the turmoil didn't end. If anything, it got worse. White Memphis was scared. Hate literature was passed out throughout the city. Some crazy called WHBQ and said that Martin would be killed if he came back to Memphis.

Some of the leaders of COME were looking at this as a good sign, as evidence that they had touched a live wire and they might be able to gain control of the strike.

I wasn't so sure. Live wires often burned.

I couldn't get Laura to leave. She was energized by Martin's speech, and she wanted to stay for the march. She had never done anything like that, she said, and I was certain her society friends would be appalled. Part of me was glad she was stepping in, and the rest of me was worried.

I was convinced Laura didn't know what she was getting into.

Not even I was sure. We were heading into new territory, and it seemed fraught with danger.

On Tuesday, I finally got to see Jimmy. I arrived just after school, hoping that Jimmy would have made it home by then.

His foster parents lived near Henry's church. The neighborhood was like mine; rows of formerly white houses in desperate need of paint lined up too close together. Garbage was piled on the curbs, and I reflected that Loeb's scabs would have to work real hard to get to all the neighborhoods he had neglected since the strike began.

I pulled up in front of a house with an overturned bicycle in the front yard. As I got out of the car, I saw a curtain swing closed. I stepped over the mounds of garbage and onto the sidewalk. As I mounted the steps, the front door opened.

A woman stood there. She was slender and big-busted. She wore a sweater that was too tight, knit pants that weren't, and a purple apron around her waist. Her face was long, her features classic, her skin darker than mine. She had her arms crossed beneath those magnificent breasts as if she were holding them up.

"Can I help you?" she asked, her voice so cold that I thought it might turn the air to ice.

I smiled. Usually women didn't react that way to me. "My name is Smokey Dalton. Reverend Davis told me this was where Jimmy Bailey's been staying."

"Reverend Davis *told* you?" She sounded like she couldn't believe anyone would talk to me, about anything.

"Yes, ma'am," I said, deciding to give her the title of respect even though she was probably younger than I was.

"Why?"

"Because I'm the one who brought Jimmy to him."

She softened at that. "Oh," she said, pushing the door open wider. "You're the one."

"Is Jimmy here?"

She nodded. As I passed her, she held out her hand. "I'm Selina Nelson."

I took her hand. The fingers were long, slender, and callused. And cold. "Smokey Dalton," I said again.

"Sorry to be so rude," she said. "It's just you never know these days, especially . . ."

She didn't finish the sentence, but I understood it. Especially with someone asking after Jimmy.

The interior of her house smelled of fresh cookies. A toddler sat in the middle of the floor, pushing a stuffed dog around as if it were a truck. A little girl, maybe about three, had fallen asleep on the couch, a blanket clutched in one hand like a life preserver. The television was on, but the sound was turned off.

It seemed like a homey place, a comfortable place, just neat enough to show that Selina Nelson made an effort at keeping it clean, and just messy enough to show that children lived here.

"Is Jimmy here?"

"In the kitchen," she said. "We were making cookies."

I went inside the small kitchen. It was neat, with nothing on the countertops except cookie sheets covered with dough. Jimmy wore an apron, which he hastily took off when he saw me.

"Hey, Smokey!"

"Jimmy," I said, and hugged him. He let me. "Looks like they're keeping you busy."

He eased out of my embrace. "It's for the kids."

"I know." All of them, I assumed. Jimmy never had the chance to do homey things.

"He made the dough," Selina Nelson said.

"But she says I make the cookies too big." Jimmy sounded like he didn't agree with her.

"If they're too big," she said, "you don't get as many."

It didn't look like that argument persuaded him.

"Why don't you let me finish and you can talk with your friend?" she said.

I looked at Jimmy. He had a dusting of flour on his nose. "We can stay in here if you want," I said. "I haven't made cookies in a long time."

He grinned. So instead of talking with Jimmy about missing school, I spent the most pleasant afternoon I'd had in weeks, baking chocolate chip cookies, stealing dough, and learning how to make raisin cookies so that they would be soft, not hard.

We laughed and made a mess of Selina Nelson's kitchen, which we eventually had to clean up, and somehow she convinced me to stay for dinner, even though I was so full of cookies I could barely eat.

And as I left, hours later, the sound of childish laughter still ringing in my ears, I knew that Jimmy had finally found a safe place at last. Maybe there, he would learn what home was. Maybe there, he would learn the value of love.

So, on Wednesday morning, my mind was filled with Jimmy and Martin and the upcoming march when I picked my mail out of its cubby on the first floor of the Gallina Building. The mailman had stuffed a big yellow envelope into the cubby, and I had a hell of a time pulling it out. With it came two circulars and a bill. I grabbed them and climbed the stairs slowly, opening as I went.

Laura hadn't arrived yet. I unlocked my office door and went inside, flicking on the light as I kicked the door closed. Then I crossed to my desk, threw out the circulars, tucked the bill in a drawer, and sat down.

I reached inside the envelope and pulled out a handwritten note, along with another bill.

"Usually," the note started in rather florid script, "I send the original to the owner of the file. After all, the doctor's gone and I don't have any more use for it. But in this case, I didn't. You'll see why. I did go to the expense of having some Photostats made. I've billed you for those. They are enclosed."

It was signed "Mrs. Beaumont Calhoun."

I felt the first bit of excitement I had felt about this case in weeks. It was a break. And I had forgotten about it. I'd been so focused on the financial records I hadn't paid attention to how long it had taken Mrs. Calhoun to get back to us.

No wonder it had taken her so long to respond. She had gone to the trouble to copy the entire file. My curiosity was peaked. I reached into the envelope and pulled out a manila folder.

Inside were tiny, fragile Photostats. I placed a piece of clean white paper on my desk and put one of the Photostats on it. I squinted at it. The Photostat was of a piece of lined paper, covered with a nearly unreadable scrawl. The date was April 30, 1939. It took me a minute to parse out the writing. It was the doctor's history of Dora Jean Hathaway's pregnancy.

She had been in Birmingham the entire time.

My mouth went dry. I wiped my suddenly damp hands on my pants and read. Dr. Calhoun was worried about Dora Jean because she had some toxemia. Her body was swelling all over, and it was still early in the pregnancy. He prescribed a home remedy that sounded just ghastly to me, and bed rest which "I doubt she'll be able to do, given their situation."

The next notation was months later. Dora Jean looked awful, and Calhoun was worried for the health of the baby. He admonished her for not coming into the office, and she had told him that she couldn't afford to pay him. He told her to keep coming anyway. He was of the old school, a family doctor who had known and cared about his patients.

The next six notations were in medical jargon. I didn't entirely understand them, but from the gist, I gathered Dora Jean was in a bad way. Dr. Calhoun wrote that he worried about the couple's other children if Dora Jean passed away. "Earl," he wrote, "doesn't dare stay home and care for them. He can't lose this job too. And there isn't a one of those children over five. I keep warning the Hathaways that you can have too many children too quick, but they haven't listened to me."

Too many children too quick? I glanced at the door. Laura

hadn't arrived yet. Which was good, because I didn't like the feeling I was getting.

I kept reading, my face nearly pressed against the top of the desk as I tried to decipher the doctor's scrawl. Laura was born at home—a one-room cabin outside of Birmingham, one room which was home to four children, their parents, and now the infant Laura. The birth was a difficult one, and Dr. Calhoun wanted to take Dora Jean to the hospital. Earl wouldn't hear of it. Laura was born in the middle of the night; at dawn, Dora Jean died.

I closed my eyes for a moment. I knew we'd find something, I just wasn't sure what. And I certainly hadn't expected it to be something like this.

I took a deep breath, opened my eyes, and kept going. Dr. Calhoun asked Earl if he wanted to give up the child. Earl said no. Dr. Calhoun argued against it, but did arrange for a wet nurse, whom Earl said he could pay in food. Dr. Calhoun wrote up a small agreement, and Earl signed it—with an X that Calhoun labeled as Earl's mark.

Three days later, when Dr. Calhoun came to his office to open it in the morning, he found Earl on his doorstep cradling little Laura. Her face was blue.

She was dead.

I wanted to lock my office door, shut off the lights, and hide. But I couldn't. I owed Mrs. Calhoun more than money. After she had read the file, she had known that Laura Hathaway wasn't the infant her husband had helped bring into the world, but she did send the file anyway. She probably figured that the deception wasn't Laura's, or Laura would never have requested the file. The old lady was sharper than I had given her credit for.

The baby Laura, Dr. Calhoun speculated, died because "her lungs were underdeveloped" and because "she didn't have a mother's nurturing." Whatever the cause, the good doctor had taken his patient's double grief to heart and had paid, out of his own pocket, to have the little girl buried next to her mother. Dr. Calhoun had even purchased the headstone.

I sincerely doubted that the Earl Hathaway who was trying to raise four children alone was the Earl Hathaway who had made his fortune in Chicago. But they were tied together somehow. Obviously, it was the headstone that gave Laura's parents the idea to ask for the dead infant's birth certificate. But the unusual part of this whole thing was that they didn't just take the child's identity. They took the identity of the whole family.

I stood and shoved my hands in my pocket. It wouldn't have been that hard to do in 1939, to steal the identity of a poor man who was raising four children. What Earl Hathaway in Chicago did had no impact at all on the Earl Hathaway from Birmingham. And next to little Laura's grave would be the grave of her mother, so the Chicago Hathaways knew they would have no problem with Dora Jean.

Documentation really wasn't an issue at that time, not for an adult. Children's birth certificates were becoming important—*records* were becoming important—but a lot of poor folk traveled during the thirties and they did so without benefit of birth certificates or passports or anything else that required proof of identity. If you said you were Earl Hathaway, you were. Only a handful of things required proof of identity and most of those were government related, from driver's licenses to high level government employment. I was sure Earl Hathaway—Chicago's Earl Hathaway—could have found a way around that.

But I had to be sure. I picked up the phone, dialed O, and asked for a Birmingham operator. Then I asked for a number for Earl Hathaway.

"I don't have Earl Hathaway, sugar," she said. "I have Earl Hathaway, Junior."

Junior. Chances were that was as good as I would get. "Fine."

She gave me the number and hung up. I checked my watch. Laura was later than she had ever been. I wondered what was holding her up.

Then I shook my head. I was becoming used to this, these daily meetings where we were alone, sifting through records. It wasn't that we talked much—we really didn't—but we were becoming comfortable with each other, a first, I think, for both of us. She had never promised that she would be in at ten. I had just assumed she would, just as she probably assumed I would.

That would change now. The entire investigation would change.

I dialed the number the operator had given me. I doubted I would have any luck. Earl Hathaway, Junior, if he was the child of the Earl Hathaway who fathered the real Laura, was—at the oldest—thirty-four years old. He was probably working on a Friday morning.

To my surprise, someone picked up on the third ring. "Hathaway's Auto Repair. Mavis speaking."

"I was wondering if I could speak to Earl."

"He's in the shop. Can I help you?"

"No," I said. "I'm calling long distance."

"Lordy," she said, and put down the phone. I heard her screech, "Earl!" and moments later her voice was echoed by a much younger one shouting, "Daddeee!"

I wanted her to pick up the phone so that I could tell her it was all right, I would dial him directly, when I heard a male voice in the distance.

"Mavis, how many times I gotta tell you—"

"It's long distance, Earl." She was speaking in a whisper, but I still heard her.

"Long—?" Apparently that caught his attention. I heard footsteps, a child's laughter, and a mumbled "Squirt" before someone fumbled with the phone.

"This's Earl."

"Mr. Hathaway?" I asked in my best educated white man voice. I kept the northern accents I had learned out, though, and let my Memphis through.

"Yessir."

"My name is Billy Dalton, and I'm from Memphis. I am investigating a case involving a man I believe to be your father. Do you have a moment?"

"Yessir." I heard the squeal of chair legs against linoleum. "Whoizzit?" Mavis whispered. Earl shushed her.

"Mr. Hathaway, are you the son of Earl and Dora Jean Hathaway of Birmingham?"

"Yessir." You'd think I was a school principal for all the inflection Earl Junior was putting into his words.

"Is there any way I can speak to your father?"

"He died ten years ago."

"I'm sorry to hear that." And I was. It would have made things easier.

"My momma's been dead now thirty years."

"She died giving birth to your sister, right?"

"Baby died too." It was so long ago that Earl Junior was able to speak of it almost flippantly. He had been five at the outside; the baby probably hadn't been a real thing to him then.

I didn't quite know how to ask the next question. "After your mother died, did your father move to Chicago?"

There was a long, long pause, and then Earl Junior snorted with laughter. Shocked laughter. "*My* daddy? My daddy never left Alabama in his whole life. Why would you ask a fool question like that?"

"Because I'm trying to find out about an Earl Hathaway from Chicago, and some of the work I did led me to believe that he was your father. I guess I'm wrong."

"Guess so." Then with slow deliberation, Earl Junior said, "How'd you know about my sister?"

I had to lie on the spot, something, fortunately, I was good at. "The Earl Hathaway I'm checking has a daughter born in 1939. I've been checking birth records all over the country."

"Well, my sister died," Earl Junior said again.

"I'm sorry to hear that. Do you mind my asking what your father did after your mother died?"

"Hell, just about anything," Earl Junior said. "He wanted to keep our family together. Almost didn't do it. But his maw helped out, and we made it. He wasn't nobody special. Jus' did what he could, when he could."

"Did he teach you how to fix cars?"

"Sure. Saw it as a necessity, not a skill."

I smiled. "Thanks for your time, Mr. Hathaway."

"Sure thing," he said, and hung up.

I cradled the receiver for a moment before hanging up myself. Within fifteen minutes, I saw bits and pieces of someone else's life. Earl Hathaway of Birmingham, Alabama, wasn't anyone special, but he had raised four children on his own, managed to hang onto them without skills, education, or a wife, and had at least one child who had grown up to own his own business—and who seemed to have a good relationship with his own child.

The real Earl Hathaway may not have been rich, but it seemed as if he had a warmth that the Chicago Earl Hathaway clearly lacked.

At that thought, the door opened, and Laura came in. She pushed the door closed with her shoulder and struggled with the sleeves of her white parka. It was streaked with dirt.

I got up to help her, but she twisted away.

"What happened to you?" I asked, wishing that today, of all days, she had arrived in her customary good mood.

"Did you know they're picketing on Main Street?"

"No," I said.

"They are. Some big huge signs saying 'Stay Away. No Shopping Today,' and some crap about decency."

I was stunned by her tone. Just the day before she had been telling me how much she wanted to join the march. "What were you doing on Main?"

"One of the stores has a counter that serves a great breakfast," she said. "I never had trouble getting in there before."

I felt myself go cold. "You did today?"

"Oh, yeah. Some teenage boy started shouting about whities not supporting the strike, and me crossing a picket line, and then some other boys yelled at me for wearing a white coat, and the next thing I know, they're throwing garbage at me." She looked at me, blue eyes flashing. "I didn't think I was crossing any picket line. They weren't parading in front of the building."

I nodded. "It's hard to tell sometimes."

"This is the kind of trouble you've been worried about."

Actually, I'd been worried about worse, but I lied. "Yes."

She wiped at her face, and her fingers came away dirty. She grimaced. "Excuse me," she said, and headed for the restroom down the hall.

I picked up her coat from where it had fallen. The soft material was wet and streaked with dirt. I wondered if it would ever come clean.

I brushed it off as best I could and hung the coat on the coat rack. Then I wiped my hands on one of the napkins I kept on my desk and put the file together. My hands were shaking. I was worried about this client's reaction to the news I was about to give her, and that was not good.

She came back in my office, her face red and shiny from being scrubbed. She carried a faint scent of the industrial soap used in the bathrooms. I wanted to put my arm around her, but I didn't.

"Did you get breakfast?" I asked instead.

She nodded. "The manager got me inside. They fed me and let me out the back. They apologized as if it were their fault."

"And then they called the police, right?"

"Yeah. But the police were busy. You know there's been some violence near the dump?"

"I know," I said.

She sank into the chair, looking drawn. "I've never been attacked like that."

I wrapped my arms around the file to keep from trying to soothe her. Then I leaned against the desk, as far from her as I could get and still seem compassionate.

"Do you need to go back to your hotel?" I asked. I tried to tell myself that I asked out of concern, but my question partly came from cowardice. I didn't want her to see the file. "I'll drive you."

She smiled at me and shook her head. "I'll be all right." She tucked a loose strand of hair behind her ear. "I guess I should get to the files."

"Laura," I said, and was going to hand her the file. But I couldn't, not yet.

"What?" She was combing her hair with her fingers.

"You could get attacked worse than that on Friday. At the march."

"I'm beginning to realize that." Then she looked up at me and saw what I was cradling. "What's that?"

I could have lied. I wanted to. But she would have to learn it soon enough.

"It's from the doctor's wife," I said. "It's a Photostat of the file we requested."

"A Photostat?" She frowned, and that wan look was back on her face. "Something's wrong. What is it?"

I took a deep breath. "Remember that I told you if we dig you might not like what we find? This is that moment. You can choose not to look, Laura. You can turn your back on all of this and go home as if nothing has happened."

Her gaze met mine. It was level and flat and assessing.

"In fact," I said. "We'll call the debt even. You won't have to pay me from your folks' will, and I'll swallow all my costs."

"It's bad, isn't it?" she asked, and in that question I knew she wasn't going to give up.

"It's not what we were expecting."

She sighed and held out her hand.

"Laura—"

"I'm an adult, Smokey. Let me make my own decisions."

I handed her the file. She took it, opened it, and squinted, much as I had.

"I can't read this," she said.

"Take it to my desk."

She did and sat at the edge of my chair as if she didn't belong in it. I pulled out the first Photostat, slipped a white piece of paper behind it, and turned away from her. I didn't want to watch as she learned that everything she knew—right down to her own name—was a lie.

For a long time, the only sounds in the room were the clink of the radiator, the sound of her breathing—even and steady—and an occasional rustle as she turned the pages of the Photostats. My heart was pounding as if I had been running. I shoved my hands in my front pockets, feeling somehow responsible. If there hadn't been money left to me, if I hadn't spent that first ten thousand, maybe, just maybe, she wouldn't be here now, learning something she really didn't want to know.

"What does it mean?" she asked, her voice rusty, as if she had never used it before. "Smokey? What does this mean?"

I bowed my head. She knew. She had to know. But she wanted me to confirm.

"Your parents found the graves," I said. "They requested the birth certificate. Laura's birth certificate, and maybe Dora Jean's as well."

"But it says here that Earl is still alive. That isn't my father?"

I turned. I had never seen an expression like that on anyone's face before. It was both hopeful and sad, frightened and curious. The emotions bled one into another and back again, so quickly I could barely keep track. And they all moved across her face without a single change in her features. Only her eyes revealed her feelings. Her wide, blue—tearless—eyes.

"That isn't your father."

"So the siblings aren't mine, either," she said, and there was sorrow in her voice.

"No."

"But how . . ."

"I've been thinking about it." I held my position in the center of the room, my hands still firmly in my pockets. "We were wrong about when your parents were in Birmingham. They were probably there in December at the earliest, maybe January of 1940, spring at the latest. It usually takes a month to carve headstones and place them on a grave. Sometimes it takes longer. It was winter. Even in Alabama undertakers sometimes wait until spring. Your parents were there, going through the cemetery, looking at baby graves."

"For me."

"For you," I said, waiting. Waiting for it all to hit.

"But why wouldn't they use my real birth certificate? I had to have one, right?"

I didn't say anything.

Then the energy left her face as she understood. "They were running from something. They didn't want to use their names."

"Or yours."

"Or mine," she whispered.

"My guess is they were looking for a way to get I.D. for the whole family. This was the first or best opportunity they found. A mother and a daughter, dead at nearly the same time. If they had checked, they would have found an illiterate laborer struggling to raise four children on his own. He wouldn't come after them. He probably didn't even know such documentation existed."

And, as I spoke, I realized that I hadn't asked Earl Junior an important question. I hadn't asked if his parents were buried together under the same gravestone. If they were, the kind Dr. Calhoun had probably placed Earl's name on it, with his date of birth, so that everything would be ready when he died. Laura's parents may have gotten Earl's birth certificate as well.

The realization must have shown on my face.

"What?" Laura asked.

I didn't know how to tell her this. I didn't want to tell her much more than I needed to. "How old were you when your parents moved to Chicago?"

"I don't know," she said. "Two. Three."

"Do you remember?"

"No," she said.

"Did they call you anything besides Laura? A pet name? Anything?"

She thought on that, then shook her head slightly. "No. Not that I remember."

"Do you remember being in Chicago during the war?"

She nodded. "Little things. Our apartment was small then. We had to walk up. There were always people on the streets selling war bonds. Things like that."

"Where was the apartment?"

She blinked at me blearily.

"Surely you know," I said. "All little kids have to memorize their addresses."

She thought for a moment, then recited a street number and name that meant nothing to me. I made a note of it. Perhaps I could check building records. Anything might be helpful at this point. "And what about Rockford? Do you know where you lived there?"

She shook her head.

"Did you ever go back there? Visit family? Visit friends?"

She shook her head again. She was looking stunned.

"What about your parents' friends? Did people from out of town visit them?"

"No," she said.

I took a deep breath and took my hands out of my pockets. I hated the question I had to ask next, but I had to ask it. "Forgive me, Laura," I said. "But I have to ask you this."

Her eyes suddenly focused on me. They seemed hard and vulnerable at the same time, as if she were steeling herself for something even more difficult.

"Did your father have any shady friends? Mob friends?"

She rose, the old indignant Laura, the one I hadn't seen for weeks. The file fell to the floor, the Photostats scattering. "I told you before. He would never traffic with criminals. Not my father. Not—"

Her voice broke and she gaped at me, as if she had just heard what she was saying. Her lower lip trembled.

"Oh, God, Smokey," she said and burst into tears.

This time I did go to her. I wrapped my arms around her and pulled her close. She was fragile, her bones so delicate that it felt as if I could crush them with the hug. Her entire body shook. I patted her back as if she were a child and tried to think of her that way, instead of the softness of her against me, the faint rose scent of her hair mingling with that industrial soap.

I didn't tell her everything would be all right; it wouldn't be, maybe not ever again. She had just discovered incontrovertible proof that her parents had lied; that her own identity, her legal identity, belonged to someone else; that she wasn't who she had thought she was. What she learned threw her entire life into doubt, and nothing would be the same again.

Her tears were soaking through my shirt. She took three deep, hitching breaths and backed out of my arms, wiping her face with the back of her hand like a lost little girl.

"I'm sorry," she said. "I didn't mean to do that. I'm so, so sorry—"

"Don't be." I kept my own tone dry and calm. No sense in upsetting her more. "I would have been surprised if you hadn't had some reaction."

She sniffled. I reached around her and grabbed a napkin off my desk. She took it, wiped her face, and blew her nose heartily. Then she sank back into the chair as if her legs had lost all power to hold her.

"What do I do?" she asked.

The question sounded rhetorical, but I chose to answer it anyway. "You don't tell anyone. Your parents spent twenty years creating this fiction, and it's a solid one. As far as the world is concerned, you *are* Laura Hathaway. The real one only lived a few days. You're not doing any harm."

"But those people, the real Hathaways—"

"Don't have a clue. I spoke to the son this morning. The father died before your father did. They're doing just fine. The last thing they need to know is that their father's identity was stolen."

"You spoke to them?"

I nodded.

"But won't that clue them to this?"

"Why?" I said. "They just think I had the wrong Earl Hathaway. And they have no way of contacting me. It'll be all right."

"The doctor's wife. She knows."

"She suspects," I said. "And she won't do anything. If she were going to, she would have already. Besides, she's a smart old woman. She knows that you wouldn't come after your own birth information if you had any idea about the scam."

I regretted the use of that word the moment it left my mouth. But Laura didn't seem to hear it.

"I'm not Laura Hathaway," she said, looking at her hands. "I don't have any identity at all."

I crouched before her and took those hands. They were cold. "You are Laura Hathaway. In that, nothing has changed—"

"*Everything* has changed."

"Nothing has changed," I said. "Except that you now know more about your parents. You were suspecting something when you came to me. Now what you have to do is go back in your mind through everything, all that you learned from them, and remember what didn't fit, what seemed to contradict. Write down their irrational fears. Make a list of the things you weren't allowed to talk about. Write down the differences between you and the other children you played with."

Her eyelashes were spiky from the tears. "Have you done this before, Smokey?"

I shook my head. "Not a case like this."

"You warned me." She bowed her head. "You told me I might not like what I find."

"Usually people hide things for a reason."

"And you don't know what that reason is?"

"No."

"Even though they sent you money?"

I squeezed her hands and stood. It all came back to that. To that money they had sent. There was a tie, somewhere. A tie they felt guilty about. But I knew I had never seen those two people before, under any name.

She wiped at her face again. "We're not related, are we, Smokey? Not even distantly."

"Probably not," I said.

"It's something else, isn't it? You've been warning me all along that it could be criminal. You're a detective. Maybe you worked on a case for them."

"I would remember," I said. But would I? I remembered my clients, but not always the people that I came across in the course of a case.

And if it had been a case, how had Dora Jean Hathaway

known that I grew up in Washington, D.C.? I didn't usually divulge personal information to clients.

Maybe I was looking at this wrong. Why would anyone feel they owed me money? Did I hold a secret I wasn't supposed to? If so, why didn't they pay me before they died? Did I render service that I was unaware of?

Or was it something else? Something related to another case, perhaps?

"I'm going to review my files," I said. "See if anything rings a bell."

"You do think this is related, then?"

"I don't know," I said. "It would be a mistake not to pursue the relationship, just as it would be a mistake to assume that my inheritance is related to your parents' unwillingness to use their own names."

She nodded and swallowed hard. I could see the effort she was making to remain calm. "The question really is, who were they?"

"Yeah," I said. "That is the big question."

And I had a hunch we wouldn't like it when we found out.

SEVENTEEN

I drove Laura back to the hotel so that she could rest. I gave her my home phone number with instructions to call me at any time for any reason. I didn't know what else to do with her. I wanted to send her back to Chicago, but I knew she wouldn't go, now more than ever. I wasn't even sure she regarded it as home any more.

The drive to the Peabody was short, but along the way I saw the pickets she was talking about. They were scattered along Main and Union, carrying signs that read "Integrity and Decency for our Sanitation Workers" and "Keep Your Money in Your Pockets." Tellingly, there were no pickets in front of the Peabody.

I pulled into the valet parking in front of the Peabody to let Laura out. She kept her head bowed, and she carried her coat over her arm. Without saying much more than a whispered good-bye, she let herself out of the car and headed inside the hotel.

No one gave me a second glance, and I didn't see Roscoe Miller. He was probably fetching someone's car. I swung through the parking area and headed back to Main.

I thought of yelling at the picketers, but they weren't the people who had attacked Laura. It had to have been Invaders or members of the Black Organizing Party. This was the first incident that I had heard of since Martin's speech.

It did not bode well for Friday's march.

It seemed a long way away. I couldn't concentrate on it or the plans I was making for the security team. All I could think of was Laura.

My guess was that Laura's parents had never been to Birmingham. They had been on the run for some years before hooking up with the Chicago mob, probably in a small way, and the mob had gotten them the identification. Very few decent people knew how to legally change their identities, let alone illegally, and most didn't have the wherewithal to get identities for their entire family. The mob probably used one of their guys, who had to find the right year for Laura, and a southern background for her parents. Then he had to find parents who had died in an unspectacular manner or who wouldn't notice if their identification had been used.

The mob guy had succeeded admirably.

If the mob hadn't done it, someone else had. Someone Laura's father had paid. Either way you looked at it, the birth certificate pointed to Earl's involvement with career criminals. The move was too sophisticated to fit the scenario I had described to Laura.

That closed all my leads. No professional would leave tracks, not that it mattered in a case this old. What it did lead me to believe was that Laura's parents were criminals before she was born. They had probably operated in the South, and had probably done something high profile.

I was hoping it would be possible to find reference to a couple, a pregnant woman and a man, who had done these crimes, but I knew it would be another needle in a haystack. It would take a lot of digging through old crimes before I found the one I wanted.

And, I had to admit to myself, even that might not work. The Hathaways had committed a crime; that much was clear from their behavior. But what if they hadn't been seen? What if no one had known what they had done? Or what if the crime was not deemed as important as they thought?

Then I would not find them this way. And I doubted the records that Laura had brought would carry any information about this, although I would go back to the office and check. I could only hope that her memory might turn up something, now that she knew her parents weren't what they seemed.

I spent the rest of the afternoon searching the Hathaways' records in my office. I dug through the pre-1945 stuff, a handful of receipts and some newspaper clippings folded together. Most made no sense to me—they were about some of the minor war campaigns, and a few were about Chicago society meetings. One seemed to predate the war—it was an ad for women's clothes, clipped in its entirety. There had been dozens of clipped ads for women's clothes scattered among the records. Apparently Laura's mother saw a style she liked, clipped the ad, bought the dress, and saved the ad. I thought it was an odd way to do business, but there was nothing normal about the Hathaways.

By the next morning, I had sorted through the 1940s papers and had seen nothing unusual. Even the clippings made a strange sort of sense. Most were about businesses, local Chicago businesses, and I suspected, after I spent some time examining the documents, that Earl Hathaway had either invested in them or bought them outright.

Laura was late. That didn't surprise me. I thought of calling the Peabody. But we hadn't really made an appointment to see each other, and I was not her keeper. She was, as she had reminded me, an adult. She had to come to terms with this strange news on her own.

Still, I held my hand over the phone for a long moment before I picked it up and used my Chicago contacts to trace the owner of the apartment building that the Hathaways had lived in when Laura was a little girl.

For once, I was in luck. The building was still under the

same ownership and managed by the owner's real estate firm. I got through to one of the firm's managers, and even though he didn't keep records from the 1940s, he did confirm that Earl Hathaway and his family had rented an apartment from him.

"I always thought it was, you know, kinda ironic, the way they lived in this two-room apartment, and he went on to own so much of the city," the manager said.

"You watched this transformation."

"I did," the manager said. "Thought I was watching a kinda history. My grandfather did the same thing, bootstrapped himself right outta poverty and into—this place, anyway."

"It's your grandfather's real estate firm?" I asked.

"Oh, yeah, but everything was hands off by the time the Hathaways moved in."

"Do you know when that was?"

"Not exactly, and like I said we don't have the records. But it was during the war. I know that."

"It was too bad you didn't keep anything."

"Yeah, well, how're you supposed to know?"

How indeed. I thanked him for his time and hung up. By then it was eleven-thirty and still no Laura. Maybe she was giving all of this a second thought. Maybe she didn't want to know any more. It was the end of the week. I could prepare my bill, with the thought that it might be a final, and then present it to her when she told me it was over.

The office door opened then, and Laura came in, wearing her dirty white coat. She looked tired and bedraggled and smaller than she ever had. Her eyes were red-rimmed and sunken into her face, her mouth a pale pink line against chalky white skin.

I stood and went to her, but she turned away from me—clearly on purpose—and pulled off her coat.

"So," she said, her voice trembling. "It's going to get worse, isn't it? Before it gets better. It's going to get worse."

I stopped near the chair and nodded. "Most likely."

"I spent all night trying to think of why they'd do this, why they'd lie like that. It would be to escape someone's parents, or to elope. They could have done that without changing their names, and twenty-eight years ago, no one would have known how to look for them."

"That's right," I said.

"So they did something. Something bad." She clasped her hands in front of her like a schoolgirl. "And all that money, it came from the same something bad, right?"

This was the kind of information we needed, information she hadn't realized she had. Information she hadn't been willing to look at, until now.

"What money?" I asked.

"When I was little, my mother used to say that everything would be all right, that soon we'd be taken care of. Then one day, my father moved us to this great place and from then on, everything was better." She put the heel of her hand to her forehead. "Or they thought everything was better. I had lessons. Elocution, and dancing, and classes, and it was so that I could be the perfect daughter. Mom used to say they'd raise me better."

"Better than what?"

"I don't know." She brought her hand down. "But that's the phrase I can't get out of my head. They'd raise me *better*."

I watched her. All the patrician confidence was gone. Beneath it was a child, a little girl who had just learned that the world was not what she expected, that it wasn't what she was prepared for, and that scared her.

It scared her a lot.

"And I don't think," she said slowly, "that my father had mob ties. He never seemed to owe anyone anything. He was pretty accepted in town except . . ."

She let her voice trail off.

"Except?" I asked.

She raised her gaze to mine. "He didn't want his picture taken. Not then, not ever. And if the papers wanted an interview, it was with the express understanding that he would do it by phone, not in person."

"What was he hiding from?" I asked, more to myself than to her.

"I don't know," she said. "I can't tell. I've been thinking all night, and all I can come up with is that they stole the initial money."

"And waited until it cooled down before using it," I said.

She nodded.

"Probably to avoid notice."

"Then the money would have to be traceable, right?" she asked.

I thought about it for a moment. "Perhaps," I said slowly. "Or perhaps they stole something they had to sell, and had to wait until they had a buyer."

We looked at each other.

"How do you trace that?" she asked.

"We dig," I said.

She frowned. "How can you do this work, day in and day out. You dig through eighty things to find a detail."

"Sometimes," I said. "And sometimes the details find me."

I took her hands and led her to the chair. She allowed me to do so and sat cautiously. I wanted to run my fingers along her cheek, to squeeze her shoulder, to make her feel better, but I didn't. I went back to my desk and sat there, hands folded.

"Now," I said. "Tell me everything you remembered."

And she did.

Laura Hathaway was a golden child. Raised primarily by her mother, Laura spent her days learning how to be part of her "social set." It was clear from Laura's earliest childhood that her mother didn't belong to that set. Her friends' mothers went to teas and benefits and concerts; her mother stayed home. Once Laura had asked her about it, and her mother had given a nervous little laugh.

"Sweetie," her mother had said softly, "you have to be invited."

As Laura grew older, her parents were invited to the more important events, mostly because of her. Sometimes her mother accompanied Laura. More often, Laura went with a girlfriend's family and made excuses for her parents. No one seemed to care that her parents didn't come, not really. All that mattered was Laura and, as her friend Prissy Golden had said, her money. Everyone knew that Laura's parents wanted her to marry well; they also knew that Laura would bring to the marriage poise, intelligence, beauty, and more money than the rest of them had combined.

"This was common knowledge?" I asked.

"Oh, yes," Laura said.

"And no one cared that your parents were so eccentric."

Her smile was tiny and tight. "Not as long as they were rich."

Laura's parents were eccentric in other ways. Her mother seemed to live for her, but her father would do anything for her mother. He rarely spent any time with Laura and often ignored her when he was there.

"That meant," she said, "I spent a lot of time trying to gain his approval."

When she got into the University of Chicago, she was convinced he would be proud of her. He barely noticed. When she decided to major in economics—and managed to get into the department, one of the most influential in the world and the most competitive in the school—he told her that the world had its own economic system, one that could only be lived.

He died shortly after her twentieth birthday, but he'd been

sick for weeks. Two days before he died, he asked to see her alone.

"You're your mother's," he had said to her. "She has dreams for you. See that you live them."

He said nothing about love or affection, nothing about his hopes and dreams for his only daughter. He only spoke of her duty to his wife.

" 'You're your mother's'?" I repeated.

She nodded. "He used to say that to me a lot when I was a girl. If I'd ask him a question, he'd say, 'You're your mother's girl. Ask her.' It was his way of acknowledging the truth in our family. He really didn't care about me. Mother did."

Interesting. I made a note of that fact. It might become useful.

Laura clasped her hands tightly together. She bit her lower lip and then said, "I don't remember much about my father's businesses, but they seemed legal enough. He never owed anyone anything."

"Did he travel?"

"Not that I remember," she said. "You'd think I'd know, Smokey."

I was beginning to believe her. It made the Washington, D.C., connection all the stranger. "And he never wanted to be photographed?"

"No."

"What about your mother?"

"I don't think photography was an issue at first," she said. "And then as I grew older and we started to go to functions together, she didn't seem to mind."

If her father had friends, they were all in his business, and she never saw them. Her mother made all her friends at the society functions. There had been no one until then.

Laura hadn't thought that strange. It was, after all, how she grew up.

"And no talk of the past?" I asked.

"None," she said.

"None at all?"

She closed her eyes and sighed. "I thought about it all night. There was no talk at all."

And that was all she knew. I asked every question I could think of, probed each part of her memory as best I could, and we learned, together, that her parents had been very disciplined in their silence.

"And I was so damned self-centered I didn't even notice," she said.

What I didn't say was that it seemed they had raised her that way intentionally. She didn't look to them because they didn't invite the looks. Her parents had been very secretive people, even from their own child.

What little she was able to tell me gave me supposition, and nothing more. It seemed as if her father was the one who committed the crime and perhaps had done it, in some way, for her mother.

I doubted Laura was his child. He was too indifferent to her, and that phrase, "You are your mother's," was telling. Yet they didn't want her to know that she wasn't theirs. Was that part of the identification deception? Or was there another reason?

Perhaps her father had hooked up with her mother after Laura had been born, after the crime—whatever it was—had been committed. Whatever crime they had committed it was apparently their last. Their lives from the day they arrived in Chicago until the day they died seemed exemplary.

"What about that mob rumor?" I asked.

She shrugged. "All I can guess," she said, "is that it had to do with the money."

I wasn't that naive. I suspected that Earl Hathaway did have ties to the Chicago mob and that was one reason he stayed away from all the social events. His wife gradually gained acceptance through her rich and pretty daughter. The family apparently decided not to push it with Earl.

But again, that was merely supposition. What seemed even more likely to me was that Earl fronted for the mob and got paid very well for doing so. That way, he kept his own record clean and still managed to make a better living for his family than he could have done any other way. The mob connection could have been, as Laura said, a rumor brought on by the family's mysteriousness and its sudden wealth. But a person in my business learns that rumors often have a basis in fact.

After she finished telling me everything, Laura leaned back in the chair. She looked even more exhausted than she had before, and I realized we had talked through lunch. It had grown dark outside, and that meant we were missing dinner as well.

"Now what?" she asked.

"Now let me feed you," I said. "You look like you're about to fall over."

Her smile was small but real. "You mean I haven't yet?"

"Not yet." I stood up from my desk and got her coat. Then I held it out to her. "I'm sorry."

She shrugged, then stood and slipped her arms into the sleeves. "You warned me."

"I know. But I didn't expect this."

"I didn't either." She turned and faced me. We were only inches apart. "And the strangest thing is, I feel like I've inherited the secret. I can't tell anyone but you."

I put my hands on her shoulders. "For now. Maybe when we find out what really happened—"

"What if we're right?" she asked. "What if my parents did steal the money that they lived on, that my father built from? What then?"

I let my hands run along her upper arms. I knew what she was asking; she was asking what I would do. Would I make her lose everything? Give it all back?

"It'll be your choice," I said. "You and I are the only ones who'll know."

She tilted her head back slightly, but she didn't move out of my grasp. "But you're an ethical man, Smokey."

It was as close as she was going to come to questioning me again. "I suspect you're ethical as well."

She closed her eyes. "But that would mean—"

"Don't," I said. "Don't make a decision yet. It's all what-ifs right now. You'll be better equipped to decide when you know what happened."

"If I know." She opened her eyes.

"If you learn it, yes," I said.

She patted my side and gave me a small, sad smile. "You promised me dinner, Smokey."

"And so I did." I let my hands fall. Then I shut off the office lights and let us into the dark hallway. I was feeling better than I had that morning, even though Laura was understandably upset. I felt like we were finally moving on this, as if there were answers out there; we just had to find them.

I kept one hand under her elbow as we went down the stairs. She didn't move away. She seemed to need the support. As we went out the door at the base of the stairs, a blast of chill air hit us. It was extremely cold, and the sky was filled with ominous clouds. The streets were pretty empty for Beale at this time of night. I hadn't heard the weather reports, but I had a feeling that something was coming.

I tightened my grip on Laura's arm. I led her across the street to the King's Palace. We walked past the arched doors and in to the main door of the restaurant. It was Thursday night, so there wasn't a line, for which I was grateful. No music either.

As we waited near the bar for a waiter to seat us, a man watched us from one of the booths. Laura didn't notice him, but I did. I recognized him as another of Joe's friends.

When he realized I had made eye contact with him, he stood and sauntered over. He was wearing a black beret, sunglasses, and a black leather jacket over black pants. As he got closer, he let the sunglasses slip to the end of his nose.

"See you brung your white bitch," he said, loud enough to carry over the conversation in the restaurant.

Laura turned. I tightened my grip on her arm.

"Ain't no one told you that black is beautiful, man? What you doing with some honky woman when you could be with one of ours?"

"We just came for dinner," Laura said, her words trailing off as I squeezed her elbow warningly. I stepped between her and the man.

"Do I know you?" I asked.

"We seen each other before."

"You're one of the men who's been sending little boys out to deliver drugs?"

Behind me, Laura hissed slightly.

The man just pushed his sunglasses up with his thumbs. "You should pay more attention. We been advising on the way things should go around here."

"As if you're an expert."

"I might be. More than you, any way. You and your white bitch."

Laura stepped up beside me. "It's not—"

"Laura," I said with great firmness.

"That's right. Least you keep her in line."

"I don't like your mouth," I said.

Laura put her hand on my arm, but the man smiled. "You don't got to like it. You just got to listen to it."

"I don't even have to do that. Come on, Laura." I took her hand and led her out of the restaurant.

195

"Why are we leaving?" she asked as she hurried to keep up with me. "He didn't have any right to say that to you. You didn't have to listen."

"And neither did you," I said. "We wouldn't get any peace and quiet in there."

"Who was he?"

"I'm not sure," I said. "I know what he wants me to think he is, but he's being awfully visible."

"What does that mean?" We were walking quickly down the street. I wanted to get to my car and get out before he had time to find his friends.

"It means he's dressed like one of the Black Panthers, but he's not acting like one."

"You mean that California group?"

"They're all over now," I said. "And they like to get attention, but not this kind. Not behind the scenes. They like to make the establishment notice them—the white establishment. They usually don't go after blacks."

"But you're with me," she said.

"Still." I didn't like the encounter. "I'll take you back to the hotel."

"No." She stopped beside my car. "Not yet. Can't we go somewhere?"

We probably could. Any one of the clubs in West Memphis or the restaurants by Stax Records wouldn't have looked twice at the two of us. But I didn't mention them. I didn't want to be in a crowd any longer.

"I'll cook you some dinner," I said. And then I realized who I was inviting to my small house. "If you don't mind seeing how the other half lives."

"Not at all," she said. I unlocked the car door and she slipped inside. I walked around, looking down Beale at the King's Palace. He hadn't followed us outside, which was good. Thomas Withers hadn't made any threats since we saw each other a week ago. Either he had decided I wasn't worth his time, or he had other plans.

I hoped that man in the beret wasn't part of the other plans.

I climbed in the car and drove off. Laura sat quietly, looking at the streets of Memphis in the growing dark.

As we got closer to my house, I began to wonder about the wisdom of my idea. The neighborhood was scruffy on its best days; almost a month into the strike, it looked dirty. Garbage cans were lined up curbside, and so were some plastic garbage bags. Most of the garbage was in stained grocery bags that were rotting over time. The stench was almost palpable. The skeleton crews put on by the city hadn't touched the black neighborhoods, only the upscale white ones.

As I parked, I felt my shoulders stiffen. I don't know what I was afraid of—Laura saying something rude, I suppose, like "You live *here*?" But she just got out of the car, stepped around the trash, and waited for me.

Even in her dirty coat and blue jeans, Laura looked out of place in the neighborhood. Something about her said money, even though she wasn't dressed that way tonight. Maybe it was her posture as she waited, the rigid back unbowed by life, or maybe it was the manicured edge she had— her hair was trimmed, her nails buffed, even her shoes looked new. Whatever it was, I saw her standing behind the garbage, near the row of shotgun houses with their peeling paint, and wondered why I had thought to bring her here.

I got out of my car and stepped through the garbage to meet her. Then I took her elbow and led her up the steps onto the porch. She waited while I unlocked the door and walked inside just behind me.

The house was dark and still smelled of the morning's toast and coffee. I flicked on the overhead light, a faint forty-watt bulb that I rarely used, and walked to an end table to turn on a lamp. Laura waited by the door, like a guest, making sure she wiped her boots on the mat, so that she didn't track across my wood floor.

I flicked on another light, and then turned off the overhead. The room looked better in indirect lighting, but it still looked spare. Compared to what Laura was used to, it probably looked small and meager. The bookshelves on the wall held only battered paperbacks and bookclub editions, not valuable hardcovers. The only art was a photograph of my foster parents, and the tiny black-and-white television set, squeezed onto a scarred end table that didn't match the other furniture, simply looked like the only company of a lonely man.

"This is the place," I said to fill the silence.

"It's comfortable," she said, and I felt myself relax by degrees. If she had said "nice" I would have thought she was humoring me. "Comfortable" seemed to be an honest word.

I took her coat and hung it on the tree by the door. Then I pulled off my own and headed toward the kitchen, thankful I had taken the time to clean up after my breakfast that morning.

"I don't have a lot," I said.

She had followed me. "I'm not that hungry anyway."

She was peering through the darkness into the rest of the house.

"It's not much," I said. "That's the bathroom, and through that door is the bedroom."

"This is a shotgun house," she said. "I've read about them. We don't have them in Chicago."

I supposed not. I opened the refrigerator, pulled out some cooked brisket I'd been planning to use on the weekend. I took cans of tomato sauce, tomatoes, and beans out of the cupboard, then grabbed an onion, Tabasco sauce, and spices, thankful that I always kept my foster mother's ingredients for chili in the house. Laura sat at the table while I cooked. She didn't say anything except to offer her assistance once, which I declined.

Then I left the chili to simmer on the stove and sat down across from her. I took her hand in mine. She didn't move away. Instead, she covered my hand with her other hand. There was nothing to say. There was nothing I could say. She had to sort through this one herself. I knew that much. I would never forget how it felt to have the world slip out from underneath you, to know that nothing would ever be the same again.

When the Grand had finally come and pulled me out of that closet, I was ten going on fifty. He had taken me to his home and broken the news to me gently: my parents were dead and I had to get out of the city for my own protection. No one ever wanted to tell me the full story—how my father, apparently, had offended the wrong people, and they had come to the house seeking revenge. They had gotten it too. My parents had a closed casket funeral that I wasn't even allowed to attend. My older, meaner cousin had tried to describe how my parents had looked when they were found, how badly beaten they were before they died. But those images didn't stick with me. Instead, it was the sound of my father's voice as he told me to hide. That had never left me.

That, and the knowledge that the world could turn upside down in the space of a minute.

I don't know how long Laura and I sat like that. Long enough for the scent of freshly made chili to waft over to us, for my stomach to growl, not once, but twice before she sat up straight and laughed. It was a soft, sad laugh.

"I'm keeping you from your dinner," she said.

"I don't mind."

Her gaze met mine. Her blue eyes were clear, but slightly swollen from a night of crying. If she hadn't been in such turmoil, I would have kissed her. But I didn't dare. The last thing I wanted to do was take advantage of someone in the state she was in.

Instead I smiled, patted her hand with my free one, and pulled away. I got up, took bowls out of the cupboard, and dished up the chili. Usually I liked to let it cook all night—

the spices wouldn't be blended to the best advantage other-wise—but I knew my foster mother's recipe would be better than anything Laura had had in the restaurants near the Pea-body.

"I wish I had some bread," I said as I put the bowl down in front of her.

"It's all right," she said.

I got two Cokes out of the fridge, pulled the ring tops, and sat down across from her. She ate as if she hadn't eaten for days. It wasn't until she was nearly done with the bowl that she wiped her mouth with her fingers, grinned at me, and said, "It's good."

"Thanks," I said, and almost told her it was a family rec-ipe, then decided I had better not. I slid my chair back and pulled napkins out of a drawer, handing one to her, and taking the other for myself. We ate the rest of the meal in companionable silence.

I hadn't done that in a long time, eaten a meal with some-one and not felt the obligation to speak. It felt good. When we were through, she offered to clean up, and I declined.

"You're probably tired," I said. "I'll drive you back to the hotel."

"Not just yet, Smokey." She drew her knees up to her chest, looking like a schoolgirl on my metal kitchen chair. "I don't know if I want to be by myself again."

I turned, feeling out of my depth. I started to say some-thing and she held up a hand.

"You're the only one who knows. I find comfort in that. I keep wondering how I could have missed it."

"Everyone missed it," I said. "Your parents planned it that way."

She nodded and rested her chin on the top of one knee, then she sighed.

I put a hand on her shoulder. "Go watch some television. I'll clean up and join you."

She smiled. "Thanks."

She got up and went into the living room. After a moment, I heard the sound of canned laughter coming from my television set.

It was nearly eight o'clock. I was supposed to meet Roscoe to go over security for the next day's march, and I was already late. I was about to go use the phone in my bedroom when I heard a weather bulletin echo from the TV. They were predicting snow for Memphis. A serious storm that had grounded all air traffic. They were warning people to get home before the bad weather hit.

If anyone showed up, Roscoe would handle it. I could stay here, with Laura.

The idea warmed me. I smiled and started cleaning up the kitchen.

When I finally went into the living room, the television was playing weird music. Laura was sprawled on my couch—the best way to watch my tiny set—only she was sound asleep. She had one arm underneath her head and another across her flat stomach. Her hair was flowing around her face, and her skin, in the soft light, looked flawless.

I had never seen anyone look so beautiful in my life.

I didn't want to wake her, but I didn't know how she'd feel, sleeping in my house. I shut off the television, but that didn't disturb her at all.

I went into my bedroom, opened the cedar chest my foster mother had given me when I bought the house, and pulled out one of the few things I'd salvaged from my childhood. It was a quilt my mother had made when my parents got together. My aunt had once explained that she had sewn a wedding ring pattern on the fabric to celebrate the marriage. In it was leftover material from my mother's wedding dress.

I carried the blanket into the living room and gently spread it over Laura. She didn't move. I turned off all but one light, then went into the bedroom. I lay on the bed, intending to think a bit about the week and what I'd learned, hoping I would be able to see something I had missed. I was fully dressed in case Laura woke up and wanted to return to the hotel. I didn't expect to sleep, but of course, I did.

I awoke to complete darkness and the faint scent of roses. I was still in my room, but I wasn't alone. Laura was beside me. I could feel her warmth. As I stirred, her hands touched my face.

"Smokey," she whispered. "Hold me."

I slid my arms around her. My fingers caressed the smooth skin of her naked back. I drew in a surprised breath of air, and started to move away when she wrapped her arms around me.

"Laura, I don't think, with what's going on—"

"Shh," she said, and kissed me.

I didn't say another word.

EIGHTEEN

The cold woke me up. My nose was an ice cube, and so was my right hand, the hand that was above the covers. A spot on the mattress beside me was still warm.

I was tangled in the sheets, naked and sticky, and feeling better than I should have. With a lazy arm, I reached out of bed and pulled back the shade. Snow covered the ground and was still coming down in big thick flakes. I could hear the wind whistling and my furnace struggling to keep up.

I could also hear my shower pipes gurgling. I pushed myself up against the pillows and saw her clothes scattered on my hardwood floor. My clothes were in a pile on the other side.

The shower shut off with a squeal, and I ran a hand over my closely cropped hair. I wasn't sure how to face her. Nor was I sure how to face myself. I had broken two rules: I had slept with a client, and I had slept with a white woman.

The second rule was unwritten, of course, but that didn't negate it. I had always secretly derided men who valued the women by the paleness of their skin. And I hadn't even slept with a light-skinned black woman. I'd slept with one so white that my sheets looked dark in comparison.

And the worse part about it was that I wanted to do it again.

The bathroom door opened, and she came out in a cloud of steam, one towel wrapped about her head like a turban, the other wrapped around her torso. Her feet were long and bony, her ankles narrow and her calves surprisingly short. I hadn't noticed any of that before.

She smiled at me. "I think I left some hot water."

"Good," I said, smiling back like an idiot.

She was looking more relaxed and the bags were gone from beneath her eyes. "Mind if I borrow a shirt?"

Then, without waiting for my answer, she went to my closet and pulled out a long-sleeved jersey top. She held it up, saw that it would run to her midthigh, and dropped her wet towel on the floor.

She didn't feel as thin as she looked. I could see her hip bones and the very edges of her ribs. Her breast were small but round, and they fit perfectly onto her slender body.

She smiled at me again—I must have been staring at her like a schoolboy—and then she shook her head. "Breakfast first," she said and pulled on the jersey. Then she slipped on her jeans without bothering to put on her underwear and toweled off her hair. She picked up both towels, took them into the bathroom, and then walked into my kitchen as if she owned it. A moment later, I heard the clanging of pots and pans.

I felt as if I had walked into a dream, as if I had made the mistake for being cautious, not her. I grabbed my shorts from the pile beside the bed and scurried into the bathroom. I usually wasn't that shy, but I usually felt more in control than I did at this moment. Laura had changed the relationship. She had changed it into something I wanted, but not necessarily something I approved of.

She had left me hot water. I stayed in it until it turned cold, leaning my face into the spray, one hand braced on the tile wall. I tried to examine the low-key, free-floating anxiety that I woke up with. It wasn't just breaking my own rules and being forced to examine my principles. It was also that I didn't know what she was about.

In 1964, a number of my friends got involved with women like Laura, rich northern white women who had come down as part of Freedom Summer. They slept with black men because they were experimenting, because they were intrigued, and because they felt it gave them some sort of political cachet. Most of those women left, and the men dealt with the consequences long after they were gone.

Consequences partly meted out by men like me, who were too good for that sort of thing. Too proud. Too willing to judge someone we felt had turned his back on his own people, his own heritage, and his own color.

Just like the man who had driven me and Laura out of the King's Palace the night before.

I shut off the shower and stepped out. The scents of bacon and fresh coffee were overwhelming, and my mouth watered. I was hungrier than I remembered being for some time. I dried off, wrapped the towel around my waist, and let myself out of the bathroom.

She was standing barefoot in my kitchen, her back to me. Her long wet hair had dripped on my shirt, leaving dark patches. She was stirring a skillet full of eggs with a spatula and didn't see me. Thin sunlight from the window over the sink caught her in a halo of white.

She looked like she belonged, and I knew then and there, no matter what happened, I would see her standing there every time I stepped out of the bathroom and saw weak sunlight fall across my stove.

I slipped into the bedroom, put on a clean pair of trousers, a fresh shirt, and a tan crew-neck sweater.

"You look good," she said when I came into the kitchen. "I've never seen you dress like that before."

"We're not going anywhere. Have you seen that snow?"

She smiled. "Where I come from we'd call it inconvenient. Here, the radio's calling it a blizzard."

"Whatever it is," I said, "it means the march is canceled. I'll wager everything else is as well."

Her eyes met mine. I smiled for the first time that morning. Her smile grew wider. She scooped eggs onto a dinner plate already laden with bacon and toast. Then she set it in the place where I had sat the night before. A glass of orange juice concentrate and a steaming mug of coffee were already in place. The tips of her fingers caressed my shoulder as she walked back to the stove.

"Laura—"

"Not yet," she said, head bowed. She scooped eggs onto her plate, then climbed onto one of my chairs.

And with that little interchange, the mood of the morning shifted. Some of the glow had left it. I ate the eggs—they were fluffy and light—and nibbled on the bacon. She was a better cook than I expected her to be. Somehow I had thought a woman raised the way she was wouldn't know how to make coffee let alone the perfect scrambled egg, and I wondered if my assumption was based on knowledge or a subtle prejudice I hadn't even known I had.

When she finished her eggs, she set the plate in the sink. Then she poured herself some coffee, added milk, and sat down, half on the chair, half off. She put one bare foot on the seat, the other on the floor, and rested the coffee cup on her upraised knee.

"You're always so serious, aren't you, Smokey?"

The bacon suddenly didn't taste as good. I finished chewing, then set my own plate in the sink without getting out of my chair. I supposed I was serious—I never laughed as much as my friends, and I was always responsible, even though my foster parents accused me of being irresponsible.

"Did we make a mistake, Smokey?"

"I don't know," I said. "You tell me."

Her smile was wide and beautiful. "You think you took advantage of me? A girl in a fragile emotional state? I snuck into your bed, not the other way around."

"I know," I said.

"But you're still worried."

"You hired me to do a job."

"As a convenience for both of us."

"And your whole life has been turned around."

She nodded, the smile fading. "I've needed someone to hold me for a long time, Smokey."

"And I was here."

"No," she said. "I waited until I found someone I wanted instead of someone I needed."

My mouth was dry. I made myself sip from the coffee cup. Her face slowly turned pink. "But if you don't want—if I did something that you're not—"

I set my cup down and stood in the same movement, crossing the small distance between us so that I could kiss her properly. She held me tightly, and I realized she had had similar fears to mine, only she had hidden them better.

I took her back into my bedroom and laid our fears to rest.

We couldn't go anywhere on Friday. Memphis was at a standstill. Outside, snow covering the garbage littering the curbsides. The road itself was pristine, the houses a matching shiny white. It was a surreal scene. It made me feel as if we found a special moment, a moment all to ourselves, and the entire world stopped for it.

We stayed in the house for the entire weekend. It was long, lazy, and glorious, and yet it passed in an instant. She wore my clothes because I didn't want to go to the Peabody with her and we ate chili until I thought I never wanted to taste it again. Neither of us wanted to go out. Neither of us wanted to spoil this magical world we had created. Neither of us wanted to see reality, at least for three private days.

We almost made it. But I woke from the nightmare, the old familiar nightmare, around three on Sunday morning with more than an ancient case of the chills. I had promised myself when I lay down on Thursday night that I would discover what I had overlooked in this case, and when I woke up, I knew what it was.

The papers I had pulled from the detective's report. I had set them aside to look at them, and I never had.

I had a feeling that something in them was important.

My movements didn't wake Laura. She was sprawled beside me, hair across her back, hands clutching both pillows. I leaned against the headboard and watched her sleep, knowing that I would have to bring the world back into our fragile new relationship in just a few hours.

I wish I could say I was at peace, but I was not.

She wore her own clothes when I dropped her at the Peabody at eight o'clock that morning. Roscoe saw me—he was taking luggage from the back of a Cadillac—and he started to wave, until he saw Laura emerge from my Falcon. She wrapped her coat around herself like a woman who didn't want to attract attention and disappeared through the revolving doors without a glance at me.

Roscoe watched in wonder. I nodded to him and drove away. The car felt empty without her. It had felt empty with her as well. We had separated at the house without saying a word. It was as if the morning after had happened on Monday instead of Friday. We acted like two drunken strangers who had met in a bar and had awakened in the same bed, uncertain as to what had happened.

I didn't know how it would go when she showed up at the office. I wasn't even certain I wanted to be there. I was tempted to work on another case, one of the ones I'd been ignoring the past few weeks, but that was running away, and I knew it.

Besides, I wanted to go through those papers.

The drive from the Peabody to Beale was much too short. Snow was piled high on all the street corners, making visibility difficult. There were icy patches on the road and my bald tires slid on a number of them. Some pickets were out, standing in front of department stores whose lunch counters served breakfast, but the morning seemed quiet. We had seen a few strikers on the way in from my house, and the morning news had promised more of the same.

The radio news was full of Martin's decision to return to Memphis. When the march got postponed on Friday, he checked his schedule and found that he could be back here by Thursday. One of the few phone calls I had received this weekend had been from Henry, making sure I knew of the change, making sure I would be at the march.

I promised I would.

I parked and went up to my office, not even stopping for my customary cup of coffee. My stomach had been upset since I woke from that dream, and I had the familiar unsettled feeling—the lost feeling—that the dream always brought. I unlocked, went in, flicked on the lights, and cursed at the heat. The radiator was clanging at full bore again.

But I didn't go downstairs to complain. Instead, I sat at Laura's customary spot on the floor, even crossing my legs as she did, and searched through the piles.

I had marked the papers I pulled from the detective's report as something to look at later. I finally found them, under a stack of dress ads. I picked up the entire mess and set it on my lap.

The papers were mostly notations, inexplicable scribbles—a phone number, a note ("meet June at 4:15")—but one was a gem. It was a handwritten receipt from a Milwaukee detective agency. Someone had billed for fifteen hours and had been paid in full. That same someone had marked on the receipt "cash."

The receipt was dated February 28, 1960.

I pulled it out, hand shaking, and as I did, I knocked over the dress ads. They scattered across the floor. I picked up the first and stopped as something jumped out at me. Words. Half of the caption beneath a ripped photograph:

> . . . *Junior Leaguers in their grandmothers' dresses* . . .
> . . . *before five thousand guests in the City Auditorium.*

I turned the clipping over. On the other side was a full dress ad, just as I thought. Discreet and tasteful. Hand-drawn in the custom of the times. I couldn't quite tell the date on the ad, but I knew it was prewar just from the fashions it showed and the coy poses of the women.

My hand started to shake. I turned the clipping back to the half-ripped photograph, the ruined caption. I looked at what I could see of the photograph. There, in the middle of the grainy newsprint, someone had penciled in an arrow. It pointed at a group of children in the background, seated on the floor near some ionic columns. The children were dressed as pickaninnies.

But the arrow pointed at just one of them.

It pointed at me.

Somehow I made it to the phone, still clutching the newspaper clipping and the receipt. My hands were shaking so badly I nearly dropped the receiver.

I dialed Milwaukee. The Gruner Agency. A man answered. Henrik Gruner. He sounded very old.

I identified myself. I didn't think to disguise my name. I asked if he had ever worked for a Mrs. Dora Jean Hathaway in 1960.

"Excuse me," he said. "I will check my files."

He clunked the receiver down, and I heard—through hundreds of miles of phone line—a chair squeak, the banging of a metal file drawer, a man's soft curse. Then paper slapped against a desk, and the receiver crackled as he picked it up.

"I have the file here," he said.

"What did she hire you for?"

"I don't usually—"

"She's dead, Mr. Gruner. I'm working for her daughter. Please. What did she hire you for?"

There must have been something in my voice. Some urgency, some raw emotion.

"Let me see," he said. "Ach, yes, that one. She wanted me to trace a young boy, a Billy Alburty."

I started. I hadn't heard that name in years. My name. The name I'd been born with.

"I found out he was adopted, found out who took him, and she had me stop there. Paid me in cash and wanted nothing in writing."

My mouth was dry. "How did you trace him?"

"You, you mean, Mr. Dalton? How'd I find you?"

Sharp old man. He was staring at the file. Of course he saw my name.

Both of my names.

"Yes," I said softly.

"Your cousin. Seems he never did like you much."

I closed my eyes. Saw my cousin's face covered in blood, the ache in my knuckles from the force of the blow. Each event, it seemed, came around.

"Did she say why she wanted to find me?" I asked.

"Nope." His voice was flat now. I used that voice with emotional clients. "Thought it seemed fairly obvious."

"I suppose," I whispered. Fairly obvious.

Of course.

Somehow I thanked him. I pressed the disconnect button as Laura walked into the room.

She stood in the doorway for only a moment, and when I didn't move, she shut the door gently. "You found something?"

I nodded.

She came over beside me and peered at the clipping, obviously not seeing anything. I pointed to the arrow.

"My mother did that," she said.

I looked at her, startled.

Laura shrugged. "She had a distinct way of marking things. I'd recognize that anywhere." She leaned closer. "What's it pointing at?"

"Me," I said.

She took the clipping. She frowned at it, turned it over, then turned it back again. "What is this? A play?"

"The Junior League Ball, held on December 14, 1939, in the City Auditorium in Atlanta, Georgia." I heard the same flatness in my voice that I had just heard in Gruner's. Maybe it was a defense. Maybe all of us private eyes developed it to prevent ourselves from feeling anything.

"You remember this?" she asked, handing the clipping back to me.

"It was for the premiere of *Gone with the Wind*." Now the bitterness was beginning to creep into my voice. "Clark Gable was there."

"And you—"

"Sang." I took the clipping from her, stared at my round and innocent face. "I sang."

"I don't understand." She hadn't taken off her coat. "Are you saying my parents are from Atlanta?"

"That would be my guess."

"And they knew you?"

"I don't know."

"But—"

"Laura." I didn't want her to talk anymore. I stepped away from her, unable to be close. My entire body felt as if a fire were burning beneath my skin, all prickly and hot. I wanted to move away from myself, but couldn't.

"I don't understand, Smokey."

I hadn't spoken of this to anyone. Not since I left Atlanta. I felt the heat rise in my face: an old familiar shame. They must have done something. That's how the feeling went. That it was somehow their fault, and somehow mine. Maybe they smiled at the wrong person, forgot to say "ma'am" when speaking to a white woman. Maybe they purposely stood up for themselves in a way that just wasn't allowed then.

Amazing how deep the training went in, how much of it I absorbed and couldn't shake free. For the first time in years, I wanted to talk to Martin, to find out how he managed to shake loose of his training, how he managed to understand that he was greater than what he had been told.

"Smokey?"

"Two nights after this picture was taken," I said, "when all the celebrities were gone, and the streets were littered with balloons and confetti, and the city fathers were arguing about whether or not to leave the Rebel flags flying in front of Loew's theater, my parents were kidnapped from our home—" my voice was shaking. Laura had moved closer—"taken to some fucking red clay dirt road, beaten until they couldn't stand any more, and maybe even my mother—"

"Smokey, you don't have to—"

"—and *lynched*." I clenched my right fist. "My cousin, my fucking betraying cousin, said my father didn't die right away. He said that they found him clutching the rope like he was trying to pull it away from his neck."

Laura put her hand on my shoulder. I wrenched away and walked to the window. Through the filthy glass, Beale looked no different. People were walking to their jobs. A handful of picketers were carrying signs down Third as if they were headed somewhere.

I couldn't breathe. My entire chest felt as if someone had been sitting on it for years, and the pressure was growing worse. It wasn't a heart attack. It was a function of memory, of a past so deep that even talking about it made my throat raw.

"Smokey." Her voice was trembling too. "You don't think my parents—I mean, were they running because they—"

"Killed my parents?" The words came out harsher than I intended. I shook my head. "Among some people, it was a badge of honor to kill niggers. It still is."

"You don't mean that . . ."

I turned, and the look on my face silenced her. I did mean that. I meant every word. And it was my own fear, my own realization which had come to me quite young that no matter what I did, I was second- or third- or maybe even fourth-class. I didn't leave the black community because it wasn't safe to leave my community. I didn't go anywhere unknown where I didn't know the rules because I didn't know what would get me killed and what wouldn't. I didn't look at women like Laura—

I bowed my head. Every single act in my life was informed by that moment, by the fear that caught and held me in that closet, when I knew—I *knew*—I would be alone for the rest of my life.

She reached for me again, her fingers brushing the side of my face. I caught her wrist and pushed her away from me.

"Don't," I said. "Not now."

I moved back a step, rested my palms flat on my desk, and made myself breathe. I had learned this trick in the service. Count the breaths, concentrate on the breaths, feel the breaths go in and out and in until the anger passed.

It didn't entirely pass. But it receded enough to allow me to talk to Laura in a civilized way.

I brought my head up.

"Do you want me to leave?" she asked. The question was gentle, gentler than I deserved. She held the clipping tightly in one hand.

"No." My voice sounded funny, strained, to me. I cleared my throat. "I—we—have to discuss this."

I walked behind my desk and took my chair, hoping it would make me feel more like Smokey Dalton the adult than little Billy Alburty the orphan sent, without explanation, to his uncle's farm in South Georgia. Sent away, gone for weeks, and then taken, not to his own family, but to Washington, D.C., to a foster family found by the Grand, a family who promised him—and tried to deliver—a good life.

"I—I warned you that there might be things here you wouldn't like." I rubbed a hand over my face. "I never expected that the same would apply to me."

"We never thought of it as blood money," she said, sinking into her chair. Her face was pale and she spoke as if she were afraid her words would offend me again.

"It can't be that simple," I said. "People who murder others don't repent, and people who committed that kind of crime never thought of blacks as human. Why would they worry about me? And why so late?"

"Maybe . . ." She swallowed so hard I could see the motion. "Maybe my father participated and my mother disapproved. Maybe—"

"No," I said. "It doesn't feel right. To me anyway. Does it to you?"

"No," she whispered. "I can't believe my father would kill anyone."

I raised my head and looked at her. Two spots of color formed on her cheeks, and her eyes swam with tears. Her lower lip trembled. She bit it to hold it in place, then, like I had done, took a deep calming breath.

"I can't believe it, Smokey," she whispered. "No matter what else he did. He was a gentle man. He never even raised his voice at me, or at my mother. She wouldn't have tolerated it. She wouldn't have tolerated any violence. One of my earliest memories of her was her sitting by the radio, listening to the war broadcasts and weeping. 'All those boys,' she would say. 'All those young boys.' "

I ran my hand through my hair. I was picking up her nervous gestures. I couldn't believe it either, although not for her reasons, but for the reasons I had named earlier. It didn't fit. It just didn't. But I was going on gut, without any proof. I needed something more.

"Whatever happened," I said, "the tie was back there, in Atlanta. Your mother knew about Atlanta. I just spoke to another detective she hired. He confirmed it. She knew me."

I picked up a loose staple and bent it between my thumb and forefinger. No wonder I didn't remember them. I didn't remember much about Atlanta before my parents died—purposely wiped out of my memory, my foster mother used to say—and I didn't remember anything about any white people. At least not individual white people. I remembered them in groups, such as the Junior League Ball, or the hostile group of older kids who had screamed obscenities at my first grade class on an outing.

I licked my lower lip, felt the control coming back, at least as much as it could. "I'm going there," I said. "I'm going to Atlanta. I'll see what I can find."

She stood as if we were leaving at that moment. "I'll come with you."

I shook my head. "It won't work."

"Sure it will. You'll need someone in the white community. I can probably go places—"

"No," I said, even though she had a good argument. I never went to Atlanta. Not even after my foster parents moved back there three years ago, after my foster father was granted a full professorship at Morehouse, with tenure. They had been so proud and wanted to show me their new house, have me celebrate his good fortune—he had only been an associate professor at Howard—and I hadn't come. I couldn't face the city. I never wanted to see Atlanta again.

And now it seemed I would have to. Taking this trip meant I would have to go into Atlanta proper, visit Sweet Auburn and the old neighborhood, take a look at the world I had left behind nearly thirty years before.

I couldn't do that with Laura beside me. And I didn't even want to think of the complications it would cause, just trying to deal with her there. Dealing with her, and the altered relationship. I shuddered. For the first time, I regretted the weekend.

"Smokey—"

"No," I said. "There won't be any argument. In fact, there's no point in you staying here either. Go back to Chicago, see what you can dig up in your father's corporate files. Leave me a number, and I'll call you."

The color had completely drained from her face. "I thought things were different," she said softly. "I thought—"

"We'd be Nick and Nora Charles, going through life in a debonair fashion, the slick detectives of the nineteen sixties?" I shook my head. "I'm still working for you, sweetheart, but the personal stake just rose."

I stood too.

She didn't move. "How could you be so deliberately cruel? Why didn't you just say 'I don't want you to come to Atlanta, Laura'?"

"I did. You didn't listen."

"You didn't listen to me."

"Laura," I said, as gently as I could. "I don't want you to go to Atlanta. My parents were lynched there."

"Thirty years ago," she said. "It's different now."

"Not that different," I said.

"Neither is Memphis. You can't say any place is safe these days."

I stared at her for a moment. She needed me. We both knew it. She was shaky and she was using me as a crutch. I had wanted her to. I still did. But, since I found that photograph, I was shaky too, and I couldn't let anyone lean on me. I couldn't let *her* lean on me. I might collapse.

"Memphis is safe for me," I said. "It has been for more than ten years. I understand it. I always will."

"Do you?" she asked. "Now?"

"Yes," I said.

She sighed and looked down. "Are you sending me away

because you believe you're protecting me? Or because of this weekend? Do you think we made a mistake, Smokey?"

I reached out and touched her face. Within the space of a weekend, the feel of her skin had become as familiar as my own. "I don't know if we made a mistake, Laura," I said softly. "Things are different now."

And they were.

NINETEEN

I couldn't leave right away, even though I wanted to. I had made promises. And I had some errands I had to complete first. I had to be at the march, but I was going to leave the moment it ended. I had to get my car ready for a winter drive through Mississippi and Alabama, two of my least favorite places. I was going to retrace the steps that Laura's parents, whoever the hell they were, had probably made when they fled Atlanta.

I did see the irony in that.

I couldn't be near Laura. I could hardly stand to look at her, and yet I wanted to hold her. I wanted to go back to our magical weekend.

But the snow was melting, and beneath it, the garbage looked more rank than ever. And I knew, no matter how hard you tried to cover up something, it never got any better.

I got her Chicago phone numbers, hurried her out of my office, and made her promise to take the next flight she could get. I didn't even offer to drive her to the airport.

Laura seemed to understand. She seemed to need the distance from me as well. Or perhaps I was imagining that. Perhaps I was imagining that because I needed to.

I had money in my accounts—Laura had been paying me

as agreed—and I decided to take a cheap hotel room near Sweet Auburn. I didn't even call my foster parents. I couldn't bear to talk with them. They would be so excited that I was coming to Atlanta. I could hear their voices in my head, their excitement, their plans.

I didn't want to tell them why I was coming. I might not even see them. I wasn't sure I could look at them either.

I went through the next two days by rote. I saw Roscoe, made plans for the march, spoke to the organizers. They were so proud that Martin had felt secure in Memphis, proud that he hadn't even sent his own people to help organize the route.

It was a detail, like so many others that week, that just seemed to float right past me.

Thursday morning, a week after my first night with Laura, dawned clear and cold. My alarm went off damned early, and I felt as if I had spent the night drinking instead of sleeping. My head was muzzy, my eyes swollen and sleep-filled. I drank extra coffee, had a large bowl of cereal, and cut up an orange, but it didn't seem to do much good. I was exhausted, emotionally and mentally, and I needed to be at my best.

The cool morning air shook some of it off, and so did the drive to Roscoe's. He brought his son Andrew and promised that we'd meet the others at the Temple.

We arrived at 8 o'clock. There was supposed to be training for the marchers at nine, run by Martin or one of his associates. Roscoe and I scouted the area. Already there were too many police for my liking and a lot of people milling about. Henry was there, and so were the rest of the leaders of COME. They hovered near the doorway as if they didn't know what to do. Someone had placed a series of placards near the door which were emblazoned with the slogan of the sanitation workers: "I Am a Man." Already some of the arrivals had picked up signs and seemed to be restless. I was too.

But we had a long time to wait. At nine o'clock, one of the ministers announced that we would wait until ten to start the march. There was no sign of Martin or his assistants. I hovered near the edge of the street, watching for Invaders or Panthers or anyone else who looked like he might be trouble. Roscoe found a few Beale Street Professionals lurking at the fringes of the crowd and asked them to go home. Before he did, he pointed them out to the march leaders who merely nodded and seemed preoccupied.

The crowd kept growing. They filled the street and were mostly silent, milling around, talking softly, craning their heads to see if anything was going to happen. At one point I stood on a car and tried to count. When I got past a thousand people and still hadn't counted most everyone, I got back down. What was bothering me was the growing number of young faces. I couldn't tell which were supporters and which were Invaders.

I had no way of knowing.

Shortly after ten, a boy not much older than Jimmy launched himself through the crowd, shouting that the police had killed someone. People were stepping backwards, startled—how could the police have killed anyone when the march hadn't even started?—when I slipped off my perch and grabbed the kid's arm.

"What happened?" I asked.

He was agitated, his eyes wide, his hands moving as fast as his mouth. He didn't try to shake me off, but instead tried to convince me. "Down at Hamilton High. They were trying to keep the kids in school and they murdered this girl."

"Who is they?" I asked.

"The police!"

"Did you see this?"

"I didn't see her get shot, but I saw the police there."

"Then stop spreading the rumor," I said. "We don't know if anyone is injured."

"She ain't injured," he said. "She's dead."

And then he slipped out of my grasp and ran into the crowd, carrying the news with him. His voice was drowned in the growing din. People were talking louder and with great nervousness. Others were shouting the same thing from the outside edge. More and more teenagers were arriving, all of them as upset as the boy. I saw Roscoe trying to calm some on the other side of the street. Henry was doing the same near the Temple but it was doing no good.

The crowd was getting louder, using the voice of indignation that would soon turn to a shout. Henry had told me the march was going to start with the training at nine and it was already over an hour and a half later. I didn't know how much longer this crowd would remain under control.

More teenagers ran from side streets, shouting about the murder at Hamilton High. Some of the Beale Street Professionals, including the ones Roscoe had asked to leave, were in the middle of the street, surrounded by people who had come to support the strike. Henry's flock. The ones he had said he was responsible for. I felt a shiver run down my back.

I turned and saw Thomas Withers. He was standing in the center of the crowd, pulling a handle off a placard, and handing the stick to the young boy beside him. The boy passed the new weapon to another boy. Things had already changed.

I worked my way to the Temple and pulled Henry aside. "They're not going to stand here much longer," I said over the growing din.

"I can see that," he said.

"What's the plan if Martin doesn't show?"

"He'll show. Abernathy went to pick him up two hours ago."

Abernathy. Dr. Ralph Abernathy, who had given a speech to the troops the night before, a speech I had forgotten about after my confrontation with Laura.

"It doesn't take two hours to get from the airport downtown."

"I know," Henry said.

"Then figure out what you're going to do, or you'll lose control of this crowd."

He nodded at me and walked to the circle of COME members. His hands flailed. Reverend Lawson shook his head, and Reverend Kyle, whom I hadn't seen until that point, pointed at the crowd.

Not even the leaders could agree. The queasiness that had lived at the base of my stomach since Monday grew.

I saw more young people mingling in the crowd. Some of them were carrying beer bottles and others were carrying bricks. Many were wearing berets and leather jackets, like the Black Panthers. I thought I saw Joe's rangy form. I hurried toward it, only to lose it in the growing crowd.

Finally, a dark sedan pulled up beside the Temple, and I thought I caught a glimpse of Ralph Abernathy inside before a group of teenagers surrounded the car. The driver moved it forward, but he couldn't seem to shake them. I raised my hand above the crowd and tried to catch Roscoe's attention. He waved, showing he'd seen me. Somehow it only took him a second to show up at my side.

We went to the car. The kids had their faces pressed up against the windows. They were saying courteous things to the men inside—

"We really respect you, Dr. King."

"Nonviolence is our way too."

—but they weren't moving. They were pressing their bodies against the sides of the car so hard they were rocking it.

Roscoe grabbed the nearest kid and flung him back. I grabbed another, taking his arm too tightly and not caring. I had a lot of anger I'd been storing and I was going to use it on this kind of stupidity. It gave me strength. I pulled the kid back, then another and another.

Somehow James Lawson had made his way to the car. He shouted at the window, "The only way we'll get away from them is get out and start the march."

I pulled another boy away, only to have him run back toward the car. But his movement freed up the door, and it opened.

Martin got out. His face was rounder than it had been the last time I'd seen him, and he looked like he hadn't slept for days. His gaze swung past me, then came back to me.

"Billy."

"Martin."

"I didn't expect to see you."

"I was hoping to see you."

And then he grinned at me like the boy I had once known, as Dr. Abernathy linked arms with him in that familiar marching style that had worked so well for so many years. One of the march organizers shoved people away. Roscoe and I took to the sides, and we tried to get Martin to the front of the group.

But the crowd had seen him, and from all sides, the shouting started:

"Dr. King!"

"We're glad you came to Memphis!"

"You're the hope of America!"

Sometimes the shouts differed, but not by much. They were warm and complimentary, and they were orchestrated, designed to distract from the march. Reverend Lawson carried a bullhorn, and he shouted at people to get in behind Martin but most were not doing it. I stayed a few paces to Martin's right, Roscoe to his left, and we watched. We watched everything.

I knew when the Beale Street Professionals peeled off, when a young man grabbed the remaining signs and pulled off their handles, and when the other signs appeared. The new signs sent shivers through me: "Damn Loeb" and "Black Power Is Here!"

The police were getting nervous. I could see it in their movements. Most of them had tactical gear I hadn't seen in Memphis before but which I recognized from television:

white helmets with chin straps, bullet-proof vests, and cattle prods. They were expecting trouble, just as we were, but once they got involved, they would add to it.

The crowd was too big. The inexperienced parade marshals, with their whistles and their horns, couldn't keep the crowd in line. More and more people ran along the sides, screaming at Martin. He focused ahead, trying to lead, and his associates stayed beside him.

Until we heard the popping behind us.

At first I thought it was gunshots, and so did several others, for we all hurried to Martin. Then the sound came again, and I recognized it for what it was—breaking glass. People were screaming and shouting, and the police started to move in. Barricades were going up.

It only took Martin a second to realize what was going on as well. "Jim!" he shouted to Lawson.

Behind us, sirens were going off. I saw three officers grab gas masks and pull them over their faces. Other officers were starting to stop and reroute cars.

"Jim!" Martin shouted again. "There's violence breaking out and I can't lead a violent march. Call it off!"

Lawson stared at him as if he couldn't comprehend what Martin had said.

"Call it off!"

I started to reach for the bullhorn when Lawson brought it up to his lips.

"The march is off!" he shouted. "The march is off! Everybody go home! The march is off!"

But no one seemed to be listening. Police whistles sounded over the screams, and then more sirens started.

"We have to get out of here," Martin said.

His associates scanned the area. We were too far from his car. To take him back the three blocks was to take him into the worst of the violence.

A chain of state troopers was starting to form ahead of us, and I cursed under my breath. They had planned for this.

The cops had thought this was going to happen and they pulled out all the stops. More people ran by, bricks in hand. Again I thought I saw Joe, but I couldn't get to him.

Abernathy was pointing at a car near the corner. A woman was driving it, and it looked as if she would be allowed through the police barricades.

"Get Martin there!" he shouted at me.

Roscoe and I used our bodies to get all of the leaders there. When we reached the car, the woman took a look, recognized Martin, and motioned him to get in. One of his assistants opened the door, and as they were sliding in, I shouted to Martin, "You'll be all right?"

He nodded, the door closed, and they shot off so fast it was like they hadn't been there. I turned around. The crowd had turned into a mob. They were running along several streets. Windows were breaking. Police were using gas a block back.

I headed in the direction I thought I saw Joe go, toward my office. But as I got onto Beale, things got worse.

We were on Third, near my office. Looters were ransacking the display window at Paul's Tailoring Shop across the street and breaking windows in the loan office in the Gallina Building. Police were chasing them with nightsticks, hitting anyone who moved. People were running with goods, shouting epithets. A teenage boy stumbled on the curb, got clubbed and thrown backwards, only to get trampled by others. I couldn't get close enough to help. I was being moved forward by the crowd, against my wishes, into the worst of the rioting.

Teenagers were standing in the street, throwing bricks and beer bottles and anything they could get their hands on. One man with a black beret had wrested a baton away from an officer and was clubbing him with it. Young boys were jumping on cars, denting the hoods and trying to shatter parking meters.

A young girl, her hose ripped, her shoe missing, was running from a policeman who was chasing her, club raised. Others were in Handy Park, trying to get away. The screaming was fierce.

I reached down, grabbed a boy about Jimmy's age off the sidewalk, and pulled him to his feet. He shoved me away and went back toward the tailor shop.

An officer took a club to the face and went down as the crowd cheered. Someone kicked him, and he put his hands up. I tried to pull people back and away. I'd lost Roscoe and I no longer saw Joe, if I ever had, but one of the Panthers, his beret gone but his sunglasses still on, continued to kick the fallen policeman.

The crowd was moving me onto Beale proper, and I tried to break out of the flow. As I did, two state troopers and a cop headed toward me, shouting at me, spittle flying through the air. I couldn't understand them and as I put out my hands to show I meant no harm, one of them shoved his nightstick in my stomach.

I doubled over, reaching for something, anything, to keep me up, but it didn't work. I was dizzy and out of breath. If I fell, I would be trampled. I reached out, grabbed nothing, and used my remaining strength in an attempt to force myself upright.

As I lifted my head, the cop before me called me a filthy robbing fucking nigger and slammed his billy club into my skull.

TWENTY

Roscoe found me. Roscoe dragged me out, half carrying, half coaxing me. He got us to my car, and he drove me to the emergency room. There he found a resident who knew us both and stitched me up quickly and neatly. The resident didn't log us in or out because, he said, the cops were arresting anyone who arrived with what looked like riot-related injuries. The emergency room was so chaotic and so full of people who were shot or bleeding that no one noticed when we snuck out the back.

Roscoe got me home and forced me to stay. "You ain't going nowhere," he said. "Not to your office, not to Atlanta. Nowhere."

"Roscoe, I have—"

"Tomorrow, Smokey," he said. "See how you're doing tomorrow."

And then he left me with my television set, to watch the rest of the rioting. I wasn't supposed to sleep for the next eight hours, and I don't think I did, not while watching Memphis eat itself alive.

Thomas Withers had succeeded, the bastard. He had turned a non-violent event into something unrecognizable, something Memphis had never seen before.

Looters were all over the city. Fires started in most of the Loeb's Laundries, the mayor's family business. Students were held outside Booker T. Washington School, and the rumor that started it all, that a girl had been killed at Hamilton High, had a basis in fact. She had, indeed, been shot. She simply hadn't died.

There was only one riot-related death, a seventeen-year-old boy whose name they weren't releasing pending notification of next of kin. I knew he was black, because the reporters kept referring to him as a looter rather than a victim, the perpetrator of his own death at the hands of police.

I hoped like hell it wasn't Joe. But I was afraid it was, so afraid that I called the police department to get some information.

They told me the boy's name was Larry Payne. They asked me if I knew his next of kin.

I did not.

My phone rang twice that afternoon. The first time was Laura, relieved to hear my voice.

"I thought maybe you'd been hurt," she said.

I didn't tell her my head ached and they were worried I had a concussion. "I'm glad you missed this," I said.

"I'm sorry to say I am too."

She hung up shortly after that. We had a lot to say to each other, but we weren't ready to say it. We had to wait until I went to Atlanta, until things calmed down.

The second time the phone rang, it was Jimmy, his high pitched voice even higher.

"I ain't heard from Joe, nobody's heard from Joe, and someone died," he said, all in a rush.

"The dead boy," I said slowly, "is Larry Payne."

"Larry?" he whispered and I heard relief in that word. Relief and something else.

"You knew him?"

It took Jimmy a moment to answer. "Yeah," he said. He

took an audible breath. He wanted to honor Larry, but he was more concerned about his brother. "And Joe?"

"I saw him, but not enough to talk to."

"How come?"

"It was a little crazy there."

Jimmy didn't respond to that. His breathing was loud and strained, as if he had been panicking all day.

He probably had been.

Finally, he said, "You sound funny."

"I got conked on the head. Pain pills," I said.

"Oh." A pause, then, "You okay?"

"Yes," I said.

He made a small sound, between a sob and a moan. Then he said, "I'm scared, Smokey."

"Yeah," I said softly. "There'd be something wrong with you if you weren't. You stay inside, with that nice family, all right? Promise me."

"But Joe—"

"Joe can take care of himself."

"You sure?"

"I'm positive," I said. "It'll be all right, Jimmy."

It wasn't until I hung up that I realized I had finally uttered one of those platitudes to him, one of those things I vowed I would never say.

Sirens wailed all over the city. As darkness fell, things seemed to get worse. I could go to my window and see the orange lick of flames against the dark skies. We wouldn't know all the damage until the next day, but it was already becoming clear: Memphis would never be the same.

Even the interior of my house smelled of smoke. About 2:00 A.M., after the last television station displayed its test pattern as it played the "Star Spangled Banner," I took another one of the pain pills the doctor had given me and wandered off to bed.

The sirens and flames filled my dreams. I kept hearing

Martin's voice, saying "I still stand by nonviolence" as he looked at me, blaming me. "I didn't expect to see you here," he would say, and I would say, "I'm here now," although that felt wrong. Joe was standing behind Martin with a brick, and as Martin spoke, Joe threw the brick. Martin ducked and the brick hit me in the head, and Roscoe said, "Keep going. Keep going. If they catch us now, they gonna arrest us." So we kept moving, and the sirens kept going all through the night.

I woke at dawn covered with sweat and sticky dark flakes of dried blood that I hadn't cleaned off when I got home. My head throbbed as if I had a hangover. I staggered out of bed and went into the bathroom.

The face that stared at me wasn't that much different from the one I had seen the previous morning. The resident's neat stitches made it look as if someone had drawn a line in my curls with magic marker.

I splashed water on myself and then made myself shower. I got dressed slowly, set the pain pills aside, and took an aspirin since aspirin didn't befuddle my brain. Then I made myself eat.

The sirens had ended. That must have been what woke me up. But smoke hung over the city like a pall. I couldn't stay in the house. I had to get out, had to make sure everything was all right.

I got into my car and drove back to Beale Street. As I did, the radio kept me company, reciting the grim news: 155 stores had been damaged or destroyed, sixty people were injured—more, I assumed, if others had done as I did—and two hundred and eighty, all black, were in jail.

The National Guard had tanks on Hernando Street. They drove slowly, sweeping the area, the white boys in uniform holding their guns like they wanted to use them. There were a handful of cars out already, but only a handful, at a time of day when the streets should have been crowded. Police also guarded each corner, some of them holding nonstandard hunting rifles. Memphis looked like a town at war, which I guess it was.

The police weren't letting anyone park on Beale. I parked between Third and Union and walked slowly through the debris. Already some business owners were assessing the damage. Others were trying to pick up the pieces.

A fire still burned a few blocks up, and firefighters were driving past. The police officers stared at me, looking at my battered face as I passed, but they didn't question me. When I finally reached Beale proper, I stopped.

The sight that greeted me was not what I expected. Bodies were strewn across the sidewalk, most torn in half. One still held a sign that read "I Am a Man." More signs were scattered along the street.

There was no blood.

I stumbled forward, then realized that what I thought were bodies were mannequins from the store windows, tossed into the street like dirt. They looked so real and so dead that I had thought someone had left bodies for later cleanup.

The fire that the fire department was still battling was at Wilson Drug. Martha stood outside, her hands clasped together. I could just make her out in the morning haze.

A tank rumbled by, and some state troopers jogged across Beale at South Main, stopping to set up some sort of barricade.

The devastation was more than I had expected, even after hearing the news. Beale was a poor district anyway, and it would be poorer now.

"Sad, isn't it?" a voice asked behind me.

I turned. Withers was leaning against the side of the Gallina Building as if he had been waiting for me. He had a bruise on his left cheek.

My head throbbed. "Gloating?" I asked.

"At this kind of destruction, all the ruined lives? Of course not." He stood and brushed off a sleeve. Then he smiled at me. "I gotta admit, though, Smokey. I thought you'd be a more formidable opponent."

I lunged for him, but he stepped away. I caught myself on the edge of the building, feeling dizzy. Damn the injury. Damn the pain medication.

"Don't worry, Smokey," he said, tilting his beret down over his forehead. "I've decided that I've had enough of Memphis. We don't have to see each other again."

Then he stepped over a mannequin in the street and walked away.

I let him go. There wasn't much I could do, short of trying to kill him with my fists, something that wouldn't go over, not with all the National Guard troops around.

He vanished down an alley and I hoped to hell he was gone for good.

I stared after him for a long time. Then, when my breathing was regular again, I went up to my office. No one had touched it. I took some cash from my safe, double-locked the door for safety, and went back to my car.

It was time to get out of Memphis.

After this, facing what awaited me in Atlanta would be easy.

Or so I thought.

TWENTY-ONE

I left at three that afternoon, after I had gotten Martha off Beale, let Roscoe know I was leaving after all, and called Henry to tell him that my services—such as they had been—weren't going to be available for the next few days.

My car was packed with blankets and a pillow in case I couldn't get a room, some clothing, and some food in a cooler so that I wouldn't have to stop in an unfamiliar town for a meal.

I drove past National Guard tanks to get out of Memphis, and it wasn't until I was into Mississippi that my stomach unclenched. That had never happened to me before. Usually Mississippi was the place that made me nervous.

The weather was spring-wretched: overcast with a drippy cold rain that promised more winter and less summer. The roads were narrow and full of winter ruts, and the places I did stop—the familiar ones—were full of unfriendly faces, people who didn't want to be working or didn't seem to have time for a traveler of any color.

I had trouble finding radio stations I wanted to listen to. All of them rehashed the riots and I didn't want to hear about it. Martin had given a press conference that afternoon from the Rosemont Hotel—I hadn't even realized he had stayed in Memphis last night—denying that he had left the march in a hurry.

He had departed, he said, because he didn't want to be part of a violent action. And he promised to be back around April third (no later than April fifth, he said) to lead a massive, nonviolent demonstration.

I shut off the radio after that. I wouldn't be able to stay away any longer than that. After what happened at the march, I knew I'd never forgive myself if I wasn't back in Memphis, trying to prevent a repeat of the actions of the day before.

For most of the drive, I found myself thinking of Laura. I no longer had any idea how to behave around her. She was a client, a lover, and had been becoming a friend. She was white and rich and from the North. Her parents knew who I was—had known me from Atlanta—and that made them even more suspect than they already were, having changed their names and moved on like they had. How much could I blame her for that? And how much was I using it as an excuse to put some distance between us?

As the highway took me through Birmingham, I felt a tightening of my shoulders. Birmingham had a dangerous feel to it. I didn't even stop.

The tighening got worse as I drove into Georgia. I hated this place. I had hated it as a boy and hated it even more now. I had once told my foster parents that I would never go back.

They pretended to understand, but they didn't. They were so proud of their move to Atlanta. The years in D.C. were years of struggle for them, not just because of my foster father's job, but because of me. Out of the goodness of their hearts, because they felt they had to do something for their community, they had adopted me. They had hoped for a good, well-behaved boy, the boy I had been before my parents died, probably the boy that the Grand had described to them.

Instead, they had gotten a sullen, withdrawn, frightened boy who read all he could, spoke to no one, and moved out of the house as soon as his age allowed. From that moment, I never looked back, although I stayed in touch. I felt I owed them that much.

They were good people. They took pride in my service record, even more pride in the education I had gotten with their help, and when I refused to do anything obvious with that education, they only mentioned it once, and then in a wistful, don't-you-think-it-would-be-better-to-become-something? manner that spoke more to them than to me. I settled in Memphis and began my career, and they said nothing. When it became clear I wasn't going to marry, at least not for a long long time, my foster mother pulled me aside and said she hoped that someday I would find what I was looking for.

The words made me cringe. I had found something last weekend, and I was turning my back on it already. I flicked on the radio, found an Atlanta rock station that was close to WDIA on the dial, and listened to it all the way in, suffering through the Beatles to get an occasional cut from the Supremes or Isaac Hayes.

The music didn't keep my mind off everything, but it helped. I got into Atlanta around eleven, found a motel near Sweet Auburn, and checked in. The motel was a roadside that had been black-owned and operated since I was a boy. It was two stories and long, with boxy rooms and an office on the first floor that was the front room of the manager's apartment. My room, on the second floor, had a double bed covered with a chenille spread, a TV chained to the wall, and a tiny bathroom with a showerhead that dripped silently, leaving a rust-colored stain from the faucet to the drain. It wasn't much, but it would do.

I locked the door, sank onto the bed, and let the exhaustion of the last week take me away.

I woke midmorning and showered. A banana from the food I'd brought with me served as breakfast. When I was cleaned up, I grabbed a dime and used the pay phone near the pop machine on the first floor, not wanting to make any calls from my room.

At first, I thought it was guilt that made me call my foster parents first. Then as the phone rang, I realized I was going to initiate a conversation we had never had, a conversation that I had dreaded for most of my life.

It was time now.

My foster mother was home and surprised to hear from me. To her credit, she didn't make much of my call or my explanation of it; she didn't try to make me feel guilty for failing to visit them in the three years they had been in Atlanta. Like she had always done, she took me for who I was. I told her I was just passing through, doing some work on a case, and that I had some questions, but I could tell from her tone that she knew those questions were important.

The drive was only partially familiar. Atlanta itself had changed in the twenty-nine years I'd been gone.

Atlanta always changed—that was its only constant. I knew that much because Atlanta was the door to the commercial South, the place that was constantly in the news. I read about Atlanta; I did not visit it, except in my imagination. But as I drove from Sweet Auburn to my foster parents' neighborhood, near Morehouse College, I was surprised at how much it of Atlanta I remembered, how much of its history I knew, and how much it was nothing like the place that still haunted my dreams.

Because Atlanta was rebuilt after Sherman burned it to the ground in 1864, it saw itself as the New South, a place that was above the hatreds and problems of the old. It wasn't, as my life, and my parents' lives attested. But it did imagine itself that way and was willing to play the game, sometimes with blacks, as in the social changes that started about ten years ago, and sometimes without, as in the *Gone with the Wind* premiere that I had once been a part of. Both exemplified Atlanta, at once patrician and commercial, Old South mingling seamlessly with the New South because it kept its seams hidden beneath a layer of civility not found anywhere else this side of the Mason-Dixon line.

That much of Atlanta hadn't changed. But the skyline had. The city I had known had been short, squat, and tree-lined, in what had once been virgin forest land. Atlanta was not settled because it was at the site of any great river like Memphis, but because it had become the terminus for several railroads. In fact, the city's first name had been Terminus. It was as different from Memphis as could be; a modern city with some of the South's first skyscrapers.

There were no skyscrapers near my foster parents' house. It was a two-story white house that dated from the 1920s, and it was in a beautiful old neighborhood. There were tall trees in the front yard and a tilled area around the foundation that suggested spring flowers. I was willing to bet there was a vegetable garden out back.

My foster mother had always been proudest of her garden, since she couldn't be proud of me.

I pulled up in front of the concrete sidewalk and got out of the car. My foster mother had been waiting on the porch. She was a stately woman in her early sixties, her hair still dyed black and ironed straight. She stood rigidly, and I still thought of her as taller than I was, even though I had her by several inches.

I walked up the sidewalk, noting the winter cracks, and stepped onto the porch. She came into my arms as if she had been holding herself back and then squeezed me so tightly it hurt.

"We missed you, honey," she said. "You'll come back tonight so your daddy can see you?"

He had a Bible class that afternoon, or he would have been here with us, even on short notice. She had explained that in our brief phone call.

"Yes," I said, even though I hadn't planned on returning, and really didn't want to. But I didn't see how I could stay away. I had never visited them here before, and my foster father would want to see me in his Atlanta home, just once.

She leaned back in the hug and stared at my face. Then she ran a light finger near my stitches. "What happened?"

"I was with Martin on Friday."

"Oh, Smokey," she said softly. "Was it as horrible as they say?"

I blinked. Her gentle words touched a part of me I had deliberately shut off. I had stared at the destruction of my hometown, but I hadn't let it reach me. It would have been too overwhelming.

"It was worse," I said.

She put her arm around my waist and led me inside. The house was bigger than I expected and had two stories, which surprised me, given that my foster parents were both getting on in years. The front foyer was dark, and I could make out the lines of a large living room, but my foster mother led me to the kitchen. She didn't show me the house, perhaps because, in her mind, I belonged there and already knew what it was like.

"I made something," she said, and as usual, it was not something small. She had put leftover fried chicken in the middle of the plastic tablecloth. Fresh cornbread sat in a basket, covered with a towel, and the kitchen smelled of baking apple pie.

I had no idea how she had prepared the pie and got it into the oven during my drive over, but she'd managed. She always did.

The kitchen was light, painted yellow, and spacious. It was warm, and that was good, as Atlanta was unseasonably cold for March. She sat me down, poured me some coffee, and then sat down herself. She pushed food at me, and I ate, startled at how hungry I was, and how much I had missed her cooking.

"What did you want to talk about?" she asked, her hands folded on the yellow checked cloth. She leaned forward just slightly, like she used to do when I was a young man coming in from a day in the D.C. high school I hated.

In fact, it felt like those times, and it made me wonder at the power of memory. Even though I had never been in this home before, it felt familiar. She felt familiar. And so did the feeling that I had when I was with her. With her, I was always a perpetual fifteen.

I swallowed the bite of chicken I had taken, then followed it with a swig of hot coffee. I picked a piece of cornbread out of the basket, more so that I had something to do with my hands than not.

I broke the cornbread apart, then wiped my fingers on the paper napkin she had provided. I didn't know how to approach this. "I'm working on a case."

She nodded.

"It seems it might have ties to me."

She frowned. "How is that, Smokey?"

I licked my lips, tasted chicken grease and butter. "Let me ask questions first, then I'll tell you."

She waited, a trait I had always valued in her. She was a steady woman, a woman who hadn't seemed ruffled by raising another woman's troubled child. She had never had children of her own and had once said she hadn't known what she missed until I showed up. By then, she said, it was too late to have any more.

I took the photos of the Hathaways out of my breast pocket and handed them to her. "Do you know these people?"

She studied them for a moment, then turned in her chair and held the photos to the light. She started to shake her head, then seemed to think the better of it. Finally she handed them back to me.

"I've never seen them before," she said. "Are they the ones that hired you?"

I shook my head. "I'm trying to find out who they are. They lived for years under false identities in Chicago. The trail has led me to Atlanta. I think they were here in 1939." She looked at me sharply, recognizing the significance of that date to our family. "Do you think—"

"I don't know," I said. "The woman left me money in her will. I've never seen them before."

She picked up the pictures again, got up, and took them to the window, frowning over them. "I'll show Oran," she said. "Maybe he'll remember." Then she raised her head as if what I had said had just hit her. "She left you money in her will?"

I nodded.

"And you don't know them?"

"Never seen them before."

She sucked in air. "A white woman," she said softly and sank back into her chair.

I took the pictures from her and slipped them back in my pocket. "We'll show Dad tonight."

She nodded, lost in thought. "I thought you said you had a case."

"I do. Their daughter hired me to find out what this is all about."

She glanced at me sideways. She knew me better than I liked to admit. "A white girl."

I nodded.

"And you agreed?"

I shrugged. "It seems we both could use the information. Better I get paid to look for it."

My foster mother smiled at me. The smile was small and sad. She waited. The question hung between us, the question I had never asked, not in all the years I'd known them.

I swallowed. "What do you know about what happened to my parents?"

She tapped a long finger on the table, then looked down at her hands. Mine were still ripping up cornbread, even though I hadn't realized I was doing it. She took a deep breath, then shook her head slightly, as if she weren't quite sure what to say.

Finally she took my left hand and held it, cornbread crumbs and all, between both of hers.

"The Grand called us in February of 1940. Your uncle had contacted him. Things weren't working out with you in Stone Mountain and he was afraid that you'd get in the wrong kind of trouble. I also got the sense that he was afraid to have you in his home."

I stiffened. No one had ever said that, but it had been clear. It was as if I were tainted because my parents were so brutally murdered, as if some sort of pall hung over me. It didn't help that my cousin was jealous of me, of anyone taking attention away from him, and he was saying the most awful things about the way my parents had died. I beat him up five times in January, and on the first of February I had broken his nose.

I still didn't regret that. He had deserved it. And after that, I had never spoken to him again.

But apparently he thought of me, enough to tell a white detective the name I was hiding under. I wonder how many others he had told.

Obviously, he had told Withers.

"The Grand was afraid you'd end up in an orphan's home, or worse." She rubbed my hand hard, unconsciously, her gaze far away. It was as if she had saved these words up for a long time, and now that she could say them, they simply poured out. "He spoke to several other families, most of whom you already knew, a number from your church. They were afraid to take you."

"Why?" I asked.

She raised her head and looked at me. Her eyes were a very clear, very light brown. "Because of your parents."

She had told me that before, a long time ago. I had accepted it then. I thought I understood it now. Why take the child of a couple who was so hated that they were lynched together?

"The Grand thought it was better that you didn't go back to Atlanta. He wanted you out of the city, out of the state if possible. He called everyone he knew. Then he called us."

"I still don't know why you took me in when all those others didn't," I said, my voice soft.

"Because we'd seen you before, when we were visiting here once. At Ebenezer Baptist. You don't remember, but I do. You had such a beautiful voice." She smiled. "And then there was Oran. He didn't want a baby. We thought we could help you, calm you down, make sure you got an education. We did that." There was regret in her voice, as if she felt she had failed.

"What do you know of my parents' death?" I asked again.

Her lips tightened together, and for a moment I thought she wasn't going to tell me. "It was pretty ugly. Everyone knew the men who killed them. No one did anything about it. The white folks thought it was justified, and so did some of the blacks."

"How can a lynching be justified?" I snapped.

She didn't pull away from me. She just stared at me for a long moment, the sadness that had always been present in her eyes when she looked at me even more pronounced. "It can't be."

"Then why—?"

"Times were different, Smokey." She bowed her head. "They wanted us to adopt you *before* we took you in. Legally adopt you. And change your name. They insisted on it."

I frowned. I still remembered that day, all those adults surrounding me, telling me I wouldn't have a home unless I changed my name. I always felt that my name had been the only gift my parents had given me, the only thing I was allowed to keep, and even that had been taken away from me. They let me keep Billy, but that was when folks started calling me Smokey, to hide even that.

I had blamed my foster parents for the name change. I hadn't realized they had been forced into it. No wonder no one wanted me. How can someone reasonably adopt a half-grown child without getting to know him first, without knowing what they had signed on for?

My foster parents had and had never uttered a word of regret.

"You always resented us for that." She spoke softly, without a trace of blame.

"Why didn't you tell me that they insisted?" I asked.

She shook her head. "Too many questions. You were going to ask too many questions, and you weren't ready for the answers."

"How do you know?" I hated the way they made decisions for me. I still hated it.

"Smokey," she said, "you were ten. There are just some things ten-year-olds, no matter how worldly, no matter what their experience, don't understand."

I slipped my hand from hers. I believed that, as an adult, but there was still an indignant boy in me, a boy whose world was destroyed in a single evening, and he didn't understand. He didn't understand at all.

"Then," she said, "as you got older, you stopped asking. You stopped trying. I even tried to bring the topic up once, and you walked away from me. You said—"

" 'Who cares about dead people anyway?' " I remembered that, the flat anger that was hidden behind the words. It was too late. It had been too late by then. I wasn't going to speak of my parents to anyone. It was very hard now.

I swallowed, tried to distance myself, made myself think as I would if this were a case, someone else's case, something I was investigating.

I thought back over what she had said, tried to analyze it critically, tried to see what didn't fit.

"Why would they want you to adopt me?" I asked finally. "First, with no time spent to see if we were compatible?"

For a moment, I thought I saw fear in her eyes, but it was banked down quickly. She glanced at the empty chair near the cookbooks, my foster father's chair, as though wishing she weren't having this conversation with me alone.

Then she said, "Because they weren't sure anyplace was safe for you."

"What did they think? That the mob would search me out, and string me up to a tree?"

"Eventually," she said through thin lips.

I hadn't expected her to say yes. My heart was pounding so hard that I could barely think. "Why? Why would they do that to me? I was ten years old."

She licked her lips, then took a deep breath. "They thought you knew."

"Knew what?"

Her eyes filled with tears. "Where your parents buried the baby."

TWENTY-TWO

I froze in place. The fragment of a memory rose: the phone, ringing on that cold winter morning, waking me out of a sound sleep, my father's voice rising—"You've got to be kidding"—and then fading into that subservient tone he used with white men in authority, men he was afraid would do something to him, his home, his family. "Yes, yes. Of course you can come here."

My foster mother caressed my cheek with the back of her hand. "Smokey?"

I focused on her face, her dear familiar face. I didn't remember seeing that many wrinkles before. Worry lines. She had worry lines. "What baby do you mean?" I whispered.

"Scarlett Ratledge," she said. "The daughter of Susan and Ross Ratledge."

Ratledge. One of Atlanta's oldest and most respected white families. My mother—my real mother—had worked for the Ratledges up until the day she died.

I was cold, even though the kitchen was warm and smelled of apple pie. "The Ratledge's baby?"

"She disappeared that Friday night. Your mother was supposed to be watching her."

I couldn't get my breath. "They thought my mother killed the Ratledge's baby?"

My foster mother nodded. "Folks in our community who believed it thought it was accidental. Babies are such fragile things. Maybe she squeezed it too hard or put a blanket wrong and let it suffocate. I've heard all kinds of theories. The white folks, now they had different theories."

I could imagine. I picked up my coffee cup but then had to set it back down. My hands were shaking too badly to hold it properly.

"They thought she killed it on purpose because she was jealous or because she was crazy. And then she took the baby away and hid the body. Or buried it. And they thought your father helped."

I couldn't imagine my parents doing any such thing. Then or ever. But it explained the fear in my father's voice that night when the knock came at the door. Had he expected it? And if he hadn't, why hadn't he? Why hadn't we all just left town as quickly as we could?

I swallowed hard. "I don't understand. Why did they think my mother took the baby?"

"She was the last one to see her, the last one to be with her." My foster mother took my shaking hand in her own. Her fingers were cold. This story bothered her as well. "You remember the *Gone with the Wind* hoopla, don't you?"

I nodded.

"The baby disappeared the night of the Junior League ball. Your momma was sitting. She was staying late, although she probably wasn't getting paid for it. She put the baby down and then went downstairs to do her chores. She said she checked on the baby about eight o'clock and it seemed fine. The Ratledges came home at midnight and let her go. It wasn't until the next morning that she knew anything was wrong. And to be honest with you, I'm not sure the Ratledges even checked on that child until dawn."

But I remembered the night of the ball and the next day. Everything seemed normal. Then I frowned. It had seemed sort of normal. My mother was in the house, but she had been worried. My father had gone to talk to some friends. He had come back saying "If they're going to do something, they would have done it already." The knock didn't come on the door until two days later. I was sure of that.

"But why didn't they just call the police?" I asked. Not that the police would have been much better. Not that my parents had a hope or a prayer once it was decided what happened to the child.

"Oh, the police knew," my foster mother said softly. "They knew. They just decided to keep everything hush-hush until the national press went away. The day after the movie stars left, that was the day everyone came for your parents."

"But my parents should have left."

"They believed something else happened to that baby. They thought that they would be all right. At least that was what the Grand said. I don't know how that could be." She ran a hand over her face. "I've thought through this, over and over, for years. I honestly think your parents were taken that night not to be killed, but to be tortured into confessing where that baby was. The fact that they died showed me that they never did say anything. I doubt they ever knew anything."

The buzzer went off behind me, making me jump. My foster mother put her hand on my shoulder as she got up. She turned off the buzzer and removed the pie. It was brown on top, with crisscrossed crust and bubbling apples. It looked magazine-perfect and was the most unappetizing thing I had ever seen.

"Why didn't anyone do anything? Why didn't the Grand help them? Why didn't they leave? This doesn't make any sense," I said.

She turned to me and sighed. "Because of the timing. If this had happened on any other day, your parents would have been dragged from their beds immediately and probably would have died then and there."

She paused, and in that pause, I heard her thought. I would have died then too. They would have taken the whole family, rather than leave witnesses.

"But this was the New South, and Atlanta was 'advanced.' And if something like that happened, even in 1939, the city would have been embarrassed. The baby's disappearance didn't even make the newspaper for a week."

My mouth had gone dry. "How did they know the baby was dead?"

She frowned at me. "Hmm?"

"How did they know? Was there blood?"

"Not that I know of," she said. "The child just up and vanished."

"Did they ever find the child?"

"No," she said. "And that's why the Grand always thought you would be in danger. There were folks who believed you knew where she was, and he was afraid they'd come after you. That's why you left Atlanta the minute the Grand found you, and why we never brought you here. That was part of our agreement. We weren't allowed to come to Georgia while there was still a chance someone would go after you."

"But you came here three years ago."

She smiled. "Atlanta was our home. Oran and I met here, went to school here. He couldn't pass up the opportunity from Morehouse. And we thought it would be safe now. I don't think most people even know about the Ratledges' baby, and if they do, they think of you as a little boy, not as a man full grown."

I nodded, but I wasn't thinking about now. I was thinking about what she had told me. "Something about that story's missing," I said, and I wasn't referring to what was obvious to me—Laura. I meant something else.

"I'm sure there's a lot to this that's missing," she said. "I purposely didn't learn much about it. I learned enough to answer the questions I thought you would ask, but you never did."

"At first I did," I reminded her.

She nodded. "At first, I couldn't talk to you."

"You thought they did it."

She shook her head. "I didn't know, Smokey. I didn't want to know. I just wanted you to be happy."

"That wasn't possible."

"I know." She took my hand again. Her touch was comforting. "I know."

There wasn't much to say after that. We sat in silence for a while, then my foster mother offered me some pie, as if she were trying to make this afternoon as normal as she could. I forced down a piece, along with the rest of my coffee. Then I thanked her, promised to be back for dinner, and left.

My heart was racing. I was breathing shallowly, and I was queasy. Laura and I had been right. I had taken blood money. The first down payment from her parents, a guilt offering that put a value on my parents' lives.

Ten thousand dollars each.

Apparently that was the going rate for Negroes in 1939.

A block away from my foster mother's, I had to pull over. I lost the pie and the makeshift lunch. I gripped the side of the car for a moment, then made myself breathe.

The queasiness was fading, but the disgust remained. I had spent blood money.

The rational part of my brain told me that I did need more information. I couldn't go to Laura with what I had. I didn't have anything.

Not yet.

I wiped my face and got back in the car, holding the steering wheel as if I were driving. Then I concentrated on calming myself.

I had always thought the attack on my parents had been

random violence. Part of me thought it was in response to the hysteria whipped up by the *Gone with the Wind* premiere. It wasn't until years later, when I saw the movie, that I made up a reason for it: the revenge sequence after Scarlett had been attacked by a group of former slaves after the war, only to be saved by Big Sam. I thought that for some reason, my parents had become targets of drunken good ole boys. It was as good an explanation as any, and it made some sort of sense out of something my nasty cousin had said to me:

"It all goes back to that *Gone with the Wind* stuff, remember?" he had said. "It was in all the papers."

He had been referring to the lost baby, which had been in the papers, my foster mother said, a week later. Only I had never seen those papers. I was protected and hidden and kept in the dark about what happened to my parents for a very long time. I guess my aunt and uncle, who were taking care of me before my foster parents took over, thought protecting me was the only way to take care of me.

And perhaps it was.

Perhaps it was.

It was the memory of my cousin's remark, though, that brought me to myself.

The papers. There had been more in the newspapers. My foster mother had confirmed as much.

Newspapers were open on the weekend. Someone would be able to help me.

I drove to the offices of the *Daily World*, Atlanta's first black newspaper, and asked if I could look through their archives.

I remembered my father reading the *Daily World* as if it were the Bible. It had always been, even after I left, the ideal of black journalism for me. But the *Daily World* had competition now. The new voice of black Atlanta was the *Atlanta Inquirer*, and it was driving the *Daily World* out of business.

That was evident even to my casual eye. The reporters lacked the enthusiasm I had always associated with them. The newspaper's pace was slow and steady. Even the paper itself looked familiar, as if no one had thought to change fonts or layout in the last thirty years.

The weekend receptionist I spoke to gave me a polite but distant smile. "We don't let just anyone go through our archives, sir," she said.

"I'm sorry," I said, realizing that I had forgotten to go through much of my usual routine with her. "My name is Smokey Dalton. I'm investigating a case for a client, and I need to look up some records. It would be kind of you to let me use the archives."

"Mr. Dalton, I can't—"

"Smokey Dalton?" A voice boomed from the back. "Billy Dalton, Oran's son?"

"Yes," I said.

A man came out of the small office. He was bald and hunched over, carrying a pipe in one hand. He held out the other to me. "Regent Porter," he said.

I had heard of him. I remembered reading his Monday and Wednesday columns when I was reading the *Daily World*. "It's a pleasure."

"What brings you to us?"

"A case."

"You're a detective now," he said, and it wasn't so much a question as a statement.

"More or less."

"I remember you at Ebenezer Baptist. Martin King, well it was clear he was going to be a preacher like his daddy, but I always pegged you for music, like Geekie Dobbs."

I froze. It startled me that someone would recognize me, know who I really was. Maybe there was something to those fears everyone had for me after all.

He smiled. "Relax, son. I've known Oran most of our

lives. And I was a friend of the Grand's. I knew about you, and I was one of only three people who did. I never said a word."

I swallowed hard, not sure what to say. Ultimately I didn't have to say anything. He seemed to sense my discomfort.

"What kind of case?" he asked.

"Hmm?"

"You said you were here on a case. What kind?"

I met his warm brown eyes. "The worst kind. It got personal a few days ago."

"Involvement with the client?"

I shook my head, even though that had happened. "The case wraps into my own family."

"Mmm," he said, and stuck the pipe in his mouth. He patted the receptionist on the shoulder, then took my arm. He led me past metal desks covered with manual typewriters that were at least twenty years old. A few of the reporters were typing. Others were talking on the phone. Half the desks were empty. Monday's paper would be thin.

"So," he said, as he led me into a back room. "It doubles back on your family how?"

I took a deep breath. I was still shaky from my conversation with my foster mother. "My parents' murder."

"A sad case, that," he said.

"How familiar are you with it?"

"Very. Atlanta's version of the Lindbergh baby. Only our accused weren't immigrants. Our accused were Negro and therefore didn't have to suffer the ignominy of a trial."

It took me half a beat to hear the sarcasm in his voice. "Do you think they were guilty?"

"Hell, no," he said, walking past a series of filing cabinets, his thick arthritic finger pointing at dates as he did so. "I think they were convenient."

He stopped in front of one of the cabinets and tugged open a drawer. In it were a series of dusty accordion files with names written on them in faded ink. He braced himself against the open drawer, then pulled out a thick file and set it before me.

"I wrote three columns on your folks. Always wished I could do more. But it was a dangerous case. The powers that be didn't like questions, and they were worried that there was a conspiracy. I guess they saw shades of Nat Turner or something."

I had to think for a moment before my history came back to me. Nat Turner, the slave who led a successful slave rebellion in 1831. He murdered his masters but the whites, in turn, slaughtered every slave for miles.

"Others were killed?" I whispered.

"Threatened," he said, "especially if someone thought they knew something." He set the file on a wobbly table underneath the only window. "There's microfiche too, but I suspect you won't need it when you're done with this."

I put my hand on the file, not wanting him to go, not yet. "You always keep your notes?" I asked.

"On the controversial ones," he said. "Habit." He flicked a file cabinet with his finger, the metal making a soft pinging sound. "Fortunately not everyone in this place is as fastidious as I am or we'd be buried in paper."

He smiled and patted my shoulder, a gesture that was oddly comforting. "Come talk to me when you've finished thumbing through everything."

I nodded, then reached forward and flicked on the metal desk lamp that stood in the corner of the wobbly table. The lamp provided a bit more light than the thin fluorescent on the ceiling. I bent over the accordion file and with trembling hands, pulled out all the manila files stored inside.

They were labeled in that same spidery hand I had seen inside the cabinet: Columns, Competition, Interviews, Lies, Photographs, and Police Reports. I opened the Lies file first because it intrigued me.

In it were handwritten notes, scrawled on yellowing paper.

> *Why assumption of murder?*
> *What happened to body?*
> *What happened to coin collection?*
> *Why not investigate noise?*
> *Back door?*
> *Always blame the Colored housemaid.*
> *No ransom note.*

I felt my stomach twist. I closed the Lies file, deciding to save the remaining pages for last. Instead I opened the Columns file and found Porter's three columns on the topic, which I did not read. Columns were usually opinion, and I wanted to form my own. I set that file aside as well and opened the Competition file.

In it were yellowing newspaper clippings from the *Journal*, the *Georgian*, and the *Constitution*. Lurid headlines that seemed to get only worse as the end of the year approached.

SOCIETY'S FAVORITE DAUGHTER MISSING

MISSING CHILD FEARED GONE FOREVER

POLICE BELIEVE BABY MURDERED BY
COLORED HOUSEKEEPER
Ratledges still have hope

I spread the articles out in front of me and began reading. In the white press, the notion of Negro guilt was there from the start. It was as if they considered no other options.

I turned the pages and read, wincing at the descriptions of my family, the way my mother was referred to as stupid and careless; my father as conniving and dangerous. In one article there was a mention of me and the fact that according to the white press, I was "missing." Only Ralph McGill's *Constitution* reserved judgment, and even worried that assuming so quickly that the Negro (and he did capitalize the word) housekeeper had taken and killed the child was perhaps the wrong way to approach the information.

None of them seemed to know at this point my parents were already dead.

I turned the fragile newsprint and then stopped, my breath catching in my throat. For on the second page of the *Journal* was a studio photograph of the Ratledges. Ross Ratledge had the long thin face that was considered both fashionable and handsome in the 1930s. But I didn't look at him much.

Instead I stared at his wife.

Looking at a portrait of Susan Ratledge was like looking at a still photograph of Laura.

I went through the rest of the files with shaking hands. The queasiness had returned, so strong that I was afraid I wouldn't be able to swallow after a while. Occasionally I had to stop and wipe my eyes, and once I stood, shoved my hands in my pockets, and leaned my forehead against the cool metal of a filing cabinet.

It didn't soothe my feverish brain. I was thinking a thousand things at once and none of them pleasant. I knew my parents; I knew they weren't killers, and so had all of their friends. But the stupidest thing about this was that Laura had been kidnapped as a baby, and no one knew. No one tried to find her. That meant there had been no ransom note.

They all assumed she was dead.

Laura. I raised my head and opened my eyes. I had no idea how I would tell Laura.

I have no idea how long I stood there, hands in pockets, staring at the gray metal of the cabinet. Eventually, I heard a door creak behind me, and Porter returned.

"Strong stuff," he said.

I nodded without turning around.

"Your parents were good people. They didn't deserve what happened to them."

I didn't even lash back at him with my usual response: *no one deserves to be lynched.* Instead I nodded again.

"Did the file help with your case?"

"More than you know," I said. My voice came out strangled and strange. I cleared my throat, took a deep breath, and silently told myself to pull myself together. I turned to him, hoping that my face looked somewhat normal. A man couldn't read about the needless death of his parents and not look a bit shaken, but I didn't want to look as devastated as I felt.

"Forgive me, I haven't lived in Atlanta since..." I couldn't finish the sentence, so I jumped to the next. "Are you still writing columns?"

"Monday's is due at six." He smiled. The look was reassuring. He had to have been my foster father's age—my father's age too—in his early sixties.

"If things go as I think they will, I'll have another column for you."

His smile widened. "That's what I was hoping for." Then he nodded at the table. "You can have the file, if you return it."

I didn't want it. I wanted to take it, shove it in a cabinet, and never see it again.

But I needed it. Laura would never believe me. *I* wouldn't have believed me. Not after thirty years of brainwashing. Not after thirty years of lies.

"Thank you," I said. I put the pieces back together carefully so that I didn't rip any clippings or lose any of the smaller scraps of paper. I reached into my wallet and took out a battered card with my name, address, and phone number on it. I had little occasion to use these things, and I usually forgot I had them. I was pleased to have one now.

I handed it to him. "In case you need to track me down."

"I suspect I could have done that with Oran or Lucinda," he said, but took the card anyway.

The queasiness in my stomach became a burning in my throat. I turned back to the accordion file and attempted to tie the top of it with the attached brown strings, but my hands were shaking too much. Porter came up beside me, tied the file, and handed it to me. He said nothing about my obvious distress, for which I was very grateful.

He walked me out of the office and to the street. When we reached my car, he shook my hand, and then he patted it just once. "Times have changed," he said, "and I have hopes for the future. Small hopes, but hopes nonetheless."

I frowned, trying to make myself concentrate.

"But," he said, "the hopes never take away the sting of the past. Sometimes, I think they make it worse."

I nodded, not sure I understood him, and not sure I agreed with him. Then I thanked him again, got in my car, and drove away.

I barely remember the dinner at my foster parents'. Mostly my foster mother forced food on me and touched my forehead to see if I was ill. My foster father, who always knew more than he admitted, finally ordered her to stop fussing.

"The boy's had a shock," he said. "Let him grieve."

And they did.

We sat in their bright living room and watched Lyndon Baines Johnson declare a limited halt to the bombing in Vietnam.

And then he said, "I shall not seek, and I will not accept, the nomination of my party for another term as your President."

My foster parents cheered, and I might have too. But I was too numb to recognize the implications, not then.

I went back to the motel room that night and didn't sleep. Twice I reached for the phone to call Laura, and twice I brought my hand back. Finally I got up and reread the file, then compared the photographs of Laura's parents—the people she believed were her parents—to the photographs in the file. I hadn't made this up. It had happened.

I bowed my head, and there, over information three decades old, I finally fell asleep.

I stayed in Atlanta one more day, ostensibly to clear up loose ends. I did dig up small pieces of information, things that confirmed what I already knew, but that was work I could have done from Memphis. In reality, I stayed because, for the first time in my life, I found my foster parents' presence oddly comforting. I finally understood what they went through to allow me to grow up in their home, and I was grateful, truly grateful, an emotion I had never allowed myself to feel toward them. If I had felt that one in the past, I might have felt all the others, the ones that swirled around me now, the ones that nearly overwhelmed me whenever I tried to speak.

It was easy to find information on the Ratledges, even though they had withdrawn from Atlanta society; apparently a white person never entirely withdraws. They still rated articles in the local papers, and they eventually had more children, who made news when they had their coming-out parties at the Piedmont Driving Club or married or had children of their own.

Laura had an entire family she didn't even know about.

I never did try to contact the Ratledges, though. Even if they didn't associate me with my parents, I knew they wouldn't believe a strange black man who came to their door saying he knew what had happened to their missing daughter. And if they ever discovered my true identity, well, it would probably only confirm—in the Ratledges' minds—the fact of my parents' guilt.

No. Contacting them was up to Laura. I had done my part. And after I called Laura and gave her the news, I would be finished with this case.

Before I left the motel, I tried to call her. The phone rang three times, but when someone answered, I hung up.

I didn't want to talk to her, not from Atlanta. I had visions of her flying here, expecting me to stay, of going to the Ratledges with her or putting her back together when it was over.

I didn't like any of those images. I had to keep the situation in my control. The problem was that I didn't know how to do that. The situation had long since left my control.

And I wasn't sure if I would ever get it back.

TWENTY-THREE

The drive to Memphis was a long one, made even longer by melting snow and slush. I kept the radio off the entire time, my mind too busy to be distracted. I had taken $10,000 from the people who had murdered my parents. I'm sure the Hathaways hadn't meant for my parents to die in their stead, but that had happened, the unseen consequences of a well-planned crime. And it had bothered one of them, probably Mrs. Hathaway, bothered her enough to offer a small token from their considerable fortune—$10,000 per person, what they considered a black life to be worth.

I had spent the money. I had none of it in reserve. I couldn't even write a check and give it all back to Laura, not without some planning.

And part of me wasn't sure I should pay it back. Part of me wanted to expose her parents for what they were and demand a percentage of their fortune—a sizable percentage.

But that would hurt Laura, and despite the growing anger I was feeling, hurting Laura was the last thing I wanted to do.

Scarlett. Her real name was Scarlett. In her birth announcement, which was sandwiched into the odds and ends

Porter had collected, the Ratledges had named her to honor Margaret Mitchell and the *Gone with the Wind* hoopla. Mrs. Ratledge had expressed in the society page her joy that her daughter had arrived early enough so that she and her husband could attend the festivities.

These people were not ones I would want as parents. But then neither were the Hathaways. Laura had a choice between bad and worse, in my opinion. And at the moment, my opinion counted for a lot.

I got into Memphis in the late afternoon. The light was diffuse, growing dark, and in the shadows, the city looked terrible. The curbs were piled with garbage, and I noted the farther into town I got, the worse the smell got. The scent of rot hung over the place like a miasma. I hadn't realized how bad it had gotten until I had gone away.

I went to my office first. Beale looked like a Third World city. Windows were boarded up. Large signs covered doorways, saying that businesses were closed. Wilson Drug was a ruined hulk on the corner of Fourth, and the air still smelled like smoke.

The streets were littered with trash. I crossed over a large pile of it against the curb and nearly slipped on some filthy water on the sidewalk beyond. Memphis was cold and dark and unwelcoming, but it felt more like home than Atlanta ever would.

I carried the accordion file inside and locked it in my safe. My office was just as I had left it, with the Hathaway's notes and papers scattered on my floor. Laura hadn't asked for them back when I made her go to Chicago. Perhaps my odd behavior hadn't bothered her. It had bothered me at the time. Now it seemed justified.

If she had gone with me to Atlanta, who knew what would have happened.

I sat at my desk and turned on the lamp. I shoved a pile of papers aside and dialed Laura's number before I had a chance to stop myself.

It rang once. I put my finger over the disconnect button. Twice. My finger itched. Three times. I was about to press the button when Laura's voice came on the line.

"Hello?"

My traitorous heart leapt at the sound. I swallowed, the queasiness from Atlanta rising again.

"Hello?" she asked again.

"Laura," I said.

"Smokey." She sounded relieved. "I've been worried about you. I didn't hear, and didn't hear, and didn't hear, and I thought maybe something bad happened to you."

Something bad had happened to me, but it had been a long time in the past. It only felt as if it were happening now. "I'm fine," I said.

"I haven't found too much here, although there are some connections of my father's that are somewhat shady. I got an old friend to tell me about them, and he hinted that those newspaper articles were right. It seems that my father did make a percentage of his early money doing things he shouldn't have."

She was talking too fast, and it struck me then that she was nervous.

"Still, I talked to his old secretary, and I should get his letters—or some of the carbons anyway—tomorrow. Then I was hoping to go through their house one last time. I have to put it up for sale anyway, and I thought maybe there might be some hidden storage places that I didn't know of. I was thinking maybe you could come up here and help me. What do you think, Smokey?"

"I think we need to talk," I said. She was talking too fast; I was talking too slow. I felt as if my entire body were underwater. "I went to Atlanta Saturday, Laura."

"You found something." Then I heard what was really going on. She was afraid. She was afraid of what I had found, afraid she wouldn't like it.

Well, she wouldn't. At least parts of it. The knowledge that she had another family, ready-made, might appeal to her. "Smokey?"

"Yes," I said. "I found something."

There was a long silence as I gathered my thoughts. I picked up a pen and held it between my fingers, twirling it.

"What did you find?" Her voice was nearly a whisper.

All the way back, I had been thinking of this conversation, playing it over and over in my mind. Sometimes, in my imagination, I took the coward's way out. I told her, starkly, what had happened and its consequences, following up her disbelief by mailing her the accordion file. Other times, I thought that too cruel. I thought telling her in person would be better. Those scenes I couldn't play. I tried to imagine myself holding her, reassuring her, but I couldn't see that. I couldn't really imagine the words ever leaving my mouth.

"Smokey, please."

"I'm sorry, Laura," I said. "I can't bring myself to tell you over the phone."

"It's bad, isn't it?" she asked.

"Yes. No. I don't know," I said. "Come to Memphis. Then you can evaluate the information for yourself."

"Why don't you come here?"

"No," I said. "You're going to want to see what I have, and then maybe go to Atlanta yourself. Come here, Laura. I'll be waiting."

And then I pressed the disconnect button and kept my finger on it, as if holding it down would break the connection forever. The silence astounded me. Maybe not telling her was the coward's way out. I closed my eyes, imagining her now, her disorientation, her worry.

The phone rang, startling me. I gripped the receiver harder, knowing it was her, knowing that she wanted me to tell her something, anything, that she wanted it to be all right.

I let it ring three times, and then I realized I couldn't let the conversation end this way any more than she could. I let go of the disconnect button.

"Yeah?"

"Smokey." It sounded as if she had started crying. "What is it? What did they do?"

They kidnapped you and left no ransom note. They stole you, Laura, and let my parents take the blame. What else do you want to know? You want to know what it was like growing up with that sort of fear hanging over your head, with nightmares of hiding in a closet while your parents were dragged out of the house to their deaths? You want to know why I can't talk to you anymore, Laura? Do you really want to know?

I cleared my throat. "Remember I told you that you might not like what we find?"

"Yes," she said.

"I found the connection between your family and mine," I said. "It's not pretty. I'm sorry I'm being so harsh, Laura. I'm still in shock myself."

"Did they kill your parents?" she whispered.

"Not directly," I said.

"Oh, God." This time she was the one who was silent. "What information do you have?"

"Proof. Of what your parents did. What happened afterwards. Why my parents were killed. Maybe I should tell you now, Laura. Maybe that would be better."

"Just the bare bones," she said. "I don't think I can live with not knowing. Not now that you know. Please tell me, Smokey, or else I'll make something terrible up."

I closed my eyes. "Your real name is Scarlett Leigh Ratledge," I said. "You were kidnapped from your parents' home when you were six weeks old. Earl Hathaway, whose real name was Ray Hunt, was working as a gardener for your real parents until the late fall, when he was dismissed for unspecified reasons. His wife couldn't have children. She was, by all accounts, a nice woman who believed that a child would somehow elevate her."

I heard Laura's breathing on the other end, harsh and ragged.

"Either to get revenge on the Ratledges one evening or to appease his wife, or maybe both, Earl Hathaway snuck into the Ratledges' house. He stole some heirloom silver, a coin collection, some jewelry that was in a family safe with a flimsy lock, and you. Apparently you didn't cry as he carried you out of that house. And then he and his wife disappeared. The jewelry was pawned in Memphis. The silver was probably melted down. The coin collection turned up nearly ten years later in Detroit. And you were gone for good."

"This is true?" she asked, her voice shaking.

"Yes," I said. "Although no one knew it, not for a fact. They all thought you were dead."

"And your family? How does your family fit in?"

"My mother was the Ratledges' housekeeper. She was baby-sitting that night. She heard nothing. She put you down about eight o'clock and didn't check on you again when she left at midnight. The Ratledges apparently didn't check when they got home, either. Nice people. When they discovered you missing, they thought my mother had killed you and had hidden the body."

"But the thefts—"

"Weren't discovered for a week. Everyone was preoccupied with the loss of the baby. Of you."

"And your parents were murdered." She took a deep, shuddery breath. "Oh, Smokey."

I opened my eyes. I didn't want her sympathy or compassion. I didn't want any of it. I wanted to be angry with her. I wanted her to go into hysterics, to fail to believe me, to scream at me so that I could scream back.

Maybe that was why I wanted her here, so that we could fight like I had never fought with anyone before, and we could end it all. Only we couldn't end it. We were tied together forever in ways I didn't want to think about.

"What kind of evidence do you have?" Now it sounded like the story was started to sink in.

"Newspaper articles, photographs, speculation."

"And it confirms what you say?"

"Yes. You'll see."

"But if no one knew that the baby was kidnapped, then how do you know it's me?"

"I have a photo of Ray Hunt, who looks enough like Earl Hathaway to convict him. I talked to his sister, who confirms that he disappeared in December of 1939. I have the word of a detective who was hired to search for you by the Grand. He found nothing once your parents left Atlanta. They covered their tracks well, even then."

"Is that enough?"

"It's not the clincher," I said. "The clincher is a photograph I have of your real mother, who looks just like you, only dressed in a 1930s style."

"But if there was a kidnapping, what about the note?"

"There was no note. I don't know if your parents planned a note and then your mother talked your father out of it so that she could keep you, or if you were taken for her all along. That part of this died with your parents."

"You sound so strange," she said. "Distant, angry."

I wrapped the phone cord around my hand. "Your parents wanted to give me money for my parents' lives, Laura. Ten thousand dollars apiece."

"They were probably trying to make amends—"

"How would you like it, Laura, if someone had caused your parents to die horribly when you were ten years old, and then years later gave you twenty thousand dollars and said, 'Here. This should make things better'?"

"But they didn't give you a reason."

"No note," I said sarcastically.

"Smokey."

"Don't defend them, Laura. Not after what they did to us both."

There was a sharp intake of breath. I wished I could see her face. I didn't know if she was shocked at me, at what I said, or at what it really meant. "What are you going to do now?"

"Wait for you," I said. And then I thought I understood what she was really asking. "Don't worry. I haven't told anyone about this. Not the Ratledges, not the press. No one. Just you."

"Thank you," she whispered.

"Don't thank me," I said. "This was something I should have known years ago."

She paused for a moment, and if I hadn't heard the faint edge of her breathing I would have thought she had hung up. "Maybe," she said, her voice soft, "maybe you should just send me that file."

"I thought of it," I said. "More than once. But I promised it would go back to its rightful owner. Besides, you left a lot of your parents' things in my office. I want them out of here."

"I see," she said as if she didn't see at all. "Is this how it's going to be between us now, Smokey?"

"I don't see how it can be any other way."

"All right." Her voice was shaking. "I'll be down there as soon as I can get a flight. And I'll make sure I have the rest of your money."

She hung up before I could protest. I placed the receiver in its cradle, then rested my head on the back of my arm. I had fired the first shot, and Laura just showed she could keep up with me. Things were going to get nasty, and I didn't know how to stop it.

I didn't want to go home. The idea of walking through my house, paid off with the money I received from Laura's parents, was anathema to me. And Laura had been there. If I closed my eyes, I could see her in my bed, her body tangled in the sheets. They probably still smelled of her, of us, of sex. I couldn't go there.

I kept my head on my arm for a long minute, and then I sat up. I had chosen this path. I could have lied to her. I could have said I found nothing. Strangely, though, I hadn't thought of that option until just now, when it was too late. She had sounded so shocked, so shaken, and I had been so cold. It was as if there were a part of me that believed she needed to pay for my parents' death, for the situation her parents—her adoptive parents—had put me in. It wasn't logical, it wasn't rational, but it was there.

I had been alone with this too long. I needed to talk to someone who wasn't involved. My foster parents had done their best after the last few days, but they were trying to deal with their son, not with the man that I had become. They had waited for that day for years, and when it finally came, they handled it well but they saw me as a boy—probably would always see me as a boy—and that had felt good at first, but it didn't feel good now.

Without really thinking about it, I grabbed the receiver from its cradle and dialed Henry. If I couldn't bring myself to talk to him about what I found, what I learned, at least I could talk to him about Jimmy.

Henry's secretary answered. She had a sweet, elderly, befuddled voice that fit the woman I had seen in the church office.

I introduced myself and asked for Henry.

"Oh, Mr. Dalton," she said. "He's visiting the family."

"What family?" I asked.

"Larry Payne's," she said as if I should have known. "The boy that got killed. His funeral was today."

"Oh," I said.

"He'll be back in an hour or so. You want me to let him know you called?"

"Yes," I said. I was answering by rote.

"There's one more thing, Mr. Dalton," she said. "Reverend Davis said that if you should call, I should tell you to contact Jimmy. He said you'd know what that meant."

Jimmy. I felt cold. I had forgotten to tell Jimmy I was leaving. "I'll do that right now," I said.

I hung up and got my coat and went to the car. I couldn't do anything about Laura, but I could see Jimmy. He was probably worried. We hadn't spoken since the night of the riot.

The drive to the Nelsons' was short. The bicycle was gone from the yard, as were all the toys. I doubted Selina Nelson had let her children outside all weekend.

Not that I could have blamed her. Memphis had become a scary place.

I walked onto the creaky porch and knocked on the peeling paint of the front door. It took a moment for it to open. Selina smiled when she saw me.

"Smokey," she said and sounded relieved. "Jimmy's been worried about you."

"I just found out," I said. "Can I see him?"

She nodded and pulled open the screen door. I stepped inside. The usual mess of toys covered the floor. This time, the toddler was sleeping in a playpen and the three-year-old girl was sitting on a booster chair in the kitchen, banging a spoon on the table.

"Jimmy's upstairs," she said. "I'll take you to him."

The stairs were made of flimsy pressboard that sagged in the middle. They creaked beneath my weight. As she led me up them, Selina picked up a stuffed rabbit, an errant jack, and a bag of marbles. She shoved them all in the pocket of her apron.

The upstairs had once been an attic, but an amateur carpenter had built walls a third of the way inside. The walls separated three sleeping areas, but there was no fourth wall on any of them, and no doors. One of the rooms, on the farthest side, had a blanket strung over the opening. The others simply opened onto the sleeping area. It was warm up here now, but I suspected it had been cold on Friday, and I knew I didn't want to be in these rooms in the heat of the summer.

There were two beds in the room directly in front of us, one made military style, and the other a tangle of sheets and blankets. Clothing was on one side of the floor, near the messy bed, and on the dresser that seemed to straddle the invisible line between the occupants were perfume bottles and hair spray and an earring tree. Girls.

Jimmy was in the next room over. He sat on a bed next to the window. The curtains were closed, but I knew that window overlooked the street. He had seen me coming.

"Jimmy," Selina said. "You have a visitor."

Jimmy kept his back to us. "Don't want to see no one," he said, his voice soft.

"It's Smokey," she said. "You've been—"

I put a hand on her arm. I knew that he had watched me walk to the front door. He knew I was here.

"Jimmy," I said. "I came to see how you were doing."

"Jus' fine," he said.

He had never been this sullen with me, not ever. I glanced at Selina. "Do you mind if I talk to him alone for a few minutes?"

She shook her head. She went back down the stairs, and I waited until I could no longer hear her footsteps before I said, "So, you're mad at me. I'm sorry I didn't tell you I was going to Atlanta. In the heat of the moment Friday, I just forgot."

Jimmy crossed his arms. "You didn't do nothing about Joe."

He had asked me, when we brought him here weeks ago, for help with Joe. I hadn't promised to do anything, but apparently Jimmy had heard it that way.

"Joe won't listen to me," I said.

"You ain't even tried to talk to him. I know."

"You know because you spoke to him?" I asked cautiously.

"I know because you left."

"I had some business that took me to Atlanta," I said, but my protest sounded lame. It didn't matter to Jimmy why I had left, only that I had.

Jimmy said nothing. His small shoulders were hunched forward. For the first time since I had known him, his hair was cropped close and he wore clothes appropriate to the weather. It even looked as if he were finally putting on a bit of weight.

I took a step farther into the room. There was another bed in here as well, but it didn't have sheets or a pillow, only a woolen blanket pulled over a stained mattress. Apparently the Nelsons had room for one more child.

At least Jimmy was getting a little privacy.

"Have you seen Joe?" I asked.

"No," he said. The word was long and drawn. I had never heard so many emotions packed in one syllable. There was anger and terror all mixed together with resentment.

"Do you want me to find him?"

He whirled. "You gonna leave again?"

I almost took a step backwards. The force of his anger was a powerful thing. I hadn't expected it from a boy so small. "I'm not planning on it," I said. Of course I hadn't planned on the Atlanta trip either, but I didn't explain the details to Jimmy.

"I think he's dead," Jimmy said, his dark eyes alive with anger.

I didn't know if that statement was one he was making to punish me or if it was based in real worry. "Have you seen something?"

"Been a week since he been home, maybe more."

More, if my visit to the apartment had shown anything.

"They throwed all our stuff in the street." Jimmy's voice hitched. "One of the neighbors saved some. It's in there." He waved a hand toward the back of the room. In the growing darkness I saw a closet door.

"Did your foster parents help you get it?"

He looked down. The question about them seemed to take some of the fury out of him. "Yeah."

"Are they treating you all right?"

"Yeah," Jimmy said again.

"You sure? Because if they aren't, I can get Reverend Davis to find you someplace else."

"No." The answer was too quick for this aura of cool he was playing at. He liked it here. It was probably the first time he had anyone ask him how school was and fix him a real meal at the end of his day, the first time he'd ever had fresh baked cookies and clean clothes.

I remembered how that felt, and I had only been without all those things for a few months when I became a member of the Dalton family. It had seemed like an eternity, and then I didn't believe it would last.

I made sure it didn't.

"All right," I said. "But if you run into troubles, you let me know."

"Sure, so you can disappear again."

I crossed my arms, much as Selina Nelson had, and leaned against the inexpertly painted Sheetrock that separated Jimmy's room from the one next to it.

"Did you come to see me and I wasn't there?"

"For *days!*" His hands balled into fists, and I saw him will the emotions back. The tears back.

The days I was gone. It must have seemed like an eternity to him. "You went looking for Joe after the march?"

"I thought somethin' happened to you and him."

The only two people who meant anything to him. No wonder he had been scared.

"I'm sorry, Jimmy. I thought you were safe here. I didn't

think you'd come looking for me while I was away." And I hadn't thought of him when I was leaving, except to be glad he was being taken care of.

"I been safe," he said in a tone that implied I was the biggest moron he knew. "Joe ain't."

Joe hadn't been for a long time. But Jimmy really didn't know that. "Did you see him while I was gone?"

Jimmy shook his head. "I looked too."

And I hadn't. Leave it to a ten-year-old to lay on guilt thicker than any I'd ever felt.

"I'm sorry," I said. "I'll see if I can find him. What do you want me to tell him if I do? That you're worried about him?"

Jimmy's lower lip trembled. He shook his head once, abruptly. He was getting old enough—or perhaps he had been born that old—not to want anyone to know he needed help.

"He's almost an adult," I said softly. "I'll have trouble finding him a place like I've found you, and even more trouble convincing him he needs help."

"They've got a bed," Jimmy said, extending his hand to the bed next to him. He hadn't mentioned this the first time I saw him here. Apparently the march and the violence had decided him. Jimmy wanted his brother beside him.

"Have you asked the Nelsons if they want Joe to stay here?"

He shook his head. He apparently hadn't considered that at all. "If he don't stay, I don't stay."

"He has to make his own choices," I said.

" 'N I make mine," Jimmy said.

"And the Nelsons make theirs. Joe has some friends that I'm sure Mrs. Nelson doesn't want around that baby I saw downstairs."

Jimmy bit that trembling lower lip. He clearly hadn't thought of that. "I still wanna know where he is."

"Fair enough. And I'll see if I can get him off the streets."

I didn't know how, but I owed it to Jimmy. Joe and I both did.

"Tomorrow?"

"I suspect it'll take me a few days to find him. How about I report to you on Saturday?" I put it off long enough to give me a chance to search.

"I'll pay you," he said and opened one grubby fist to reveal a crumpled five dollar bill. "It ain't much, but they don't give me much. I been saving it."

"Is that your lunch money?" I asked.

"So what if it is? It's mine, ain't it?"

"I think the Nelsons want you to eat with that money."

He waved a hand at me. "I'm stuffed. They give me plenty."

And from his perspective that was probably true. I stared at that crumpled bill.

"I don't want your money," I said. "I owe you this. I should have been here."

"I wanna pay." His chin jutted out stubbornly.

I shook my head. "I need to find Joe. For me. All right?"

After a moment, his chin moved back into place. He closed his fist on the five. "All right," he said.

"I'll report to you on Saturday, whatever I find."

"Jus' tell me when you find him," Jimmy said.

"I will," I promised.

Somehow I managed to smile at Selina Nelson and wave as I said good-bye. Somehow I managed to seem as if nothing was bothering me, even though Jimmy's anger had shaken me almost as much as my discoveries in Atlanta.

Still, I couldn't stop moving. I was tired and discouraged. I felt as if the bottom had dropped out on me in the last few days, and I was afraid that I was hitting freefall and unable to stop.

I went to Henry's office. He was alone at his desk, the desolate view of the garden behind him. When he saw me, he started to smile, stopped, and said, "Tell me about Atlanta."

And so I did.

TWENTY-FOUR

Henry got me home that night. He didn't literally drive me there, but he calmed me, talked to me of things I wouldn't have normally listened to, such as God's plan, and the Way Life Should Be.

After I told him what I had discovered and its relationship to Laura, my client, he had said, "Aren't you glad you finally know?"

"No," I had answered.

He had given me one of his looks, one of his don't-lie-to-me looks, and said, "Smokey, something has always eaten you alive. Perhaps it was this."

Perhaps it was, but I was unwilling to admit it. But I had heard him when he said that God gave us trials for a reason. Normally I would have scoffed at that, but this night, I found comfort in it.

I said nothing about the fact that Laura had been my lover, but it was clear Henry knew. He had known before I left. He, good friend that he was, said nothing about it either, but he gave me that extra strain of compassion, something I sorely needed.

I went home and slept for the first time in two days.

———

The next morning, I got up and decided to fulfill a promise. I went searching for Joe.

I didn't have a lot of energy, but I knew I'd never forgive myself if I failed Jimmy again.

Finding Joe proved as difficult a task as I had thought it would. I went to the apartment building first just in case he had shown up to claim his stuff. He hadn't. In his former apartment lived a new family who didn't look like they could afford rent either. Already the place was squalid and filthy, smelling of baby poop and unwashed sheets.

Downstairs I found the landlord, who informed me that he had gone through all the city's eviction procedures before throwing the Baileys' stuff on the streets, which meant he had followed a five-month program. He did let it slip that Joe and Jimmy's mother had sent a rent check two days before. Unfortunately it had covered only one month, and he applied it to the amount due. I convinced him, using Jimmy's talent at guilt, to give me their mother's address, figuring if nothing else, the state could use it to officially declare the woman unfit.

But the landlord hadn't seen Joe or any of his friends. I left my number with him just in case, promised him that he'd get more of the money owed him if he called me when he saw Joe, and let it go at that.

Then I went to all the wrong corners, the places where I knew drugs changed hands, from the riverfront to Handy Park, searching for Joe. A few of the dealers knew me, and so did some of the vets. Most of them had seen Joe, but not recently. He had let his little brother handle deliveries, but even that stopped over two weeks ago. Joe had been doing small-time dealing since January. When the deliveries stopped, most everyone figured someone else had caught up with him. Being druggies, they didn't bother to go find out.

Still, I thanked them for their time but did not give them money since most of them would use it to shoot up or buy weed. Instead, I promised them a good meal and a place to bunk if they showed up at Henry's church, and I mentally made a note to myself to let him know of that promise.

I tried to find out more about the Invaders, but all I learned was that I was too old to be told where they were. Their headquarters, such as they were, shifted from place to place, as did their roster. No one would tell me if they were really being run by the Black Panthers, as some said, or if some of the national figures like Stokely Carmichael had indeed shown up. I was a brother, yes, but I was an older brother, and dressed like I wasn't cool, so no one trusted me.

It was a strange position to be in, and a shift even from the summer before. Everything in this town had changed and I didn't know exactly when that change had happened.

I decided to drive around the city one more time and then go home. Martin was coming back to town. He was giving a speech tonight, and then he would lead a nonviolent demonstration on Friday. Henry wanted me there, not as security—this time Martin was providing his own—but for me.

This time I was free to say no.

Henry also said that Martin met with the leaders of the Invaders. They promised him there would be no violence this time. They promised him that he would be the one in charge.

Finally, I saw Joe in a place I didn't expect to. I was driving past one of the cemeteries when I saw a familiar figure leaning against a tree. Joe. As I pulled closer, I realized he was watching two grave diggers cover a coffin in dirt.

I didn't have to get close to know that the coffin belonged to Larry Payne.

Joe wore a battered leather jacket and no hat. His jeans were torn and dirty, his brown shoes scuffed. He didn't look like someone strung out on drugs. He looked like a boy who hadn't eaten well, yet who had found something to consume his life.

"I've been looking for you, Joe," I said softly, but I startled him. He jumped, then turned.

"I heard," he said, his practiced nonchalance so clearly false after that involuntary movement.

"You could have come to see me. Jimmy's been asking after you."

He had the grace to flush. He looked down, toed the edge of his shoe against a crack in the dirt path. "Guess I owe you for that one, man."

"He's been worried about you." I decided to go for the guilt. If I went for blame, Joe would be gone in a heartbeat.

"He's doing good now. You got him with some decent folks."

"It would have been better if you had seen to him yourself."

He shook his head. "I can't take care of no kid."

"Maybe you can't," I said, "but you are the older one. It was—"

"My responsibility? Well, fuck that. It was Mom's responsibility and where the hell is she?" The words burst out of him. He grabbed a crushed beret from the pocket of his leather jacket and put it on, as if daring me to comment.

"Still in Florida. She finally sent a rent check."

"Too late."

"That's right," I said. "Jimmy salvaged what he could of your stuff. You were evicted, you know."

Joe shrugged. "So what? Everything's fine now. You got Jimmy three squares, and I got my place, and Mom's got hers. Ain't nothing to worry about no more."

"Jimmy wants to see you."

"Fuck that," Joe said. "He don't need me."

"Tell him that yourself."

Joe leaned into me. He was as big as I was, but leaner. Still, the movement was threatening, and the feeling I had—that this boy actually had a chance against me—startled me, even though it passed quickly. "Who the hell are you anyway? You ain't got nothing to do with us."

"I do now," I said. "You put me in that position when you had your little brother running drugs."

"It wasn't drugs," he snapped.

"Then what was it?" I tried to sound like I believed him, but it was clear I didn't. He had been running drugs, and we both knew it.

Joe leaned back. "You don't listen, do you? You see it all, but you don't get it. It ain't about drugs. It's about whitey and taking away his world. Damn near did it too, Thursday."

"Got your friend killed," I said. "I didn't hear of any white men dying."

Joe glanced at the grave. He couldn't pretend he didn't care. His presence here showed he did.

"It was a start," he mumbled.

"A bad one," I said. "The businesses that were destroyed were mostly black-owned."

"We was planning to move out of downtown."

"Well, you didn't move fast enough," I said.

"Next time we will."

"There won't be a next time," I said. "The leader of your group promised Dr. King."

"Dr. King, Dr. King. Je-zus." Joe's eyes grew wide. "You don't get it, do you? Dr. King don't speak for nobody. He had his chance. It didn't work. Now it's our turn. And we're gonna make this whole thing work."

"Who told you that violence would work? The men I saw you with? Thomas Withers? He was in the service with me. He's FBI."

Joe laughed. "And I am too."

"I mean it, Joe. They infiltrate, try to ruin something and put the blame on the rest of us."

He shrugged. "Don't matter. He's gone now."

I felt a shiver run down my spine. So he had left after all. "He was willing to leave you on your own?"

"Said we know what we're doing now. Said we done good."

"Yeah, if you wanted to discredit the strikers and Dr. King."

"Dr. King. He ain't nothing but an old man with old ideas."

"He's as old as Withers."

Joe's eyelids narrowed. His skin was sallow and his fingernails dirty. He smelled like he hadn't bathed in a long time. Maybe I was wrong. Maybe he still was doing drugs.

"You don't know nothing, man."

"I know trouble when I see it."

"You keep saying that, but you don't do nothing. That's what you're all about. Not doing nothing."

"Except taking care of your brother," I said.

Joe raised his chin. He was slightly taller than I was. I had to look up. "I ain't got a brother no more."

"But you do, Joe, no matter how much you deny it."

Joe's eyes narrowed, and for the first time, I saw the bluster fade. He glanced over his shoulder as if he thought he were being watched, then he leaned into me again. Only this time, there was no menace about it.

"It's better for the kid to stay away," he said. "Smokey, this is bad shit. It ain't no place for Jimmy."

"It isn't any place for you either."

"Yeah, it is. It's the first place I belonged. But that don't make it right, what they was making Jimmy do."

"So he was delivering drugs for you."

"I told you, man. It wasn't about no drugs. It was about money."

"You're selling drugs to make money?"

He shrugged. "It's quick."

"It's no place for Jimmy."

"That's what I'm telling you, man." He glanced behind me, as if he were trying to make sure we weren't being watched, and leaned just a bit closer. Then he whispered,

"That's why I don't want to see Jimmy no more. They want little kids to run the stuff because little kids don't get stopped."

"You're protecting him?"

"Yeah."

"And you don't think this is bad for you."

"I'm old enough to make my own choices. And this is my choice, Smokey." Then he leaned back and glowered again. "You got that, man?"

"I do," I said. "I could haul your ass out of here, get you some help."

"I'd jus' come back. I'm telling you, man, this is where I belong."

"It'll kill you, Joe."

"Life'll kill me, Smokey."

I stared at him for a moment. I've had this moment with friends before. He wasn't going to change. I couldn't make him. But I had to try one last time, give him one last chance. "What do I tell Jimmy?"

"Tell him to stop looking for me. He's a pest and he don't belong in this mess. Tell him to leave me alone. If I ever want to see him again, I'll find him." Then Joe turned and hurried off.

I stood in the middle of the path. The scrape-scrape-scrape of the grave diggers' shovels was my only company. Joe ran to the road and disappeared.

TWENTY-FIVE

Joe had left Jimmy to me, and I didn't know how to face it. How do you tell a boy whose mother abandoned him that his brother wanted nothing to do with him either? I asked Henry, and he had no words for me except an offer to go with me.

But I knew it was something I had to do alone. Something I had to do carefully or Jimmy would blame me instead of Joe. I called Selina Nelson while Jimmy was still in school and warned her. She offered to tell him too, and I refused. Better to have him hate me for telling him the news than to have him hate the first people to care for him in a long, long time.

I went to the Nelsons' after school let out for the day. The weather was horrible—unseasonably warm, humid, and rainy, with severe thunderstorms predicted for the evening. We'd been having a lousy spring in all ways. The radio told me that Judge Bailey Brown had, at the request of the city's attorney, granted a temporary restraining order, preventing Friday's march. He would have a hearing on the matter Thursday morning.

Henry had told me that Martin's people would have training sessions in nonviolent techniques Friday before the march. When I spoke to Henry, I asked if those plans had been changed. He promised to get back to me.

Martin was supposed to fly in that day and give a speech that night. As the clouds in the sky grew darker and darker, I wondered if he had indeed made it or if he had been delayed, just as he had been on the twenty-eighth. But it didn't matter as much this time. He was arriving early to take care of things before the march started.

If the march started.

Henry was right. This time, they wouldn't need me.

I wondered if the weather was delaying Laura's flight as well. Yesterday, she had said she'd take the first plane to Memphis. I hadn't heard from her yet.

Of course, I had been out of my office all day. Part of me wondered if that was intentional.

I pulled up in front of the Nelsons', and this time Selina was watching out the window. The rain was coming down in sheets, and I ran from the car to the house. When I got inside, I shook the water off and let her take my coat.

"Is he upstairs?" I asked.

She nodded. "I haven't told him you're coming."

I took the steps two at a time. When I reached the top, I went to Jimmy's bedroom. He was sprawled on the bed, a battered history textbook open before him. When he saw me, he smiled.

The smile faded when I didn't smile back.

"You okay?" he said.

"Yeah."

"Is Joe?"

I shook my head. I sat on the edge of the bed, and Jimmy scrambled into a sitting position.

"What's wrong?" he asked.

My heart was pounding. I didn't know how to tell him. "He's—with the wrong people," I said.

"I *know*."

"No," I said. "You don't. He doesn't want to see you."

Jimmy leaned back as if I had slapped him. "Why not?"

"He's afraid. Afraid for you."

"But he could come here. He could—"

"He doesn't want to leave them. He says he likes being in the group."

Jimmy frowned, as if the information made no sense. "But if he don't want to leave them and don't want me there, then when do I see him?"

"When he's ready."

"When's that?"

I shook my head. "I tried to talk to him, Jimmy. He doesn't listen anymore."

"No," Jimmy whispered. "We're family."

"He says you have a new family now."

"No." Jimmy's voice rose. "I just live here. He could live here too."

"He doesn't want to."

"*You* say."

"He says."

"He should tell me himself."

I managed a small, rueful smile. "That's what I told him."

"And?"

"He did, Jimmy. By leaving you alone."

"*No*." Jimmy shoved me, nearly knocking me off the bed. "You lie."

I stood. "I'm not lying, Jimmy."

"You are too. You hate Joe and you're lying. You just want me to stay here."

"I do want you to stay here. You're safe here."

"I hate it here. I *hate* it. I don't want to stay. I want to go to Joe."

I shook my head. "He's in a gang, now, Jimmy, and it's not safe for you. He knows it. He's afraid they'll use you like they did before."

"They didn't use me," Jimmy said. "I offered. So I could stay."

"That's not what you told me when you came to see me at my office. You wanted me to get you out, get Joe out."

"And you *didn't*."

"That's right," I said, crouching so that I was at his eye-level. "I couldn't help Joe."

He stared at me for a long moment, then he slammed his history book shut. "Get out."

"Jimmy, I can—"

"Getoutgetoutgetout."

"Jimmy, you can always call me. I'll try to keep track of Joe—"

"Get out!" He screamed that last so loud that his face turned red and little bits of spittle caught on his lips.

I backed away. I didn't know what else to do. "I'm sorry."

But he didn't seem to hear me. He had flung himself face down on the bed and was pounding it with his fists and feet. Selina was running up the stairs. She shot me an apologetic look and then went to him.

"You'd better go," she said as she hurried across the floor. And, coward that I was, I did.

I drove aimlessly for a while, not sure of where to go or what to do. Jimmy's reaction had shaken me more than I cared to admit. I had thought the boy would at least talk to me. But he didn't. It seemed no one did.

The weather was growing worse, and the severe storm warning had been upgraded to a tornado watch. I found myself outside the Mason Temple along with camera crews from the Memphis stations as well as CBS, NBC, and ABC. They were expecting Martin.

I almost left. Somehow, in the back of my mind, I had thought the crowd would be small because of the rain, and I might be able to talk to Martin, about Joe, about Jimmy, maybe even about Laura. But when I saw the camera crews there, I knew that I wouldn't get a chance.

Still, I couldn't bring myself to drive away. I slipped inside and discovered that the crowd was indeed small. Thunder boomed, and lightening flashed, and a few people looked around nervously. I took a seat toward the back. Henry was up front. He smiled at me, then raised his eyebrows in question.

I shook my head.

As I did, Ralph Abernathy walked up to the pulpit, followed by Jesse Jackson. The crowd stared at them. They had been expecting Martin. I had been expecting Martin, and I was disappointed. Dr. Abernathy stared at us for a moment, then held up a hand and went to one of the ministers in the front. Then they disappeared through a side door.

The pew was wood and unpadded, uncomfortable against my butt. It had been a long time since I had sat down in a sanctuary. Since I was a boy. I used to refuse to accompany my foster mother, saying that church did no good.

Only I was wrong. In the black community, in my community, the church was a power for good. Martin knew that. His lieutenants did too. So did Henry.

I saw Henry stir, and I knew that if I wasn't careful, he would come to me. I didn't want to talk yet. I was numb. I closed my eyes and saw Jimmy's angry flop on the bed, Laura's confusion and disappointment. And her face as she cooked me breakfast.

Her beautiful face.

Then applause started around me, happy, joyous applause. I turned and saw a tired Martin walk down the aisle. His stride was purposeful, his manner confident. He looked nothing like the man I'd helped escape from the riot only a week before.

He didn't see me in the corner. He went to the pulpit and looked out at all of us. Only then did his gaze fall on me. His eyes widened with slight surprise. I was not known for attending Martin's speeches—at least, not as a simple listener.

That night, he was inspired.

He talked about how great it was to be alive, how wonderful life was, even when it was full of trials, and then he spoke to me. Or so it seemed.

And I remember every word. He said:

"Let us develop a dangerous unselfishness."

And then he told the story of the Good Samaritan, told it in a way I'd never heard it before, full of sympathy and warmth for the men on the road to Jericho who had passed the injured man by. But, Martin said, they asked the wrong question. They asked, 'If I help this man, what will happen to me?' instead of asking, 'If I don't help this man, what will happen to him?'

"That's the question before you tonight. Not, 'If I stop to help the sanitation workers, what will happen to all the hours that I usually spend in my office every day and every week as a pastor?' The question is not, 'If I stop to help this man in need, what will happen to me?' 'If I do not stop to help the sanitation workers, what will happen to them?' That's the question."

And his words still ring through my head, not the words that everyone quotes, but his words about helping others in need. People I had been turning my back on. Jimmy and Joe.

My own community. I had skills that could help them, skills we could use.

"Let us develop a dangerous unselfishness."

And let us do it now.

I left keyed up and full of resolve, more alive than I had been in weeks. I spoke briefly to Martin, but he was tired, and we weren't able to talk alone. Others crowded him, wanting his time. Reporters shoved toward him, wanting to know how he felt about the march, about Johnson's announcement, about the future of the Poor People's Campaign.

So after a few moments, I moved around the edge of the crowd and walked to my car. Halfway there, I stopped and looked up. The rain was still coming down in sheets. The thunder rumbled, but far away now. Looking up at the rain gave it a whole new perspective: the drops had a symmetry, a beauty I had never noticed before. I didn't mind getting wet. I liked seeing things anew.

A dangerous unselfishness.

I smiled and ran the rest of the way to my car. At first I couldn't identify what I was feeling, the sensation was so unfamiliar. It wasn't until I arrived at home that I actually knew.

I was feeling hope.

TWENTY-SIX

But hope is a fragile thing. And the next day, as I waited for Laura, the hope slowly faded.

I went to my office early, full of an energy I hadn't had since the march a week before. I called the number Laura gave me and left a message with her service to have her contact me. Then I called Selina Nelson and asked how Jimmy was doing. He had cried himself to sleep, she said, and was quiet before he left for school that morning. It would take him time to get over this, but she was sure that it was for the best.

I was sure of that too. Jimmy was looking healthier and stronger, and Joe's deepening involvement in the Black Power movement did neither of them any good.

Then I started to call old clients, touching base and making sure that everything was all right. I avoided calling Henry; I figured if he needed me, he would contact me.

It was well after lunch when there was a soft knock on my door. I was sorting papers. I didn't even look up as I called, "Come in."

The door opened and Laura entered. She was wearing her rabbit fur coat, blue jeans, and those white kid boots. It was as if she were dressed in a mixture of styles on purpose—

the jeans as a nod to me, and the rest to keep her own identity.

I took in all of that in an instant. I stopped when I saw her—all of me, literally, from my breath to my heart to my legs. It took me a moment to recover.

During that moment, she didn't move.

"I was beginning to think I'd never hear from you again," I said.

"You had severe weather," she said. "I couldn't leave Chicago until this morning."

"How are you?" I asked.

"A little cold," she said. "The hallway's chilly."

I looked pointedly at her and then at the door, and she got the message. She closed it softly and stepped inside.

Despite the fluffy rabbit coat, she looked as if she had lost weight. Her face was haggard and drawn, her skin sallow. I was torn between the desire to touch her and the need to punish her parents.

As usual, my office was an oven, waves of heat spilling from the radiator. But she didn't remove her coat. She was hugging it to her body as if it were a lifeline.

"You'll melt," I said.

"I'm not planning on staying long enough."

I set down the papers I was holding. "You might want to."

"You were very clear on that phone call—"

"I was angry," I said. "I just found out why my parents were lynched."

Her cheeks were bright red, her eyes glistening. Her hands crept up to the collar of the fur and held it closed. "Because of me."

I shook my head. "Because of your parents. Your adoptive parents, or whatever the hell you want to call them."

"How can you be sure?" Her voice was high and wispy like a little girl's. "How can you know that they did it?"

Instead of answering her, I went to my safe, spun the combination lock, and clicked the door open. I took out the accordion file, took it to my desk, and pulled out the clippings file. Then I spread that on the desktop and searched until I found the article I was looking for.

It was the one with the photograph of her parents, her real parents, Ross and Susan Ratledge. I handed it to her.

Laura let go of the collar with one hand and kept the other around her neck. She took the yellowed newspaper and stared at it for a moment. All the color left her face.

"That looks like me," she whispered.

I nodded.

"But Smokey . . ." She took two hesitant steps to the desk and placed the clipping on top of the file. She shook her head and her eyes welled with tears. "Smokey, God forgive me, but how do we know that your parents didn't take me and my parents somehow—"

"Rescued you?" The words came out harsher than I wanted. "My parents didn't run. They had two days. They thought they would be fine. Does that sound like guilty behavior to you? My parents didn't change their name. My parents didn't have a criminal record. My parents hadn't vowed revenge on the Ratledges. My parents—"

"All right," she said, her voice breaking. "You've got to understand how hard this is for me."

"For you?" I leaned forward on my desk. "For *you?*"

"Yes," she whispered. "I don't even know who I am any more."

I almost went to her. Almost took her in my arms. Almost held the woman whose parents, the people who raised her, took my parents' lives and tried to give me a pittance in return.

But I couldn't. Despite what I'd felt during Martin's speech the night before, despite my new resolve, I couldn't comfort Laura.

"You're Laura Hathaway," I said, my voice cold. "Daughter of Earl and Dora Jean Hathaway, one of Chicago's richest couples."

She shook her head. "You can stop that. You could let me go on and then blackmail me."

"Who fed you that shit? One of your advisors?"

"No." Her free hand had gone back to her collar.

"You thought that up all on your own?" I was more offended than I should have been. "Don't you remember the promise I made you? I said you could walk away at any time, and only the two of us would know. I promised you that."

"But things are different now."

"Not those things, not for me," I said. "I keep my promises."

She looked longingly at the file on my desk. God, I could read her. I could read her like I hadn't been able to read anyone in my entire life. She didn't want to believe me. She wanted to examine the material for herself, and even then she wanted me to be wrong.

"Go ahead and look at it," I said as I rounded the desk, keeping my distance from her. I grabbed my coat. "It'll take you a while, so I'll step out. Remember something else, though. I promised the man who gave me this file that I would bring it all back to him. *All* of it. And I keep my promises."

She nodded. She was miserable, and I was doing this wrong. Only I was miserable too. I didn't really want to soothe her. I wanted her to know what it felt like, to have the world shift and change without a moment's notice.

I slipped on the coat and left the office, slamming the door behind me. I wasn't hungry, but I went to the King's Palace anyway. They usually left me alone there, and I wasn't in the mood to chat. I ordered coffee and a piece of pie, then proceeded to pick at it while I brooded.

I had never felt like this before, so confused and tangled

that I couldn't find any way out of my own emotions. Most of them were directed at Laura. Part of me wanted to take her back to my house and keep her there forever, telling her that this didn't matter, we'd see it through, and part of me wanted to hurt her so badly that she would never look at another man again.

I was frightening myself, and I didn't know how to stop.

I gave her an hour. Then I went back to the office, shaking with a caffeine high and the cold.

Laura was still at my desk, but she had her head buried in her arms, her golden hair spilling around her shoulders. Her coat was in a pile on the floor. She didn't raise her head when the door opened, and for one heart-stopping moment I wondered if she had done something foolish.

I let the door close softly, but at the click she stirred and looked up. Her hair was as messy as it had been when she woke up that Friday morning, the first morning, but she looked nothing like that woman. Her eyes were red-rimmed, her face lined.

This time I went over to her, and she rose, falling into my arms. I held her and she held me and neither of us moved for a long, long time.

I should have kissed her then, but I didn't. There still remained a chunk of ice in my heart. Eventually she let me go and wiped her face with the back of her hand, like a child.

Neither of us seemed to want to speak. Finally, she said, "I think I have to go to Atlanta."

"You can forget about it, pretend you don't know," I said.

She bent down, picked up her coat, and flung it over my chair. "Can you?"

Of course not. That was what I was struggling with. But I didn't say so. "Those people, they're just your biological parents. They named you Scarlett."

"And went to the *Gone with the Wind* premiere in Confederate costumes owned by some family member. I know."

Her smile was small and didn't go to her eyes. "But it doesn't matter *who* they are. It matters *that* they are. Do you know what I mean?"

The hell of it was, I did. She had to do this. She started this odyssey with her mother's death, and damn her, she would take it to the very end.

"What do you want me to do?" I asked.

"Come with me." The small smile faded. "But you won't, will you?"

I shook my head.

She blinked hard. Her eyes were still red. "I'm not—I didn't intend this," she said. "I didn't know."

"I know that, Laura. But it doesn't matter. It happened."

"To them," she whispered.

"To me," I said. "I took your mother's money."

"Oh." She sat on the chair, on the coat, and tried to pretend that she wasn't uncomfortable. "And you think that implicates you somehow."

"Doesn't it? I knew there was something wrong with that money then."

"She was trying to make amends."

"You can't pay for a person's life." This time, I managed to get the words out without acrimony. "They weren't the best parents, but they were mine, and they died horribly. My cousin told me it took them hours to die, judging from the condition of their bodies. Tortured to death, Laura. Tortured."

"Because of me."

"Not you," I said. "Your parents."

"I'll bet they didn't know," she said. "I'll bet they were appalled when they found out."

"I'll bet you're right," I said.

She lowered her eyes. "It doesn't make things better, does it?"

I shook my head.

"And the rest of the money, you don't want it, do you?"

"No."

"But it's yours, legally. Can't you start some fund or something?"

"You start it, Laura. And put in the money I send you as well. I'll pay the other back."

"You can't afford it, Smokey."

It was my turn to smile. "Sure I can."

She raised her head. She thought I was bluffing. She thought I would hurt myself to return that money.

She was right.

"I don't want it," she said.

I shrugged. "It doesn't matter what you want, Laura. It's the right thing."

She stood, removed the coat, and clutched it over her arm, much as she had done that first day we met. She looked as uncomfortable too, but more miserable. "When this money isn't between us, Smokey, do you think—"

I put my finger over her mouth. Then I ran it over her lips, caressing them, and touched the softness of her skin. I wasn't sure I'd ever do that again. "You need to go to Atlanta without me," I said. "You need to see your real family and make your own decisions."

She closed her eyes, but leaned into my touch. "Maybe I want to stay here."

"I don't want you here," I said gently. "Not until you're done with this."

Then she kissed my palm and moved her face out of my grasp. She opened her eyes, and for the first time since I had returned, they were clear. "And what about you, Smokey? When will you be done with this?"

It was a good question.

I had no answer for her.

TWENTY-SEVEN

I stood at my window and watched her walk across Beale Street. She didn't look back. She made her way toward Union and the Peabody and I wondered if I would ever see her again.

It was nearly six. I supposed I should go home, make myself dinner, maybe read a bit, but I didn't feel like it. I didn't feel like doing anything.

Then the phone rang.

I turned and picked it up, thinking it was one of the clients I had called earlier, or maybe Henry with a request that I come to dinner.

Instead, Selina Nelson said, "I'm sorry to bother you, but I can't find Jimmy. I was wondering if he's with you."

"No, he's not," I said, feeling the inside of my stomach twist.

"He went to school," she said. "But one of his little classmates said Jimmy wasn't there the last hour. I think he's looking for Joe."

I closed my eyes. That was what I would do. I would try to find my brother and see if the words reported to me were true. Why hadn't I seen Jimmy's action coming?

"I'm sorry," I said. "I should have thought this through."

"It's not just you," she said. "I've been taking care of children through the church for nearly ten years now. You'd think I'd know too."

"Well," I said, sighing. "Here's what I suggest. Call Henry and have him get a group together of as many people as he can find. You got paper?"

"Yes," she said.

"Here's a list of places that Jimmy might search." I rattled off the names of the places I had been over the last week, places I had told Jimmy about, places where Joe had been seen, or had hung out. Selina Nelson asked me to slow down, and as I did, I heard shouting from the street below.

Male shouting, angry shouting. A woman wailed.

"Something's going on," I said to Selina. "Hold on a minute."

I went to the dirty window and peered out. I saw people milling in the street, their bodies shadowy against the age-old grime. The street had been nearly empty just a few minutes ago.

What had happened?

One woman fell to her knees, her arms stretched above her head in supplication. Horns were blaring, and the shouting continued.

I went back to the phone. "Selina, can I call you back?"

"I'm not sure I'll be here," she said. "But I think this is enough to start. Is everything all right there?"

"I don't know," I said. "Something's going on. After I find out what it is, I'll start looking for Jimmy. I'll call you if I hear anything."

"I'll make sure someone does the same for you," she said, and we hung up.

I grabbed my coat and ran out of my office, slamming the door behind me. I took the stairs four at a time and was on the street within seconds.

A man had his face in his hands and was leaning against the brick of the Gallina Building. Another man was shaking his head, and a woman was sobbing so hard that it seemed like she couldn't get any air.

"What is it?" I said, grabbing one of the employees of Schwab's who was standing in the middle of the sidewalk looking lost.

"Didn't you hear the gunshots?" she asked. "Down at the Lorraine. They say Dr. King was shot."

"Who says?"

"Everybody. They been running through the street, shouting it."

The man's voice I had heard while I was talking to Selina. I hadn't heard the gunshots—the Gallina was too well built to pick up a sound from several blocks away—but it was possible. It was possible.

"I knew," she said. "I knew something was going to happen when they gave his room number last night on the evening news."

I focused on her. "What?"

"The news. They announced that Dr. King was in town and staying at the Lorraine, and then they said what room number he had."

"Oh, shit," I said. Those white sons of bitches. They'd finally nailed him.

I didn't even thank her. My brain had shifted from Jimmy and Laura and the speech to Martin. If we lost Martin, then what?

Then what?

I ran down to the end of the block and turned on Second, going the same way Joe had gone after he had tried to rob Capital Loans. Other people were running with me, their faces blank or full of a vain hope. Sirens echoed all over the neighborhood, and police were beginning to appear like magic. There had to be fifty already. At Linden, I followed the crowd west to Mulberry, and more and more people joined us.

Mulberry was already blocked off, mostly with cars. Several firefighters from the nearby station were hauling barricades. I slipped past them. At the Lorraine Motel, an ambulance was just pulling out. There were police all over the balcony, in front of the main doors, and in the parking lot. Some were holding rifles and a few were pointing. On the street below, two of King's friends were talking to an officer who wasn't taking notes.

It was true then.

It was true.

I felt as if I had been shot in the gut. I doubled over, unable to catch my breath. Someone took my arm, and I shook him off. Then the grip came again, firmer.

I looked up. It was a white officer wearing black horn-rimmed glasses. He had an unlit cigarette in his mouth and a rifle in his left hand. He was holding me tightly with his right. He was maybe thirty years old and just beginning to get a paunch. I could take him if I needed to.

"This area's restricted," he said.

"Who was shot?" I asked.

"King."

No title of respect, no nothing. Just King.

I was shaking. "Did you get the shooter?"

"You have to leave," the officer said, his grip tightening.

Officers were standing on all sides of the street but didn't seem to be doing anything. Others were removing bystanders. Near the fire station at the other end of the block, I saw two officers struggle to shove a little boy in a squad car.

The little boy had his hands splayed on the side of the car, and he was shouting. He turned his head slightly.

It was Jimmy.

"I'll leave," I said, as calmly as I could to the cop holding me.

Jimmy was fighting so hard that one of the cops yelled for another. More people slipped past the makeshift barricade. If the cops didn't have the shooter, finding him now might be impossible.

"Just let go of me and I'll walk out of here," I said to the cop.

I must have said it with enough force because he let me go. I started to turn to throw him off, make him believe I was leaving the restricted area. Then I switched directions and ran down the middle of Mulberry toward Jimmy.

Cops reached for me. I dodged through them. It was only a few yards to Jimmy, and it only took me a moment to cover the distance. No one seemed too concerned about me, or the others who were infiltrating the crime scene. I'd never seen such passive police.

Except for the ones fighting with Jimmy. I didn't hesitate. I got to Jimmy's side, elbowed one cop in the stomach, and shoved the other away.

A third came toward me, and I kicked him before he could get close. The driver of the squad car started to get out, but by then I had Jimmy's arm.

"We're getting out of here," I yelled.

He didn't have a chance to respond. I yanked him forward, and we cut down Butler to Second. I was running, and Jimmy was struggling to keep up. Half the time I pulled him along. The cops were following us this time and yelling. One pointed a gun at Jimmy, and I dodged into a group of people, hoping no cop would be stupid enough to fire into a throng of innocents.

I pushed our way through and onto Second. When we got there, we found chaos. A growing crowd watched, and more cops milled. I had never seen so many cops in my life. It was as if they had been there already, as if they had been waiting for something.

The cops behind us shouted and pointed at Jimmy. I glanced over my shoulder just in time to see that and the communication that went from those cops to the ones in front of us. Some leveled weapons at us.

Jesus, I thought. They think Jimmy killed him?

I pulled the kid as hard as I could. The bystanders were beginning to realize something was happening, and they formed a group between us and the cops. A man who looked vaguely familiar tried to shove us toward a VW Bug, but I refused to go. I wasn't going to accept help from anyone I didn't know. We wove our way through the crowd, and others started running off in different directions, some of them grown men with kids.

They were helping us. They were acting as decoys, even though they didn't know what happened. It was an axiom down here: if a black man was running from cops, he needed protection.

I thanked a god I wasn't sure I believed in for that.

Jimmy and I took advantage of the decoys to get us to Vance and then Third. There we stopped.

No one was following us any longer. We had lost the police.

I was breathing hard, and Jimmy was breathing harder. I gave us a moment to catch our breath. It had grown dark. The sirens were still wailing, but at a distance now, and I suspected that was only the beginning.

"Take off your cap," I said when I could, "and give it to me. Then turn your coat inside out."

Jimmy didn't ask any questions. He was clearly terrified. He took off his cap and gave it to me. I stuffed it in the pocket of my jacket. Then he removed his coat, and we turned it inside out.

"When we walk, put your head down, and if someone stops us, make like you've been crying. All right?"

"We're gonna walk?" he said, his voice trembling.

"Yeah," I said. "Running's too suspicious."

It was a wonder we hadn't been shot, considering how trigger-happy police usually were after an incident like that. I walked us down Third all the way back to Beale. People were standing in the streets, many clutching transistor radios, listening for news. As Jimmy and I walked, we learned that Martin had been taken to St. Joseph's Hospital and that police were still searching for a suspect.

The crowd, at this point, was strangely hushed, and we were too as we walked. It wasn't until we had turned on Beale and were almost to my car that someone screamed, "He's dead!"

A woman held her transistor up, and the voice of the announcer repeated the information.

Screams started again, and this time, it was as if everything broke. People began shouting, some shoved each other, still more cried. The place was going to erupt again, and I had to get Jimmy out of there.

I shoved him into the passenger seat of my car, then got into the driver's side and started it almost before I was settled in. I drove through the crowd slowly so that people would move, and they hit my hood, shaking the entire vehicle. When we could finally break free, I turned onto a side road.

Jimmy turned on the radio, and the news was being repeated. Martin was pronounced dead at 7:05 P.M. at St. Joseph's Hospital. We listened on the drive, watching as people poured out of their houses, their businesses, their cars, as if they couldn't remain inside with the news.

Already there were reports of breaking windows on Union and claims that someone had started a fire downtown. I shut off the radio, not ready to process the news yet, and drove toward home.

My neighborhood was silent. Either no one had arrived home, or everyone had left. I got Jimmy out of the car and helped him up the stairs and into the house. I didn't turn on any lights in the front, only in the kitchen. I didn't want anyone to know we were there.

"You all right?" I asked.

"Yeah," he said. But he didn't look all right. His face was

gray and his eyes luminous. He perched on the edge of a chair as if he expected me to make him get up.

"You want something?" I asked, even though I didn't know how he could eat, not now.

"Water," he said.

I got him a glass and then poured myself one too. I was thirsty and hadn't realized it. I was still shaking, and part of my mind was trying to deal with the day's events. I focused on Jimmy. It was easier.

"What happened?" I asked.

"They said they wanted to shut me up."

"Who, the police?"

He nodded and looked away.

"Why were you there?"

"I was looking for Joe."

My mistake. I had told him that I had searched for Joe in that area, in the Canipe Amusement Company on South Main. That explained why Jimmy was there, but it still didn't explain how I found him and why the police wanted him. "And what happened, Jimmy, that the police got you?"

"I went to them." His voice was so soft that it was a whisper. He had my attention now. Jimmy knew better than to go to the police.

"Why?"

He raised his head, took a deep shuddery breath, and said, "I seen it. I was in this lot across from the motel, and there were these guys, sitting on some cardboard, and they say, 'Hey look, it's King.' So I look up, and there was Mr. King—"

"Dr. King," I said, automatically.

"Dr. King," Jimmy said, allowing the correction, "and then I heard this shot right behind me. This guy jumps out from the bushes and he runs across the lot in front of me, and I don't get to see his face, and as he's running, he's taking his gun apart. When he gets to the corner of the lot,

305

he throws part of the gun into some bushes, and puts the rest in his jacket. Then he jumps into the street and starts to walk like nothing's happened."

I was cold. I watched Jimmy. His eyes were bloodshot and staring down at the water glass as he spoke. It was as if he were seeing it all over again.

"And I seen them men on the balcony with Mr.—Dr. King and they was pointing at me, and he was on the ground, and I go to them bushes and I see the gun barrel, and I think somebody's got to know."

I made myself take a sip from my glass. My hand was shaking so hard that I could barely raise it to my face. I brought the glass back down.

"So I go to the fire station, and there's these white guys there, and I tell them, 'I seen the guy,' and they pull me into this corner and start asking me questions like what did I see and who I was and where did I live."

"Did you answer them?"

"Sure," he said. "But they didn't go nowhere, and they didn't tell nobody, and then they tell me to wait, and finally these other guys, the ones you saw, come and get me. And the first guys says, 'He seen stuff he shouldn't have,' and the others say that they'll shut me up."

"All this in front of you?"

He shook his head. "Off to the side where they think I can't hear, but I heard 'em good enough. Before I can get out of there, they grab me and take me to their car. I fought 'em, Smokey. I fought 'em real hard, but I didn't think they'd let me go. Then you came."

His voice trembled at that last.

"What did you think was going to happen to you?"

"I dunno," he whispered.

"What did you see that you weren't supposed to see?"

"I dunno that either," he said. "Only, there were a lot of cops there, weren't there, Smokey? For that part of town? Joe used to like it there because there wasn't any cops."

I hadn't been thinking clearly. But he was right. There were too many cops, and too soon. I had gotten to Mulberry by six-twenty, no later, and the place was crawling with police. They shouldn't have arrived yet, at least not in those numbers, not even with the fire station nearby.

"What do you think was going on, Jimmy?" I asked.

He raised his eyes to me. "They didn't act scared, Smokey," he said. "It was like they knew something was gonna happen. It was like they knew."

TWENTY-EIGHT

I stood. If the killing of Martin had been planned, as Jimmy said, then Jimmy's life was in danger. He had seen the shooter, and he had told the police both who he was and where he lived.

I held up a finger to him, indicating that he should remain quiet, then I picked up the phone and dialed Selina Nelson.

"It's Smokey," I said, without much preamble. "Do you know what's happening?"

"It's horrible," she said, her voice thick. "And Jimmy's still missing."

"You haven't found him yet?"

"No, and I can't find anyone to look. They're all busy. My husband's out now, but I'm worried. They say that looting is going on."

"I know," I said. "I saw it start."

"Smokey," she lowered her voice. "The police were just here. They wanted Jimmy."

I felt the hair on the nape of my neck stand up. "What for?"

"I don't know. They wouldn't say. What are they doing here with the whole city coming apart?"

Good question, and one I couldn't answer. "What did you tell them?"

"Only that he's been missing since this afternoon."

"Nothing about Joe?"

"A little, but that's all."

"Not anything else?"

"No," she said.

"Good. Keep it that way. I'll call when I have news." And I hung up. Jimmy was watching me.

"She'll worry," he said.

"I know," I said and bit back the rest of it. If he had stayed home, like I asked, instead of looking for Joe by himself, then everything would have been all right. If he had stayed home. But he hadn't. "You realize this is serious, don't you, Jimmy?"

He nodded.

"You will do everything I tell you?"

He nodded again.

"All right," I said. Sirens flared and died nearby. I tensed. "If someone comes to the door, you hide in my closet, and you don't make a sound. You got me?"

"Yes," he whispered.

And for the first time, I wished this house had a cubby behind the closet like the house I grew up in in Atlanta. There was no perfect hiding place here. But then, no one would drag me off either. They weren't looking for me, they were looking for Jimmy, and I would bet that most of the search would wait until things in Memphis calmed down.

Still, for good measure, I closed all my curtains, made Jimmy stay low, and turned on the television rather loud. I got him to the couch and let him rest there while I took the easy chair near the window. My shape could be viewed there, and it would look, to anyone observing, like I was watching television alone.

Before I sat down, I got my gun and placed it on the end

table beside me. Better to be safe. And I had no idea what exactly safe was.

"There's not much more we can do tonight," I said to Jimmy. "The city's going to be locked down. But be prepared to do what I tell you tomorrow, all right?"

He nodded from his position on the couch, looking more frightened than I had ever seen him.

"Smokey," he asked in a very small voice, "did I do something wrong?"

"That's the hell of it, Jimmy," I said, wishing the world were different. "You did everything right."

The entire country erupted that night. People poured into the streets in over a hundred cities. Fires burned in Harlem, Detroit, and Baltimore. In Washington, D.C., whole sections of the city burned. Stokely Carmichael—who had been there all along, not here as reported—urged blacks to go home and get guns. The white media reported the white deaths— a man dragged from his car and beaten; the shooting of the white neighbor of a black man in Minneapolis who had sworn to kill the next white he saw—but they underreported the black deaths, which were often at the hands of police.

In Memphis, four thousand National Guard troops stationed themselves all over the city. The riots, looting, and fires were horrible, but only lasted the night. In Washington, Chicago, and other cities, they continued into the next day.

Jimmy fell into a fitful sleep on the couch, and I watched the television until all the stations went off the air. I thought of calling Laura, but I had no idea what I would say to her.

So I turned on the radio and sat guard all night, listening to the reports filtering in and the sirens that echoed around us. Once I thought I saw burning in the distance, but I wasn't sure. In any case, it seemed to be gone within a short period of time.

The hope I'd awakened with that morning had died as if it had never been. I had only felt this way once before in my life—when my parents died. And then, as now, I was helpless to do anything about it. The only difference was now, I had a young boy in my care. A boy who needed me.

At eight o'clock the following morning, Memphis was quiet. The sirens were gone, the rioters dispersed. The television news gave me a rehash of the assassination, and none of the details sounded like the ones that Jimmy told me. They also reported on the chaos all over the country, the violent response to the death of a man who believed in nonviolence above all.

I almost put my own gun away. I didn't need it after all. No one had caught up to us yet. Then I had second thoughts. With my plan, I might need it. I rummaged in my drawers until I found the shoulder holster and put it on, slipping the gun in it. Then I put a shirt over it. Normally I wouldn't have risked carrying a concealed weapon, but things were normal no longer.

Jimmy still slept on the couch, covered in a blanket I had pulled off my bed. I figured that he should sleep as long as he needed to. The next few days would be difficult on him. I already had a plan.

Unlike my parents, I wasn't going to assume that because no one had come, no one would. I wasn't going to wait around for someone in authority to come after Jimmy. I was going to get him out of here. Then we would decide what else needed doing.

I called Henry and asked him to come over.

"Do you know what's going on, Smokey?" he asked. "I can't come there."

"You have to," I said.

"There's going to be a press conference this morning, and they need help with the arrangements—"

"No, Henry," I said. "You need to come here."

"Smokey—"

"Did the police visit you last night?"

"At the church," he said.

"And they weren't asking about Martin, were they?"

"No." He drew the word out, and as he did, I heard the moment when he understood me.

"Be here as soon as you can," I said and hung up.

By the time Henry arrived, Jimmy was up and in the shower. I was making the last of my eggs and had coffee percolating on the stove. The shower shut off just as Henry knocked. I had given Jimmy some old clothes of mine. They wouldn't fit, but they would do.

I let Henry in. He looked fifteen years older and more tired than I had ever seen him. He hadn't slept either.

"The whole world has ended," he said.

It felt that way. I had no response.

"Come into the kitchen," I said.

Jimmy was out of the shower, his hair still glistening wet, my Boston University sweatshirt, which he wore, damp at the shoulders. I served him some eggs, offered some to Henry, who declined, and gave them both coffee. Then I poured myself a cup and sat.

"I need you to stay with Jimmy, Henry," I said. "Don't let anyone in and don't tell anyone he's here."

"What happened?" Henry asked.

"Jimmy can tell you after I've left." I leaned forward. "We've got to get out of Memphis before he gets traced to me, and he will get traced to me."

"Smokey—"

"You'll understand soon enough," I said.

"Where are you going?" Jimmy asked, and he sounded scared.

"To my office. We need money to travel on, and I don't have it here."

"I can give you some," Henry said.

"It won't be enough." Having something to concentrate on kept me fresh. I felt more alive than I had since I learned of Martin's death. As long as I focused on Jimmy, I'd be all right.

"You're coming back to Memphis, aren't you?"

"I don't know," I said.

"But Joe—" Jimmy started.

"Joe wanted me to keep you safe," I said. "That's what I'm doing. If you stay in town, you know what will happen."

Jimmy's eyes filled, but he said nothing. Henry put a hand on his shoulder.

"I'm counting on you, Henry," I said. "He has to stay here."

Henry nodded.

"One more thing," I said. "Call Selina. Tell her, somehow, to put Jimmy's things in a bag and leave them at the church. Do that without using his name. We'll drop you there on our way out of town."

"But I brought my car."

"Have someone come back for it."

Henry blinked hard, as if he were trying to force himself to concentrate, and then he said, "This is bad, isn't it?"

I nodded. "If I don't get Jimmy out of here, I can't guarantee he'll live a week."

Jimmy raised his head at that.

"I'm sorry," I said. "It's true, and you know it."

He closed his eyes. "I know."

I nodded, then stood. I put a hand on his other shoulder. "Tell Henry," I said softly. "When he sees Joe, he'll explain. Believe me, Joe will understand too."

And then I left.

A thick cloud of smoke hung over Memphis. There had been more fires than the radio had reported. Entire sections of the city were destroyed. National Guard troops once again patrolled in tanks.

There were very few cars on the road, but I was startled to see airplanes circling the airport. Life was still going on.

It was hard to believe. It did feel, as Henry had said, as if the world had ended.

I wondered if Laura was in one of those planes, heading to Atlanta. Off to meet people who probably were happy that Martin was dead.

Beale wasn't the mess it had been a week before. There was very little left to destroy. Most of the windows hadn't been replaced yet. There was no Guard on this street, although there was a blockade on Main, and the radio said there was no going near St. Joseph's or the Lorraine Hotel.

I sat in my car for a moment, trying to recapture the feeling I'd had the day before, trying, even, to remember what it felt like. But it was gone. I was feeling nothing.

I got out and went inside. I hadn't locked my office the night before, but surprisingly, no one had come in. I went to my desk and got the checkbook—I would stop at a bank on the way home, remove most of the cash, and give the stubs to Henry. He could pick up my mail and deposit the checks I received from the bills I'd mailed the day before. I'd figure out a way to pull the money out without being traced, but I'd worry about that later.

Then I went to my safe and opened it. The accordion file stuck out slightly. I would have to have Henry return that. I sighed at all the unfinished business, and then removed what cash I had inside.

I had just closed the safe when someone knocked on my door. The sound startled me. I reached for the gun and rose, holding it.

"What?" I yelled.

The door opened. Laura was standing there. She looked at me, then the gun, then back at me.

"Can I come in?" she asked.

I lowered the gun and motioned her inside. She closed the door gently.

"I thought you were in Atlanta," I said.

"I couldn't leave. Not after this."

I stared at her as if I hadn't seen her before.

"I wanted to call you last night, Smokey," she said, "but I didn't think it was right. Not yet. But all last night, I thought about you. I thought this is just a small piece of the shock you felt when your parents died in just the same kind of way, and I wondered how people ever got over it, whether they did get over it. And then I thought about what happened when I was just a baby, and I thought how unfair it is, all we have to deal with, all the legacies we're left. And I realized I hadn't told you something."

"Is that what you're still doing in Memphis?" I asked. "Coming to see me?"

She nodded. "I wanted to make sure you were all right. You're not, are you?"

I stared at her for a long moment and didn't answer. How could I be all right? What did she expect? Did she expect me to swallow all of it, like a midwesterner, and pretend none of it happened?

"They think the shooter was white, don't they?" she asked softly.

I nodded.

"That makes a difference, doesn't it?" she asked.

"Only in that it was expected," I said.

She closed her eyes. "Dr. King was a friend of yours."

"Not really," I said. I had wanted to see her so badly, and now I didn't know how to talk with her. "Memphis isn't safe right now."

She opened her eyes. "Nowhere's safe right now. Chicago's on fire. There are riots in Washington, D.C. The whole country's going to burn."

"Probably," I said.

Her lower lip trembled. "I need to go home, Smokey. I need to go to Chicago, sort things out, see what I can do with that money I was left. It didn't all come from my father's theft. And I might have to meet those people who are my real parents. I don't know anymore."

I wanted to go to her. I wanted to touch her, but I couldn't move.

"I was thinking maybe there are some other things I could do with that money," she said, "especially now. Help I could give. The Poor People's Campaign's already set up. It'd be a shame if it didn't happen, wouldn't it? Dreams don't have to die, do they?"

I didn't answer her directly. She could throw money at Martin's campaign if she wanted. It wouldn't be the same without him. But I couldn't say that. She seemed to need hope. "That would be good."

"I came here to see if you would help me."

I smiled. "You can help yourself, Laura."

She shook her head. "No," she said. "In Chicago."

I could, I suppose. Take Jimmy and go to Chicago. It would be a start. A different start. Only I couldn't picture it. I couldn't see myself beside her anymore. She looked almost alien to me, with that light, light skin.

"But that's not going to be possible, is it?" she said softly.

"Not now." My voice didn't sound like my own. It was so flat, so lifeless.

She nodded. "I knew it when I opened the door."

The silence hung between us. I couldn't think of anything to say. I should have told her I was leaving. I should have told her everything. But I couldn't. It just didn't feel right anymore.

After a moment, she adjusted her purse strap and smiled at me just a little. "Well, if you change your mind, you know how to reach me."

"I do," I said.

She grabbed the doorknob, turned it, and pulled the door open.

She was going to leave. Suddenly I didn't want her to.

"Is that what you came to tell me?" I asked. "That you were going to use your parents' money to do some good now?"

She shook her head. She looked down. "Yesterday," she said, "even before—well, you know—I was thinking about you, and I realized I hadn't told you." She raised her head, her blue eyes shining in the dim light. "I love you, Smokey." I felt my breath catch in my throat.

"But last night, when everything fell apart, I realized that isn't enough. Is it?"

"Yesterday," I said. "I would have told you that it was."

TWENTY-NINE

We took off that afternoon, Jimmy and I, for parts unknown. I wasn't driving the Falcon. Henry had nixed that. He had given me one of the church's cars, a relatively new green Oldsmobile, and had taken the Falcon in exchange. He was worried that eventually we would get traced through it. He was probably right.

Jimmy and I followed the Mississippi north at first, because I couldn't think of anywhere else I wanted to go. I wasn't even sure I wanted to go there. I figured on a few days of driving while I settled down, and then I could make some decisions.

I still haven't made those decisions, but I need to. Jimmy is asleep beside me, curled up against the passenger door, my jacket over his thin body. He hasn't smiled in days, weeks, and he is wearing down.

So am I.

The cornfields all look the same, and the smell of manure is getting to me. I have to find us a home, and soon. I wish we could go back to Memphis, but we can't. I'm not sure we can ever go back to Memphis again.

By our third day on the road, I figured no one was looking

for us. At least not nationally. The entire country was searching for a single white shooter, the specter that was coming to haunt the good old U.S. of A., the lone gunman. We were safe, as long as we didn't return to Memphis. Until that point, I had been running on gut instinct. But the more I learned, the more I realized the instinct was correct.

Understand, I've never been a conspiracy theorist. I believed that Lee Harvey Oswald worked alone, and I didn't believe that if Southeast Asia fell to the Communists the rest of the world would follow. I did believe, though, that Jimmy was right; the police had known in advance of Martin's shooting. Not from people like Withers. He had done his job, whether for the Panthers or the FBI. He had discredited COME, the sanitation workers, and Martin. He had set the stage for something that he didn't even know was planned, and then he had left. He believed in something I didn't understand, something that allowed him to betray his own people without a twinge of conscience.

No. The plot to kill Martin probably happened after the riot, when Martin announced he'd come back. As Jimmy and I drove, we learned a lot of things from the continuous radio reports. We learned that a bounty had been put on Martin's head not too long before. The black stations were reporting that Martin's usual local security team—who happened to be black—were not assigned to him this trip. They had been replaced with a white team that conveniently disappeared about ten minutes before six. All the black cops in the area were asked to leave. Some, who would normally have been at the fire station because of Martin's visit, were asked to stay home.

Then there were discrepancies about the shooter. The police claim the shots came from a rooming house on South Main, but Jimmy saw a man in the bushes and heard the shot come from directly behind him. And the weapon is a problem as well. The cops said they found a weapon in Jim's

Grill, completely assembled and wrapped in paper. Who has time to wrap up your weapon after committing an assassination? No one.

The shooter had taken his gun apart as he ran, just as Jimmy saw, and threw the rifle butt away. No one was supposed to see that. But Jimmy had. When those first erroneous reports had come across the radio, Jimmy had argued with them. Then it became clear that this was the story, the story of Martin's assassination that would be fed to all the media outlets.

Jimmy's eyes got rounder, and he grew quiet. We now knew what he had seen that he shouldn't have.

It's too dangerous for him to go back. And that breaks my heart. He had a good home with the Nelsons. He had a start.

Now it's up to me.

I have to do better than I ever have in my life. Jimmy depends on me. I cannot get lost in what should have happened, how I could have prevented things.

Because, the more I think about it, the more I know I could have. The key was Withers. If I had stopped him, if I had told the right people about him, if I had warned Martin's lieutenants myself instead of putting it on Henry that Memphis was on the brink of serious trouble, then the March twenty-eighth riot wouldn't have happened. Martin wouldn't have been publicly embarrassed; he wouldn't have had to return, and that wouldn't have given those white bounty hunters time to find him.

Although those hunters had help. These are the thoughts that scare me even more than I want to admit. Never before had the news organizations reported where Martin was staying, right down to the room. It was as if someone had hung a target over that balcony, daring others to shoot.

There were too many police in the area, and they were too calm. A national figure had been assassinated with over fifty police officers in nearby neighborhoods. That doesn't happen, or if it does, people get fired.

No one did.

They knew. Even Jimmy, a ten-year-old boy, could see it. The police knew it was going to happen, and it happened with their permission.

There has been a lot of speculation on the radio about why Martin died now, and the reasons seem obvious to me. As he said, assassination attempts had become commonplace for him, but they had escalated in recent weeks. His airplane coming into Memphis was delayed because of a bomb threat. And then there was this.

It happened because people were afraid. Lyndon Johnson had resigned. Eugene McCarthy, an unlikely candidate, had risen to a real power. Bobby Kennedy was launching a viable campaign by saying things Martin had been saying for years.

The time had come. People actually believed a black presidential candidate had a chance, and there was only one viable candidate. Martin. It didn't matter that he said he didn't want it. It didn't matter that he probably wouldn't have run. What matters is perception. And people perceived—the wrong people—that Martin was going to try for the presidency.

I couldn't have changed that part, any more than I could have done something about the police. I could simply have prevented the events that led up to this debacle. With just a few different actions, I could have made sure that Martin wasn't in Memphis on April four.

But I didn't. I hadn't. I had been too wrapped up in Laura, in Jimmy, and in the past, in the events that began at the Junior League ball, all those years ago.

I cannot forgive myself for that. But I cannot change things either. Because I did not act, I am in this car with a little boy who has lost his entire family, who has witnessed a murder and cannot help solve the crime.

I am the only one who can help him, and I will help him. I just have to figure out a place to settle.

Henry wants us to go to the SCLC headquarters in Atlanta and have Jimmy tell them what he knows. My foster mother agrees. She has offered to care for Jimmy. It would be so easy to let her do so. But Jimmy doesn't want to go to Atlanta, and I don't want to shove my problems on my foster parents any more. Jimmy and I will deal with this together.

I have told Henry to give the SCLC Jimmy's name in case they need actual eyewitnesses one day, in case they believe they can go up against the Memphis police and whoever else had a hand in Martin's death. I have told Jimmy that giving out that information won't hurt, since the police have his name anyway. But I'm not willing to do more than that. And Jimmy thought even that was too much.

I have given Henry permission to rent out my house and to deposit the money in my account. He is also canceling the lease on my office and selling the meager equipment inside, after he puts the files in storage for safe-keeping. He has already returned the file to Porter.

Jimmy and I need time to heal. The money, what little of it there is, will give us some of that time. And then, I suppose, I'll have to find a job somewhere. But I will deal with that when it happens.

Just as I will deal with the legacy left me by Laura's parents. I have always looked at its effect on me. Right now, though, I must look at its effect on Jimmy. If I pay the money back, I have no resources, and I need them to care for him. I'm sure Laura will understand, perhaps better than anyone.

I doubt I will go back to Memphis, even after things settle down. Jimmy doubts it too, although we do not talk about it. We talk about other things, like the way the land gets flat in the center of the country, and the spectacular length of the sunsets.

I have told him that we are family now, and will remain so, always. I have told him about losing my parents and how my foster parents cared for me. I have told him family means many things.

He has said nothing about that, but he has listened. And that's a start—for both of us.

Because once again, my life has changed overnight. If I have learned anything, it is that nothing goes as I plan. I need to adjust, to move, to allow myself to go with whatever happens, however it happens.

I wish I had done that more with Laura.

I think of her sometimes, usually at sunrise, when the light is so golden that it makes the land seem brighter than it can ever be. And, despite myself, I find hope in that light.

It is as Martin said on the last night of his life. Only a man who has seen the darkest night can appreciate the light.

I am just beginning to appreciate it. And for the first time, I am turning toward it, believing it will lead me home.

ACKNOWLEDGMENTS

Writers usually work alone, but without the people listed here, this book wouldn't exist. I owe a great debt to Merrilee Heifetz for believing in this project; to Kelley Ragland for her insightful analysis of the manuscript; to Paul Higginbotham for observations and his excellent critical skills; and to Dean Wesley Smith for his willingness to read several drafts and to help each one become better.

I also owe a debt to a place. The National Civil Rights Museum in Memphis, Tennessee, provided the most moving experience I have ever had in a museum. The displays bring the civil rights movement, its triumphs and its tragedies, to life. The museum is attached to the Lorraine Motel. Room 306 has been restored so that it looks the way it did on April 4, 1968, and is a sad reminder of what could have been.